Into the Ink

Jacob Mical

Printed in the United States of America

3rd Edition, 2025

ISBN 978-0-9989328-2-8

A Mical Books Production

To Lauren, my angel, your love and support have meant everything to me along this journey.

To the praiseworthy patience of my long-time friend, Kristin Coker. Your encouragement and red pen have been nothing short of priceless. I thank you.

Into the
Ink

Prologue

The old man leaned heavily on his staff, breathing deeply, grateful for the support against the weight of age on his bowed shoulders. The twilight was deepening into full night around him, and a low mist was floating over the grassy fields as he hurried on without looking back. The witch would undoubtably be along sooner than he liked. He came to a halt, and after looking up at the sky one more time to ensure his position, he closed his eyes and slowed his breathing. His meditation deepened and he lost all sense of time and space as his mind reached ever inward. His soul was smiling as he felt the great energies of the universe flowing within him. He called to them with his thoughts, losing himself in the swirl and flow. Somewhere in the back of his psyche, he was aware that this was the culmination of everything he had lived his life for. All his study and practice; his triumphs and his failings; his victories and defeats had all brought him to this moment. Everything rested on the completion of this spell.

All of that fell away as he began to chant a verse in an ancient tongue he had penned himself. The words soon took on a life of their own causing a great wind to arise, buffeting the man. A brilliant blue light joined the wind and seemed to increase its intensity. The man bellowed the last few lines, throwing all his magical might, everything he could summon, into the spell. The light swirled in the wind, spinning and whirling like a tornado. It was all the man could do to maintain his balance, holding on to his staff with all his remaining strength. The ground began to rumble and shake, stealing the man's precarious footing and tumbling him to the ground. He rolled back over and squinted through the tumult in the direction of the still swirling tornado of bright blue light. As he watched, an enormous stone block erupted out of the ground, rising, rising, always rising to tower over him. More stone structures burst through the turf to stand tall, forming a ring around the tornado of light. He had to scramble aside to avoid the flying clumps of dirt and rock, some of which were larger than he was.

Luckily, the ground settled, and the noise abated, but the magical wind in the middle of the stone circle still spun round and round, seemingly contained by the structures. They were very interesting to behold, the closest two towers of stone connected by a huge slab lain to rest atop them creating a portal or doorway of sorts. It filled the old man with wonder and awe and lifted his heart into the heavens. His work was complete, and he could go to his rest as soon as…

"What have you done?! What is this?"

The witch had appeared, at last. Of course, she would have heard the uproar of what he had done and come to investigate. Just what he was hoping.

"This is the end of a chapter, the turning of the page. I cannot defeat you, as you love to point out, and I cannot stop you from your chosen path. You leave me only one option."

With a sudden burst of energy that took the black-hearted witch completely by surprise, the old man moved forward taking his staff in both hands. He thrust it out towards her before lifting it high above his head. He shouted what sounded like the completion of a spell as he swung his arms down, driving the butt of the staff into the ground. The tornado of light still swirling in the stone circle let out a deafening roar as if the volume had been turned on and sped right for the stunned sorceress. Before she knew what was happening, she was engulfed and seemed to be flying directly in the center of the swirl of blue light. She felt a curious squeezing sensation. Then there was only blackness...

"Stonehenge, one of the most famous relics of the Ancient world—"

The man standing at the front of the classroom broke off at the sound of the door as all heads turned to Jessica Kashmir entering the room. Kash didn't recognize the man standing at the front, and for a second she thought she had run all the way across campus, late, just to come to the wrong class.

"Ms. Kash, how lovely of you to grace us with your presence, and only ten minutes late today." Despite the near constant sarcastic tone of disapproval from her regular professor, she was happy that his presence confirmed she was in the right classroom.

"Sorry for the interruption, Dr. Radcliffe, please continue," Kash's professor said to the guest speaker.

"Thank you, professor. Stonehenge represents incredible mystery and wonder..."

Kash tried to take notes, she really did. Getting up early for this class had been a struggle all semester. Even though it was fascinating, she found herself dozing off. She only awoke when Dr. Radcliffe had finished, and the professor rapped sharply on his lectern.

"So, for two of you, this could be the opportunity of a lifetime. All the details are here on the sign-up sheet. I will see you next class."

Kash shoved her things into her bag unceremoniously and moved against the traffic of departing students down to the front.

"Professor, what opportunity were you talking about?"

The man gave her a wry grin and shook his head before responding. "Well, Ms. Kash, Dr. Radcliffe is going to take two of the best and brightest in the Archaeology program to Stonehenge with him in the summer. However, nearly the entire department wants to go, obviously, and it will be very difficult for you, I'm afraid, to be chosen."

"We'll see about that," she replied and furiously scribbled her name at the bottom of the nearly full page.

Part 1: Awakening

Ch. 1 Was it a Dream?

A sharp kick to the leg awoke Kash from her slumber. She barely heard the muffled apology from the drowsy person next to her who simply turned the other way in her seat to face the aisle. Kash ignored this to look out the window of the airplane at the brilliant light peaking over the sea of clouds stretching out before her. She ran her hands over her face, trying to physically erase the sleep from her head. As soon as her mind came fully awake, her excitement brought a small grin to her face.

This was it. This was the day that all the sacrifice paid off. Late nights at the library, long hours in the lab, and she hadn't been back to her apartment in so long she was half wondering if the landlord thought she had moved out. It was all behind her now. Since Kash was old enough to read, she had wanted to take this trip, had fought tooth and nail, and given everything she possibly could to get here. Looking out the window of the plane as the British coastline came into view, she let out a long deep breath as if to physically exhale the past and move into her future. This dig was going to define not only her career, but the course of the rest of her life as well and she knew it. Success, of any kind, would open more doors than she knew, at least she suspected as much. Beyond that, however, was her ardent desire to discover any of the many secrets she knew lay hidden beneath Stonehenge. She thought of her failure to be selected for this very trip in college and smiled. It had fueled her desire and passion to make it there or die trying. Her research began with the various previous archaeological adventures undertaken at the famous site, and she was running over them in her head all night long.

Most had provided more questions than answers, but all had inspired her to believe that the most important secrets of the structure lay in the main ring of stones. These structures were the most impressive and seemed to be the central focus of the formation. She remembered different bits and theories from all the books she had been over countless times. The site still held untold mysteries despite years of study. An energy existed there that Kash meant to experience and hopefully find the source of. She was desperate for her efforts to prove more fruitful than her predecessors. Her plan was solid, and she was determined to see it through.

The next few days went by slowly with none in the team expecting to find much in the beginning of the hunt. The restrictions placed on such digs as these by the British government certainly made it difficult to discover much, but the limited digging they were allowed to do was proving unfruitful. Undeterred, Kash kept the morale high and worked with purpose, encouraging her team. Late in the afternoon on the fourth day, Kash was taking a break from the actual digging, simply admiring the beauty of the stones. Her dirty blonde, almost brown hair blew in all directions uncontrollably in the stiff breeze. Her lithe form casting a long shadow drew her fierce green eyes to the base of the closest stone structure.

Walking through the center, towards it sent chills up and down her spine, her excitement and joy meshing with the energy of the ancient structure. The sun was beginning to set, and she could see the light dancing across the enormous stone just in front of her. Something flashed blue and made her do a double take. She moved close to the ancient rock to run her hands over it. It seemed the same as the others, nothing remarkable to distinguish it. She was certain she had seen a flash of light, however. She crouched down to look near the base where it met the ground, pushing her hand against the rock to steady herself. A sudden darkness engulfed her, but she was somehow still aware of herself. It was as if the light of the sun had been stolen, and she felt an odd squeezing sensation.

Kash thought that she was lying down but still couldn't see anything. She decided she must have hit her head and gave it a little shake. This attempt to clear her senses did no more than make her head hurt, but eventually she struggled to her feet. There seemed to be low chanting somewhere in the back of her consciousness. Was it getting louder? The sudden intrusion of swirling blue light blinded her. An explosion behind her eyes brought her to one knee, so acute was the pain. The sound of the wind was intensifying, the howl deafening. Curiously, Kash could not feel anything. Her mind was telling her that this tornado of blue lights and swirling wind surrounding her should be throwing her around like a rag doll, but it wasn't. Was she dreaming?

Kash was just convincing herself she had hit her head harder than she first thought when the strength of the tornado seemed to fade, and torches sprang up around her. Presently, she was aware of the underground chamber she was in, the shadows of the dancing flames flickering on the earthen walls. She reached out to touch the dirt, hoping that physically handling something might ground her reality. Just before her hand brushed the long tendril of a root running through the wall, a voice called out softly.

"Jessica Kashmir."

Kash froze. This dream was getting stranger and stranger. A slight shuffling brought her gaze to a stooped figure slowly moving across the room to stand before her. He was robed in the same blue as the swirling tornado. His staff was taller than he was and there was a glowing blue gem fit tightly in place at the top.

She knew her imagination was running wild here and could only shake her head and go with this hallucination or dream or whatever it was.

"I have awaited your return for time untold. Your travels have taken you far and wide, but it always began right here. You have known that your entire life, have you not?"

"I... um..."

"You seem unsure. Time has that effect on some, yet you have put considerable study and research into getting back here. I figured you might not know me when the time came, but this is the last magic I can conjure, and you are my only hope at salvation."

"Salvation? Last magic?"

"Yes, and if this spell fails then so too will my strength fail, and I will be lost to this world. All I have fought for these long years..."

He certainly had the "wizard" look and seemed old enough, so she figured she should just go with it until she woke up. The possibility of her not awakening from this reality had been held at bay by curiosity, but it suddenly rushed back, setting her heart pumping. She needed a deep breath to steady herself before speaking.

"So, you are some sort of wizard?" It didn't sound as bad in her head but out loud made it seem perfectly ludicrous.

Their eyes met for the first time and Kash could see an ancient wisdom there that made her feel small, as if she were looking into a bottomless depth. His silver hair seemed to shimmer as he looked her over. Eventually, the man smiled as he responded:

"My name is Merlin and yes, some have called me wizard before. Sorcerer, Devil, Spellcaster, Druid. I have held many monikers. My longevity is predicated on the completion of my last and greatest spell. I had not originally planned to exist this long; this life was not meant to be mine. The spell cannot be placed upon its maker. I had intended it for another, one much more deserving and much more honorable. He was supposed to transcend the bounds of mortal men and rule in Camelot forever. Alas, I was unable to convince him of his true destiny, to the ruin of all. The city was always fated to fall, but I knew its king was meant to outlive her. Arthur, to my great regret, did not agree with me. His honor would not allow him to let his knights die alone, defending everything he stood for while he escaped. I suppose I should have known that from the start, but here we are."

There was a faraway look splayed across the man's weathered features as his voice trailed off into silence. Slowly, from thin air it seemed, he produced a decrepit looking scroll in tatters clearly losing the battle with deterioration. He seemed unconcerned about its state of disrepair as he handed it to Kash. She accepted it gingerly and carefully unrolled it for a look. Celtic symbols were splayed across the page and familiar sparks of blue light started dancing along the paper. She instinctively let go with a yelp, but the ancient paper seemed to grow solid and floated in midair, shimmering with the same soft blue light.

"You will see that the magic is still strong, you have only to read it, and the power is yours. All stories must needs have a beginning and it is comforting that this was always yours."

"I have no idea what you are talking about, Merlin, is it?"

"So, you say, but I know better. Your journey through the pages begins here. There is no other beginning to your story. Think about it, Kash. You wanted to find the secrets of

Stonehenge, have even dreamt of coming here for most of your life. You are here now with the greatest of all secrets this stone formation contains right in front of you. Read the words aloud and your journey starts. This is only the beginning."

The cryptic speech left her off balance. Everything seemed to stand still as if the scene was waiting for her to continue. She stared and stared but all the self-proclaimed Merlin did was stare back, smiling bemusedly. He seemed perfectly at ease despite the odd gravity his words were weighing upon Kash. Still uncertain of the validity of her current reality, the only conclusion she could come up with was to read the scroll. It seemed to be what the scene was waiting for. Perhaps she would wake up if she read it. There didn't seem to be any other way forward. Shaking her head once more, she moved over in front of the still glowing parchment. The words were Celtic, and her studies had provided her with knowledge of many dialects in the region, but there was something about it that stumped her.

"It is the language of the arcane, the symbols of the Druids. Your studies in language have already given you the key. You must look through the proper lens of faith and the words will flow through you."

Again, Kash had no idea what the man was babbling about, but she looked back to the scroll all the same. Confusing as his words were, she thought she recognized something more as she studied the crisp writing. Deep within her, a voice she hardly recognized emitted from her own mouth and read the words as if they were her own. The characters leapt from the page swirling around her with that same blue light. The tornado grew and grew, and she covered her head against the roar, forgetting that she couldn't feel any wind. She noted the symbols from the scroll swirling amongst the blue sparks this time and noted how beautiful it all was before her consciousness faded away into blackness.

▄▄▄

Kash's senses returned slowly, her awareness coming back to her at a snail's pace. Vaguely, she recognized a hospital room as her eyes opened with effort. Then her clarity and memories came flooding back in a sudden rush that overwhelmed her and had her swallowing deep breaths in rapid succession. Just as her heart rate was returning to normal, a young nurse walked in wearing standard blue scrubs.

"You're awake then, are you? Well, it's about time, you've been here three days. I expect you've tired of my company and decided it's time to leave." The middle-aged woman was not unattractive and very cheery. Kash obviously had no recollection of having met her before, but she smiled politely anyway.

"Um..."

"Take it slow, dear," she crooned sweetly. "The man that brought you in said you had had an accident but couldn't give me any details. He's just down the hall, should be back any moment. Anyways, you're as healthy as you could be. Not a scratch on you."

"How is that possible?" Kash's thoughts escaped her lips before she could stop them. "I mean, did you check my head?" She felt around on her skull for a gash or a lump; something. There was nothing. The nurse wasn't lying, she didn't even have a headache now that she had been awake for a couple minutes. The lady only smiled without bothering to answer, obviously trusting that Kash's self-examination would suffice to quell her doubts. The silence dragged on into borderline awkwardness as Kash replayed the events in her mind. The nurse didn't seem to notice but eventually stood up before saying:

"Well, I must get going but your discharge papers are waiting for you to sign them at the desk, your clothes are right over there. Have a good day." With that the nurse turned on her heel and was gone. Kash dressed slowly, wondering just what was going on. Behind the front desk was another nurse, this one younger than the cheery face Kash had awakened to. She was about to say something to her when she heard her name.

"Professor Kash, thank god you're awake."

It was Blake Wilson, one of her assistants on the dig. He seemed wound a little tight sometimes, but he was a brilliant archaeologist and very well read in general. His skills made him an asset to the team, but she didn't expect him to be the one they left behind to look after her. Even still, she was certainly relieved to see his short, jet-black hair and tall muscular frame. She would have guessed he ran or swam or something; his athletic build was clear evidence of this. There was relief etched into his strong features and his dark eyes exuded concern as he moved up to her.

"Here you are, Ms. Kashmir," the nurse interrupted sliding a pen and her discharge papers over towards her.

"Thanks," she said without looking at the nurse.

"Wilson, hey, what happened to me?" she asked her colleague.

"I'm not sure, we lost sight of you for just a moment and then nothing. We looked for almost an hour in a wider and wider arc around the stones. We were baffled and then I walked back through, heading to the other side from our equipment and there you were, slumped against one of the main rocks. There was no way we could've missed you. I swear I walked by the spot five times. I still can't wrap my head around it but at least you're fine and weren't hurt. Do you remember anything?"

Should she tell Wilson what had happened? Would he believe her? Was she sure herself what had actually happened? The memory burned in her mind like a bright flame. She could remember every second like it had just happened. The "wizard" said he was *Merlin*. He also spoke of King Arthur and Camelot. *That Merlin?* She shook her head. It had to have been a dream. The doors of the elevator opened before her and she stepped on, Wilson hot on her heels. She didn't answer immediately, still unsure if she should share what she saw with him. While they were colleagues, they had never been more than that. She wasn't one to trust easily and anyways she was sure he would just insist that it was a dream. How could he not? She could already hear herself and how ridiculous she sounded trying to tell him she had met Merlin and read off an ancient magic spell. She laughed, finding some mirth at how crazy the dream, for that's what it had to be, was. Wilson smiled bemusedly, clearly unsure of the source of her laughter.

"What?" he asked hesitantly.

"I had a really wild dream while I was out. There were silent tornados of light and wizards and druids. Obviously, the magic of Stonehenge at work, right?" She smiled to assure him it was all just some fever dream. "I'm actually feeling great if you want to head back out to the site."

"Well, we were shut down. When the authorities finally tried to figure out what happened to you, they discovered we had continued in your absence and our lack of an explanation did little to convince them we should be allowed to carry on. So, we actually have a plane to catch."

"What, no...we. I didn't even get to..."

"I know, but there's nothing we can do. Our permit was revoked."

"Dammit!" she swore. "Damn you, Merlin." She didn't know why she said it, but it did slip out audible enough for Wilson to hear.

"Merlin?"

"Yeah, he showed up in my dream, don't worry about it," she responded quickly with a shake of her head.

This was devastating. She could not think of a worse outcome for the amazing chance she had been given. Sullen didn't get close to describing Kash's mood as they made their way into the airport and through security. It all slipped past her in a blur anyway. One moment they were waiting to board, the next she was staring out the window at the clouds again. It was a stunningly beautiful day as they flew across the ocean back towards the states, but it was unable to lift her from her doldrums. Eventually, they landed safely back in California. They rolled to a stop and were told they could disembark. Kash rose from her seat and reached for the overhead compartment. Her shirt lifted a little, revealing the skin at the small of her back.

"Wow, you have tattoos?! I never knew that; is that some kind of ancient script or something?"

Kash froze, her breath caught.

"What did you say?"

"The tattoos, on your back. It looks like some kind of old language. What do they mean?" Wilson seemed genuine and he wasn't really the type to play this sort of practical joke.

"I don't have tattoos," she replied.

"Umm, that's not what it looks like from here."

"What are you talking about?!" she asked incredulously as she lifted her shirt and tried to twist her head around to see for herself. She couldn't make out what was actually there but was certain there was something. Without another word, she turned and ran off the plane, pushing past other passengers in her haste. Angry shouts followed her out onto the tarmac, but she hardly cared. Fear was spiking hot adrenaline through her veins, and she could hear her blood pounding in her head. She tore into the building and made for the nearest bathroom as fast as she could. Pulling her shirt up when she arrived in front of the mirror, she let out a gasp of surprise and horror. The letters were unmistakable. They were the exact same Celtic words she had read off the scroll in her dream, the exact words that had jumped off the ancient paper and swirled around her with the blue light. She was hallucinating, she was tired and dehydrated and…she pinched herself so hard she nearly drew blood. Nothing happened, the tattoos were still permanently etched into her skin.

She moved out of the bathroom slowly, quite literally dazed from shock. Still not completely convinced she wasn't crazy and hadn't hallucinated the entire episode, she almost walked right into Wilson who was moving up frantically.

"What was that all about?" he asked, concerned, and slightly out of breath having chased her through the airport.

Kash just shook her head, no idea what she was going to say. Apparently, she had been visited by a wizard she wasn't entirely sure wasn't a fictional character. She had always thought the stories about him were just that, stories that somehow managed to maintain some sliver of curious credibility through the years. She decided she would have to do some research and see if she could find any connection in the old stories between Merlin and Stonehenge. Mind made up, she moved with determination and without a word to Wilson, for the door of the terminal. He didn't know what to make of it but followed in her wake, chalking it up to the strange experience Kash had had on this trip.

Ch. 2 The Other Library

Wilson walked across the grounds of Stanford University, headed for Kash's office. Nearly a week had passed since their return from the dig, and he hadn't seen or heard from her at all. While they were not the best of friends, theirs was more of a professional relationship, he had always been fond of her and impressed by her work. This radio silence was odd, however, not least of all because of her reaction to the tattoos. She seemed genuinely surprised when she saw her own back. There were many details of the dig that still needed to be completed, and he needed to discuss some things with her. He figured she would reach out to him two or three days after they returned but had heard nothing. His report was complete, so he decided he would hand deliver it himself and check on her at the same time.

Wilson made it to her office, lifted his hand to knock but stopped with his hand in midair when he heard a crash behind the door. What was going on in there? With a bemused smile he proceeded to knock. The shuffling and noise inside came to a halt.

"Who is it? What do you want? Go away!" came Kash's sharp reply.

"Um, its Wilson, is this a bad time?"

"Oh, Wilson, it's you, uh...hold on a second."

He waited patiently, listening to the sounds of a quick straightening of the office. When the door opened, he made sure to paint a smile on his features, at least a bemused one.

"Come in, Wilson, how are you?" she sounded tired and breathless.

"I'm well. I was actually coming to ask you the same thing. Haven't seen you around campus and just wanted to give you my report on the dig. I figured we would meet to finalize everything at some point."

"Oh, right, sorry about that. I have been, um…" she paused, not knowing how to describe the somewhat manic week she had had since last she saw him. The librarian was starting to hate her because of the copious amount of time she had spent there over the past few days. She was doing research on Merlin and really wanted to keep it a secret. Hopefully, she could figure everything out without alerting anyone that anything was amiss. Apparently, she wasn't doing a good job. She took a deep, steadying breath before continuing.

"You're right, I'm sorry. I've been distracted."

"Anything I can do? I realize you've been through a strange ordeal so, just let me know."

Kash looked at Wilson in a new light suddenly. He had been here the whole way, right? He had helped her back in Wiltshire, and he was here now. She decided to throw caution to the winds and hope he didn't think she was absolutely crazy. How could he? He's the one who pointed out the tattoos, right?

"Close the door, sit down. I'll tell you what I have been doing all week."

Kash told her story, fully. She started with the fact that she had always been fascinated by the stories of Stonehenge, had always felt compelled by its mystery and wonder to study it and know its secrets. She told of how she thought she had hit her head and how Merlin had come to her. At this point in the story, she could tell she almost lost Wilson but to his credit he remained silent and listened. When she told of reading the spell from the scroll and the letters becoming the tattoos on her body, she noticed it pique his curiosity and interest. By the time she was describing her week in the library, she knew she had him.

"So, that's what I have been up to. I kind of dropped all of my other duties. I'm glad it's summer and I don't have any classes right now. So, what do you think? If you think I'm crazy, be honest. I have no other explanations…" She threw up her hands when she was done as if to signify her helplessness.

Wilson chewed it over for a minute before speaking. He wanted to be sure he understood her position completely before he got on board or didn't.

"So, let me get this straight. You were pulled into some magical secret chamber of Stonehenge and there confronted by Merlin, the sorcerer of legend, and read off a magical spell from a scroll he had which then transferred to your body as tattoos?"

"Concisely stated," she replied with a grin. "So far, I haven't found anything in my research to suggest I'm not a lunatic, but I have come across a couple of different mentions of Merlin and Stonehenge at the same time. Our library is not exactly overflowing with works on Celtic legends or Druidic tales of magic. There are a rather large number of books on Arthurian legends, but Merlin has a cursory role in most of the ones I've looked at."

Her eyes went wide, and she gasped.

"I've just remembered something Merlin said during the dream, or whatever it was. He spoke of Arthur and said that the spell was not meant for its creator and Arthur was supposed to read the scroll. Arthur refused, according to Merlin, anyway. Something about honor and dying with his knights. Did I use a spell meant for King Arthur?"

"You know this sounds insane, right?" Wilson said with a shake of his head. "Despite that, I think I can help. Or at least, I know someone who can. I'm good friends with the head of the English department and he sent me to this library off campus one time when I was doing some research for our trip, actually, not too long ago. This library has the biggest collection of books I have ever seen on ancient Britain. The librarian is also a collector of old and rare books so he might have some knowledge that could help you find information on Merlin. In fact, he's an old friend and professor of mine. Want to go see him?"

"Absolutely."

The quick drive to the off-campus library did nothing to abate the nervous excitement Kash always had when faced with a puzzle. Of course, she had never been in this particular situation, and she supposed that added to her anxiety somewhat. The library did not look like much when they pulled up. It was squeezed between two other buildings and did not seem wide enough to Kash. She said as much to Wilson as they crossed the street headed for the double doors.

"It seems that way from out here but it's bigger inside and it extends backwards quite a distance."

The librarian hardly stirred when they moved through the doors into the quiet place. He did look up and smile warmly at Wilson when they moved over to the desk, however.

"Professor Wilson, how are you, my friend? How was your trip?" The man seemed friendly and Kash returned his warm smile before he looked back to her companion. She could tell he was older, but he wore his graying hair and smallish glasses well. He was just taller than her, and his button-up shirt did nothing to keep her from noticing he obviously exercised regularly. He had an air of intelligence and wisdom about him. He seemed to fit perfectly here at the old library, it put her quickly at ease. There was something about his voice that stirred some memory in the back of her mind, but she couldn't place it.

"Dr. Radcliffe, I am excellent, and the trip was eventful but ultimately unsuccessful. It is what brought us here today, though."

"How do you mean?" he replied quickly.

"Well..." Wilson paused and looked at Kash expectantly. "Where are my manners, I apologize. Dr. Radcliffe, this is Professor Jessica Kashmir, a colleague of mine at the university and the leader of our expedition."

"It's wonderful to meet you, Ms. Kashmir."

"Kash is fine, thanks. Do I know you from somewhere?" Kash asked curiously. She had been eyeing the man with a look of familiarity as if she could not place where she had met him. Was this...

"You wouldn't happen to be the same Dr. Radcliffe who spoke at the university about Stonehenge and then took a couple of students with you a few years ago would you?"

"Yes, actually, I am," Radcliffe replied with a bemused glance at Wilson.

"You probably don't remember, but I came in late one day to a class you were giving a lecture in. I never could manage to get out of bed that early back in those days," she said with a grin.

"Sorry, I gave a number of guest lectures back then," he replied with a return smile.

"Anyways, long story short, we need to do some research on references to Merlin in Arthurian legends. Wilson said you might be able to help us find a connection or at least a work that mentions Merlin and Stonehenge. I specifically would like to know if Merlin ever went there or did anything there. Did it mean anything at all to him?"

Radcliffe did not respond immediately other than to nod his head in concentration. He thought a long moment before responding.

"I personally cannot recall any specific mention of Merlin at Stonehenge but there are numerous works where Merlin appears, written by many different authors. Most believe he was a character based on a real man but there doesn't seem to be scholarly agreement on a factual account of Merlin being a real person. Geoffrey de Monmouth wrote a few works in the 1100s concerning the life of the sorcerer. We have some of them, but they are quite hard to come by these days, at least unedited and unabridged or 1st edition. It has usually been passed through so many different authors' hands it's hard to know if the original intent of Monmouth himself was upheld. Shall we have a look, anyways?"

He smiled at them expectantly and both men looked to Kash.

"Lead on," she said with a wave of her arm.

Dr. Radcliffe moved past them and they fell into step behind him. There was no one else around. Kash hadn't noticed it at first because not many people visit libraries anymore, but they were alone as far as she could tell. It struck her as odd then and she was about to voice her thoughts when she heard the librarian say:

"Ahh, here we are, *Prophetiae Merlini* by Geoffrey de Monmouth. This is an English translation, of course. I think the Vatican has one of the only remaining Latin copies of this work. Anyways, this is one of the more famous works about Merlin that Monmouth did. He saw Merlin as a prophet and a sorcerer. This book was influential and taken quite seriously in its day."

"Right, anything about Stonehenge?" Kash asked expectantly.

"Not that I remember. It was mostly about war. Well, if there is a work in this library that can help you, it will be right in here somewhere. It was really nice to meet you, Kash. I hope you find what you're looking for. If you need me, I'll be at the desk. Good to see you, Wilson."

"And you as well, Dr. Radcliffe. Thanks." They shook hands and the librarian moved away. "Well, where to begin?" Wilson asked Kash with a smile. She shook her head before replying.

"I guess the one he pulled down will do. I will grab a couple more that seem like they might reference Stonehenge. Why don't you work on the Arthur angle?" Kash knew they would find something eventually. Hopefully, it was only a matter of time.

"Sounds good," Wilson replied as he turned to the shelves.

Ch. 3 *The Prophetiae Merlini*

Daylight had almost faded completely and Kash grabbed one of the library's reading lamps to combat the growing darkness. Wilson was off somewhere in the stacks and Kash rubbed her eyes, sure they had been there for hours. She was about to pull another large volume to her when Wilson came around the corner.

"Hey, you want to call this a day? We can come back in the morning."

Kash wasn't ready to leave yet, she was never ready to quit for the day unless she had made some sort of progress. So far, they had gotten nowhere.

"I want to check one more book. This one, oh yeah, I haven't looked at this one yet. Didn't Radcliffe say it was one of the earliest books Merlin is in?" She held up the *Prophetiae Merlini*.

"Yes, that's the one." Wilson replied tiredly. He sat down next to her as she opened the weathered book. There was something immediately off about this work that they could not place until it began to glow with a familiar blue light. Kash gasped.

"What?!" Wilson exclaimed just before there was a roar of wind emitting out of nowhere and then everything went dark. The noise didn't abate, however, just continued to howl. Kash and Wilson could feel themselves being squeezed tighter than they ever had and spinning around but nothing was discernible in the blackness aside from a violent swirl of blue light. As quickly as it had begun, everything was still, and the lights faded.

Kash was flat on her back, looking up at the branches of a tree softly swaying in the gentle breeze of the cool night. The light was dim, and she could tell she was in a forest as she sat up and looked around. Wilson was just coming to and sitting up a few feet away.

"What…?" he started but his voice trailed away.

Before Kash could respond to Wilson's obvious confusion with an admission about her own, she spotted a cloaked figure striding towards them through the trees. The staff was immediately familiar and the stone set at the top was unmistakable.

"Merlin!" she called.

"Yes, it is I. What are you doing out here?" the wizard started to ask but trailed off. He turned his head in confusion, looking between the two of them. It appeared that he may have recognized Kash and was trying to place where from. A sudden intensity overtook him, and his eyes went wide.

"My lady Kashmir. How wonderful to see you, I had not thought to find you here in these woods. I suppose it does not matter which but only that you have sought me out."

Kash was grateful for a familiar face in this unknown place but had no idea what he was babbling about. He had to remember their meeting based on his memory of her name. Or was it some magic trick? Of course, it was magic, but did he really know why she was here or was he just playing along after discerning her name somehow?

"That is why you have come, is it not?" the sorcerer continued when neither Wilson nor Kash seemed about to respond.

"Um...we came..." she had no idea how to voice her swirling thoughts. With the appearance of Merlin as she remembered him, she had accepted that they were in a story but didn't know how to go further. Disbelief momentarily suspended; she was still way out of her depth.

"You wish to know more about the spell. I see you have chosen a companion and bestowed some of the words upon him already. An interesting decision. Perhaps you thought it too much power for just one?" He cocked his head to the side curiously.

"Hold on a second," Wilson was still reeling but he had finally found his voice. "Let me get this straight, you're Merlin, the legendary sorcerer?"

"I don't know about legendary, but some call me Merlin, yes."

"Right, that means we are in some story. Your prophecies. Written by Monmouth. And we have been transported into them by magic. You said she had bestowed the words on me. What are..." Wilson lifted his shirt and spun around on sudden inspiration and saw the flowing script of the same tattoos he had seen on Kash back at the airport.

"Yes, this is an important power and mission you two have undertaken."

"Wait," Kash interjected. "Mission? We just want to know how to get home."

"Yes, I expect you would but by reading the scroll at Stonehenge you accepted the charge along with the power.

You see, the spell you worked your entire life to read will be one of the more potent spells I will conceive in my lifetime."

"Will be?" Wilson asked confusedly.

"Yes, Mr. Wilson, you have travelled to one of my earliest appearances in literature thus I have yet to create the spell you are using."

"I don't understand, how do you know anything about it then?"

"Well, you see, when I met the lovely Ms. Kashmir here back at Stonehenge I had been in a magical stasis for a long time. Only this spell was holding me to life. My story was completed when she read the words and received the power. However, now that she has returned to me using the spell, she has opened my eyes to everything."

"Why did you create this spell, Merlin?" Kash asked quietly, knowing this was the answer they truly needed if they were ever going to understand what was actually going on.

The wizard turned to her slowly, his smile fading a little. "There will come a day, a part of my story, where I will meet one with powers to rival even my own. The realm of magic is diverse, varied, potent, and dangerous. There are those who would choose to ignore this and use it for personal gain at the expense of those around them. In the days of Arthur there will be a Fey by the name of Morgen, Morgana to some. One of my greatest foes. She will inspire my foray into this realm of magic, an ancient and deep pool.

"By now, I trust that you have accepted your new reality. One in which your power to travel through the tales of others is strong. You need only to open the vessel and read with intent the part of the story you wish to enter. The magic of the spell will do the rest. It took me half a lifetime of study and practice to learn the secrets of this power. I would not have normally meddled in this area, creation magic is frightfully strong and volatile, but Morgana was going to gain this power if I did nothing. I am quite sure she figured it out and was deducing an even more sinister method of draining the stories she travelled to of their magic by changing the very story itself. If she were allowed to do this the entire literary world might crumble and all of history would be irreparably damaged, not just my own but yours as well."

Kash looked at Wilson, whose bewilderment was clearly etched on his face. Despite the abnormality of the situation, if Kash was hearing him right then these tattoos were magical and allowed her to travel to stories as she had obviously done to get here. Her imagination's desire to run wild at the possibilities was held in check by the seriousness in the sorcerer's voice. He seemed to be genuinely afraid of what Morgana was going to attempt in the future, at least the future of their present moment in the *Prophetiae Merlini*.

"We're not going to have to battle Morgana, are we?" Wilson's question brought her from her contemplations to see Merlin grinning at the man bemusedly.

"No, sir. Luckily for you, and everyone else for that matter, I was able to defeat and banish her. I suppose she will still harbor resentment for the way her tale played out. Hers is a sad story. I never thought she deserved what the authors of the world did to her. However, this spell holds her in check and that responsibility has passed to you now."

"What do you mean? What did they do to her?" Kash asked, her curiosity at his somber tone making her think Merlin actually pitied his future rival.

"This was her inspiration and in turn my own for the very spell you now possess. You see, a character in a story is bound by what its author writes about them. This is the magic of creation. Morgana sought to break these bonds. In the early days, not so long from now, when I first meet Morgana, she is not filled with hatred and evil but gentle and benevolent. In fact, she will lend her healing magics to me once upon a time."

"What happened?"

"As time wore on in your world, the ideas about magic began to change. It became something too unnatural, too strange and authors began depicting it as evil and dark. Magic users in the stories were maligned and hated. I escaped only due to my connections with Arthur. For some reason, Arthur's virtue always seemed to rub off on their descriptions of me. The same cannot be said for Morgana. Her part in the stories darkened and she became an enemy of all living and natural things. I had no choice. I had to defeat her, had to take her magics from her. If she were allowed to complete this spell, all would be doomed. I created my own version as a failsafe in case I was overpowered and defeated myself. Even though I proved victorious that spell was put in place and upon my last page, I entered the magical stasis that you will pull me from to complete my final chapter."

"So, where does that leave us? Do we just have this power forever? What are we supposed to do with it?" Kash was hoping he would give her some direction, but she could tell that he was preparing to leave them. There was an air of finality about his stance and smile.

"Do what you will, just remember that the characters are bound by their authors; you can sate your compulsions for entertainment, but this spell was created to keep the stories true, to keep the stories from being irreparably marred. The magic of their creation is held together by the ultimate completion of the story. If this completion is hindered, it could alter reality in unknown and dangerous ways. That was

Morgana's plan. She would turn the stories to her will just to spite the authors who defined her existence and pushed her to the darkness. You must write your own stories but beware of succumbing to the same darkness she did. I have all faith in you, Jessica Kashmir, and Blake Wilson. Make me proud. I will see you back at the beginning."

With a smile and a wink, he moved slowly through the trees, leaning on his staff. Kash looked to Wilson bemusedly. When she turned back to look, the trees had already stolen the wizard from her view.

"Kash, do you remember him saying how we get out of the stories?"

"Merlin!" Kash called immediately, hoping the wizard was not too far away. For a moment, there was silence, then a soft voice floated back to them from the direction Merlin had gone.

"Find the matching script."

"Find the what? What does that even mean?" Wilson was clearly nonplussed by the hint. Was that even a response to his question? How did the wizard hear that from so far away?

Kash thought hard for a moment, not even acknowledging that Wilson had spoken at all. The matching script? As if it was there all along, she suddenly understood. Smiling at Wilson, she lifted her shirt a bit and turned around.

"There will either be matching tattoos between us and as you only have one it will be easy to discern if that's the one or not, or the name of the story we are in will be on me somewhere."

Wilson looked at what he could see of his only tattoo, and he couldn't really make out much but moved over to examine Kash's back more closely. It took less than a second to find what he was looking for. *Prohpetiae Merlini,* as plain as day, small, but easy to see within the larger, flowing letters of the original spell.

"Found it!" he exclaimed excitedly. "Now what?"

"Um..." Kash wasn't sure. "Can I reach it? Is it in a spot I can touch?"

"Nope."

"Let me see your tattoo, turn around."

On sudden inspiration once more, Kash looked closer at his new tattoo and sure enough, she could make out *Prohpetiae Merlini* quite clearly.

"I think maybe we have to touch each other's tattoos and..." it sounded much smarter in her head. She shook her head to indicate that it wasn't right. Wilson just shrugged in response. She thought of Dr. Radcliffe then and wondered how long they had been gone. He would probably be trying to close the library soon. She turned to Wilson to see him staring at her wide-eyed.

"What did you do?" he asked, panicked, for the blue swirl of lights had appeared around her, but only her.

"I don't know," Kash shouted over the wind, but there could be no way he had heard her. What had she done? She could feel herself lightening and starting to spin. She could not leave Wilson here. She remembered she was thinking of the library before all of this started so right before the darkness swallowed her, she was able to shout.

"The library!"

The swirl of blue lights winked out as quickly as they had appeared, but Wilson was certain he heard a shout. Was it

Kash? Did she say...? He thought of her returning to the library without him and from nowhere, to his great relief, the now familiar blue swirl of lights erupted from thin air and the wind spirited him off to the blackness.

Ch. 4 Exciting Possibilities

Dr. Radcliffe was confused. He had literally just seen the pair. Where were they now and why had they left such a mess on their tables? They were professors at the university. Surely, they had more respect for him and his job than to leave everything laying around. He moved to the next row and then the next one and on and on until he came to the wall. Nothing. He was beginning to think they had left without saying anything to him despite him being positioned at the door all afternoon. No one had come or gone. He shook his head and walked back towards their books, debating with himself on whether or not to leave the mess for the morning. He had almost reached the tables when there was a loud crash and someone swore loudly. Radcliffe rushed around the last shelf to see Kash and Wilson splayed out on the floor, a chair toppled over next to them. For a moment, Radcliffe was too stunned to say anything. He was here only moments before, where had they come from?

"Are you guys alright?" he asked hesitantly, clear suspicion etched on his face.

"I think so," Wilson said as he let out a deep breath of relief. Despite still being off-balance, he couldn't hide his relief at having made it back. Kash looked around and couldn't help but return the look with one of her own. She was less shocked by it all, but then again, she hadn't been almost left behind either. She chuckled and turned to Dr. Radcliffe.

"Sorry, I wasn't paying attention and leaned back too far in the chair." She smiled at him and hoped this would suffice to defeat his obvious curiosity. Had he noticed their absence or seen any of the blue swirling lights?

"Right," he started slowly, not fooled by the flimsy dodge. "Anyways, I need to lock up, do you think you could put all this back for me? I'll wait by the front." Radcliffe decided not to ask too many questions as he wanted to close up and get home. He moved off and left Kash and Wilson still sitting on the floor.

"So, what do we do now?" Wilson asked quietly as they collected the books and moved amongst the shelves, replacing them as they went.

"What do you mean? We can do whatever we want! I wonder if we must be here, using this library's books or if we can read any book, anywhere? I guess it doesn't matter, we can go back to my office and try another one tonight."

Kash could tell she was a bit more excited than Wilson was. He seemed hesitant to travel into another story. He never answered her as they shelved the last book, the *Prophetiae Merlini*, which made her smile again. She paused as she lifted the old book to look closer at the faded cover. Her grin grew wider at the sight of the new way the title was written. She was sure the font had been different before but now it was a spot-on match to her new tattoos. She thought it was quite fitting.

"What is it?" Wilson asked of her hesitance. She turned to the man and held out the book for him to see.

"Notice anything different?"

He noticed it immediately and his face adopted a curious expression. "I wonder why it did that?" he mused aloud.

"Obviously because we journeyed into the pages. Do you think we appear in the book now?" She tucked the book back under her arm and moved off without waiting for an answer.

Dr. Radcliffe spotted them coming around the nearest shelf and noticed the book Kash was carrying. He opened his mouth to protest but the woman beat him to the punch.

"I know it's late, Doc, but I would really love to take this one home overnight. We're both coming back first thing; I promise I'll bring it with us."

Dr. Radcliffe shook his head exasperatedly. "Alright, but Wilson, I'm coming after you for another copy if you don't bring it back. No, don't worry about putting in the system. I know where you two work." He grinned but Kash couldn't tell if he was joking or not.

"We understand, thanks a million, we'll see you tomorrow?" she replied brightly, anyways.

"Yes ma'am, good night."

▬▬▬

Kash reclined in the comfortable chair she kept in her office for times when she needed to relax. Now was one of those times and she rested her head against the chair and closed her eyes. She was running over everything that had happened to her since she went to England. It all seemed surreal, like a dream she could not escape. Or was it a dream she didn't want to wake up from? A smile creased her lips as she thought of the possibilities this newfound power presented. She was just pondering where they might go from here when she heard Wilson knocking at the door.

"Come in," she said without opening her eyes or moving at all. Wilson strolled in happily, having completed his mission of grabbing some books from his own office. These were candidates for travel, at least the ones he thought might be exciting. He looked to Kash as the woman opened her eyes and smiled.

"So..." Wilson wasn't really sure where they should begin.

"So..." Kash replied and smiled knowingly. "I've been thinking we should try a favorite and well-known story first, one well-known by the both of us."

"That makes sense. Anything particular in mind?" Wilson replied quickly.

"Well, not really but you're more well-read. Let's see what you brought from your office."

"I'm afraid I don't have many works of fiction on my shelves here. Mostly ancient history and archaeology. Fascinating stuff but mostly without any true plotlines. However, I do have a copy of C.S. Lewis' *Chronicles of Narnia*, as well as *Don Quijote*. One Miguel de Cervantes is responsible for that one I believe. And of course, my favorite, *The Lord of the Rings* J.R.R. Tolkien. I really do love the way Mr. Tolkien weaves a tale."

Wilson looked up from the books he was holding to see Kash smiling bemusedly at him.

"What?" he asked with a grin.

"It's fitting that these are the only novels in your office dedicated to the history of Ancient Britain."

"I think so," Wilson replied with a shrug before continuing. "Which one should we try first?"

"I suppose your knowledge of Mr. Tolkien's work is best. I think I remember reading it once some time ago. I have seen the movies though. Fantastic."

"I don't think we should rely on movie lore. If we travel into the book itself, I feel that version of the story will be what we find. Any discrepancies could lead us astray. That's alright, however, I have read it many times and am quite comfortable with how the story goes. Shall we?" He finished by putting the other books on the desk and holding out his single volume, leather-bound copy of *The Lord of the Rings*.

Kash took the book from him gingerly and moved to sit behind her desk. A nervous excitement was quietly building and both her and Wilson could feel themselves adding to each other's anticipation. Kash opened the book and flipped through the pages for a second before turning back to Wilson.

"Which part of the story should we venture into?" she asked.

Wilson didn't immediately respond. It was such a long, detailed story. They could do a million things and go to one of any number of places. He thought of what he would like to do most in that world and smiled. It had nothing to do with battling against evil and trying to destroy the ring. He wanted to meet Gandalf, one of his heroes of the entire fantasy genre.

"What if on this first jaunt we avoid too much danger and craziness? What if we stuck to the Shire and just met Gandalf near the beginning of *The Fellowship of the Ring*? Merlin didn't say anything about being harmed or killed whilst in these stories, did he?"

Kash nodded, more than willing to go along with his logic and not worry about anything too wild until they were more seasoned and comfortable.

"Sounds good to me," she agreed as she looked back to the book and opened it near the front. Wilson turned a couple pages for her until he was satisfied. She began to read without hesitation but by the time she had reached the bottom of the page nothing had happened.

"What's wrong? Shouldn't it be working by now?" Wilson asked.

"I thought so too, let me try reading the next page."

Kash thought hard about how it had happened back in the library with the *Prophetiae Merlini.* She was drawing a blank. She had simply opened the book to one of the first pages and it started glowing blue. Nothing like that was happening here as she read the next page about Gandalf coming to see Bilbo. She looked up when she reached the bottom of the page and shrugged.

"Should we try one of the other books? *Narnia*?" Wilson suggested.

"No, I doubt if this one is ineffective that those will be any different."

"We could try the *Prophetiae* again."

"No, I don't want to go back there. Besides, I have never read that one, have you?"

Wilson shook his head. She had a point, they would most likely be lost in that one and they had only gotten back by luck in his estimation. He was stumped, unsure of where this left them. His face intimated as much to Kash when she looked up at him again. Thinking hard, Kash considered everything Merlin had said about magic and about the spell they were using. She thought of how they returned and the hint they were given after Merlin had left them. "Find the matching script" were his words. Or at least, she thought they were Merlin's words. She was quite certain nothing would surprise her at this point. She was missing something here and she knew it. She just couldn't put her finger on it. She pulled out the copy of the *Prophetiae Merlini* from Dr. Radcliffe's library. She ran her hand over the old cover and marveled at the way the letters of the title had changed to match her own tattoos…

She looked up at Wilson, suddenly excited.

"We were told to find the matching script to get home, right? What if the matching script is the way this cover is changed? What if the way we got home was thinking of the place we had come from? If the library itself is somehow connected to the magic through the books, it must mean that only books from that library will work with the spell." Her smile was triumphant as she looked at her companion. He wore a curious expression, seeming uncertain.

"Yeah, maybe…" he paused for a moment, considering her theory. Deciding to leave the questions and mysteries for the morning he said, "Well, I suppose we'll find out tomorrow when we go back. Anyways, I am going to head home for the night; you need me to do anything for you before I go?"

"No, thanks," Kash replied. "I'm going to stay a while and read some of the *Prophetiae Merlini*. Perhaps it will provide more insight than we know. Have a good night. Meet me at the library bright and early?"

"Sounds good," Wilson replied with a smile as he collected his books and left the office.

Ch. 5 The Witch Queen

"Well, you did say you would be here in the morning," Radcliffe said matter-of-factly when he walked up the steps to the unlock the front door of the library. It was fifteen minutes before opening time and Kash and Wilson were already standing on the top landing holding steaming hot coffee.

"Yes, sir, indeed. This one is for you." Kash held out a third coffee for the librarian to take.

"Why thank you, good lady," Radcliffe said with an exaggerated head bow that made Kash and Wilson smile. They moved inside and Radcliffe started to speak before realizing the duo had already taken off. "Make yourselves comfortable, I'll be up here if you need me," he called to their retreating backs. They seemed to be heading to the scene of their "tumble" from the day before. He shrugged and moved them to the back of his mind. If he had a nickel for every eccentricity he had noticed from a professor at the university, he certainly would not be a librarian.

"Thanks," he heard Kash call out as they turned the corner out of sight.

Kash produced the *Prophetiae Merlini* immediately upon their arrival at the same table they had used the day before and gingerly set it down as if in a place of honor. Wilson glanced at it with wry smile and a lift of the eyebrows to Kash as if to ask: "where to begin?"

Kash took the cue and grinned back before moving off along the row of books, slowly, reading the spines as she went. She shook her head, muttered a denial, shook her head again, and turned quickly when she reached the end of the aisle to head back towards the table.

"These won't do," she said curtly as she moved past Wilson.

"Dr. Radcliffe!?" She found the man just returning to his desk when she moved up.

"How can I help you, Ms. Kash?" he asked politely.

"We were actually wondering if you happened to have a copy of *The Lion, The Witch, and The Wardrobe* here in the library?"

"*The Chronicles of Narnia?*" Radcliffe returned, bemusedly. "Umm, well, I have a collector set in my office of all of them, but how does that connect Merlin to Stonehenge?"

Wilson exchanged a quick glance with Kash. His was the quicker response.

"We wanted to review the bits about the stone table in that story to see if they hold any similarities to a couple of the descriptions of Stonehenge we have come across."

Again, Radcliffe had the distinct impression that this was a dodge if not a complete fabrication, but their expectant looks eventually defeated any curiosity driven follow up questions.

"Right, well, hold on, I'll go get it for you."

When he returned, he held out the copy of the second book in the series but retracted it quickly when Wilson reached for it. "Now, this set is very dear to me and even though I donated it to the library, I would still be quite inconsolable if it should be damaged in any way." He figured he didn't really have to say that, but thinking of the way they had left the work tables the previous evening before, their mysterious reappearance elicited the comment anyways. He finally handed it over and Wilson thanked him and smiled. Radcliffe could tell both were patiently waiting for him to leave, so he simply nodded and moved back to his office. When he was gone, Kash looked to Wilson.

"So, last time I simply opened the *Merlini* and we were transported there. Do you think it matters what part of the story we enter? Do you suppose we have to start from the beginning?"

Wilson pondered this for a moment then simply motioned towards the table where the *Merlini* still lay. He reverently placed *The Lion, The Witch, and The Wardrobe* on the desk and opened it up some ways in. Before he could speak his thoughts, the blue swirl of light appeared, and Wilson looked to Kash to see her excitement as all went black and they were squeezed through the darkness.

When their vision cleared, they saw that they were in an old house. Wilson knew immediately they were in the professor's house and had not actually made it into Narnia. The rain lashed at the windows and Kash grabbed Wilson's arm tightly as they both watched a small girl run out of a room just ahead and to their right then head down the hall away from them. Lucy Pevensie, Wilson assumed, had not even turned around. They were grateful for this and moved towards the room she had just left. Kash poked her head in to see what was in there with Wilson right behind her. As Wilson looked over her shoulder to see what had caught her attention, they both saw the wardrobe that must take them to Narnia.

Kash didn't hesitate but moved across the room and opened the door. As Wilson followed, he remembered a detail about Narnia that gave him pause. Kash was already wading through the coats, so Wilson had no time to voice his concern before being forced to follow her. He thought that the text mentioned that only kids could travel to Narnia, but as Wilson moved into the wardrobe behind Kash, he heard her soft gasp of delight as she emerged out the other side into the softly falling snow. They kept the presence of mind to grab a couple of the coats and moved off into the forest. Soon the lamppost they were both unconsciously looking for appeared before them.

"Now, what? Isn't the faun's house nearby?" Kash asked.

"Mr. Tumnus, yes. If Lucy and Edmund have both already been here, then he is actually in a bit of trouble. Let's see if we can get there before the Queen comes along."

Wilson hurried off with Kash in tow. Neither were quite used to so much snow and the going was tough for a while. Neither were they sure they were travelling in the right direction. Wilson had chosen at random but after only a couple of minutes, they heard a shout and great crash not so far off. They looked at each other and silently agreed to see what was going on. Luck was with them as they realized they had chosen well in their original direction. However, when they arrived at the clearing where they supposed the noise had come from, they quickly dodged behind a tree. There was a large sledge sitting in front of a small cave opening. The Witch Queen of Narnia sat in the highest seat and was glaring in their direction. Had she heard them?

Huddled behind the trees, Kash thought she could feel something at the edge of her sensibilities. There was an energy in the air, some aura that exuded power and strength. The only thing she could think of was the witch's magic. Was she casting a spell? Did she know they were there?

"Tumnus, the faun. Where is the girl? You were specifically told to keep any daughters of Eve or sons of Adam detained until my arrival were you not?"

"There was no girl, I promise," they heard a feeble voice respond weakly.

"Lies. I have already spoken with the son of Adam. He told me quite an interesting tale about his sister and a faun. Take him."

Kash chanced a look around her tree and noticed the Queen was not looking their way. She watched as the dwarf servant pulled a shaky Mr. Tumnus up onto the bench below the Queen. Her face went white, and her nostrils flared as she shot her arm forward. In her hand, the tip of the wand touched Mr. Tumnus, and his look of horror was permanently etched into his new stone features. Kash let out an involuntary gasp and spun back around her tree, praying she hadn't just given them away.

"What was that?" both heard the Queen say sharply.

There were footsteps coming their way and Wilson shot Kash a panicked look. Before they could decide what to do, the dwarf hopped between them with a yelp of surprise.

"Ahh, what're…" his voice trailed away, and he stumbled backwards a bit as they moved out into the open to stand before the Queen atop her sled. The witch's eyes went wide, but she quickly stifled her surprise and painted a superior look on her features.

"And what manner of creatures are you two?" she asked in what she must have thought was a polite voice but sounded full of malice to them.

Wilson thought hard, what explanation would she believe? The prophecy dealt with kids and not adults. He had no idea how their being here would affect the story nor did he have any clue what could keep them from joining the faun at the ice castle encased in stone. This time it was Kash's mind that was, thankfully, working quicker.

"We're from a distant land, come to pay homage to the rightful Queen of Narnia. We have heard many stories of your brilliance and your grace. Therefore, we decided to travel to your fair land and visit you. Where we come from, everyone looks like this, but we envy your obvious strength and magical might."

The Queen seemed immediately suspicious and she narrowed her eyes but remained silent for a moment, obviously contemplating this answer. They certainly resembled humans, but they were older and taller than any boy or girl she had seen. Could they be descendant from the Jinn, just as she was? Maybe they had a bit of giant blood in them, she decided, which could only be good for her.

"Well, you have found me and now, you must serve. Your giant kin have all bowed to my rule and I am sure they will be happy to meet you, even if you are only partly of the race." She wasn't certain she had it right but their response to this suggestion would allow her to gauge where they stood.

Kash looked at Wilson and they both felt that they had no other choice but to go with it. They weren't sure she wouldn't just turn them into stone and so they silently agreed to accompany her until they found an opportunity to get away. They clambered up beside her as her grin widened and Kash was certain that the energy she felt earlier was coming from the Queen herself. Her magic seemed strong and imposing. Kash hoped this ruse of theirs would hold because she was certainly intimidated. Looking at her thin, tall but obviously strong frame and her piercing, cold eyes, Kash wondered what they had gotten themselves into as the sledge sped along towards the evil Queen's palace.

Ch. 6 A Frigid Sanctuary

One wild, cold ride later the sledge came to a halt just before the path up to a castle of ice. The many towers and pillars gave the place an angular and sharp look. It produced an eerie yet hauntingly beautiful effect that gave both Wilson and Kash pause. When the Queen stopped to see what they were looking at, she grinned in recognition of their awe.

"Tis a wonderful place to live, do you not agree?"

"A bit chilly but it's magnificent," Kash replied with a grin at the witch that clearly proved to Wilson she had quickly moved past any fear of their host. They both looked to him and he nodded as enthusiastically as he could, painting an agreeable smile on his features. This seemed to satisfy the Queen who chuckled a little bit and turned back for the stairs up to the front gates which were wide open. There was a huge wolf, its gray fur sleek and its hackles raised standing just inside.

"Be at ease, Maugrim, these are travelers from a distant land, come to aid us in our war."

The great wolf harrumphed dramatically and dropped back down to the floor of the courtyard, eyeing Kash and Wilson as they moved past him.

"My head of secret police. He is the best at what he does and is loyal to a fault." The Queen told them as they followed her into the courtyard proper. Looking around proved to be somewhat grim, and they tried their best to keep horrified expressions from taking over their features as the dwarf grunted and groaned under the weight of the stone faun he was pushing into a corner.

"So many strangers coming to Narnia means we won't have long to wait. Besides, the son of Adam is already on his way here with his brother and sisters. When he arrives, this war will be won before it has truly begun. The prophecy will be squashed, and my rule will remain forevermore."

The Queen directed these words at the strangers, still not completely convinced of their allegiance but supremely unafraid of them. Perhaps her words would have some effect that would betray their true feelings and intentions here in Narnia. As she studied them, however, they didn't seem at all bothered by her proclamation. There was something about them that tugged at her, something just beneath the surface that she couldn't put her finger on. No matter, as long as she kept an eye on them, she figured they could cause no real harm.

"Feel free to move about the castle as you please, but do not leave. We will march soon."

"Yes, your majesty," Kash replied with reverence and surprised Wilson and herself a bit with a perfect curtsy. Wilson followed suit, bowing low and mumbling his own acquiescence. The Queen's smile told them their deception had worked, or at least kept them from being turned to stone for the time being. Without another word, Kash grabbed Wilson's hand and led him away, gently but quickly, while they still could.

"What now?" Wilson asked when they were out of earshot.

"Well, she's waiting for Edmund, right? He'll show up eventually and the story will move on. I think we should take her advice and explore the castle. Could be fun." She grinned at him and moved off in the direction of the main tower. As Wilson followed her, he couldn't help but notice how the light bounced off the ice and shimmered in her hair. The playful grin she shot at him as she opened the door and moved inside made his insides squirm ever so slightly. This gave him pause and he smiled, somewhat amused at himself for such thoughts. With a small shake of his head at his own expense, he followed Kash through the portal to see her already heading up a set of stairs to the right. She increased her pace as he made the bottom, and it was all he could do to keep up with her. When he emerged into the late afternoon sun all he could see was her girlish smile despite the beauty of the scene stretching out before him. He didn't know why he was seeing her in this way now. Perhaps it was the situation being so magically influenced. Maybe it was circumstantial based on their being on an adventure together, but she was undeniably beautiful standing next to him with the snowy landscape reaching as far as the eye could go.

Kash met his gaze and could tell that the man was deep in thought and she got the distinct impression his thoughts were of her based on the way he was looking at her right now. Her mind whirled, not having considered the fact that such an adventure might produce some sort of amorous bond between them. She smiled warmly but turned away from him and leaned on the banister, looking out and dispelling the moment. Wilson followed suit, allowing his thoughts to shift to the scenescape before them. He thought he could see the late afternoon sun glinting off the sea in the distance. There was a particular shimmer in one area that he thought might be Cair Paravel, the Pevensies eventual seat of power once they defeated the Queen and won the war. After a long while of the two of them lost in the moment, neither willing to break the silence nor the peace of the scene, the reality of their situation came back to them fully as Kash spotted the unmistakable form of a boy moving up the hill. Even from here Kash thought she could feel a strong energy emanating from him, but she told herself it was her imagination or perhaps, the Queen was nearby. It was confusing but she didn't take time to consider it as they watched the young boy cower by the statue of a lion, clearly afraid to pass. They looked at each other and smiled at Edmund's expense despite his arrival meaning the story would move along now.

"So, any ideas?" Wilson broke the silence.

"Sure, she is about to ride out on her sledge with Edmund and the dwarf, but she will send Maugrim ahead of her right? Suppose we inserted ourselves into the wolf's party and steal away from him once they have the scent and the chase is on? The wolves will not be paying attention to us, and we'll be able to sneak off. What do you think?"

It seemed solid to Wilson except for convincing the Queen to let them out of her sight and the man pointed this out to Kash as they moved down the steps.

"Let me worry about that," Kash said with a mischievous grin that Wilson was becoming increasingly fond of.

When they arrived back to the first floor and the main hall, they caught their first glimpse of Edmund as he stood before the Queen. Kash could clearly feel a similar energy coming from the boy which confused her for a moment; she didn't remember Edmund doing any magic. The Witch Queen's energy was much more imposing and stronger, but Edmund's was still there. Kash wondered at this but put it to the back of her mind as she tuned into the conversation.

"How dare you come alone?" said the Witch, rising to her full intimidating height and towering over the young boy. "Did I not tell you to bring the others with you?"

"Please, your majesty," squeaked Edmund, "I've done the best I can. I've brought them..." he trailed away when he noticed Kash and Wilson arriving but looked back to the Queen and continued when she looked at him expectantly, pointedly ignoring Kash and Wilson. Wilson thought he sounded rather whiney and felt that Mr. Lewis described this boy properly in the book. He tuned back in just as the Queen was calling for her sledge.

"Should we...?" he started to ask Kash, but she was moving forward as the Queen demanded her dwarf servant bring the "human creature" some sustenance. He followed her to stand before the Queen.

"Your majesty," Kash began reverently, "I wouldn't presume to suggest anything to your excellence, but I imagine you will be sending the wolf to check out the beavers' house. As we have yet to prove our worth, we were hoping we could accompany the esteemed Maugrim and aid him in this task."

The Queen narrowed her eyes, still obviously somewhat suspicious of them. She was sizing them up as she thought the offer over. How did they know of the beavers?

"Pray tell how you will keep up with the likes of Maugrim and his ilk. They will outpace you quickly and cannot afford to be slowed," she replied icily.

"We're quicker than we appear, your grace," Wilson chimed in with what he thought was a confident grin. The Queen slowly turned her withering gaze upon him and decided these two were harmless.

"Is that so? Very well, then. Regardless of your skills in the woods, our muster will meet at the Stone Table. If you are unfamiliar with this place, Maugrim will be happy to show you."

"Not to worry, your majesty, we'll prove we're worthy of your candor and hospitality."

"You have an odd speech about you, I cannot place it. Where did you say you were from?"

There was an awkward pause, but Wilson came to the rescue again, having a more extensive knowledge of the actual map of Narnia than Kash did.

"We traveled over the mountains to the west and south of Calormen, northwards from our home in the foothills on the opposite side. We are quite experienced in the wild."

"Calormen. I have never been west of that kingdom, nor south. If your words are true, then I deem you worthy of this chase. Go with Maugrim. Do not disappoint me."

They didn't have to be told twice as the tone of her voice was quite threatening. They bowed their way out of the hall and nearly ran right into Maugrim himself who was waiting for them by the door.

"Come along then and keep up. We won't be slowing or stopping. Her majesty may believe your story, but I certainly don't. So, make no mistake, I will leave you behind without a second thought." The enormous gray wolf followed this with a low growl, practically daring them to say something against his speech. They both held their hands up to indicate they had no issue with this which seemed to satisfy him as he turned and loped off.

Ch. 7 The Christmas Gift

Kash and Wilson followed, quickly realizing they would have to jog, at least, to keep up with the wolf. The snow wasn't piled deep, but the humans had a much tougher time of moving through it than did the wolf. Maugrim seemed to be trying to pick up a scent and was moving slowly. So, at first, they were able to keep pace with him. After they had struggled against the snow for about a mile, the gray tuft of fur that was the wolf's tail just visible ahead of them, the wolf stopped and let out a long howl. It was quickly answered from not far away and the responding howls soon morphed into wolves themselves as three more of Maugrim's companions emerged out of the trees.

"Now, our pace quickens, if you can't keep up you will be left behind. Her majesty may think enough of you not to destroy you but my opinion is well below this. Good luck finding the Stone Table." Maugrim chuckled at himself and gave a low growl as he turned and ran off, the new arrivals in tow. Wilson started to run after them, but Kash held her arm out, effectively halting his momentum before it had begun.

"He doesn't seem to care if we follow them, so I say we don't." This turned Wilson to look at her as she continued. "You have at least a little bit of knowledge of the geography, right? Let's head for the Stone Table and we'll meet up with the characters there. The Witch's army doesn't show up until later. The timing might actually be perfect."

Wilson mulled it over. The wolves had certainly already left them well behind and he didn't really have any desire to keep Maugrim company either. That really only left them with the one option, so he nodded his agreement with her reasoning, and they moved off in the opposite direction.

■■■

The wolves had run off at a quick pace, following Maugrim's lead but sooner than any expected, the large gray leader stopped and turned back. Unbeknownst to Kash and Wilson, the wolves had circled back and overheard their conversation. At Maugrim's direction, when Kash and Wilson left the area, they had a shadow with them, moving silently, stalking its prey, easily following their tracks and scent through the snow.

■■■

They moved slowly, not in a hurry. The farther they went it felt like the snow was lessening; the sun warming up the world around them. Wilson knew this was part of the story, the Witch's hold on the kingdom of Narnia was weakening, the ice literally melting. The farther they went the more the natural world around them awoke. Birds they had yet to hear were chirping and the sights and smells of a forest in Spring kept their heads swiveling as they moved along a well-defined path. Kash even took Wilson's arm in her own on impulse and he didn't shy away from her. He smiled warmly but said nothing, soaking in the beauty all around them and allowing themselves to be swept up in the reawakening of Narnia.

The sun had reached its zenith as they moved into a small clearing. Their winter coats no longer needed, they removed them and laid them out on the grass, deciding to take a break from walking and rest for a while. They had not been lounging long when the woods around them seemed to go quiet and the hairs on the back of Wilson's neck stood up straight. Kash seemed not to notice, her gaze locked on the sky above her,

her eyes glassy as if her mind were far away. Wilson looked around, his unease growing for some reason he couldn't grasp. Before he could figure it out, the mystery revealed itself as one of the wolves Maugrim had called slowly stalked into the clearing. If wolves could grin, Wilson was sure this one wore the evilest smile any wolf had ever given. Kash stood up immediately and moved close to Wilson as he did the same.

"Well, well, well. Looks like Maugrim saw right through you two, didn't he?" the wolf said with a low growl before continuing. "I guess we'll have to go see him and find out what the Queen thinks of this treachery. Or perhaps Maugrim will just let us eat you and we can tell her majesty you got lost and we never found you. Perhaps, *I* could just tell Maugrim the same and we can skip all the running back and forth and I'll have the feast all to myself."

The wolf's grin widened, if that was possible, and it stalked forward confidently. Panic shot through Kash and Wilson but before the wolf pounced, they all heard bells jingling in the distance. The sweet music filled the air as it drew nearer and nearer. The wolf began looking around, its demeanor quickly changing. Wilson smiled wide, confident that their safety was now assured, and strode boldly forward a step.

"It looks to me like you know what that sound precedes, don't you? I would run now if I were you." Wilson said to the wolf supremely. Kash was a bit confused, not really thinking about the story, considering they were not near any of the characters and therefore distanced from it, at least to her reckoning. She was surprised then, when the wolf took Wilson's advice and ran off in a hurry just before a great red sled sped into the clearing and came to a halt in the spot the wolf had recently vacated.

"Father Christmas," Wilson breathed.

"Indeed, Blake Wilson. Hello, Ms. Jessica Kashmir."

They watched in wonder and awe (not least of all because the driver of the sleigh knew their names) as Santa Claus himself clambered down from the sled to stand before them with a cheery smile on his face. Kash could feel a wondrous, positive energy radiating strength and joy from the large man.

"You two are some distance from home. I wonder how you came to be here in Narnia? I suppose the Witch's hold on the land has weakened more than I thought. This is wonderful news." His smile took in his ears and Kash and Wilson felt warmth exude from him and spread through their bones. His energy was as strong as the Queen's but nicer, somehow more comforting. Neither said anything, just wore awed smiles as Santa moved back to his sled and rummaged around in a big red sack. He didn't seem to find what he was looking for as he moved to stand back in front of them empty-handed.

"Now, the Pevensies, who have, perhaps, a graver responsibility before them, were each presented with individual gifts to aid them in the challenges to come. You two have a longer journey ahead of you but I, unfortunately, have only one gift for the pair of you. Your tattoos have more power than either of you have considered."

They were stunned for a moment. How could Santa Claus, or anyone in this story for that matter, have such knowledge of them? He had known their names but the shock of actually meeting him drove that from their immediate attention. How would he know of the tattoos, or that they had any power at all? Did he know they were not characters in this story? Did he qualify as a character in this story? Yes, he was in the original text, but his story wasn't exclusive to Narnia either. Did he have a similar power to theirs? He continued when neither of them seemed about to answer or indeed, even able to.

"Your ability to travel here comes from the magic of these tattoos you have, yes? But have you considered that you might also have other abilities to travel within this world as well? The same magic that brought you here could transport you anywhere in this land, should you so choose. Cair Paravel? The Stone Table? The Final Battle? All of these are within your grasp. You must only believe and imagine yourself being whisked away in a swirl of blue light. Well, not unlike yourselves, I have a long road ahead of me. Narnia is not yet saved from the grasp of the Witch Queen. There is still work to be done. I wonder if you two will have a role to play in the battle to come. Hmm?" With a pensive nod and a quiet moment, Father Christmas smiled at them, clambered back up into the sleigh and it sped away, the tinkling of the bells slowly fading.

Ch. 8 Aslan's Gathering

They stood in silence for a few moments, both contemplating his words and their meaning. Which part of that did he consider to be a gift? How did he seem to know more about their tattoos than they did? Kash looked at Wilson to see all the same questions on his face. She shrugged when his gaze met hers.

"Maybe, he's right. Maybe we can simply will ourselves to the Stone Table and the blue light will appear to take us there."

Her tone clearly revealed her excitement to Wilson who was still pondering the possible explanations for Santa's depth of knowledge. As his thoughts moved on and he considered it, he figured it wouldn't hurt to give it a try and besides, if it worked and they didn't have to walk the entire way, all the better. So, he smiled and nodded his agreement, holding out his hand for her to take.

"Do you remember the description of the place from the text? It's in the middle of the forest but there is a big clearing at the top of a huge hill."

Kash nodded and closed her eyes along with her companion, taking his hand and trying to impose an image of his words in her mind. Wilson did the same and before they could wonder if it was working, a blue swirl of light whipped up about them and they were squeezed into magical darkness. Kash shook her head to clear the queasiness when her eyes opened once more.

Luckily for them, they had appeared directly before the table itself, and the encampment of Aslan was arrayed on the other side of the hill. Grateful that their appearance had gone unnoticed, they moved in the direction of a great pavilion at the back of the many tents.

"Should we be concerned about our reception here?" Kash asked Wilson, indicating her thoughts were on meeting the great lion or at least some of his followers.

"I don't think so," he responded with some thought before continuing. "These are the good guys, right? I mean Aslan's group will certainly be more friendly and welcoming than the Queen. Besides, this is where a number of scenes in the rest of the book take place. We need to figure out where the story is, anyways."

Kash agreed but didn't say anything, simply motioned for him to continue on. She hadn't actually read this story in quite a while but seemed to remember the description of the kids meeting Aslan involving the lion having quite the presence. She had already felt the Queen's energy and Father Christmas'. Edmond and even Maugrim were the same way. Each felt different but clear. Did all characters in this story possess such an aura? Aslan was the most powerful character in the entire book so his must be the strongest and clearest of all. She wondered if she would feel this in other stories as well and filed the thought away for contemplation later as they began moving through the first few tents and campsites. Looking around, however, caused these thoughts to melt away.

There were Naiads and Dryads playing beautiful music who smiled at them as they walked by. A bull with the head of a man gave a grin and Kash gasped to see a great eagle alighting next to the bull. A centaur moved into the path, crossing in front of them and continuing through the tents on the other side. Wilson had stopped to follow the magnificent creature's passage and only snapped out of it when Kash giggled in his ear and linked his arm in hers, as delighted as he to see all of these fierce but gentle creatures smiling and laughing. They both knew that it was the presence of Aslan and the great lion's return to Narnia that had everyone in such a good mood and the joy was infectious. Wilson stopped again and pointed behind Kash, causing her to turn to see what he was looking at. Back the way they had come there were more newcomers following their footsteps.

They both moved out of the main path and behind one of the tents, hoping they hadn't already been noticed by the Pevensies as the children moved past them and on towards the waiting lion. Their gaze followed the kids up the hill to see Aslan for the first time. Even at such a distance, Kash could feel the strength exuding from the wondrous lion. Great and terrible at the same time, Kash felt that she should look away but was unable to tear her gaze from the flowing mane. Suddenly, the massive head turned, and Aslan's piercing eyes locked with Kash's. Despite thinking they were too far away, Kash was sure the lion was looking right at them. Wilson tensed, obviously sensing the same thing. They both felt rather exposed at that moment but curiously without fear of what would happen should Aslan summon them to stand before him. As quickly as it had come, the moment passed, and Aslan's attention returned to the children who were even then stopping in front of him. They turned away and Kash could tell that Wilson was thinking hard.

"What is it?" she asked concerned.

"Well, I'm trying to remember the next thing that happens in the story. Aslan says something about a feast but takes Peter aside to show him the far-off castle. Yes, that's it! But I think Maugrim is about to attack the camp."

Wilson's tone grew more insistent with every word he spoke and as he finished, he moved back around to the front of the tent, Kash fast on his heels. Sure enough, they could see there was some sort of commotion at the front of the camp that was moving along the other side of the rows of tents towards the pavilion. Wilson took off before Kash could think or say anything and she had no choice but to follow at a run.

The entire camp was now astir, and the chaotic effect the wolves' appearance was having on the goodly creatures was serving Maugrim's purpose perfectly. Wilson saw him chase Susan Pevensie up a tree and begin trying to climb it. Kash could barely keep up, but she could feel Wilson's intention as the man pulled up short ten feet away from the dangerous gray wolf.

"Hey, why don't you run along now, Maugrim, while you still can," Wilson said more bravely than he actually felt. He was trusting in his knowledge of the text, however, and he felt just a bit more comfort as Kash rushed up beside him. The wolf stopped trying to climb the tree and spun quickly. It looked like it would pounce immediately but the sight of Kash and Wilson gave him pause.

"So, as I suspected, you two have betrayed your Queen." Maugrim snarled dangerously.

"We betrayed no one. I don't remember swearing fealty to her." Kash shot back at him, surprisingly unafraid; not something the wolf was used to.

"Hmph, no matter, I'll just have to make you!" he roared with a quick step and a leap for Wilson's throat. Wilson dove aside, tackling Kash out of the way. He rolled over quickly to see the wolf laying atop a young man, quite dead. Wilson grinned, grateful that his suspicions about Maugrim's demise were fulfilled.

"Wow, thanks," Kash said, still out of breath, laying underneath Wilson where they had crashed down together.

"No problem," he said, pausing for a moment to look into her eyes before remembering where they were. Peter Pevensie gave a groan from beneath the gray wolf, breaking Wilson's trance and he got up, pulling Kash up behind him before going to assist their savior. As he neared the young man, he could clearly feel the strength exuding from him. Wilson figured this made sense, he was a king after all, even if he had yet to be crowned. He was fated (along with his siblings) to save, then rule Narnia. It made perfect sense to Wilson but as he was mulling this over and helping Peter to his feet it occurred to him that there was no hiding from any of them now and he had no idea what he was going to tell them when they asked who he was. Before this thought even caused Wilson's mind to race, Peter really studied Wilson for the first time.

"Thank you, sir. You look remarkably human to me but you're an adult."

"Uh, yes, I am," Wilson stammered, not sure how to respond. He was saved from having to as Susan dropped out of the tree and Aslan and the others approached.

"This is Blake Wilson and Jessica Kashmir. They have travelled quite a distance to be here, not unlike yourself, Peter. Not unlike myself. I sense that they will not hinder us in the trials to come." Aslan spoke up and once again, Kash and Wilson squirmed a bit at yet another character knowing so much about them. The lion was currently looking them up and down with scrutiny. They felt bare and exposed but not uncomfortable, just as before. His great eyes seemed to bore straight into their souls and the power radiating from the magnificent lion was immense. For some reason they could not understand they knew they would speak with Aslan later and so they bowed before slipping away back into the campsite.

"So, what happened to staying clear of the story for a bit, huh?" Kash asked with a huge grin.

"Ha-ha," Wilson deadpanned but was unable to resist returning her smile.

"What now? Didn't they chase one of the wolves back to Edmond and will be bringing him back at some point?"

"Yes, but that doesn't happen until morning. We should see if we can use one of these tents for the night." Wilson started off towards the nearest structure. Kash slowly followed, pondering her memories of the text, and trying to reconcile them with the Aslan they had just met. Her contemplations were interrupted when Wilson came back over to her.

"It appears as if Aslan has provided us with tent of our own. The faun there said it was on the other side just on the edge of the trees." He held out his arm expectantly and she looped hers in his as they made their way across the camp. The sun was sinking into the trees, and the evening was darkening about them as they found their tent and bent down to move inside. They had been provided with two bedrolls and some blankets. It seemed cozy enough and they were both quite tired from the day's adventures. Kash immediately plopped down on one of the bedrolls then propped her head up on one hand to look at Wilson who was sitting down beside her.

"So, do you suppose we should spend the night here? Can we? Do you think the spell will let us? How did Aslan know who we were?"

"I certainly think we should spend the night here and at least witness the final battle; besides I still think it would be interesting to talk to Aslan. I think he knew us because he knows pretty much everything that happens here, right? I mean if Santa knew us then it makes sense that Aslan would.

Did you get that same feeling he wanted to speak to us later? It was weird but seemed so clear. I think we should be able to stay if we so choose. We only left the *Merlini* because we wanted to."

Wilson's logic was sound and Kash was also excited to converse with the great lion. She didn't really want to fight in a battle though. They would have to either watch from afar or try and leave before it happened. She simply nodded to Wilson who lay down on his bedroll right next to hers. For a second their eyes met, and they both paused. Kash hovered over the man as a little bit of tension seemed to sneak between them, but Kash gave a sheepish grin and a laugh as the moment passed. She lay back and stared at the top of the tent. Both lost in thought, neither spoke again until sometime later as Kash was drifting off to sleep, Wilson murmured, "Good night," in a drowsy voice and rolled over the other way. Kash smiled to herself a little before closing her eyes and letting sleep take her.

▄▄▄

They awoke the next morning to hear the camp all astir. It seemed as if everyone was packing up. As soon as they had moved outside into the gleaming sun, a couple of wood nymphs came over and began taking down the tent. They were all smiles and happy chatter. Kash and Wilson excused themselves politely and walked through the busy camp once more to try and find Aslan. Looking around, Kash felt her before she spotted the Queen moving down the main path towards the hill where Aslan waited.

They knew this part and knew that the Queen was demanding Edmond's life based on the old magics. They also knew that Aslan had an ace up his sleeve and would sacrifice himself in Edmond's stead. This would evoke an even deeper magic and they both would be spared. Kash wondered as she saw the Queen and Aslan walk off alone together if Aslan could somehow avoid the torture and humiliation he was about to endure. Wasn't he the most powerful character in the story anyways? Despite knowing how it all turned out, it still didn't really sit well with her. She vaguely remembered that the evil beasts shaved him at one point and remembered how Lucy and Susan watched and cried. Having met the lion herself, she understood exactly how Lucy and Susan felt. She voiced her thoughts to Wilson who seemed intrigued but insisted that it had to be that way, and they shouldn't interfere. Kash knew he was right but couldn't quite get past it in her mind.

The Queen would eventually be roared out of the encampment and their walk to the next camp began. Wilson could feel Kash's mind churning, desperately trying to think of a way to influence things without changing the outcome. He sympathized but knew any major interruptions could really change things in unexpected ways. Merlin's warnings still rang in his mind. He had been confident that his involvement in the scene where Peter killed Maugrim wouldn't alter things that much at all. The story was progressing to its most important points and Wilson could only assume that their trying to influence things at this stage would have more dramatic effects. Looking at Kash as they moved along at an easy pace, he thought she looked like she might be preparing to do something of the sort.

"We should tail Lucy and Susan tonight," she said suddenly but not unexpectedly.

"You think so? What for?"

"Well, suppose Aslan doesn't come to see us, how will we get to speak with him?"

Wilson narrowed his eyes suspiciously but smiled quickly to cover it up.

"I don't really want to witness those scenes but if we could catch up to him before, we might get our chance."

He decided he would keep an eye on things but go along with her at the same time. Hopefully, Aslan's determination to see his plan through would win out, not unlike it does in the story itself with Lucy and Susan. Eventually, the troupe came to the Fords of Beruna, the place where they would camp tonight before the final battle tomorrow. Again, the same faun came up to them as the camp was constructed around them and showed them to theirs. They thanked him for his kindness but never went in. They knew as the night deepened that Aslan would be heading back the way they had come, back to the Stone Table and the Queen.

Ch. 9 What the Lion Said

On sudden inspiration, they had moved out ahead of the lion and his juvenile shadows. Since they knew his destination, they figured they could head him off before he made it back to the Stone Table. They eventually found a cluster of trees that afforded some cover but was also directly in the path they had travelled earlier in the day. Figuring Aslan would have to come this way, they sat down behind the trees, peeking out from time to time to look the way they had come. They didn't have long to wait before a peculiar feeling overtook the both of them. Kash sorted it out quickly, recognizing the presence of the great lion. Aslan's energy was unmistakable but before she could figure out what to do, the lion spoke.

"You can come out now," he said with a soft growl.

Wilson and Kash didn't hesitate and moved out to stand before Aslan. His golden mane shimmered in the moonlight when he moved, and his fierce bronze eyes looked right into your soul. In spite of this, Kash managed a smile.

"To what do we owe the pleasure of your company here in Narnia, Ms. Kash and Mr. Wilson?"

It was a simple enough question but neither of them quite knew what to say. They both decided that concocting some story would be pointless as the lion would certainly see right through any deception. So, before either could produce anything coherent, the lion continued.

"Be at ease my friends, I mean you no harm. You have certainly found adventure and excitement here, but I must warn you that the impending battle is very real. To insert yourself into such would be most perilous."

They didn't know what to expect from him, but they certainly didn't think to be warned against the battle. It sent Kash's mind to a million different questions, not least of all the full extent of the lion's knowledge of them. It made her reword the question she had been puzzling over ever since they left the camp that evening. She remained guarded about the knowledge she possessed of the story ahead of this moment.

"Is there not an easier route to defeating the Queen? Her treachery knows no bounds and she will not honor anything she said back at the Stone Table. Perhaps..." She trailed away as the lion gave her another piercing look that stole her momentum.

"Remember that the easiest solution is not always the right solution. The Queen cannot be allowed to win but the old magic must be appeased. There is no other way. My fate is written." The lion looked at Wilson who smiled into his somber features and nodded. Kash was highly dissatisfied but knew that the lion had moved past any arguments she could muster.

"I am curious about one thing, though, Aslan," Wilson spoke up. "We're adults, I mean, that is to say I was under the impression only children were allowed to travel to Narnia, something I didn't think about before we came here."

"Hmm," the great lion pondered this for a moment before looking back at them. "Well, professor, it could be that the Queen's hold is weakening, her reign coming to an end, the same thing that allowed me to return. However, children are the only ones allowed to enter here from your world due to the strength of their imagination, the strength of their belief that anything is possible. Many are those in your world who lose this along the way. I can see that the pair of you still let that candle burn, albeit with stricter lenses."

He moved past them but turned back for a final word. "Belief is your strongest weapon now, belief in yourself, belief like the children have. Whether you choose to aid us in the battle or not, carry this truth with you. Farewell, Jessica Kashmir and Blake Wilson."

With that he moved on through the woods. Wilson and Kash stayed where they were, pondering the lion's words until they felt more than saw the Pevensie girls trying to be as quiet as possible in their own pursuit of the lion. Kash smiled and Wilson returned it warmly, neither wanting to break the silence and alert the girls that they were there. After giving the children enough time to pass them by, Kash and Wilson moved back the way they had come.

▬ ▬ ▬

The next morning dawned bright, the sun glinting and gleaming off finely polished armor and shining helmets. Kash and Wilson moved along slowly at the back of Aslan's marching forces. They were uncertain of where they might fit in but were hoping they would be able to aid or at least not get in the way of the goodly creatures. They eventually filtered out of a narrow valley and onto a large open field. Kash and Wilson climbed as high as they could along the ridge where the valley gave way to the plains below, hoping to stay clear of the main fighting but still be able to see what was going on. They didn't have long to wait as the Queen and her forces appeared in the distance, moving steadily forward.

There was a moment of eerie silence when the two armies stopped and stared across the no man's land at each other. Then without warning, a minotaur in the Queen's ranks bellowed an earsplitting roar and the stand-off was broken.

The charge of both armies shook the ground beneath their feet and the clash of metal on metal was only drowned by the shrieks and cries of the various creatures. The lines were quickly blurred in the melee and who was who became very hard to discern. The Queen, however, was easily spotted and her power bared was a terrible sight to behold. She was waving her wand this way and that and those unfortunate enough to be caught before her were instantly turned to stone. Kash and Wilson couldn't take their eyes from her and in a momentary lull in the fighting around her, she looked up the ridge and seemed to lock eyes with them. Their worst fears were confirmed a moment later as she let out a scream of rage and began moving in their direction. She cleared the edge of the battle, leaving the way open between them and raised her wand with a wicked grin. As her arm reared back, preparing to shoot forward and launch some devilish spell, Edmund shot out of the morass of bodies behind her and swung his sword with all his might. It connected midway along the wand and the magical implement shattered into a million pieces. Momentarily stunned, the witch scrambled to spin and face her assailant.

Kash and Wilson didn't wait around to find out what happened next and ran down the hill towards the entrance into the narrow valley, back the way they had entered earlier. When they had put some distance between them and the battle, they paused, hands on knees, sucking in air in big gulps. They listened closely as what sounded like another charge thundered back to them.

"Aslan and the girls must have made it back to the field to reinforce Peter and Edmund," Wilson said breathlessly.

"Should we go and see their victory?" Kash asked and took a step in that direction, recovered a bit from their run. Wilson smiled and thought for a moment before slowly shaking his head.

"I have a better idea," he said as he held out his hand for her to take. She took it and before she knew what was happening, she was squeezed into the magical darkness with a swirl of blue light. When she opened her eyes, not knowing what to expect, she was standing before four immaculate thrones in a magnificent hall.

"Where are we?" she breathed, swiveling around to take in all the wonders and the roof of ivory.

"This is Cair Paravel, the palace that, even now, the victorious Pevensie children are marching towards to claim these thrones as their own. I thought we should see it before we left. I thought I glimpsed it from the tower at the Queen's castle. It's much more spectacular up close." He smiled at Kash, who grinned back and turned around looking towards the open doors in the east. They could hear the seagulls cawing and the ocean waves rolling in. Wilson followed Kash over to the door and they looked out. The setting sun shimmered across the blue green water and Wilson thought it reached all the way to the beautiful smile painted on Kash's features, her soft hair billowing in the sea breeze. She returned his look with a knowing one of her own and they stared into each other's eyes for a long, wonderful moment. Without dropping their gaze, they silently took each other's hands, and the swirl of blue light appeared and disappeared as quickly as it had come, squeezing Kash and Wilson into the magical darkness.

Ch. 10 Enough Thinking

The library was quiet when they returned, still holding each other's hands. They both opened their eyes, smiling before breaking away. Wilson looked out the window on impulse to see that the sun had not seemed to climb too high in the sky yet. How long had they been gone? He was curious about how time would pass outside the story while they were in it. He looked around for a clock and the one on the wall told them it was not nine o'clock yet. They hadn't even been gone an hour! He was stunned. Hardly any time had passed at all but they had spent nearly three days in Narnia.

"What is it?" Kash asked, suddenly sensing Wilson's confusion.

"Well, we spent two nights in Narnia but only a few minutes has passed here." His tone revealed his depth of thought as he stepped to the end of the row and peeked around it to ensure Dr. Radcliffe wouldn't overhear. Kash didn't immediately respond, considering the possibilities for herself. She seemed unconcerned after a moment's contemplation.

"That's a good thing, right? I guess it makes sense. Hey, maybe time passes as if someone was reading the novel while we're in it," she joked with a laugh. Wilson cocked his head to the side as if her suggestion wasn't as ludicrous as she seemed to think. "Anyways, I thought that was perfectly wonderful. Did you notice how all of the main characters seemed to give off a strong energy or aura? At first, I thought it was just the Queen's magic but all of them kind of felt the same."

"Yeah," Wilson said, absentmindedly, lost in thought.

"I felt Aslan's presence the keenest, obviously. What did you make of his suggestion that belief in ourselves is our strongest weapon?"

Wilson seemed to snap out of it and looked back at Kash before answering. "I'm not sure, there seemed to be a number of characters that knew more about us than I expected. Father Christmas chalked it up to the Queen's winter waning and even the Queen herself seemed to be thinking along those same lines. Although, meeting Santa Claus was fruitful and interesting."

"His arrival was timely, that's for sure. I wonder if our ability to travel within stories will extend to others or was exclusive to that book. Does Santa's "gift" stay with us now that we have left?" She used her fingers to make air quotes as she said "gift".

"Hey, I certainly thought it a good present. Even if we can't do that in other stories, I was grateful we didn't have to walk all the way to the Stone Table." Kash nodded and smiled in response. She locked gazes with the man, her thoughts wandering, and put her hand on his, about to mention some of the more amorous moments of their adventure when Dr. Radcliffe came around the corner.

"Walk to the Stone Table?" he asked with an incredulous look. Neither immediately answered, turning to one another but not knowing what to say. The silence became awkward, and it seemed as if Radcliffe was perfectly happy to wait for a response. Eventually, Wilson spoke.

"Umm, yeah, you know how the Pevensie children have to walk through Narnia to get to the Stone Table. I am just glad I didn't have to make that journey."

At this point, Radcliffe knew they weren't telling him something. He was a clever man (at least he thought so) and could tell when someone was dodging the truth and trying to hide what was really going on. He slowly let a small smile find his features and gave an exaggerated nod clearly telling the other two he didn't believe a word of what Wilson was saying. "Right..." with a wave he moved on past them towards his office, closing the door behind him.

"You know, keeping all of this from Dr. Radcliffe is going to be difficult," Kash said looking in the man's direction.

"You're right, these flimsy dodges are not going to suffice to keep his curiosity at bay forever. I don't think it's a good idea, however, to tell him what we are doing. I feel like this should be kept as quiet as possible."

"I agree..." they both trailed away, thoughts on Radcliffe and what might be next. Eventually, Kash would break the silence, her mind moving on quicker. "So, I think we should try something a bit different this time." She paused and tilted her head to the side as if in thought. "You have quite an extensive knowledge of classic literature do you not?"

"Well, I don't know about extensive, but I have certainly read my fair share. What classics might you be talking about? Are you sure you want to jump right back into another story?"

Kash didn't respond except to shoot a wicked grin that Wilson couldn't help but return, the small squirm of his stomach reminding him how much he was coming to enjoy this woman. She got up and headed towards the librarian still sitting in his office. She lifted her hand to knock when she arrived, but Radcliffe had spotted her and met her at the door, pulling it open before the first knock landed.

"What can I do you for, Ms. Kash?"

"Would you be so kind as to point me in the direction of your classics section, please and thank you?" she said with an expectant look, unable to contain or conceal her excitement. Radcliffe returned a bemused expression, again not worried about the fact she was up to something he was currently unaware of. Out of sight out of mind, he told himself as he headed off towards the fiction section without a word to the professor who followed in his wake. She was unbothered by this somewhat muted response, but Radcliffe couldn't yet know why. Wilson joined them just as they arrived at the proper aisle.

"Here we are, the classics."

"Thanks again."

With a nod as his only response, Dr. Radcliffe moved off in the direction of the front desk.

"The classics?" Wilson inquired.

"Yes, sir. Any one of them could be quite the adventure, wouldn't you agree?"

"Fair enough. What're you thinking?"

"Enough thinking," she replied with a wicked grin. "Since you have an extensive knowledge of these particular works, why don't we just pick one at random? How about this one?" She closed her eyes and reached out for a book. Pulling it from the shelf, she didn't even look at what it was as she flipped it open. To her immense delight, the familiar blue swirl began, and she reached back to grab Wilson's arm as they were sucked into the darkness. Everything stilled and the pair of them examined their surroundings. They had been transported to a graveyard in the dark of night. There was a chill in the air and a light mist hung low over the ground, obscuring some of the headstones.

"What was that?" Wilson began hotly. "What book did you just grab? Not all these stories are sunshine and rainbows, you know? In fact, most are quite the opposite."

"Geez, sorry. I thought it would move us past all the decision making. What harm could it have done? Do you know where we are? I didn't get a look at the book I grabbed, obviously."

Wilson couldn't be sure but as they stood there, he noticed the approach of four dark figures from across the graveyard. He grabbed Kash's arm and pulled her down behind a headstone with him. He peered over the side to see what they would do. A sense of foreboding was stealing over him and his mind was racing through all the novels he had read for some clue. He watched the four figures move up to one of the more ornate tombs and enter, emerging soon after and moving off into the nearby trees. They disappeared, leaving Wilson and Kash still completely unaware of where they were.

"Should we go talk to them, maybe we could figure it out just by seeing who they are? I opened the book maybe just past halfway, that means we are in deep in the novel and one of those men might be the main character. They would be able to tell us what story we are in."

Kash's logic was reasonable, but Wilson knew there were other factors to consider. They couldn't just walk up and ask what characters these men were. Plus, it was clearly the middle of the night and Wilson's mind was not remembering any happy stories that had graveyard scenes at night. He eventually shook his head as Kash studied him for a response but never said anything. He was struck with an idea that he certainly did not like and was desperately hoping he was wrong. He poked his head back out from their hiding spot in the direction of the tomb. His heart sank at what his eyes were showing him. A ghostly white figure was moving through the cemetery towards the tomb. He watched the four men converge upon the figure, now revealed to be a woman holding a small child. Wilson's horror only grew as he watched the scene unfold. He knew it well. These four men were battling Lucy Westenra, a vampire.

"What's going on over there?" Kash asked breathlessly from Wilson's side.

"That's one of Dracula's victims. Dr. Van Helsing and the others are trying to keep...well they're trying to survive if my memory of the text is correct. They will not return to actually kill her until tomorrow. You've brought us to Bram Stoker's *Dracula*."

"Really? That's awesome!" Kash replied a bit loudly and not at all in the vein that Wilson was hoping.

"Keep your voice down," Wilson whispered sharply. "We mustn't be seen by any of the characters over there."

"And why not? Why shouldn't we interact with them? We spoke with Aslan, didn't we? Does it not intrigue you at all? That's Dr. Van Helsing over there, don't you want to meet him?"

"Look, I get it, this is awesome and unique but it's also incredibly dangerous. I doubt we get any second chances. If we get bitten and become vampires..." He left his fears unsaid, hanging in the air like a gruesome elephant between them but he could tell that Kash did not share in these fears at all.

"We're not going to get bitten, alright? Everything is going to be fine. All we have to do is shadow the story but stay out of the way, just like before. So, what happens next?"

Wilson shook his head in frustration at her persistence but thought back to the novel anyway to try and figure out their next move. He recalled that the story shifts to a scene out at the asylum and the Count's estate at Carfax. He gasped aloud then laughed at himself a bit.

"Mina Harker is about to be bitten by Dracula. That's the next major event in the story. The other characters travel around London, sealing off the Count's various coffins. When they are all sealed, the vampire will flee back to Castle Dracula, but he doesn't arrive..." Wilson slowly fell silent, a sudden glint in his eye reflected by the predawn light beginning to show the land around them.

"What is it?" Kash asked curiously, then went on without waiting for a response. "Do you think we should try to save Mina from being bitten?"

Wilson shook his head quickly at that notion. There was no need to risk themselves in such a manner, Mina will be fine when Dracula is vanquished in the end. No, he had something different in mind. If they had knowledge of the future of this story, why shouldn't they use it? He looked back to Kash who was peering at him intently. "We know where they are going. We know what happens in the end. I say we travel to Transylvania with the story, and we can watch it unfold or...I don't know but if we aren't going home, I definitely think we should stow away aboard a boat bound for the east."

"The east?" Kash asked, thinking hard, trying to recall what she knew of the rest of this story. It had been some years ago since she had read this particular work, wasn't it all journal entries? She remembered the castle and Transylvania but not what happened there in the end.

"Yes, but we don't know when all of this is going to happen. Dracula flees when they ambush him in London, at his house in Piccadilly. We need to know when that is going to happen. We have to go to Dr. Seward's house. That's sort of the story's headquarters. There we can discern the passage of events."

It seemed logical to Kash, so she nodded and fell in beside Wilson as he moved off. He was walking purposefully as if he knew where he was going, so Kash didn't ask questions. She was curious, however, what their interacting with the characters would do to this story. Narnia seemed harmless enough, but this tale was wholly different. Something in the back of her mind that wouldn't go away was gnawing at her sensibilities. The idea of meeting Count Dracula, or any vampire for that matter, was exhilarating and exciting. Obviously tinged with a bit of fear but she wasn't too worried. That's what surprised her the most when she thought about it. Shouldn't she be more afraid? Wilson certainly seemed to be against the idea of tangling with Dracula or Van Helsing for that matter. They should definitely go at least talk to the main characters though. What were they doing here if not to interact with the story? She didn't want to change anything, the story would end the same, just as Merlin said it had to. Therefore, there couldn't be any harm in taking advantage of the situation.

Ch. 11 Unexpected Interactions

Her step was much lighter than Wilson's as they neared town. She had no clue where they were going or where they were or if Wilson had any ideas either, but she trusted in his knowledge of the book. Soon, Wilson stopped in front of a house and looked around before moving up to a window to try and peer in. Just then a man emerged from the house, pulled out a pistol, and pointed it right at Wilson. He fired before Wilson could cry out and the bullet just missed him, smashing through the window behind him and scattering glass everywhere inside and out. Kash ran over and thought she made out a winged creature flying away over the house. Was that a bat? She looked back to see the man leveling the pistol Wilson's way and heard him ask:

"Just what are you doing over there, sir?"

Kash could see the deer in the headlights look splayed across Wilson's face. The near miss obviously shook him. She could tell he was thinking hard as he slowly raised his arms. Kash could also feel that same energy she was feeling in Narnia when close to characters of the story. She wasn't sure who this was in front of them, but he had to be an important character. Wilson regained his composure before addressing the armed man's question.

"Mr. Morris, right?" Wilson asked haltingly.

"You know me? Who are you?" the man who had to be the character Quincey Morris replied quickly.

"Yes, and no. It is a long story, don't worry about it. I am unharmed and whole. We can just forget about all of this and

81

we'll be on our way." Morris turned to look at Kash suspiciously while still holding the gun on Wilson. They could both see the wheels turning in the man's head, however, they both knew he would never figure out who they were if they didn't reveal themselves. Morris seemed to calm somewhat and slowly lowered the gun, but his curious expression did not abate.

"You two do not belong here. Go back to where you came from." The sudden change in demeanor and the cryptic nature of his statements were curious to Kash. Wilson didn't seem to notice and grabbed Kash on his way past the man with a "you go it" and a wave. Kash looked over her shoulder to see Quincey Morris staring at them as they moved off. Before she turned back around, he had disappeared into the house. Would this encounter change the sequence of events at all? What scene was that? She hoped Wilson had more of an idea. She just couldn't shake the nagging feeling that Morris knew they were not from this story. The way he had told them they didn't belong and to go back to where they came from was very odd. If he knew they weren't characters, did that mean he knew he was one? How could he have made such a differentiation if he didn't? She was about to share her thoughts with Wilson when he beat her to the punch.

"Did that seem odd to you?" he asked her, stopping once they had moved out of sight of Dr. Seward's house.

"Which part?" she laughed. "The part where you almost got shot or the part where Quincey told us to leave his story?"

"So, you caught that too. I had the weirdest feeling that he knew we were intruding on his novel. Now, I certainly do not want any more run-ins with the characters. I thought I was dead."

"Why was he shooting at you anyway? What scene was that? Did you see the bat?"

"The bat? Ooh," he breathed as he recalled that Quincey went outside to shoot at the bat during one of the meetings at the house. "Well, at least we achieved our goal. I know what part of the story we are in. It shouldn't be too much longer until the novel takes everyone back to Castle Dracula and the mountains of Transylvania.

━ ━ ━

Back at Dr. Seward's house, Quincey Morris had told the group about the bat, but he only mentioned the two strangers to Van Helsing. He *was* the imminent expert on all things unusual.

"Dr. Van Helsing, these two were foreign, in every way, so why would they be peering through the window? What is their interest in the good doctor's house? Do you think they suspect our work with Lady Westenra?"

"I do not believe we should concern ourselves with this mystery duo. From your account, it seems they are benign to our cause and let's hope ignorant, as well."

"Maybe, but I expect we will see them again before all is finished. They gave me an odd feeling as if they were not supposed to be here..." he went quiet and didn't meet Van Helsing's withering stare. The two men let the silence spiral on as their respective considerations filled their thoughts. Eventually, they snapped out of it, and with bigger problems set before them, they let it slip to the back of their minds for the time being.

━ ━ ━

The ship still sat gently rocking in the harbor the same as the day before. Kash was becoming impatient with Wilson's hesitation and need to be certain. He didn't think that the ship's captain would give them passage for the money that had traveled into the story in his back pocket. They had both accepted they would have to sneak on board and stow away, but Wilson was unsure if this was the correct vessel. Kash didn't know how he would figure this out before it was too late, but she wished he would hurry up. Boredom was not something she expected to experience on this adventure, and she had said as much to Wilson at least twice now. She had just made up her mind to say something similar once more when he grabbed her arm and told her to watch closely.

"Is that—?" Kash started but Wilson cut her off.

"Yes, if I'm not too terribly mistaken, that was Dracula's coffin, or at least the last one the main characters have not destroyed yet. That means that this is the right ship, and I expect it will be leaving soon."

"Do you think he was in there?" she asked a bit too excitedly for Wilson's liking.

"Let's hope not," was all he chose to reply as he moved off towards the boat with Kash falling into step behind him.

"How are we going to sneak on?" she whispered in his ear.

"I don't think we are going to," Wilson answered slowly, leading Kash's gaze with his own to the captain who was staring right at them. His leathery skin was sunbaked a deep brownish red, but they couldn't look away from his beady black eyes that were currently shooting as much suspicion directly at them as Kash had ever experienced.

"Oy, you there!" the man waved at them to approach. There was nothing they could do but obey as all hope of secrecy slipped beneath the gentle waves rocking the boat.

"You don't belong here," he began hotly when they moved in front of the burly captain. Just like with Quincey Morris earlier, Kash had the distinct impression that this character knew they were not a part of his story at all. The man went on, drawing Kash back from her contemplations.

"Your presence here is a danger to us all."

"Sailing across the sea is a dangerous business," Wilson replied diplomatically, "we are simple travelers hoping to find passage with you, sir, into the east."

"You don't have any money. Can you work the lines on deck? Doesn't look like it to me. Why should I endanger my crew for your sake when I receive nothing in return?"

"A fair question." Wilson looked to Kash who could tell that he was running out of answers quick and was searching for some way to convince the man but was struggling mightily. She decided to give it a try herself and gave Wilson what she hoped was a comforting nod before stepping forward.

"Good Captain," she began but before she could go any farther the man interrupted her.

"Ahh, yes, right this way Miss. We have been expecting you. You and your manservant are most welcome." This abrupt change in demeanor was admittedly odd but Wilson's shrug as he mouthed "manservant" at her mirrored her own confusion. They both looked back to the expectant captain holding his arm out to show them the way. What had just happened? They both shook their heads and didn't voice their questions as they were led aboard. The captain moved below decks and opened the door to the hold.

"There are a couple of extra hammocks back there, unfortunately the only cabin beside my own is occupied and I was paid handsomely to ensure the cabin was not disturbed by anyone. We will set sail very soon." With that he left them in the hold, doing nothing to quell their curiosity or their growing suspicion this might have been a bad idea. It had to be Dracula in the other cabin. All Wilson wanted was to reach their destination and they had hardly left the dock. He already decided it wasn't going to be a pleasant trip.

"Are you sure about this?" he asked his companion who turned back to him with that disarming grin of hers. Despite how beautiful she looked in the low light of the sole lantern, he still felt uneasy. Why were they allowed onto the ship in such a manner? Who was expecting them? None of it sat quite right with Wilson. He was about to say as much when Kash spoke.

"Where is your sense of adventure? I know I have never traveled across the sea on a ship, have you? Loosen up, everything will be all right. We'll steer clear of all the vampires and see where this story takes us." It wasn't easy but she kept up a constant stream of comforting words and assurances over the next few days as they made their slow way, leaving England far behind.

Ch. 12 Dracula

Four days out of London, Kash was enjoying the sun and sea up on deck. She had decided not to get too caught up on how the captain had mysteriously acquiesced to their desires when he spotted her, despite wanting to stop Wilson. So too did the crew seem not to care or even notice they were on board. Yes, it was strange, but she didn't want to stir up any commotion out here on the water. She would feel much more comfortable interacting with the characters again when they made it back to land. Certain Wilson would agree with her, she hadn't really discussed it much with him, knowing that he would caution her again. She didn't need another lecture. A loud creak of the wooden boards beneath her spun her around to see the captain approaching. There were a number of crew members surrounding him, speaking very quickly in what she thought might've been Romanian. Here knowledge of Eastern European languages was limited at best. The man turned and held his hands out and said something emphatically and the rest of the men stopped talking and moved away slowly. Kash could tell that a couple of them were not happy with the result of the conversation.

"Everything alright, Captain?" she asked politely.

"Ahh, yes, of course, Miss. Do not worry. Some of my crew are a bit superstitious and are afraid of the contents of our cargo. They would have me abandon the item I was paid so handsomely to deliver. It is nonsense."

"Why would they want you to do that?"

"They believe it is cursed. We have had a disappearance, and the mystery has stirred their imaginations. I am sure the sailor simply stumbled overboard whilst drinking on watch. Besides, I must fulfill the contract. No need to trouble yourself over such things. I just wanted to inform you we will be arriving sometime late tomorrow on the Romanian coast." Without another word he walked away across the swaying deck.

Kash found it quite amusing that the captain was completely ignoring the truth shouting at him right alongside his own crew. Cursed was putting it mildly, she thought, as she moved across the deck. But still, to meet such a legend of classic literature...wasn't that the best part of having this power? What was the point of such abilities without actually making use of them? A budding curiosity had formed in the back of her mind and had been gaining momentum in the tedium that was travelling by sea in the late 1800s. Hardly aware of her movements, as if in a daze, her feet carried her across the deck and towards the doors leading below. Walking down the hall, almost to the captain's quarters, she stopped to listen. The faint noise of the gulls and the men on deck above her floated down through the open portholes but there was nothing from within the captain's quarters. To her excitement, there was also no sound to be heard coming from the other cabin, the one no one was supposed to enter.

She knew the Count had to be in there; it was daytime, and she assumed he would return to the coffin during the hours of sunlight. She took a deep breath to steady herself, vaguely wondering where Wilson was and if she should get him first. She knew he would strongly object to what she was about to do, so before this stopped her, she pushed gently on the door and to her surprise, it swung in without a sound. A musty smell that reminded her of death filled her nostrils upon her entrance into the dark cabin. All the windows were covered, blocking any and all light from sneaking through. Unsurprised by any of this, Kash moved over to the simple wooden coffin laying in the middle of the room. This made it cramped in the smallish space, but she didn't mind, having been in many such spots throughout her career as an archaeologist. Her palms were a bit sweaty, and she smiled at her own nervousness despite wanting to continue. Reaching out to grasp the lid of the coffin she pulled it open and once again, it did not make a sound as it slowly lifted to reveal Count Dracula laying peacefully inside.

The vampire looked strong and in good health. He must've fed well on the missing sailor before throwing him overboard. She stared for a moment in the low light and held her breath. There was an aura of great power that emanated from the creature, as strong as Aslan but even more terrible than the Queen had felt. She wanted to close the lid and run out of there suddenly. Fear had crept up on her and white-hot adrenaline coursed through her veins. She grasped the lid to slam it shut but before she could do this, the vampire's eyes popped open eliciting a sharp gasp from Kash. The fiery red glare set upon her froze her and chilled her to the bone.

"Was it fortune alone that brought you to my cabin just as the cursed sun sets? Or is another to blame? I sensed your presence and wondered when you would come, for I knew you would. Someone who has traveled such great distances would never be able to resist." His hungry grin did nothing to quell her rising anxiety. She couldn't seem to hold on to any thoughts for more than a second. Her head felt foggy as if there were some mist filling her mind and slowing it to a crawl. In the recesses of her consciousness, she heard someone shout "magic". That was it, Dracula was a magical being and thus, his magic was inducing this haze, not unlike his methodology with other victims. She shook her head as the image of her being bitten flashed in her mind, sharpening her senses once more. She was able to move back a step and regard the slowly rising and wickedly grinning vampire.

"You have some resistance to my charm it would seem. No matter, there are others on board. Now, about this insatiable thirst for answers that has brought you before me. Do you know what it means to wield true power? Yes, you may have some limited experience with the supernatural, but I assure you, it pales in comparison to what I can give you."

Kash noticed he had looked down as if to indicate he knew her powers came from her tattoos. She felt extremely uncomfortable with the fact that Dracula seemed to know she was not from his story and had travelled there through the use of magic. She took a steadying breath, reminding herself that she could resist. When she truly considered the vampire's words, she realized he was trying to convince her to *let* him bite her. Her mind flashed to images of three scantily clad lady vampires flying around a gothic looking village. She looked up at the unmistakable strength standing before her, offering that very same power to her. Her instincts had her backing up until she bumped into the door. The firmness of the wood behind her gave her the courage to pause and think. If she was honest with herself, she was certainly curious now that the option was laid out before her. She looked at Dracula again to see the vampire take a step forward, easing towards her. A darkness seemed to rise up behind him and Kash heard a noise outside as she flung the door open almost knocking Wilson to the ground along with his lamp. There was a loud hiss as Kash rushed out and slammed the door behind her.

"Wilson," she said breathlessly. "Grab the lantern, we should get out of here before the captain comes to see what's going on."

"What were you doing in there, I had already searched everywhere else. I didn't want to tell anyone until I was sure I couldn't find you. Was that Dracula himself? What were you thinking? Let's get up to the deck!" Kash didn't need to be told twice and moved quickly back up the steps and through the door out under the deepening gloom as the night slowly came on in full.

"What happened in there?" Wilson asked when they had moved out of earshot of anyone else. They were sure to keep their lantern right beside them.

"I don't know, it's a bit foggy to be honest. I was able to resist his magic a bit, I think, but I am certain he almost bit me. He certainly wanted to, and he seemed to think that *I* wanted him to. I swear he knew I wasn't from his book though. There was no denying the way he talked about me having traveled such a long way to get here. He knows we're not characters in his story." She gasped at the end of this and looked up in alarm before continuing. "That must be why we were allowed onto the ship so easily! Dracula must've known I would seek him out."

"You didn't want him to bite you, did you?" Wilson asked quietly, uncertainty clear in his voice. Kash's initial silence spoke volumes to the man, and it almost stretched into discomfort before Kash looked down and responded.

"I admit I was curiously drawn to the idea of being a vampire. Vampirism may have its drawbacks, but it also has its advantages." This shocked Wilson to hear her saying these things. He wondered then if Kash had ever actually read the book they were in.

"You realize how this story ends, right?" he asked her cautiously.

"Yes, yes, I know." Her reply did nothing to convince Wilson she was telling the truth so he interrupted her before she could say anything else.

"When Dracula is destroyed later on, all of those who he has turned are destroyed with him. Allowing him to bite you would only lead to certain death. I'm not sure we should be mixing our abilities with ones that do not exist in our world anyways."

Kash just nodded, unwilling to argue with him and not sure she wanted to. She didn't entirely agree with his last statement and tried to resist letting her mind become annoyed with Wilson's continued fear mongering. Besides, regardless of what the man thought, she had read this story, and she remembered that Mina Harker, whom they spoke of earlier, survives being bitten. That didn't mean she wanted to as well but the areas she was exploring were grayer than Wilson believed. His clear concern was touching and gave her pause. He *had* just saved her from almost certain disaster. She looked back into his strong features and smiled warmly, moving close. She paused to look him in the eye then reached up and kissed him gently, whispering "thank you" before moving off, looking over her shoulder at him with a sheepish grin.

Wilson was stunned for a moment and stood staring at her as she moved across the deck. Slowly, a small grin appeared on his face as he pondered the feelings that were steadily growing for his impulsive companion.

Ch. 13 At the Castle

The ship had passed into the Black Sea by the next dawn with no further incident, bringing Wilson to Kash who stood at the rail, staring at the distant coastline they were keeping close to.

"What now? Do we just see this through to the end? The other characters are ahead of us if my estimation of the date is correct. Its sometime in October, I think. Van Helsing and the rest may have already reached the castle and could even now be eliminating Dracula's wives and sealing him off from the castle. Maybe, I can't be sure of the timetable. The story mostly stays with the others and not with the Count's retreat."

Kash let him ramble on. He tended to think aloud when she was around, which seemed to help him keep his thoughts organized. She didn't mind; it allowed her to consider all he was saying without having to respond much. Despite his constant worry, she was undoubtably grateful that he was here and smiled at him before turning back to the wind and the waves. Her mind wandered to the castle that was somewhere ahead of them. She certainly wanted to see it. A Gothic castle and the home of Count Dracula, no less. She looked to Wilson to see an alarmed look on his face.

"What did you do?" he asked as the familiar swirl of blue lights began to spirit her away. Kash reached out and grabbed the man by the wrist and was vaguely conscious of him having come along for the ride with her. Her relief was immense when she saw that they were standing on a high battlement on the wall of a magnificent castle. Although, she wasn't exactly sure what had just happened. She had been thinking of Dracula's castle and Wilson had been speaking of Van Helsing being here and then...what? They were transported to a different part of the story just by them both concentrating on it at once, just as Father Christmas had said. Just as they had done in Narnia.

"We just moved through the story, didn't we? I guess Santa's gift does extend beyond Narnia. That's good to know." Wilson's statement brought her mind back to the castle and where they were.

"I think so," she was going to continue with her thoughts, but they were interrupted as Wilson grabbed her by the arm and pulled her down behind the back crenellations overlooking the courtyard below.

"What?! Ow!"

"Look, it's Van Helsing and Mina Harker. They have come to destroy the three lady vampires and seal Dracula from his own castle." Wilson looked back to see Kash already moving off, heading for the stairs down into the courtyard.

"What are you doing?" he whispered intensely as he moved to catch up with her. She didn't respond, just kept after the fading footsteps of Van Helsing and Mina. Kash turned a corner ahead of him and by the time he made it around the same corner she was nowhere to be seen. Cursing under his breath, he increased his pace to the next turn where he faced with a decision. Left, or right? It was hard to see anything in the dim light and the darkness stole the end of the hallway in both directions. He heard a clatter and waited a second to discern its direction. He took off down the right-hand passageway, wanting to call out for Kash but knowing that was not the smartest idea. He really hoped she wouldn't try to interfere with the characters again. This was an important moment in defeating Dracula and if she did anything to change the story now, the consequences could be catastrophic. He had to find her; he sped up as he turned the next corner into still more darkness.

▄▄▄

Kash had turned the first corner, her excitement lending speed to her steps, and didn't notice the deepening of the blackness behind and around her. Her lack of sight slowed her pace considerably and she moved towards the wall, putting her hand out to feel her way along it. She never found the stone but kept moving into the blackness. She was sure she had turned to the left and the wall should've been there, but it wasn't. Had she moved through an open door or archway? Without warning, the blackness began to lift and standing before her were three beautiful young women. She could immediately feel and recognize the aura of power they were exuding. It lacked the intensity that Dracula himself emanated, even with all three of them here, but Kash knew they were still potentially dangerous.

"What do we have here?" the middle one said, gently brushing her long auburn hair out of her face and grinning, revealing long, sharp canines.

"Our Lord and Master has sent us a plaything." All three vampire's eyes flashed, staring hungrily, as one, at Kash. She suddenly felt that same fog creeping into her sensibilities. There was a different feel to it this time however and she could hear the three calling to her somewhere in the back of her mind saying: "join us, come to us." They beckoned to her even as they edged closer, and it took all her willpower to clear her mind and take a step back. The fog lifted somewhat, and her vision cleared. The lady vampires were no longer smiling but neither were they approaching still.

"Hi," Kash stammered, immediately berating herself for her timidity and reminding herself she had power here as well. She stood up a little straighter before continuing.

"I have been wondering, ever since I met your master," here she paused to smile at the shocked look on their faces, "whether I would have the chance to meet you three. You are a very traditional part of the story but are perhaps not as threatening as Dracula himself."

"We can be threatening enough for the likes of you," the raven haired, taller vampire hissed. The blonde laughed and the three began to sway in a wide circle around Kash.

"You're curious about this life and this world, aren't you, traveler?" the original speaker asked huskily, as if to a lover, without breaking the dance. Kash spun and tried to keep up with their movements at first but eventually gave it up before she became dizzy.

"I will admit, your beauty and grace are enticing. Living forever is also attractive."

"Ahh, many may think that, but they have not tried it, they have not had to see the rise and fall of centuries. There are things about this life we wouldn't wish on any. Our Master brooks no arguments from us but he is not always unkind. It is not such a horrid existence." They stopped abruptly and seemed about to close in on Kash, suddenly very serious.

"Let's leave this one be, sisters, she knows not what she is asking. Travelers such as yourself should continue to be so. Why would you bind yourself to our Master? Why would you bind yourself to his fate?"

Kash got the curious feeling once more that these characters knew she wasn't a part of their story. They hadn't reacted at all when she mentioned them being a "traditional part of the story". Did the vampire's words indicate she would be stuck here in the story if she allowed them to bite her? She wasn't seriously considering this, but they seemed to know things about her power that she didn't. She opened her mouth to ask a question of her own but the three vampires starting hissing and screaming, in agony it seemed. One by one, they turned to dust that gently floated down to the ground around her. Dr. Van Helsing must've completed his work here in the castle, she thought. She stood there, thinking hard. So much had happened in what seemed like such a short time. Just a few days ago she had been on her dream dig at Stonehenge. Years of study and work had provided her with the opportunity of a lifetime. She smiled at the absurdity of where her path had led her. She was just convincing herself she wasn't crazy, but she still had a ton to learn about her tattoos when she heard heavy footsteps pounding down the hallway outside the nearby door.

"Kash, oh thank God, I found you. What happened back there? You turned the corner and were gone. I thought I had turned the same corner; I have no idea how I missed you. I think enough time has passed since Mina and Van Helsing went into the castle. Should we go back up to the battlements and see what we can see?"

"Yeah, sure," Kash replied slowly, her mind still on her recent conversation with the lady vampires. Wilson gave her an odd look to question this hesitance, but Kash only smiled and said, "lead on."

Ch. 14 Isn't the Story Over?

They had only made it as far as the courtyard when Wilson was grabbing Kash and dragging her down behind some crates once more. She was about to protest when she heard a woman's voice saying something followed by a growling response. She paused, then stood up as the duo walked out of the front gate and off down the road. They waited a while to ensure the characters could not look back and see them before following. Wilson started explaining how they had reached the very end of the story and all that was left was to destroy Dracula himself. They followed through the deepening snow, staying close behind Van Helsing and Mina Harker. The weather made it tough for them to keep the duo in sight but also ensured they would be equally tough to spot on the mountain should the pair turn around. Wilson held up his hand for her to stop and they both watched Van Helsing pull out some binoculars and look out. They tried to follow his gaze when they saw the man point out something in the distance. Van Helsing and Mina started off once more, unaware of their two extra shadows in the deepening gloom. Their urgency was apparent and soon they came upon their quarry. Kash and Wilson hid in the nearby trees and watched the scene unfold.

Two men they assumed were Jonathan Harker and Lord Godalming pointed rifles at the team of gypsies carrying the familiar coffin of the Count. Kash could see the man Wilson named as Quincey Morris and another she assumed was a character as well. Wilson would later tell her it was one Dr. Seward, the owner of the house where he was almost shot. Kash was fully expecting the blue swirling tornado to pop up when the dust of Dracula's body began to fade away like the lady vampires back at the castle. Much to her surprise it did not, and Wilson looked at her helplessly, clearly expecting the same thing.

"Isn't the story over?" she asked him.

"Well, yes..." he didn't seem to have any answers either. "And no," he continued suddenly, excitedly. "There is a note at the very end of the novel from Mr. Harker. It says seven years have passed. We're not going to have to stay in this story another seven years, are we?" His question wasn't necessarily directed at her, but she shrugged anyways, as at a loss for ideas on what to do next as he was. They watched as the man named Quincey succumbed to his wounds and uttered his final words. Much to their surprise, all the characters suddenly turned to look in their direction, staring as if they knew Kash and Wilson were hiding in the trees. They both ducked down instinctively, not knowing whether they were hoping they hadn't been seen. Kash saw the bewildered look on Wilson's face and shook her head. Resolving not to be afraid of characters in this story anymore, especially since these were the good guys, she stood up and turned around to face them.

Her smirk and subsequent laughter made Wilson jump up to look as well. The characters had all disappeared and, in the spot where Quincey Morris had died "a gallant gentlemen" stood the swirling tornado of blue lights. Wilson's relief was evident as Kash offered her hand and a smile. They moved back through the portal, hands clasped together, thinking hard of the library. They were not startled at all this time when they returned to the very row of books they had departed from, to see Dr. Radcliffe bending down, picking up the copy of Dracula they had dropped. His back was to them, and he curiously did not seem to have noticed they had just appeared from a swirling tornado of blue lights. The man stood up straight and turned with a yelp of surprise.

"O my god, professor Wilson, you scared the hell out of me." His hand covered his heart, and he blew out a long sigh before turning a curious eye on them. He seemed about to ask them a question, but Kash interrupted him before he could.

"Sorry, I think I may have knocked that one off the shelf. Can I see it for a second?" She smiled sweetly at the frowning man. This seemed enough to head off any forthcoming questions of curiosity as he held out the novel. Kash immediately noted the change in font on the cover and held it out for Wilson to take note of the same thing. He nodded without saying anything and they both looked back to Radcliffe with a smile as the silence spiraled into awkwardness. Dr. Radcliffe was the one to eventually break it.

"So, you guys have been spending quite some time here in the library the last couple of days. How's the research going?"

"Research?" Kash asked confusedly before she could stop herself. Radcliffe looked at her curiously for a moment.

"Yes ma'am, your research about Merlin, the fabled sorcerer," he said slowly.

"Ahh, yes…Our research is going well. Smoothly." She looked at Wilson pleading for him to say something and rescue her foot from her mouth. He only chuckled before turning back to Radcliffe. Wilson could clearly see the suspicion etched on the librarian's face.

"So, you said a long time, I seem to have left my phone at the office. How long would you say we have been here?"

"At least two hours, so far, today. You were here all afternoon yesterday."

"Right. Thanks." Wilson and Kash moved passed the confused and somewhat bemused man. Kash smiled and Wilson nodded before they turned the corner and moved across the library back to where the *Prophetiae Merlini* lay on the table next to the copy of *The Lion, the Witch, and the Wardrobe*.

"Two hours?! We were in Dracula for days."

"Almost a month, actually. We saw things recorded in the journals of the Dracula characters spanning about a month's time and we were only gone two hours in our own time." He repeated it in his head trying to make it sound more sensical, but this certainly failed. Kash had a skeptical look on her face but if Radcliffe was correct about how long they had been here today, then there could be no doubt. They entered the story at the end of September and left at the beginning of November.

"Time passes faster in the stories relative to our world, remember? We haven't seemed to age either. That's incredible. We could spend years in a story, supposing the story itself lasts that long, and come back as we are now. Obviously, I have my doubts about extremely long durations but that definitely reinforces my confidence we could spend a lot of time in these stories."

Kash was happy he was excited about it for a change. She smiled at him and nodded, allowing her own thoughts to wander the avenues of possibility. She didn't think there was any time to waste but was also unsure of which story to pick. Some reflection and meditative thought would do her some good, she decided.

"Hey, why don't we call it an early day, today? I would like to really think about the next story we travel to and do some planning. I'm going to head back to my office. You're welcome to join or…" she trailed off as she stood up.

"Yeah, good idea," Wilson replied. "One more thing before we go, let me see if "Dracula" has appeared in your tattoos." Kash smiled and nodded. Spinning around and lifting her shirt just a bit, she looked back over her shoulder at the man. He was nodding, obviously having spotted the word immediately.

"You know, even if I didn't know these tattoos were magical, I would still think them amazing."

"They do have a certain allure." Kash responded as she lowered her shirt once more and they headed for the exit. Dr. Radcliffe was standing behind the front desk, reading something. He looked up as they approached.

"Thanks again, Dr. Radcliffe. I imagine we will be back bright and early, tomorrow."

"My pleasure, professor." With that they left, trying to ignore the librarian's curious stare as they went.

Ch. 15 Something Historical

Wilson moved down the hall slowly. His face was buried in the *Tales from the Arabian Nights*, a potential book he was thinking of suggesting for his and Kash's next adventure. She seemed like she wanted some space when they had arrived, so he had set off on a stroll around the grounds. He loved the various stories in this work and thought he might reread one or two of them to refresh his memory. Eventually, he found a quiet place beyond the astronomy building underneath a wonderful tree with a magnificent view of the mountains off in the distance. The evening gloom would find him still there, nearing the end of *Aladdin and the Wonderful Lamp,* as it was one of the more popular stories and he read rather quickly. Feeling cheerful and satisfied as he always did at the end of such tales, Wilson stood up to find Kash and suggest they travel to Ancient Persia.

It didn't take long for the man to make it across the campus to his colleague's door. He lifted his hand to knock but noticed it was slightly ajar before he did. The small opening in the door afforded him a view of a tiny sliver of the room. Kash was seated across the office at her desk, scribbling furiously in a nicely bound leather journal. He didn't want to startle her, so he knocked softly and slowly pushed the door open. The woman looked up at the slight noise.

"Oh, Wilson. Come in," she said brightly.

She went back to scribbling. Before Wilson had settled in the chair in front of her desk, she had obviously completed her journal entry because she closed the tome and placed it gingerly in the desk drawer. She looked up at him expectantly.

"So," he began without much conviction. "I, um, wanted to talk, well, obviously about what the next move is but also about...about Dracula." The hesitant manner of his speech told Kash he had been waiting for the right moment to share his thoughts on her solo excursions during their time in the story.

"Alright, what exactly is it you wanted to talk about?"

"Well, it was clear to me that you sought out Dracula on the ship. No one was supposed to go in the cabin yet, somehow, I knew that was where I would find you. I am certainly glad I did, too. It seemed like you were in a bad way when I arrived."

"That's because I was."

She thought back to the heaviness of the vampire's very presence. His magic was hypnotizing, alluring and powerful all at once. She understood why some of the characters were unable to resist the Count. She was still uncertain how *she* did it. Obviously, it had to do with the magic of Merlin's spell, but Dracula still almost overpowered her. Perhaps this was because deep down she knew there was a part of her that was curious about that life. She looked at Wilson, understanding then that this was why he was bringing it up.

"Dracula's magic is strong, and it was only Merlin's power and your timely arrival that saved me from sharing in his same fate. I knew in the end the vampire was destroyed but that didn't change the allure of that strength and power. No, but when I met his wives or mistresses or whatever they are—"

"Wait, you met the lady vampires? All three of them? You didn't tell me that," Wilson interrupted.

"Yeah, when we got separated at the castle, I think they tricked you into running past and lured me into a side room or something. They had power as well. It was interesting that I could feel the difference in their magic and Dracula's. Maybe possessing these tattoos has attuned me to other magics in literature just as it did in Narnia." She cocked her head to the side in thought.

"What did the women say? Did they do anything? You seem whole; they didn't attack you, did they?" His concern was touching and Kash smiled at him, her mind revisiting for a moment the kiss they had shared.

"No, they tried the same tricks Dracula did and they certainly *wanted* to bite me. They wanted me to *let* them, actually, despite what they were saying to each other. They kind of talked at me and never really to me. Anyways, Van Helsing destroyed them before they finished toying with me."

"So..."

"It was actually those three that showed me I would never have let them bite me, in the end. I simply didn't know how the two magics would interact. Would I have had to stay there forever? I knew that Vampirism has its allure but being stuck there outweighed any such thoughts and anyways, subservience to anyone, let alone Count Dracula, is too high a price to pay. It wasn't all scary though, was it? Think about it. We confirmed a few things did we not?"

Wilson's relief was evident to Kash although he simply nodded before responding. "Indeed, we did. Perhaps a plan next time and not a sudden jump into the unknown." He grinned in spite of himself.

"Well, yes, that too. I was referring, however, to the fact that we traveled, magically, from the boat to the castle, confirming that particular ability. Also, it seems obvious now that the characters have power of their own. Each one has a certain intensity, but not all characters are created equal it would seem. Dracula was as strong as Aslan but opposite, you know? Where Aslan exuded comfort, Dracula's energy felt like a sweet, enticing poison."

"I was wondering about that, actually. We got on the boat quite easily. Did Dracula know we were coming? Did he know you would seek him out? Leastways, we also know that the power of the tattoos gives us some resistance to that type of magic. I can't say I'm unhappy with how that tuned out either." He finished with a laugh and shot a playful grin at his counterpart. She laughed and matched his smile with one of her own. She was about to point out the book in Wilson's hand, a potential candidate for travel she was assuming, when he spoke again.

"What about Quincey Morris? The way he said you do not belong here was curious, don't you think?"

"I suppose," she replied pensively after pondering her memory of the occasion for a moment.

"I just had this weird feeling that he knew we were not from the story."

Kash narrowed her eyes in thought, unconvinced. "You think? Maybe he just knew we weren't from England or maybe he thought we were dressed oddly. He certainly couldn't know we had traveled there magically. Does magic even exist in that story? I mean, this kind of magic. I guess vampires are magical creatures. But still, he may have looked at us sideways, as you say, but it's quite the stretch to think he knew we weren't characters in a novel. Would that not imply he was aware of his own nature as a character in the novel?" Kash could tell her words were not dispelling Wilson's worry nor were they moving his mind from his consideration, so she continued in a more conciliatory tone.

"Look, we'll make a decision on the next one and then do our homework. We'll be really careful and then we'll have the upper hand on any characters we meet because we already know all about them."

Wilson remained silent for a long while, considering everything that had gone before. She was right, he told himself, this opportunity she had literally stumbled upon was something extraordinary at the very least. If they went in with a plan and a goal in mind, then he felt that they could really explore the extent of this power. However, he knew they would have to choose wisely and exercise extreme caution. Eventually, he held up the book he had brought along to show her.

"*Aladdin?* I haven't read that one in ages. I may have only read bits and pieces of it, anyways. I'm guessing you have read through it all, multiple times and this is where you want to go next?"

"Well, there are a number of different stories in this work. *Aladdin* isn't the only one. There is also *Ali Baba and the Forty Thieves* or *Sinbad the Sailor.*"

"Oh, not that one, I have had my fill of historical sea travel. It might be cool to go to Agrabah, but I don't know. There are a lot of fantastical things there, I guess. Lots of magic. I was thinking something a bit more our speed, however. You like your sci-fi/fantasy and there's nothing wrong with that but what about history? What about the things we have both studied for so long? I know! We could go to Troy during the war for Helen. *The Iliad!*"

"That's not a bad idea at all," Wilson mused, not really attached to the idea of traveling to Agrabah and liking what Kash was thinking as well. He began to run over the story in his mind. Wasn't the original text a poem?

"You know what? Homer wrote another epic poem as well. *The Odyssey* with Odysseus would be a wild trip. Ahh, but that takes place aboard a ship, for the most part. *The Iliad* it is."

Kash's smile took in her ears. She had been toying with the idea of something historical that she would be more familiar with. She had actually read this one multiple times. Having once laid the groundwork for a trip to where some thought Troy's ruins to be buried. She had reread the work hoping to find some clues. She wanted to go over it again, however, before they actually ventured there. Besides, a summer in Troy would be quite lovely. She imagined moving through the great city, arm in arm with Wilson. She looked at the man again, the first inklings of a plan forming in her mind.

"I might need a bit to refamiliarize myself with it, though. I don't have a copy here, but I think our library does. I'm going to go see."

"Yeah, I have a copy in my office I'll go look at. We could meet back her tonight, or should we meet back at Radcliffe's library in the morning to compare notes?"

Kash smiled at the hopeful tone in the man's voice but told him they should meet tomorrow. He returned her smile and promised to be there in the morning. She headed for the campus library, her thoughts swirling like the blue light they had been travelling on.

■■■

The next morning found Kash and Wilson once again moving up the stairs of the library to stand before the locked door. They both held steaming cups of coffee, having been up half the night reading, and studying.

"I thought I might find you two had arrived before me again."

Dr. Radcliffe moved up the stairs and past them to the door. Unlocking it, he bowed them inside with a dramatic flourish. Kash's smile at him was the only response required, and his nod back was all the permission they needed to head into the depths of the library. They quickly made their way back to the classics section. Kash stopped and pulled down the copy of *Dracula* they had travelled into and placed it on a nearby table as she had done with the *Prophetiae Merlini* and *Narnia* before their last jaunt. Wilson's curious look prompted her to say something.

"Just in case, I want to replicate the circumstances of our last trip," she explained.

Wilson simply shrugged, not really thinking it mattered either way and willing to let Kash take the lead. Eventually, they found the library's only copy of *The Iliad*. Wilson removed it from the shelf reverently and went back to the table where *Dracula* lay with the newly morphed cover, next to their other adventures to date.

"The question is, where do we jump into the story?"

"That's easy. I thought about it last night and I think we should use the time relativity to our advantage. We should start right at the beginning, the first scene where Agamemnon demands Achilles' woman after one of the battles. This will give us plenty of time to explore Troy. Just think of all the archaeological discoveries and corrections to history we can make. Especially since we are much more prepared than last time. Trust me."

"That's what you want to go for? Archaeology?" Wilson's tone clearly indicated his incredulity.

She painted a bored expression on her face and stared at him for a second. "Didn't you do any research yourself? Do you not have any ambitions for this trip? There are a plethora of characters and scenes to explore. I know there are mysteries you want to solve, at least for your own curiosity if not for anything else. We have an incredible opportunity before us, and we should make the most of it." With no further hesitation, Kash went back to the copy of *The Iliad* and opened it to the very first page. Almost before she began to read, the swirl of blue lights erupted around her and Wilson. Just as they were disappearing into the blackness, Dr. Radcliffe came around the corner of the aisle and dropped all the books he was carrying. The last thing they saw before being spirited away was the shocked expression of the librarian as his mind tried to reconcile what his eyes were showing him with any normal circumstance of reality.

Ch. 16 A Prophetic Encounter

Kash could smell the brine of the ocean immediately, before she even opened her eyes. Wilson, as expected, instantly expressed his concern about Dr. Radcliffe having seen them.

"What're we going to do? Radcliffe certainly knows something unusual is happening now."

"Yeah, yeah, we'll deal with it when we get back. There isn't much that he can do while we're away and there's no telling how long we'll be here. Remember we won't be gone long there, regardless of how long we spend here." This pacified his anxiety somewhat, at least enough for him to look around and take a measure of where they were. Kash was already moving, having figured they would arrive in the Greek camp down on the beach. Thankfully, there was no one close by, but she could see a large group of leather clad men milling about not far down the shore. She led the way into the nearest tent and began rummaging around for something suitable to change into. She knew their 21st century American clothing might bring way too much unwanted attention. Her goals in this story required more subtlety.

"What're you doing?" Wilson asked her back as she moved around the tent.

"Looking for something to wear. You should put that armor on right there. We need to blend in. Aha." She stood up holding a long robe. "Turn around, or go outside," she told him with a sheepish smile. Wilson returned a bemused grin but did as he was told and moved out of the tent to try and put the armor on. Kash emerged a few moments later dressed in the robe she had found. It was almost too short for her tall frame, and he could see the lower half of her shins sticking out the bottom of it.

"You are too tall to be a woman in this time," he pointed out as she moved up to him.

"Actually, brave warrior, I am blessed by Aphrodite and therefore my height is a thing of grace and beauty. You must pray to Ares to give you strength. How does that sound? Too much?"

"No," Wilson snickered. "Just try to avoid being too longwinded with any of the characters." He started to move off towards the gathering of soldiers, but Kash grabbed his arm.

"Not that way, we need to make it to the city. I'm throwing in with the Trojans. Besides, I don't want to sleep in the sand."

"*Throwing in with the Trojans?*" Wilson asked as he struggled up the dune behind Kash. "You know they lose this war, right? What is it with you and being fascinated with the losing side?"

Kash didn't answer, just pushed on to the top of the hill. Her grin took in her ears. There it was, the great city of Troy. She stood there for a moment, considering everything she had ever read, studied, and heard about this place in her career. How many archaeologists would give their right arm for a chance like this? She had to take a deep, steadying breath. Nervous excitement was rushing through her veins, and she was vaguely aware of Wilson coming to stand beside her and behold the walled city across the plain. They stood in silent contemplation for a few moments, the sun setting and the shadows of the early evening beginning to steal the light.

"We need to go if we are going to make it in before they close the gates. We should also move around the city to the other side. The main gate might be difficult to get through this time of day. I imagine they will close at sundown if they aren't already." Wilson said. He looked at his companion, and she nodded eagerly. They set off at a swift pace but found that the distance was farther than it appeared. The side gate was literally closing when they ran up, huffing and puffing. The guards standing there crossed their spears in front of them to halt their progress.

"Please, my good man. We've traveled a great distance and then some to come to your city. We heard of the Greek attack, and I wanted to do my duty to King and country. You must let us inside or we won't last the night out here on the open plains with the Greeks just over the hill on the beach." Kash was pleasantly surprised that Wilson had taken the initiative with such flare and confidence. It made it easy for her to stay silent as the guards looked them up and down.

"Your tongue has an odd manner." The guards eyed them with great suspicion for a long and uncomfortable moment before throwing a hand out to halt the man turning the portcullis. They were passed through and only had to stoop a little bit to fit under the gate. It didn't take any time at all for the man on the crank to get it lowered behind them.

"Good thing those weren't the main gates, right?" Kash asked as they moved through the bustling city as it prepared for nightfall.

"Agreed. I think we appeared on the beach too far to the side. The main gate is…" He had already seemed to lose his bearings and spun around in a circle.

"Not to worry, we'll find it again, eventually. For now, let's find a place to spend the night."

"I think if we head towards the citadel, we should find the residential section of the city. Some of my reading last night involved the possible layout of this place."

"Excellent, there might be a barracks where we could use the same story from the gate or maybe we can convince someone to let us stay in their home." Kash didn't necessarily like the thought of spending the night with a group of soldiers and was hoping that the latter proved to be their fate.

They drew nearer and nearer to the royal palace but there seemed to be less and less people about. They turned a corner and found themselves right underneath the walls of the citadel. A noise came from somewhere just ahead of them and they stared along the wall for the source of it. A richly dressed, magnificently beautiful woman was scurrying towards them. The woman didn't seem to notice they were there until she was right on top of them. She let out a gasp of fright and tried to turn quickly but Kash moved out of the shadows and said, "Wait."

The woman stopped and slowly turned back to face the approaching Kash and Wilson. Unexpectedly, Kash could feel an aura of power coming from this woman. It was curious, not unlike the way being around Dracula and the other vampires felt but this was quite different. It did seem to lend credence to the fact that the characters all seemed to feel this way to her. Who could this be then? There was no way their luck was that good. Was this Helen herself? She silently laughed at that. What would Helen be doing outside the citadel after dark practically running along the wall here?

"Greetings," Kash finally started but was interrupted before she could figure out what to say next.

"Who are you? You have a strange way about you."

Wilson looked to Kash confusedly before they both turned back to the woman.

"Yes, we have traveled quite far to seek refuge and possibly glory in the war."

"You have not," the woman stated simply before walking around them, examining them slowly. "You're from across the sea, if not farther, but you do not seem Greek to me. The exact locale escapes my mind but regardless, you have most certainly not come to take part in our war. What has drawn you so near to the palace this night?"

Kash, less stunned by the woman's seeming knowledge that they were not from around here, smiled at the woman and decided this wasn't Helen after all. There was something nagging at her though, as if she should know who this was standing in front of her. She was saved having to invent something else to say by Wilson's voice bringing her back to the conversation.

"We are actually seeking shelter for the night. Not at the palace of course. We certainly didn't think to be invited into the citadel but were hoping there would be a barracks or home we could stay for the evening in this area."

The lady ran her hand through her long, dark hair and was silent for some time. Wilson was taken aback and quite uncomfortable with the situation. Their unexpected acquaintance seemed to calm, however, and took on an almost superior air. Kash could tell the woman was sizing them up and coming to a decision.

"Well, you two are blessed by the gods. They have seen fit to allow you to come upon me at a most inopportune time. In exchange for your silence about our meeting, I will allow you to share my home for the evening, but we must be quick and we must be quiet." The woman moved past them quickly, bidding them to follow her. They moved off in the opposite direction along the wall and before long came to a small door in the stone they had not noticed before. She rapped upon it three times, paused and then three times again. This signal did the trick as the door swung open and they heard a quiet, urgent voice say, "Quickly". They followed their new friend through the portal and were immediately accosted by two palace guards.

"Stop, they're with me. You will tell no one of this."

The soldiers lowered their weapons and openly scowled at all three of them and Kash got the feeling that they were rather reluctant to obey the woman. They did as they were told, however, and the trio moved off into the winding passageway of the royal citadel itself.

"Wait, are you a handmaid, or..." Wilson's curiosity echoed in the dim light of the close walls. The woman turned back to look at them incredulously before responding.

"I am Cassandra, daughter of Priam who is King of Troy. Surely you knew this." Her grin was a bit telling to Kash but left Wilson completely off-balance. Cassandra was one of Priam's more referenced daughters in the ancient stories and literature about this time in Troy's history. She was supposedly given the gift of foresight by Apollo but angered the god and was cursed so that no one would believe she spoke the truth. Kash figured this could work in their favor. If Cassandra were in contact with Apollo and the gods then perhaps, their running into her would prove quite lucky indeed. She also wanted to pick the woman's brain to see just how much characters knew about them. Although, as far as she could remember, Cassandra had a minor role if any in the actual story of *The Iliad*. Kash simply figured, as she had hoped since they arrived in this story, that they didn't necessarily need to maintain proximity to the main characters of the text itself. Dracula's ship from England wasn't described in any detail in *Dracula*, so she was hoping her magic would allow her to come and go at her leisure here in this world. She was certainly going to operate under that assumption until proven otherwise. Besides, if she thought about it, this was the perfect person to serve as their first contact with the characters. Not to mention she was the daughter of the king himself.

Kash hurried to catch up with Cassandra, who had resumed her march through the corridors, pulling Wilson along with her. Turning a corner into a stairwell, their footsteps echoed in the narrow space as it began to climb. They couldn't tell how far the stairs had risen but they came to a landing and moved into another corridor. Eventually, Cassandra slowed and moved through an archway into a spacious chamber. The walls were lavishly decorated with tapestries and there were many rugs laid upon the floor. The bed was massive with four posts to the ceiling and hanging coverings shrouding the bed itself. The room was open onto a large balcony and the slight breeze felt cool and refreshing in the hot night air.

"Leave us," Cassandra instructed her two servants that were waiting for her when they entered. The two young girls walked out of the room briskly. "So, he clearly stole that armor, and you don't have any idea how to keep that robe tied properly do you?" Kash had been having trouble with the garment since she put it on. She hadn't noticed anything out of the ordinary about the armor Wilson wore but she wasn't an expert on that either.

"And...?" Kash asked leadingly.

"And I have seen it in my dreams that travelers from far away would come to Troy. Travelers not involved in the war and yet they will have great influence therein. Apollo may have cursed the minds of others to disbelief but that does not defeat the truth of my visions. You must be the travelers I dream of. Borne upon the blue wind, they came sweeping out of the sky. I have seen it. Just last night. I went out tonight to consult with a trusted advisor and whom did I run into? It cannot be denied; my prophecy is fulfilled."

Although Kash was expecting to be known by the characters, this was a bit strange. Cassandra had the power of foresight and prophetic visions. Blue wind? Was she talking about the blue lights that swirled around them as they traveled into the stories? What else could it be? A knowing look slowly spread on the woman's face as both Wilson and Kash's stunned silence spiraled on and on.

"Fear not, this can only be a blessing from the gods. Our meeting was not by chance." This relaxed Wilson a bit and Kash seemed to be moving on from her initial bewilderment as well.

"My lady, you speak truly, we have come a long way and are supremely grateful for your kindness. I was wondering if you could tell me more of your visions? Perhaps we could help discern what it all means?" Kash looked to Wilson to see him wearing a confused expression. She gave a comforting smile and a nod, attempting to dispel any nervousness Wilson might have about her speaking so candidly with the princess. He decided to trust her and as Cassandra looked at him then back to Kash with a bemused expression, he felt it might be good to see what the seer actually already knew. Despite his interest, he found his mind wandering as the two ladies bantered back and forth. Eventually, his head began to nod, and he drifted off to sleep. Lady Cassandra and Kash continued their conversation well into the night and it wasn't long after Wilson's contented snores brought smiles to both ladies' faces that they paused and moved out onto the terrace under the wonder of the night sky.

"So, tell me…" she paused, causing both to realize Kash had yet to introduce herself.

"Oh, my name is Kash…Kashmira and my slumbering companion is Wilsonious." Cassandra stared for a second and Kash got the feeling the princess caught her slip and recognized the dodge. She seemed to let it go, however, as she continued.

"Yes, Kashmira. You have an interesting way about you, you both do. He, at least, wears his heart on his sleeve making his desires easy to interpret. Most men are. However, your energy is much more guarded, as if you have yet to fully give in. Love is always felt keenly and is obvious to those around you."

"Love!?" Kash echoed incredulously but she could hear the forced nature of her response in her tone, as did Cassandra who smiled at this recognition. Kash tried to push past the moment.

"My energy? What do you mean?"

"You have an aura about you that exudes confidence and willpower. It also tells of the bond you two share, however much your mind keeps your heart in check. It might be somewhat masked by the foreign nature of your presence, but love isn't hard to spot to the wizened eye."

Kash remained silent for a while, pondering the princess' words. She hadn't yet admitted it out loud, but she couldn't deny the obvious connection growing between her and Wilson. She looked over at him, sleeping soundly on a cushioned divan, and smiled to herself. Cassandra had said that this made her energy strong and recognizable. The idea gave her pause because it sounded as if she was having a similar effect on the characters that she and Wilson were experiencing from them. Apparently, Cassandra could feel an aura exuding from Kash, just as she felt from many of the characters they had met so far. Could this be why some of them seemed to know they weren't from the story they were in? It still didn't seem right to her that *any* character would know of their own nature as participants in a book. Cassandra seemed to know many things that would point to this awareness, but Kash couldn't be certain. She also did not want to really push it farther and risk revealing her own true nature but if Cassandra's words were true and she and Wilson were exuding an aura of their own… This opened all kinds of possibilities that Kash hadn't been expecting. She was saved from having to return a response as Cassandra went on.

"You two certainly have a unique way about you but your true nature is no different than my own. We both long for companionship, trust and love, as all do. It is a powerful emotion and all you have to do is believe in each other and this belief can be your strongest weapon."

That was a curious turn of phrase, Kash thought, and it made her look at Cassandra suspiciously. The air of mystery about the woman was evident and it made Kash believe the woman knew more than she was letting on, but it wasn't a discomforting thing for Kash. She could tell Cassandra was a friend and she decided she liked the woman. It was curious that she used similar words to what Aslan had told them just before they parted with the great lion. More than one character had spoken of belief now and Kash wasn't exactly sure what to make of it. She looked back at Cassandra, her hesitance to deny the princess' words speaking volumes about the validity of the woman's statements. Kash let it fall to the back of her mind and stared up at the stars, feeling Cassandra doing the same beside her. They would sit for a long while in silence, enjoying the peace of the night, neither speaking until sleep eventually drove them both to retire for the evening.

Ch. 17 The Temple of Apollo

The sun's light opened Wilson's eyes, reminding him of where he was and what had happened last night. They were in the royal palace of ancient Troy. Not so ancient at this point, he mused. He looked around for Kash and Cassandra, but he was quite alone. He turned back to the magnificent view from the balcony. The surface of the distant sea glittered and sparkled, bringing a peaceful smile to the man's face. At least for a moment. He was worried about what Kash intended to do here. A weight was growing in the back of his mind, and he knew it would be brought to the forefront before too long. His contemplation was interrupted by the sound of girlish laughter coming up the stairs.

"Do soldiers let the day slip away as such in your land?" Cassandra asked him with a grin as she moved into the room, Kash following closely behind. Kash chuckled a bit at the thought of Wilson being a soldier.

"I am no sol...I mean..."

"This is already known to me, but neither is the potter or the fishermen a soldier until the enemy appears at the gates. So, which are you?"

Wilson smiled back at the woman. He decided he liked her and the way she spoke. "I'm not a fisherman or a potter. I am an archaeologist and professor at an esteemed university." Cassandra's confused expression returned Wilson's memory of the epoch they had traveled to, quickly making him qualify his statement.

"Ah, that is to say, I am a historian and a teacher."

"A learned man, then. Kash has told me many things of your homeland and it sounds a delight."

Wilson looked at Kash then with concern. Kash smiled disarmingly, providing Wilson with at least a little bit of comfort. He was intensely curious as to what she had shared with Cassandra but didn't want to invite too many questions, so all he did was nod.

"So, Cassandra, what of the war? What of the Greeks? Why do they not resume their assault today? Has Apollo spoken to you of this?" Kash felt it time for her to intervene and steer the princess from such dangerous waters.

"Apollo's gift shows me many things but does not require the divine presence to impart its visions. As for the invaders, they quarrel amongst themselves causing the present delay. This is in our favor as we have the favor of the gods."

"Can I ask you, princess, about Apollo?"

"You wish to hear the tale, do you not? The tale of my gift and my curse."

"Well," Kash looked to Wilson, his expression begging her to exercise caution. She wasn't very inclined to do so and decided it was past time Wilson get on board and go along with her plans. She plunged ahead, indifferent to what Wilson would think of her leading questions.

"Actually, I am more interested in your interaction with the god. Did you visit Olympus, or perhaps, Mount Ida? Did Apollo come to you?" Cassandra's eyes narrowed in suspicion, clearly indicating the woman would draw conclusions of her own about Kash's interest. She felt she could trust Cassandra, however. There was nothing in her studies or memory of Cassandra's life that suggested otherwise. Kash supposed the woman just wanted someone to believe her for a change.

"Men do not visit the garden of the gods. They can, perhaps, be taken there by divine influence but such places are inaccessible to those subject to mortality's grip. Apollo saw fit to come to me and his gift remains but not his blessing. My penance is servitude to the gods and my punishment is belittlement and disbelief. Shall we visit the temple of Apollo? Perhaps the answers to the mysteries you seek will reveal themselves to you in that most holy place. Come."

▬▬▬

The great temple dedicated to Apollo was on the opposite side of the city from the citadel. Their journey through bustling streets was pleasant and uneventful. Wilson wondered why they did not have an escort of soldiers. Did the princess not warrant protection? This question was answered by the many passersby who greeted Cassandra warmly. He could tell the people were flourishing under her father's rule and held no contempt for the ruling family. They arrived at the magnificent temple without incident and moved inside. The ceiling flew away in the open space and the many decorated columns were spaced about the sunken middle of the chamber in a circle. There stood a great altar, presumably for sacrifices made in search of divine favor. Opposite the space from where they entered stood a golden statue of the god Apollo himself. Cassandra moved right up to the base of this statue, Kash following closely behind. The princess prostrated herself before the edifice with no hesitation. Kash turned to Wilson with a "when in Troy" look and followed suit. Wilson decided to examine the altar and let the ladies do their thing.

"Great giver of light, our lord Apollo, hear our prayers and grant us your favor. We are your humble servants."

"Would you teach me to pray like that?" Kash asked. "I am afraid disbelief has plagued me most of my life and the gods of my world have not shown themselves to humans for some time. But if Apollo would shine his light upon me, I would worship and bow before his radiance."

Wilson's head perked up from across the chamber at that. Those were alarming words to hear. Just how deep was she trying to go here? He remembered her early questions about the gods and Mount Olympus and his eyes widened. She wasn't going to try and reach the mountain of the gods, was she? He moved closer to hear what Cassandra was saying back to Kash.

"Apollo accepts all genuflection and devotion. I was priestess before his divine visit and I continue my service, as promised, despite the double-edge of his gift. I will train you in the lord's ways. You will make a strong priestess." The ladies stood up and looked at Wilson. "And you, my dear. What has fate in store for you, I wonder? My visions spoke of distant travelers but not their intent or what designs they have. Tell me, Kashmira has chosen, what will you choose?"

"Kashmira?" the man mouthed confusedly. Kash's guilty smile almost made Wilson shake his head in bemusement before he remembered Cassandra was asking him a rather important question.

"I, um…"

"Perhaps service to the god Ares is in your future. All the gods must have followers, devout or otherwise. While we follow all the gods and are beholden to their whims, we can seek the favor of one or the other just as they bestow their favor on one or the other as they see fit. The god of War does need soldiers for his endless army. No? Well, you said you are a historian, perhaps, the goddess Athena would welcome your gifts. The library of the muses would suit your professed talents better. Who am I to say, though? Even the gods must bow to Fate. Let us visit the great palace library, the royal historian can appoint you a place."

Wilson was pleasantly surprised at this turn of events. He knew they would have to fit in somewhere and he was desperate to avoid the battles outside the city walls. The library could certainly be a way to accomplish that. He was worried, however, about Kash or Kashmira, as it were. It did seem a stroke of luck having run into Princess Cassandra, but he still had an odd feeling about all of this. A priestess of Apollo wasn't the worst way Kash could've chosen to fit in. Wilson decided to be grateful for their fortune so far and exercise patience. Once they were established in the city, he could worry about corralling his companion's dangerous budding ambitions. "Lead on," he instructed their new friend.

Their journey back across the city was even less eventful than their trip to Apollo's temple. They were admitted through the front gate of the citadel this time without question. The guards here were obviously used to Cassandra having friends in tow. They made the library with the glares of the guards being the only incident along their way. Whilst it certainly lacked the modern technology of the Dewey Decimal system, Wilson was still delighted and surprised at the library here. It was small and all the "books" were actually scrolls made of some paper Wilson was unable to identify.

"Ahh, Princess Cassandra, your presence graces us like the light of Apollo."

"Your words warm the heart, my dear friend, Cliffradus. I have brought you a new recruit for your incessant translating and copying and study. This is Wilsonious, a learned historian and teacher. Be gentle, he wears his caution as a badge of honor. Perhaps your tutelage will cure the storm that rages in his heart and mind. And now, Kashmira and I must return to the temple of Apollo, there is much to do." Cassandra turned to leave and Kash moved to stand before Wilson.

"I'll come visit you soon. Cassandra says there are rites and rituals to be performed. I think this place will do you some good. Maybe they will teach you to read the language."

"Are you sure splitting up is a good idea?" Wilson asked.

"C'mon, where is your sense of adventure. Besides, this is right up your alley. Imagine the knowledge and history stored in this room. I know I want to come back to look at some of it. Besides, we must fit in here somehow. Just try to remain as unassuming as possible and do some reading. I'll be back tomorrow." Wilson watched as Kash followed Cassandra back between the pillars and out of the small library.

"Shall we begin?" he heard an old voice ask behind him.

Ch. 18 Mysterious Encounters

The next few days were peaceful, ironically enough, for Kash as she went about her daily duties at the temple. Peace wasn't something you often found in times of war, but Kash knew about where they were in the story and wasn't worried. Knowing that the battles would resume soon, her resolve to avoid the actual fighting was quite strong. She figured she would spend those hours with Cassandra, wherever the princess went during such times. Maybe simply staying here in the temple where she had been allowed to take up residence was the best plan. She decided she loved it here. If this was Ancient Greek daily life, then it wasn't so bad. She obviously missed some of the 21st century amenities she had grown used to but she never minded not having those on digs in hot deserts for days at a time.

She was currently waving a fan back and forth to try and battle the summer heat. She was supposed to be studying the ancient scrolls displaying the methodology and proper protocols for sacrifices to Apollo. Everything had to be just so on and around the altar and it was required to know all of it in order to participate in the ceremony. However, the heat was stealing her concentration and the tiny diagrams on the weathered scrolls made her squint, which hurt her eyes before too long. Thankfully, she was familiar with it already. She heard someone shuffling into the hall and she stood, more than happy to see if it was Cassandra coming to rescue her from her tedium. Unfortunately, it was not, only a pair of worshipers come to pray before the statue of Apollo.

"Kashmira."

Kash spun around at hearing her name to see a tall soldier moving her way. She thought there was something familiar about him as soon as she saw him but couldn't place it. His armor was ornate, and his dark hair and beard did nothing to hide the intense yet calm look of his eyes. He put her at ease despite giving off a serious air. She wasn't sure who it was, but she thought she might know him.

"I was told you were spending more and more of your days here with Apollo. Cassandra speaks very highly of you. Whilst many will show joy and friendship, few have been able to keep the attention of my sister the way your presence has."

"Your sister?" Kash echoed, comprehension suddenly invading her mind. "Hector? I mean, my prince!" she corrected herself with a bow. The man smiled warmly and nodded.

"Indeed. In the days before your arrival, our beloved Cassandra's sullenness knew no end. Her smile had not graced my sight in days. War can weigh on the heart, yet I was struck that a different notion pulled her gaze downwards. At times, her prophesying brought small comfort but these fantasies cannot alone bear her sadness forever. And yet, your arrival has buoyed her spirit to new heights. Your influence is strong, and I am grateful. It does my heart well to see Cassandra's smile."

"Yeah, Cassandra is great. She—"

"She says you came here on a blue wind, just as she foretold not two moons ago."

"A blue wind?" Kash was sure to sound confused. She thought she knew where this was going now. Since Apollo cursed Cassandra to be disbelieved by everyone around her, Hector wanted to know why she thought that Kash was prophecy fulfilled.

"Yes, she proclaimed you as a great adventurer. The tales of your exploits are grand, Cassandra would have us believe. I thought I would come meet you myself. Would you enjoy a walk upon the plains? We will stay close to the city; besides, we do not expect battle to be joined today, it should be safe within the shadow of the great walls. You can tell me of your travels."

■■■

"So, your homeland. Regale me." Hector was clearly trying to figure her out as they walked through the front gates and onto the dusty plain. Perhaps he was just being overprotective of his favorite sister, but Kash was still a bit off guard. While she thought she recognized his energy as a character, and he certainly claimed to be a main character, he had a way about him that made Kash uneasy. Not as if she were in danger but more so that this man was not telling her something or was deceiving her in some way. Not being able to place it, she didn't see any harm in attempting to dance around the truth with her answers. Smiling, she began to tell stories based on some of the digs she had been on. They had made it almost all the way around the city and back to the wall abutting the great temple with Kash thinking all was well and Hector was starting to trust her. As they made it back into the city and up the front steps of the temple, Hector asked the question he had obviously been waiting to since he sought Kash out.

"This blue wind that brought you here…?" He broke off, his look at her and his silence a clear question.

"Ahh, yes, well Cassandra does have quite the imagination."

"She does, indeed. I take it "blue wind" is the name of your sailing vessel?"

"My sailing…Yes, yes, it is. Our ship is called "Blue Wind."" Kash decided to let him believe whatever he wanted to believe. She wanted to save face with Cassandra but also did not want to alarm the characters into asking of her true origins.

"I think I would like to see this great vessel. Will you take me to it, some time?"

"Sure, shouldn't be a problem," Kash lied, hoping she could figure something out before he made her show him.

"Cassandra did speak truly about the strange manner of your tongue. It does not detract from your grace, rather adds to your beauty. My lady." With a bow, the great general of the Trojan army and the crown prince moved away and out of the temple leaving her standing there staring. She still felt odd about this encounter, something in the back of her mind ringing alarm bells. Unable to quite figure it out she let it go, for now, and moved back to her studies.

▄ ▄ ▄

Wilson's first few days in the ancient city of Troy were certainly less adventuresome and uneventful than he thought they would be. He had learned to read ancient Greek surprisingly quickly, which was just as well. He assumed it had something to do with the magic of the tattoos and his familiarity with language. Regardless, he was grateful this gap in his façade was filled before any suspicion could come from it. The royal scribe was a talkative, white-haired old man. Wilson could tell he had not had anyone spend any time with him here in the library for quite a spell. Wilson didn't mind the chatter; he hadn't been tasked with anything too difficult as yet. Having offered his services, the scribe had asked if he would assist in making copies of the various works, a never-ending task in those days, it seemed. The work was dull and long, but Wilson was getting to read many things he most certainly would not have before Stonehenge and everything after. He also had not seen Kash in a couple of days but was aware that they would ask more and more of her in the temple the longer she was there. He thought to visit her soon and was about to ask leave of the scribe when he heard a noise coming from the hallway just through the archway into the library. He looked up to see a stunningly beautiful woman moving towards him with such grace it stole his greeting from him completely.

"Ahh, yes, my lady Persephone. Surely, your radiance is a gift from the gods to light this dark room and bring joy to our eyes. Have you met Wilsonious? A great historian and shaper of minds; he comes from lands far away to study our ways and aid the great city of Troy in the days to come." Wilson smiled at the woman and was vaguely aware of his own bemusement at the old scribe's penchant for the dramatic.

"A scholar and so handsome? The gods must be smiling upon *me* today." The woman's coy manner and the way she looked at him stole his breath once more. Her golden hair flowed in radiant waves down her back and her brilliant green eyes exuded an alluring intensity that swallowed the man up. For some reason, before he was able to get a hold of himself, the image of Kash's smiling face flashed into his mind. Eventually, he unwound his tongue and composed a response.

"It is lovely to meet you, lady Persephone. Our friend, Cliffradus, speaks truly. Your beauty is a light shining upon us. To what do we owe the pleasure?"

"I was studying the scrolls about the Greek enemies encamped on our shores. The other assistant, Peleus, was aiding me. I must say you are much more pleasing to my sight."

"Peleus was sent by royal decree down the coast. His journey will keep him away from the city for some days."

"The gods favor me a second time, it would warm my heart if your new friend would aid me with the scrolls today." The royal scribe bowed low then looked to Wilson, motioning for him to follow the lady Persephone. Wilson nodded and moved after the woman, hoping his understanding of the scrolls would prove useful, limited, and new as they were. When they were out of earshot of the old scribe, the woman turned around to face Wilson. As he moved to stand before her once more, the same image of Kash flashed in his mind. He didn't quite know what to make of it but was saved having to figure it out just now by Persephone's voice.

"It is obvious to me that your heart belongs to another and yet, perhaps, I might steal it away. Blindness has plagued you, but your eyes have opened to Fate. Or have they? I wonder…"

"What?" Wilson had no idea how to respond. What was she even talking about? He thought for a second his command of the language had failed him. Her sudden air of mystery was a bit alarming. He was beginning to think the woman had come here to see him and not to study the scrolls. He couldn't recall if the lady Persephone was an important character in the *Iliad*. She went on before he could figure it out.

"Your pursuit begins in earnest. Go now, your fate awaits." Without another word, this mysterious lady moved past him and out of the library. He moved back over to where the royal scribe was sitting behind his desk writing out yet another work from the endless pile waiting to be copied.

"Is the lady Persephone always like that?" he asked the old man, hoping he would have some insight.

"Who?" the man asked without looking up.

"The lady Persephone, just now? She said she was working with Peleus. The scrolls?"

"There is no Peleus here, and it seems the heat is going to your head. No one has come this morning. Fever dreams. You should take water and rest." The royal scribe went right back to his work after this, clearly satisfied the encounter was at an end. Wilson stared for a few moments, deciding whether to point out the man himself had spoken to the woman. He moved away, thinking it better not to make any waves and try to figure it out on his own. Again, he searched his memory for a Persephone in the story but drew a blank. He had a strange feeling he should know what had happened but couldn't place it. He went back to his table, shaking his head in wonder and frustration.

Ch. 19 Pressed Into Service

Wilson spent the night in fitful sleep. His dreams were full of the swirling blue wind, the lady Persephone, Kash's smiling face and the cacophony of fierce battle. He awoke to the dawn, the lady's final words echoing in his head and that same image of Kash.

"Your pursuit begins in earnest. Go now, your fate awaits."

Had he hallucinated the entire thing? The old scribe had even spoken with her before proclaiming Wilson insane. It made no sense. All he was left with was a desire to see Kash. Hopefully, she would be able to unravel this mystery. He rose from his bed at the back of the library where he had been granted a place to spend the evenings and donned the robe he had been given. The scribe was nowhere in sight, so Wilson decided to head to the temple of Apollo, hoping he would find Kash there.

Kash stood and moved away from the statue of Apollo, having finished her attempts to practice the way Cassandra prayed. She was about to return to her chamber when Wilson moved up the steps with a wave.

"Wilson, how wonderful to see you."

"Kash, I am glad I found you. I had a really strange visit yesterday."

"Really? So did I. Well, I guess it wasn't so strange." Kash thought the afternoon with Hector was rather enjoyable aside from tiptoeing to avoid suspicion.

"What do you mean? Who visited you?" Wilson asked, temporarily forgetting his own encounter and the reason he had come to see her.

"It was the prince, Hector. I think he wanted to see me for himself. He seemed concerned about his sister. Cassandra and I have spent some time together and apparently, she has mentioned me to her brother. He came to see me and asked about how we got here. I think he was just being protective of Cassandra, but I did get an odd feeling from him."

"Odd, how so? And what did you tell him? You know we must be careful around the characters." Kash rolled her eyes at this, clearly growing impatient with his caution.

"It wasn't the same as with Cassandra, or Dracula, even. It was a wholly different sensation that confused me but I just kind of went with it. I didn't reveal anything to him, except I may have let him believe we came here on a ship called "blue wind" and that he could see it sometime. Not sure how I'm going to wriggle out of that one if ever I need to, but I suppose we'll burn that bridge when we get there."

"You did what?! Hector is the *crown prince!* If he comes back and decides he wants to see the "ship", what are you going to do?! Best case scenario, he'll throw us in the dungeon. Worst case...I don't even want to think about it!"

"Woa, calm down. It'll be—"

"Don't tell me to calm down! This is serious! Would you want Hector to reveal that you lied to our new friend Cassandra? What would she think? What happens when one of these characters figures out exactly what we can do and decides to try and come back with us?"

"What was I supposed to tell him, huh?" Kash replied, her volume increasing with her indignation.

"I don't know, but that was such a risky thing to say. If we're found out...I'm just saying we need to be more careful." Wilson replied, deflating just a bit.

"Alright, all right. I will. Wait, didn't you say that you had a strange visit, also?"

Wilson took a deep breath, not quite believing that Kash was taking his warnings seriously. Her stubbornness was cause for concern, but he still wanted to know what she thought about the lady Persephone, so he pressed on. "Yes, I did. A lady Persephone came to me in the library. She first claimed to want to study the scrolls about the Greeks and that she had worked with another before I was there. The scribe greeted her warmly and seemed to know the man of whom she was speaking. She indicated she wanted me to help her in his stead, but I am pretty sure she made all of that up. When we moved away from the old man, she turned and was different. She talked about stealing my heart and being blind. She said my pursuit begins because my fate awaits. Then she left, it was really odd. Crazier still, when I went to ask the scribe about her, he acted as if she was never there. He told me I had a fever dream and should go lay down. It was quite bizarre." Wilson didn't mention his dreams or the fact that he had seen her face during the encounter and the night before. He watched as Kash mulled it all over. She certainly seemed intrigued by the story.

"You said the librarian, uh, scribe, denied her ever being there at all? That *is* wild. Your pursuit begins?" Kash gave him a mystified look, clearly indicating that her confusion matched his.

"What're you going to do now? Try and find her again?" she asked him.

"I don't kn—" Wilson turned at the tolling of bells echoing over the city. "What?"

"The Greeks, they must be attacking." Kash said breathlessly.

"You there," a guard by the door said, pointing at Wilson. "Come, gather your armor, the war resumes."

"I'm not—" Wilson protested but the soldier ushered him under the archway and down the steps, his powerful grip on Wilson's arm giving him no choice but to allow himself to be half dragged away.

"Wilson!" Kash shouted, moving after him but the soldier had already pushed him around the corner and out of sight. Kash stood frozen at the top of the great temple steps. What should she do? Wilson was about to be pressed into the battle. She had to find Cassandra; the seer was the only one who could help. Turning back into the temple, she moved through its quickly emptying halls, frantically searching, hoping against hope Cassandra was here. Finally, having circled the entire place, she realized the princess was not in the temple and likely secured in the royal palace. She moved out of the building and raced down the steps. She certainly hadn't meant for Wilson to get caught up in the battles outside the walls. She had to make it across the city and find Cassandra.

Kash passed many woman shepherding children into their homes, kissing their husbands and sons who were rushing to the gate. She was able to reach the palace without being held up or hindered by anyone but was stopped by the guards. She did not recognize them, and they clearly did not remember her. They crossed their spears in front of her well before she moved to stand in front of them.

"Good sirs, I am friend to Cassandra and here at her beckoning. Please, allow my entrance so I may find the princess."

"The princess is with her royal father, overlooking the battle."

"You must allow me to join her, I promise she will name me friend and be grateful to those who allowed me to find her side." The guards certainly looked unsure but one nodded to the other before speaking again.

"Come, I will announce you, and if you are found to be false, you will be thrown from the walls before you can even look upon the royal family."

Kash thought this harsh but felt safe in her belief that Cassandra would welcome her while the battle raged. They moved through the palace in no particular hurry, doing nothing to quell her rising anxiety. Eventually, they moved up a final staircase and out into the open air. This section of the palace had been joined to the city walls affording the royalty of Troy a panoramic view of the entire plain between the city and the beach where the invaders camped. Kash gasped involuntarily at her first sight of the battle. Cassandra was there and must've heard their approach because she turned at the sound.

"Kashmira. Thank the gods, come witness the spectacle of our forces victorious. My brother will repel the invaders. Come meet my royal father." She grabbed Kash by the hand, dismissing her escort with a stern look, and pulled her over to where a tall woman was standing next to a white-haired man who was seated and wearing a crown. His fierce blue eyes instantly reminded Kash of the prince and despite his age, King Priam of Troy looked strong. Kash was also immediately aware of the aura of power coming from the man. This even rivaled the strength of Dracula. Such an important figure must lend power to his presence. Kash wondered at how different this man seemed than Hector, his son. She didn't currently have time to contemplate this mystery, however, she reminded herself. She was standing before a king. Cassandra bowed and pulled Kash down to follow suit.

"Father, may I present the lady Kashmira. She has sailed from distant lands to our great shores seeking adventure." The king smiled at his daughter before turning his gaze upon Kash. Curiosity blossomed upon his features and Kash felt his penetrating look peering into her very soul. She was certain, without the man having even spoken, that he knew she was not from his story. She heard Wilson's voice in the back of her mind screaming for caution. She began to fumble for something to say as the silence wore on but was saved.

"Cassandra names you friend and I have seen marked improvement in her character since your arrival. The gods have truly blessed us with your presence." The king smiled warmly but his features suddenly twisted in alarm. He stood up and boldly strode past Kash, proving in no uncertain terms there was still strength left in his old frame. He moved to the edge of the ramparts and looked out. Kash quickly discerned the cause of his concern. A single soldier was moving out in front of the rest of the army, clearly bellowing a challenge. The approaching enemy soldiers stopped at the call of their commander. A large man moved out from the ranks, looking to accept the challenge of the lone Trojan. Before the duel could begin, the Trojan warrior turned and tried to hide himself amongst the rows of his fellow defenders. A horseman, clearly the general of the army, Hector, Kash presumed, moved after the fleeing soldier. Kash thought she remembered what was going on here.

Paris, the prince of Troy and the man who had stolen Helen away from her Spartan husband, was the Trojan warrior. That made the man who had accepted the challenge Menelaus, king of Sparta. As the scene played out in Kash's mind she came to another realization. If her memory served, Helen was supposed to be up here with Priam during this part. She looked at the woman who she had at first assumed was the Queen. She was undeniably beautiful and Kash thought she might could feel the woman's presence, but it was all overpowered by the strength exuding from the King. She couldn't be sure. She looked at Cassandra and the two ladies' eyes met. Kash looked in the direction of the woman she thought was Helen, clearly asking an unspoken question of the seer. Cassandra nodded her understanding.

"Helen, this is the lady Kashmira." Cassandra said, looking over at the woman. Helen turned to regard them and moved to stand next to Kash.

"Kashmira, such a pleasure. Alas, our meeting could not be more ill-timed. I fear greatly for my prince's life. Menelaus will surely slay him." She turned away with concern etched into her features. Kash looked back out over the wall to see Hector leading Paris back to the front. Just then the King was summoned to the field.

"I must go down and agree to the terms of the duel."

He moved past them and most of those gathered around him fell into line behind the guards. Kash was left standing with Cassandra, watching Helen, the last to depart down the stairs. They turned back to the field when the royal entourage moved to the front of the troops standing before the walls. They seemed to be discussing and agreeing to terms. This meeting did not last long and the king marched back for the large gates of the city.

"Cassandra, Wilsonious is down there! A soldier forced him to go out to the field. He is no fighter. We must get him out of there." Cassandra's worried expression spoke volumes and Kash knew there was nothing they could do. They both looked back to the field as Paris and Menelaus prepared to duel.

Ch. 20 Realizations

Down on the field, Wilson stood at attention in the rank and file of the Trojan army. He was close to the middle, so the King moved right past him on his way back into the city. Wilson saw Paris move out in front of the army and issue his challenge and knew that it would halt the battle, at least for the time being. He watched as Menelaus and Paris prepared to face off in the no-man's land between the armies.

Paris dodged the Spartan king's thrown javelin and launched his own. His enemy spun, the missile flying harmlessly past, and roared as he charged. They came together in a clash of steel as sword met sword. They moved around each other in a fury, exchanging blows and throwing dust into the air. Wilson winced, despite expecting it, when the Spartan king broke through the young prince's defenses and scored a hit on his leg. The wounded Trojan fell to the dirt and was promptly, unceremoniously drug back towards the cheering Greek army. Before the pair had gotten halfway, Wilson smiled widely. He spotted the great cloud of fog moving up behind the ranks of Agamemnon's forces. It soon covered the entire army and continued to advance until it swallowed Paris and Menelaus. Wilson knew this was the work of the gods, Aphrodite, he thought he remembered. Once the fog lifted, Wilson was the only onlooker completely unsurprised that the Trojan prince had disappeared. He knew that the young man had been spirited away to the safety of the palace. Wilson continued to observe, powerless to influence the scene at all, as Agamemnon proclaimed Menelaus the winner of the duel and demanded Helen be brought down from the ramparts. This was never fated to happen and Wilson looked around for the man, Pandaros, he thought the man's name might be, who would fire his bow at Menelaus, thus breaking the truce and rejoining the battle. The men around him began to advance, Wilson invariably moving in his place with them. He had certainly not signed up for being in a fight. Fear and adrenaline spiked like a rocket through his veins as the screams and wailing of battle filled the air around him. He looked ahead and saw a cloud of arrows rocketing out of the sky. He raised his shield above his head and ducked for cover. Three hard thuds knocked into his arm as a body was thrown to the dirt right beside him, two arrows sticking out of his back, the shafts still quivering. He stood, lowering his shield once more, a sudden burst of energy and rage spurring him on beside his fellows. A roar erupted from his lungs that Wilson knew nothing about. He pulled his sword and charged the enemy ranks. The warriors around him responded with their own ferocity and the two armies clashed together in a tangled mess of steal and limbs and blood.

The battle raged on below Cassandra and Kash as the royal entourage returned to the viewing platform. Wilson was down there somewhere, and she couldn't help but worry. Taking a deep breath, she reminded herself that there was nothing she could do. Going out there herself certainly wasn't an option. The only choice left was to go ahead with her plan. If she succeeded, then she might be able to devise a way to remove Wilson from the battle as well. She thought hard about what was next in the story, knowing timing was critical here. Her eyes scanned the battle desperately as she inched closer to the edge of the wall. A particular Greek drew her gaze, and she thought she might could feel his aura. It was strong and so was he. In the original story, Athena inspired Diomedes to great heights and blessed him with the ability to discern the gods from men. She also knew that many of the gods had cameo appearances in this scene. She watched the warrior closely, knowing that he would chase after Aphrodite when she came to protect Aeneas, her son. Just as she remembered, the story unfolded below her. Diomedes was even then grabbing the warhorses of Aeneas as a prize.

Kash's eyes went wide as a figure stepped up, seemingly from nowhere, to face the blessed Greek warrior. Kash looked on, knowing it was Aphrodite on the field. Even at a distance, her energy was unmistakable. The familiarity of her being a character in the story was there but the strength she was emitting was incredible. It rivaled even the King who was standing six feet away. She supposed it made sense; Aphrodite was a goddess after all. Diomedes, inspired by Athena, drove Aphrodite from the field. It was in that moment that Kash realized Aphrodite was fleeing to Olympus. She tried to follow the goddess but lost sight of her. Kash closed her eyes and thought about the very next part of the story where Zeus admonishes Aphrodite for fighting in the battle. She was hoping to access the magic of her tattoos as she had done in *Dracula*, but before the blue wind even began to appear, she stopped, realizing she had momentarily forgotten she was surrounded by story characters and probably shouldn't produce a storm of swirling blue wind. She didn't know if it would work anyway, the mysteries of blending her magic with that of the Greek gods were completely unknown.

There was no time to ponder this as the story out on the battlefield kept rolling right along. Hector made his way over to Aeneas and began to move back towards the walls. Another realization hit Kash like a thunderbolt as she remembered her encounter with Hector a few days ago. She knew in the story it was Apollo and not Hector that spirits Aeneas away down the coast but her eyes were telling her a different story. She grabbed Cassandra by the sleeve and pointed to Aeneas and the man holding him up.

"Who is that man there? The one dragging poor Aeneas from the front?" She pulled Cassandra close trying to create a line of sight down her arm for the princess.

"I know not, but his efforts are nothing short of heroic."

"That isn't the prince? Your brother, Hector?" Kash asked urgently.

"My brother is battling magnificently on the other flank, just there. The light of Apollo shines bright on his armor." Cassandra pointed, leading Kash's gaze and solidifying her certainty. She moved off without another word, trying to find a private place and attempt her magic again. She had already lost sight of the god helping Aeneas. She grinned in satisfaction at having recognized that the man's energy was akin to that of Aphrodite's. She paused for a second to consider why it was that Apollo would seek her out personally in guise. She grinned even wider at what she was about to attempt, thinking she would just have to ask the god himself. She found a deserted corridor and leaned back against the wall, closing her eyes, and breathing deeply. She filled her mind with the image of the temple at Pergamos. She knew that's where Apollo was taking Aeneas. If she could somehow make the magic of her tattoos take her there, she could speak with Apollo himself. Just as she hoped, it didn't take long for the swirl of blue lights to spirit her away. Kash smiled as she felt herself melt into the blackness in a flash of blue.

━━━

Wilson didn't think he had ever been so scared in his entire life. This was not like the movies or the books or anything he had ever read about war. This was horrific. He knew it was luck alone that he was still breathing. He was right in the thick of the fighting with dust floating around, choking, and blinding him. All he had was to keep moving and try to avoid everyone.

This was a flawed plan, he knew. Sooner rather than later, he was going to have to fight someone. Sure enough, turning, Wilson saw a warrior charge him. There was wildness in the man's wide eyes that could only be the heat of battle. Adrenaline alone moved Wilson's feet to meet the charge and lifted his shield arm to block the first blow. It had tremendous weight behind it that nearly knocked Wilson down. He jumped back, out of reach of the next swing, backing up even more. The man grabbed his sword with both hands and raised it above his head, preparing to bring it down with all his strength. On instinct, Wilson charged forward, sword leading, driving the blade deep into the man's chest, his momentum taking both to the ground. He wrenched the sword out of the dying soldier and stood up. Just ahead of him there was a large Greek warrior battling fiercely and felling many Trojans. Wilson felt as if he might know this man based on the energy he was putting off. It was remarkably familiar as if the man might be mentioned in the text. Wilson thought about where they were in the story and decided this was Diomedes, inspired by Athena. His eyes widened as he remembered that Aphrodite herself would show up soon to battle the man.

Watching Diomedes almost cost Wilson dearly as a scream from right next to him made him look around in time to dive aside, narrowly avoiding being skewered on the end of a javelin. Just as Wilson dove aside, another soldier ran right behind him and took the bolt in the chest. It propelled the man backwards and down to the ground. Wilson blew a sigh of relief, despite the death all around him. He was certainly happy that wasn't him. He looked back to Diomedes then to see him battling another warrior Wilson thought might be a character. Aeneas? He turned his head in curiosity, thinking he had hit the mark. Like himself, many of the soldiers had backed off from the Greek hero and were watching the fight unfold. Wilson was eager for a sight of Aphrodite and maybe Apollo. Ares was supposed to make an appearance as well.

As he watched, Aeneas was defeated and then from nowhere someone else stepped out to face Diomedes. Wilson's stare widened considerably as the lady Persephone stood before the great warrior Diomedes. That was supposed to be Aphrodite. Did that mean that the goddess had come to visit him in the library? He was stunned. What his eyes were telling him and what his memory of the text were telling him were far apart. The only way to reconcile them was the fact that Aphrodite had visited him in disguise. But why? It did explain how the goddess' influence confused the royal scribe, but he couldn't fathom why she would want to speak to him. He ran over all she had said to him again. The image of Kash flashed in his mind giving him pause. He turned to look over his shoulder at the city walls on sudden inspiration. He could see the back of the palace where the wall joined it, and the king would be watching the battle. Was Kash up there? He felt like she was and that she was watching the battle unfold.

Wilson turned back to see Diomedes wound the self-named "lady Persephone" and the goddess flee the field. He was unable to discern where she went in the thick of the battle, but he did spot someone dragging Aeneas away from the front line. With a nod of recognition, he thought that it must be Apollo. The aura of strength coming from them certainly backed up this assumption. Wilson's attention was drawn to the prince Hector rallying his troops with a roar. The noise was deafening as a magnificent warrior charging next to Hector attacked the Greek forces in a fury. A wildness of his own seemed to fill Wilson at the sight of Ares, the god of war, himself.

▬▬▬

Kash opened her eyes to find herself standing on the front steps of a magnificent temple. It was immediately apparent that the temple of Apollo here in Pergamos was more splendid than the one she had called home over the last few days. She looked around in awe and wonder as she moved into the structure. How had they constructed something so grand and incredible?

"Kashmira." Her thoughts were interrupted by the man who claimed to be Hector calling her name.

"So, this blue wind of yours is a fast ship."

"You knew that already, though, didn't you, my lord Apollo?" Kash was confident that she would be able to converse and interact with the god as the characters of the *Iliad* had. This boosted her nerve when the god moved to stand before her with a smug expression.

"Indeed, my lady, Kash. So, in this distant land of yours, do all have the abilities to travel great distances with such quickness?" His use of her real name put the woman off-balance. She needed to remind herself that she was speaking with the god Apollo himself. He was obviously going to know things others would not. The question was how much did he know? Yes, he was a god, but he was also a character in the *Iliad*. Perhaps there was a limit to his knowledge and power after all.

"No, not all. I simply stumbled into the one who bestowed it upon me. His power was transferred, and here I am." Her memory of thinking she had actually stumbled and hit her head when she first encountered Merlin gave her an ironic smile as she studied the god standing in front of her.

"Yours is a great power and it makes sense you would be attracted to my service. However, I can see through you, I know your true intentions. Despite it being exactly what you had planned, I will take you to Olympus with me. You will find your visit there to be more than you expect. Shall we?"

"What of Aeneas? Will he be all right?" Apollo looked at her curiously as if he didn't think she would worry about the man at all. It made her wonder, once more, exactly how much the god knew about her. He had yet to mention Wilson, either. Apollo then turned his head to look behind them, leading Kash's gaze with his own. Aeneas was being helped to his feet by two of the temple attendants but looked back as he was being led away. He locked eyes with Kash for a moment, his knowing gaze piercing into Kash and sending a shiver through her spine. She looked back to Apollo whose visage was the epitome of superiority. The god held out his hand without a word, answering her question with a nod. She slowly reached up to take it and felt a familiar sensation as a swirling wind arose around them. This time, however, it was bathed in golden light so brilliant she had to shut her eyes tight. The pressure was more intense than she was used to, and she thought her breath was being squeezed out of her as she felt herself melt away.

Ch. 21 The Greatest of the Divine

Wilson couldn't believe what he was seeing. At first, Ares had driven all before him with unmatched ferocity. Hector rallied behind the god and the Trojans pushed forward. Diomedes, still blessed by Athena, stepped up and halted all the momentum by defeating Ares, who retreated from the field. The Greeks turned the tide and pushed the Trojans back. Wilson moved amongst the soldiers running for the gate. He noticed Hector ride by and was able to sneak into the city behind the prince. He found a deserted alley and sat down to rest, breathing heavily. He tried to recall the next parts of the story, grateful to have survived the nightmare of battle. He felt it had something to do with Hector visiting his family. Regardless, he was happy that there was also a lull in the fighting. He thought back to seeing the lady Persephone stabbed in the hand by the great warrior Diomedes. He was still amazed that the goddess had come to see him herself. There was something in the back of his mind that told him he knew why but was struggling to admit it. The image of Kash floated to the forefront of his thoughts in those moments of contemplation. Aphrodite was the goddess of love and every time he thought of her the image of Kash flashed into his mind. He remembered his anger the last time they had spoken with a wave of guilt; he had to find her.

Wilson rose to his feet shakily. Surviving a vicious battle was tiring work. He shed his armor and weapons and left them in the alley. He poked his head around the corner of the opening to see if anyone was around. This area of the city was deserted. Now was his chance. He exited the alley at a brisk walk. The citadel loomed large before him as he got closer and closer to the wall. Wilson hoped the guards would let him through. He was nearly at the front gate when he skidded to a stop in front of the place where they had met Cassandra. On impulse, he knocked on the door in the same fashion as Cassandra had done that night and to his pleasant surprise the door swung open.

"Quickly," a gruff voice said as a strong pair of hands grabbed Wilson and dragged him through the portal before slamming it behind him and then slamming him up against it.

"Wait, who are you? How did you know lady Cassandra's code? Speak! Now!"

"Calm, my friends, he is no foe." He was saved. Cassandra was coming down the stairs to his rescue. "Wilsonious, come along, we have much to discuss."

Wilson eyed the guards as he gladly followed the seer up the stairs and to her chambers. When they arrived, Cassandra moved out into the open air of her balcony before turning to address Wilson.

"The lady Kashmira has disappeared. She departed the high walls of the palace after Aeneas was injured. I went after her, but she was nowhere to be found. Where would she go? The temple? What do you know?" Wilson shook his head, taking a moment to digest the information. He honestly had no idea where she would go. The temple was as good a guess as any. Then he thought back to what she said about Hector coming to visit her. If the lady Persephone *was* actually Aphrodite, could it be that "Hector" was another god in disguise? Apollo was the one who rescued Aeneas from the field, the very same moment Cassandra claimed Kash had disappeared.

"I know not, my lady. She is quite strong-spirited. I fear she may well be in danger though. War is a tense time. The temple of Apollo would afford her some security. Perhaps we should search there." Cassandra nodded slowly and moved back across the room, Wilson allowing himself to be swept up in her wake. He had no idea how any of this would play out but having been pressed into the very real danger of the battle, he was definitely not underestimating the potential for disaster here in this story. All he knew was he had to find Kash before this spiraled out of control completely.

Kash breathed deeply once more, gratefully gulping in as much air as she could. Travelling with Apollo was somewhat different than the travel she had experienced between stories thus far. She could feel the power of numerous presences around her as she gathered her senses. Her eyes went wide when she recognized the aura of many different gods. She must have made it to Olympus. Looking up, she spotted Aphrodite as Apollo went to join her. They were in a magnificent palace; the pillars and the statues all reminded her of pictures of Greek architecture and décor. The ceiling flew away as Kash gazed upwards, absently scanning the various statues and works of art leering down from on high. Everywhere she looked there was gold and jewels but what drew her eyes most were the gods themselves. They all appeared human enough, but Kash could feel the strength from each one keenly.

"The lady Kashmira, or is it Kash? Welcome to Olympus." The speaker's voice was like rolling thunder and her eyes were drawn upwards to the power of what could only be Zeus, seated on a great throne farther down the hall that crackled with electricity. Kash's mind was blank, and she could barely stand such was the weight and majesty of the god seated before her. She thought she knew and had properly anticipated the effect that Zeus would have. After all, she had felt Aphrodite and Apollo up close. Zeus was an altogether different matter, and she was barely able to breathe as she struggled to keep her feet in front of the gigantic throne.

"Yy...yes. Thank you, your greatness."

"I see your plans; I see you mind. Your world is intriguing to me. Tell me, why leave? Why come here to our world? You have achieved a measure of power and yet you desire more. Or do you simply seek to explore your full potential?" His voice created a storm that nearly knocked her from her feet. She couldn't tell if he was doing this for dramatic effect or if he genuinely didn't realize it. She had to scream at the top of her lungs to even hear herself over the roar.

"I feel the same about your..."

"Ahh, yes, sorry." Zeus waved a lightning bolt about lazily and the storm abated, rushing away as if it were never there. Finally, Kash was able to stand comfortably in front of the throne.

"My curiosity was not unlike your own, I wished to see the world through the eyes of Troy."

"You cannot hide your mind from me, mortal. Your experience and wisdom led you to the power you knew was here. You aspired to come to Olympus before you even traveled to this world. Do you deny it?" Kash didn't immediately respond, caught off guard by the depth of Zeus' knowledge about her. Apollo didn't seem to know much but this was clearly not the case with Zeus. The god continued before she found an answer.

"You believed your power would be great enough to allow you to travel here or at least convince one of us to bring you here. I wonder what gave you such hubris." Lightning crackled around his head as he seemed to be talking to himself almost.

"Ahh well, when humans find something unique, they always try to use it to gain advantage. You are no different. Of more import and interest is your ability to travel to Troy in the first place. This blue wind ship of yours is quite useful. Traveling to and from our world as well as around it is your power to use at will. I wonder if this is the same power that will return you to your home or is it another spell? Hmm." Kash couldn't figure out if he was fishing for answers or not. The uncertainty of his level of knowledge had her off-balance. His ambiguity was maddening, and she was at a clear disadvantage here in this verbal sparring. She considered everything she knew about Zeus and everything she had read or studied. Anything she thought might be useful in this situation, but she was struggling. She needed to keep him talking.

"Why would my return home be of interest? Am I not welcome here?" Zeus smiled at her daring, deciding he might like this one.

"Well, who can know what Fate has in store for you? Destiny comes for all mortals as their story comes to a close. What of your story, my lady Kash? I do rather enjoy that moniker. It suits your aura." Fate? Her Aura? Again, her thoughts spiraled, leaving her almost unable to respond. She was constantly fighting to keep control of her mind here, which was suspicious. Was there some kind of magic being directed at her she wasn't aware of? She spun around and eyed those gathered around her intently. Before she spun back around, Zeus seemed to be thinking along the same lines.

"Leave us!" he commanded to the rest of the gods, his voice booming out with thunder and lightning once more, brooking no argument from any of them. They all slowly filtered out of the hall, Aphrodite and Hera (Zeus' wife) dragging their feet somewhat at the door. Kash looked at Aphrodite and their eyes met, Kash doing her best not to blink in the face of the goddess' vicious stare. She wasn't sure why she was receiving that glare and stored it away to ponder over later. She turned back to Zeus, reminding herself she had more important matters to discuss in front of her.

"I suppose Fate will find me at some point, hopefully on a sunny day a long time from now. You're right, I did intend to come here when I chose this world to travel to. I am not exactly sure what I hoped to find; I suppose the archaeologist in me wanted to meet the Greek gods. I surely wanted to see Troy and now that I have, I am sad I have traveled to the time just before its destruction. There must be something you can do; you are the greatest of all the gods."

"Indeed, my powers do rival the others. I am not, however, all powerful. There are laws of this world that govern my potential as well. You suppose Fate will find you someday. Fate always finds us. Is that not a beautiful thing? Fate connects us, Fate binds us. It is one of the few things the divine and mortals share; their adherence to the inescapable."

"So, you, Zeus, the greatest of the divine, cannot influence the destiny of man? You have no ability to direct the actions of mortals?" Kash was unsure exactly why, but she was intrigued by this humility from the most powerful being in the whole story.

"That is precisely my role; I influence, I change, I direct. None of these actions, however, have the power to alter the outcome. The ending remains the same. I feel you wanting Troy to survive this war. You already think that your time in the great city will fall short of your desires and expectations but if you could extend that time, perhaps reside in the city with your beloved...? You seek to save the Trojans, yet you know they are destined to succumb to deception. Not even I can alter this and will not attempt to do so. You shouldn't either. As all tales have endings, so must this one and it cannot be changed." Zeus was looking down at her smugly, as if he knew her thoughts exactly. It was certainly intimidating, especially since he was right on the money. His mention of "tales" was curious but the more she pondered it the less so it seemed. Wouldn't the greatest, most powerful character she had yet met know he was a character in a story? Surely, since the other characters she had interacted with seemed to, as well. What would that mean? Did his talk of destiny infer he would try and stop any attempts she made to save the city? She thought of Cassandra then for some reason. Didn't the seer try and warn everyone about the huge wooden horse? She looked back to Zeus who still wore a knowing grin.

"You know, back home there are many who do not believe in predestiny, many who would like to think they control their own fate. This belief is based on the idea of free will. We make choices every day and then live with the consequences. It cannot be any different here." Zeus' smile became almost sinister as his eyes widened a little bit before responding.

"Stubborn. Good. Wisdom comes from experience."

The god lifted his arms, and a great wind began to howl and swirl around her. She felt herself being lifted from her feet, ever rising. She looked to Zeus to see his smile as he stared after her, the storm carrying her away. Beneath her was a dark cloud that felt substantial as she put her weight upon it and relaxed. The crackling blue energy all around her seemed to be shooting lightning amongst the clouds while she was spirited away. The world flashed by beneath her and she had no way of knowing where the storm was taking her until she spotted Troy on the horizon. Speeding right for the city on a thunderstorm was another unexpected pleasure of her trip here and she smiled when she was gently deposited on the top steps of the temple of Apollo. She moved in without hesitation, heading towards her room for some needed rest and contemplation.

Ch. 22 A Lovely Visit

They moved into the temple urgently, heading straight for Kash's chambers. There was a small door at the back of the main hall and Wilson let Cassandra take the lead. The woman obviously knew her way around the place much better than he did. They moved through the portal and down a long hallway with numerous rooms and doorways on either side. They neared the end and Cassandra stopped.

"This is the one." She knocked and they both listened for any movement inside. After a pause, Cassandra knocked again. Nothing.

"Kashmira?" Wilson said hesitantly, the altered name feeling awkward as he said it. He looked at Cassandra who shook her head and moved past him back down the hall without another word. Wilson hurried to keep up before asking the million-dollar question as they moved back into the grand hall where stood the great statue of Apollo and the holy altar.

"What now? Where could she be?" Cassandra didn't answer but led his gaze to the approach of a magnificently beautiful woman that Wilson recognized instantly. His eyes widened to saucers as the lady Persephone moved to stand in front of them.

"My lady, Cassandra, how lovely to see your radiance this day."

"Thank you," she replied with a bow of her head. "Your wonder never ceases to bring a smile, my lady." With that, Cassandra moved past Persephone and out of the temple, leaving a thoroughly confused and stunned Wilson alone with the smiling beauty of Persephone, who he knew to actually be the goddess Aphrodite. He stuttered and stumbled over something to say but all he was able to get out was an indecipherable gurgle. The goddess laughed gently at him before speaking.

"Oh, Wilson, your gentle and kind heart is a wonder to behold. Rare amongst men and most of the gods for that matter." Her blatant revelation that she knew of his knowledge of her true nature kept him off balance and reeling. He understood that was by design and took a deep breath trying to slow his heart rate and collect himself. Eventually, he was able to formulate a response.

"My lady, Perse…Aphrodite. Your grace is most wonderful to behold." The goddess grinned from ear to ear again and laughed a bit more at his hesitance.

"You're too kind, and your meekness aids your desire, at least in my eyes, but mine isn't the opinion that matters." This statement was odd and Kash flashed in his mind's eye once more. Wilson thought he was beginning to catch on to what Aphrodite wanted from him, and he became suspicious of these flashes all of a sudden. Were they divinely inspired?

"What do you continually see when you look upon my visage?" the goddess continued. "No mortal man can look upon me and not see the object they truly desire. Love holds more power than you can imagine, my dear Wilson. Even more than you already possess. Do you not see that love is what brought you on this adventure in the first place? Its influence is clear in your eyes, in your mind, and in your past. You were fated thus from the beginning. Love is what brought you here and what drew me to stand before you now."

He thought back to when he had agreed to join Kash's team to go to Stonehenge. He couldn't figure out what had attracted him to the project or why he had been invited in the first place. She had claimed it was due to his expertise in British history, but he didn't think his specialty could necessarily add enough to the expedition that he should be invited along. He wasn't, however, prepared to pass up an opportunity to work at Stonehenge and thus heartily agreed when asked to join. The subsequent wild ride seemed one of circumstance way more than choice as he replayed the events of the past few weeks in his mind. As he thought of the kiss they had shared, however, he found himself quite grateful for those circumstances. Aphrodite was claiming it was all in the name of love. The more he thought about it the less sure he was, and he looked back to the goddess to see her give him a knowing smile.

"She is currently safe, well as safe as mortals can be in the presence of the gods. I know you feel you have lost her but take heart, for the power you two share has intrigued Zeus."

"Wait, what?! What power? Intrigued Zeus?!" Wilson's incredulity demanded he interrupt.

"Yes, I assume she is still on Olympus. I wasn't privy to their banter; however, I do know that your abilities to travel around my world, and to and from your own, are quite unique here. It would seem that your beloved has designs on our story. She has taken a liking to the great city of Troy. She would not see it destroyed. Fate has sealed your course, but I wonder what destiny has in store for the one who would try to change it. In her great hubris, your lady Kashmira has erred. I hope the Greeks are merciful."

With another smile that brought Kash to his mind, Aphrodite turned slowly and left Wilson standing there, his mind racing. He thought about everything he knew of the story and when Kash would go to the beach, supposing he interpreted the goddess' last words correctly. What would she do or say? Would she approach Agamemnon himself? If Aphrodite was to be believed, she had already spoken with Zeus, so what was a human king compared to the greatest of all the gods? He then considered how some of the human characters in the story were deceived by divine influence. Was that what was going on here? The goddess knew a lot about him and Kash and their unique abilities. How much had she told the gods? How much had they inferred?

He was at a loss. Cassandra seemed to have abandoned him completely, for she had left when Aphrodite showed up and was nowhere to be seen now. He had nothing else but to continue his search for Kash. As he had no idea where to start inside the city he decided to see if Aphrodite's clue about her approaching the Greeks held any merit. If he could make it to the beach without being spotted, he might be able to stake out Agamemnon's tent until Kash showed up. It was the only idea he had, so he moved out of the temple and back to the alley where he had left his armor and weapons earlier. If he had stayed in the temple, pondering his direction for only a few moments more, he would still have been there when Kash returned from Olympus, thus revealing the divine deception of the goddess. As it was, their paths were not destined to be reunited just yet.

Grateful the equipment was right where he had left it and unbothered, he figured the armor would mark him clearly as an enemy down on the beach, so he strapped the sword to his belt and left the rest. He only hoped he would get there before she did. He didn't think he would be able to pull off a rescue against trained fighters. Kash was the only familiar thing in this entire world, and it was with thoughts of her that he moved out of the city and off towards the beach as stealthily as he could manage. He recognized where the story was as he moved out past the returning Trojans, dusk beginning to bring the night around him. A truce had been agreed upon and there would be no fighting while each side collected and buried their dead properly. The time was perfect to sneak onto the beach, Wilson just hoped he wasn't too late.

Ch. 23 A Dance of Words

Wilson poked his head up over the dune and dropped back quickly, lying flat out on the sand as a sentry walked by just below him. Despite the truce and the fall of darkness, the camp on the beach was not quiet. The guards were all still on alert. It seemed as if the invaders didn't quite trust the Trojans to uphold the truce. Wilson supposed this was fair, and smart. After all, the Trojans had been tricked into breaking the last truce, which wouldn't inspire their enemies to be confident this one would hold very long. He slowly raised his head back over the wall of sand and was glad to see the patrol had moved on. Now was his chance. He climbed over the dune and clambered down the other side. Rushing to the nearest tent, he moved around the back of it and crouched down. Wilson had no idea where Kash might be, but he had to start somewhere. He kept to the outskirts of the camp and continually ducked into the shadows to avoid detection.

He was lucky and had managed to make it almost to the other side of the encampment completely without being seen. He grabbed the side of the tent he had come to and leaned on it for support, breathing heavily, having run the last open expanse to the shelter afforded by this structure. Unbeknownst to him at first, he had chosen to stop and stand very near the opening of this particular tent.

"Wilson?!" he heard whispered incredulously. "What are you doing here?"

An arm reached out and pulled him inside before he could do or say anything. Kash stood before him with a concerned expression on her face. She seemed different to him somehow, but he couldn't place it. He had more pressing issues at hand, so he shrugged these thoughts away before responding.

"Looking for you, of course."

"You shouldn't be here. If they catch you..."

"What? It won't be any worse than what happens if they catch you. In fact—"

"Alright, alright," she said before he could gain a head of steam. "You're right. Maybe we should just go." She looked at him intently as she said this but turned away again, seemingly indecisive.

"Go?" he echoed, not expecting that. "What about trying to stop the Greeks? What about trying to save Troy?"

"Yes, I have grown to love the city but what can we do against Fate? The city is going to be destroyed no matter what we do. It's only a matter of time. Stories must have endings. Right? We cannot avoid this one." Wilson grew increasingly confused as she went on. This didn't seem like the Kash he knew, who was quite stubborn and loath to give up at all, especially not this easily.

"What happened on Olympus? What did Zeus say to you?" he asked, thinking he might have found the root of her sudden reversal.

"How do you know about that?" she asked, surprised at his knowledge of what she had been up to.

"Does it matter? I know you went there. Did Zeus convince you it wasn't worth trying to interfere with the characters and the story? I know I couldn't, I suppose divine intervention and all." Wilson chuckled a little bit at his own joke. Kash stared at him intently, clearly trying to discern where his information was coming from and just as clearly discomfited by it. Eventually, she spoke, changing her demeanor completely and stepping forward.

"Well, it doesn't really matter what Zeus said. We should go. If the Greeks catch us here, we're doomed. Let's go home."

"Home?" he echoed, confused once more. "Home? As in home, home, or Troy?" The man certainly didn't think she would want to return to the library so soon. Had Zeus spooked her? Surely, she wasn't done in Troy yet. There was plenty left to learn and study. But then again, Wilson didn't presume to know her true motives for coming here. She had to have been prepared to meet the gods having chosen this story herself.

"Home, of course. We share only one home. You know, where we came from. Not Troy."

Wilson's instincts were screaming at him. Something was off here. Kash would never refer to the library or the university in such a way. His suspicious mind careened down the corridors of a million different possibilities. Were the gods deceiving him again? The lady "Persephone" had come to him twice now in disguise. Aphrodite passed herself off as someone else, but he thought that was simply to nudge him into pursuing his feelings for Kash. Wasn't it? There was something about the way Kash was looking at him expectantly. If she wanted to go home, why wasn't she thinking of the library and bringing the swirl of blue wind? This was wrong. Was Aphrodite here again, trying to get him to take her back with him to his world? Could it be? The goddess knew quite a bit about them. Did Kash's meeting on Olympus inspire the gods to want to leave their own story? That seemed farfetched to Wilson. He knew something was amiss, but his mind wasn't prepared to make such a leap yet. He looked back to Kash, an idea forming in his mind.

"Alright, go ahead, I am right behind you." If he was wrong, and this really was Kash, she would simply will herself back to the library, if not...

Kash, or this woman who looked like Kash, and who Wilson was increasingly believing was Aphrodite in disguise again, shook her head and moved closer to him.

"Together, we have to do it together, remember?" Wilson grinned, confident now his guess was right, and he was being deceived. Sure, they wanted to remain together whilst traveling between stories and their world, but Wilson remembered barely making it back from the *Prophetiae Merlini* which proved that they could make the journey alone. A fact Kash seemed to have forgotten.

"No, my lady, we do not. You certainly do not remember the *Merlini*, because you were not there, *Aphrodite*." Wilson's confident tone was vindicated when Kash smiled and didn't deny his statement. She took a step back and turned away, moving to the other side of the tent. She looked over her shoulder at him and grinned, telling Wilson plainly that it wasn't the last time he would see her before he could make it out of the story. A commotion outside the tent turned his head to the opening. When he looked back, the goddess was gone. A jumble of voices reached his ears, growing louder with each passing moment. He had been tricked by the goddess, but he would have to worry about that later, he realized. He didn't want to be found here. There was no telling how the Greeks would treat intruders.

Drawing his sword and moving to the back of the tent, he didn't hesitate to slash a hole in the canvas. He forced his way through and out into the night. He hadn't gone two steps when he heard a shout.

"You there, stop!"

He took off as fast as he could across the sand, fear barreling adrenaline through his veins. The camp around him sprang to life and he was quickly surrounded and tackled to the ground. His hands were bound, and he was roughly hauled to his feet. None of his captors said a word as they marched him back the way he had come. The group came to a halt outside a nearby tent that he had just run past. A guard moved inside, and Wilson heard an exchange he couldn't quite decipher. The soldier returned quickly and grabbed Wilson, shoving him inside and to the ground before a man seated next to a table strewn with scrolls and the remnants of a meal.

"Who are you? You are not Greek; nor are you Trojan. Where do you hail from? Speak!" Wilson had no way of knowing who he had been brought to, but he could feel that it was a character of some importance. The man looked strong, and fit. His beard was full and his eyes bespoke wisdom and patience. He certainly didn't seem bothered too much about the disturbance to his dinner despite his questions. The man took a sip from his cup and observed Wilson intently. Wilson struggled to his feet, his bound hands not doing much to aid in this process.

"My lord, my name is Wilsonious. I come from a land far away."

"I gathered that, Wilsonious. What business do you have sneaking into the camp and interrupting my supper? Perhaps I should have these men execute you as a Trojan spy right here and now." Wilson's eyes widened, hoping this wasn't Agamemnon. The commander of the entire army was certainly not known for his kindness or mercy. The man in front of him seemed more reserved, however, which gave Wilson some small measure of courage and hope.

"I am no spy, my lord. I am a simple traveler in the wrong place at the wrong time."

"A traveler equipped with a Trojan sword," the man commented blithely as one of the men who brought him in held up Wilson's weapon for the leader to see. Just then another man moved into the tent and bowed before the seated man.

"My lord, Odysseus, the King Agamemnon has demanded the prisoner be brought to his tent at once."

"It seems your fate is no longer mine to decide my friend. Let us see what our gracious leader has in store for you." Odysseus rose from his chair and grabbed Wilson by the arm, personally leading him out of the tent and across the camp. They reached a huge tent that dwarfed all of those around it and moved past the guards without stopping. There was a makeshift throne set up at the back of the structure and Odysseus moved Wilson to stand right before it.

"My king Agamemnon, I give you Wilsonious, a self-proclaimed traveler from a far distant land who was trying, somewhat unsuccessfully, to convince me he is not a Trojan spy."

"Ha, I knew the wretched Trojans would endeavor to break the truce once more. They broke the first one, why wouldn't they do it again."

"I swear, king of kings, I am not Trojan. I was deceived into believing a dear companion of mine had come to your camp. I came for her but was discovered by your men before I could find her." Wilson hoped this would suffice to explain his presence without raising too many questions about Kash, or Aphrodite as it were. He certainly couldn't tell the king he had spoken with the goddess in the tent before he was taken. They would think him mad.

"Why should I believe you? A woman, you say? Well, if there is a woman who wasn't supposed to be in the camp here now, I imagine she has been caught as well. My men are probably enjoying her as we speak." Wilson wasn't really surprised to hear him say something like that, but neither was he worried. Kash wasn't even here, and he doubted very much that any of the soldiers had captured Aphrodite.

"My king, I was deceived. The woman I speak of was never here. It was my folly to be so easily duped."

"Hahaha. Of course, the simple minded can be convinced of anything. I, however, am anything but. Your Trojan tongue cannot deceive me. We will sacrifice you to Ares, that he might bless us in the battles to come."

"Ares fought against you, great king," Wilson blurted, hoping against hope he could find some way to talk himself out of being executed. Agamemnon cocked his head to the side, surprised to be addressed thus by anyone, let alone a prisoner. His curiosity defeated his rage, thankfully, and he posed a question rather than just have Wilson's head off right then and there.

"And you know this how? We won the day, and the Trojans were the ones who sued for peace, not the other way around." Agamemnon was clearly unconvinced.

"That is true, but your hero, the great Diomedes, battled Ares so fiercely that the god retreated back to the safety of Olympus."

"You seem to have extensive first-hand knowledge of the day's events. Pray tell me, traveler, how is this? It almost seems as if you were on the field yourself. If you fought for the Greeks, you would have no hesitation declaring such. However, your words mark you clearly as a Trojan and a spy."

Wilson realized his mistake halfway through the king's response. He thought he was surely doomed at that moment. He searched desperately through his mind for something, anything to save him.

"My king, I was pressed into their service and only fought to survive. I care nothing for the Trojans, the glory of your army was splendid to behold. Allow me to join your ranks that I might prove I am not a Trojan or a spy." It was a desperate move, but he thought it might be the only option left before him.

"And why would I spare a traitor to his own people?" Wilson didn't know what to say; the man's obstinacy was proving too high a wall to tear down. He was grateful, then, when Odysseus spoke up behind him.

"If I might, my king, the circumstance seems suspicious, and his words paint a grand picture. As we know, actions speak louder than any words. Allow this man, Wilsonious, to fight at my side and with my company. We will keep watch over him and see if he will prove his worth. At first sign of betrayal, he will be killed. After all, in the midst of the battle, where will he run to?" Agamemnon took a long moment of silence to consider the proposal before waving his hand.

"As you will, but if his treachery brings ruin upon us, on your head be it." With a nod and a bow, Odysseus grabbed Wilson by the arm once more and marched him out of the tent. Once outside, one of the guards came and cut the rope binding his hands.

"We will outfit you tomorrow, for tonight, I will show you to the tents serving as barracks. My men will be given orders to kill you if you so much as look like you're trying to escape. They're not all very bright so I wouldn't make any sudden moves if I were you. We shall see if your words ring true and you really are a warrior. I think you were simply dancing to save your skin, but I suppose your story will come out eventually." With that, Odysseus walked away, leaving Wilson confused but grateful to still be breathing. He could hardly believe his luck as he moved into the tent that was nearly full with makeshift cots. He was shown to one near the back and he lay down without speaking or looking at anyone. He shut his eyes trying to rest, knowing he had barely managed to escape the executioner and hoping that he would find a way to get out of the impending battle. He eventually drifted off to sleep, thoughts of Kash filling his mind and spilling into his dreams.

Ch. 24 An Unexpected Slip

Dawn came, bringing with it the sounds of a camp awakening and preparing for battle. Before Wilson was fully conscious, he was roughly shaken awake and opened his eyes just as a breastplate, sword and shield were dropped onto his stomach. He got the distinct impression the soldier bringing the gear rather enjoyed tossing it at him so. The man did smile as he turned and moved out of the tent. Wilson sat up and tried to grab the rather bulky equipment but failed and scrambled to collect everything as it dropped to the sand beneath him. Finally managing to orient himself and strap on his sword, he moved out into the morning sunshine and the cacophony of a mustering army and held his hands in front of his eyes, nearly blinded by the glare. This was now the second set of armor he had been given and this one fit even worse than the last one. His movements were quite restricted and he laughed at himself as he said a silent prayer for protection. His mirth was derived from his curiosity if any of the gods in this story had heard such a prayer. It didn't matter, he supposed, he could do nothing to escape the battle he was being forced into. If he did, he would be murdered on the spot. So, his limited options were to be killed now or in a little bit. He thought about returning to the library for a moment as he considered this, his heart rate increasing, but he knew he couldn't leave Kash. Before he could figure out what to do, he heard his name shouted.

"Wilsonious, form up! We march for the city!" He searched for the speaker and noticed Odysseus himself jogging up to him. "Let's go, time to prove your honor." He grabbed Wilson and dragged him along, shoving him into a line of soldiers and standing just in front of them. He looked around one more time as if for stragglers before moving forward with the rest of the army, Wilson in tow. More adrenaline poured into his veins as they made the top of the dunes and the city walls came into view. He could see the Trojans flowing out of the gates and forming up outside the walls. The two armies both halted their marches, staring across the no man's land between them. There was a slight pause where the only sound was the swirling of the wind. At a signal from Agamemnon, the Greek forces charged. Wilson let out a battle cry with the rest of them and hustled to keep up so as not to be trampled. Their run was met by the Trojans and the soldiers came together in a mass of blood and tangled weapons. Wilson just managed to dodge a thrown spear and tumbled into the man next to him. With no time to consider his cushion, for he knew the spear thrower was wading in right behind it, he swung his sword as he bounced back. Another sword descended at the same moment and the blow nearly took Wilson's arm off. He was almost spun in a complete circle and he decided to roll with the momentum but his enemy was right there when he came back around. Wilson thought he was doomed in that moment but a javelin flew over his shoulder and lifted the attacker from his feet, dead before he hit the ground.

With no time to look for his savior or thank him anyways, Wilson regained his balance and ran off, trying to stay alive and avoid all the arrows and spears flying through the air. Dust was swirling everywhere, getting into his eyes. He squinted ahead, having lost track of the battle lines and hardly able to tell friend from foe. A Trojan ran at him, sword aloft, with a feral growl. Wilson matched the man's yell with one of his own and leapt forward surprising his opponent. No more so than Wilson himself when his sword slid into the man's chest and Wilson's momentum carried them to the ground, the Trojan's sword flying from his grasp. He was struggling to pull his blade free when he felt a tug on his arm that coincidentally aided his efforts. Wilson stood up quickly, lifting his sword as he did, expecting another charging enemy.

"C'mon, Wilsonious, we must pull back." It was Odysseus and Wilson fell into line without hesitation. He knew that Odysseus ultimately survived this story so he vowed to stick close by the character's side. It was as good a plan as any in the midst of a battle. Wilson's strategy would prove successful despite many near misses and close calls. Wilson's heroics aside, the Trojans pushed the Greeks back to the beach and at day's end, found themselves encamped just over the dunes. The Greeks fell back behind their shield wall and the fighting subsided for the day.

Stripping off his armor and laying down on his cot, Wilson could not believe his luck. Both his good fortune in surviving another battle and his misfortune to be in the battle in the first place. He was confident that staying close to a character thick with plot armor was a good strategy but it wasn't foolproof by any means. He wasn't sure he could make it through another day like that one. He had to escape, had to at least try. He decided to let the camp die down a bit before trying to sneak out. He stared up at the top of the tent in the deepening gloom, his thoughts wandering. Kash swam into his contemplations and he wondered what she was doing. Hopefully she was safe in the temple of Apollo. He decided to sleep for a couple of hours and it was with thoughts of finding her and returning to the library and their own world that he drifted off.

▬ ▬ ▬

Kash awoke with the dawn, unsure of her next move. She had a goal in mind but she was uncertain how to achieve it. Surely, if she convinced King Priam that Cassandra was telling the truth they would heed the warning about the Trojan horse. She didn't know how much time she had left before that happened even though she knew it wasn't actually a part of *The Iliad.* She did know that it was how the war ended, regardless of which book that part of the story unfolded in. There was a bit of her that was curious about how that would play out, but she was fairly confident that it would happen, at the very least. She felt like Wilson might have some insight. His knowledge of the text of both this story and *The Odyssey* rivaled her own. Maybe he would be able to help. Although, she knew convincing him to go along with her plan would be more difficult still, despite her belief that her end game would be appealing to him. Regardless, she had to find the man first. She desperately hoped he wasn't involved in the fighting. If he was not, then he would most likely be in the library.

Arising and donning her robe, she moved out of her small room and down the hall to the main chamber. She bypassed the statue of Apollo and the holy altar, completely disregarding her morning duties, and moved out of the temple. She figured her cover as a priestess would be wearing thin by now anyway and there was no one to admonish her, so she thought nothing of it. She moved across the city quite quickly, her familiarity with the place increasing every day. The front gates of the palace only had one sentry at them and he nodded and smiled at Kash in recognition, making no move to stop her progress into the royal residence. Kash wondered at that, not expecting such an easy welcome but neither did she stop to inquire of her good fortune. Even though she had been in the palace a couple of different times, she still got turned around in the winding corridors and myriad adjoining rooms. Eventually, she found her way back to the grand anteroom with the giant staircase. She had already climbed this and couldn't figure out how she had made it back down to the ground level. Before she could unravel the mystery, Cassandra came striding gracefully down the steps, calling her name.

"Kashmira, thank the gods. I have been ever so worried. Your disappearance has caused me great sorrow. How happy I am to look upon your beauty once more."

"You're too kind, my lady. I have been in and out of the temple, my studies and duties have had me quite busy these past couple of days." Cassandra eyed her somewhat suspiciously but didn't say anything. She simply wrapped her arm around Kash's and led her up the stairs. Kash realized her wrong turn as they made their way, seemingly to the parapets to watch the battle joined. When they moved out on the terrace, Kash made it a point to stay well clear of the main characters and tried to stay as unassuming as possible. They were all preoccupied with the battle and didn't pay her much heed anyway. This was just fine with Kash and she pulled Cassandra aside as the two armies charged each other on the field below.

"Have you seen Wilsonious? He was pressed into the battle a couple of days ago and I have not seen him since. I fear the worst."

"Oh, well, I am not sure. I know he survived the battle you and I beheld because he came to me looking for you. I left him at the temple of Apollo. My dreams have been troubled of late. I would not tell you but they are full of your presence and that of your love, Wilsonious. They are not pleasant portents. Despite my heart wanting to tell you he is well; I fear he may have found himself in the battle once more. There was more to my dreams, but I am having trouble sorting through them. What are you going to do? Please, my lady, do not disappear again, I beg of you."

Kash didn't know how to respond. She had clearly made an impression on the young seer, as evidenced by her insistence Kash stay by her side. She had to find Wilson, though, he was the only one who could help her figure it all out. Not to mention the budding feelings for the man she was failing to keep under the surface. She was also quite fearful about his survival of the fighting. She realized in that moment that she had missed him over the last couple of days. His constant worrying had been bothersome, but she was coming to see how much she needed and cared for him in this unfamiliar place. Her regret that she had thought it a good idea for them to split up lent fuel to her determination to find him as she remembered their last less than peaceable conversation.

"Sorry, my lady, but I must find him. I cannot sit around doing nothing. Besides, the ending will not wait for my indecision." Cassandra gave her a confused look as she turned on her heel and ran back down the stairs into a long corridor. She vaguely recalled how to get to the library, deciding to cover all possible places he could be before trying to figure out how to extricate him from the battle. She wasn't even sure he was in the battle anyway, so she headed in the direction she thought was the right way towards the library. Luck was with her and she managed to recall the correct path with only one wrong turn and a small backtrack. Just as she hoped, she found Cliffradus, the royal scribe, hard at work copying out a ridiculously long scroll that trailed away onto the floor behind the desk where he sat.

"My dear Cliffradus, how are you today?" she greeted warmly.

"My lady, forgive me but I do not remember your name, and your face escapes my memory as well."

"I am Kashmira, friend to Wilsonious, the man who has been helping you in your work these past few days," she returned with a smile.

"Ahh, yes, Wilsonious. Has his fever abated? He was quite bothered the other afternoon."

"Fever? I am not sure what you mean, sir."

"He wasn't either." The man put his head down and continued scribbling. Kash let the silence spiral, thinking hard about what he could be talking about. Wilson had mentioned that he had been visited by a strange woman here in the library. Was it possible he had been visited by one of the gods as well? A bit more fear coursed through her at that thought for it couldn't mean anything good.

"Well, have you seen him recently?"

"Not since that day, perhaps he went to the houses of healing and has found some respite there."

"Thank you, kind sir," Kash replied and the man nodded curtly, returning to his work. Kash didn't think the scribe had any more valuable information for her, but she was almost certain Wilson wasn't in any house of healing. So, he hadn't been back to the library. Where could he be?

▬▬▬

Wilson awoke abruptly a few hours later. The contented snores of those around him reminded him of where he was as his senses returned fully. Slowly sitting up and looking around, Wilson decided it was now or never. As quietly as he could, he extricated his sword from the pile of equipment beneath his cot. Unsure of how to proceed or how loud cutting through the canvas would be, Wilson had to pause. Someone grumbled in their sleep behind him and his heart skipped a beat. He knew he had to act fast and so moved the sword tip right against the side of the tent. Little by little he applied more pressure until the blade poked through with a ripping noise that sounded like a bomb to Wilson in the quiet night. He held very still for just a moment, ensuring there was no movement behind him, before sliding the sword down enough for him to slip out into the night. When he came fully out of the tent, he crashed into something solid as he began to run and tumbled to the sand. Before he even looked up, he knew he was caught.

Night was falling as Kash exited the city. The Trojans had won the day and pushed the invaders back down to the beach. Hector had ordered this advantage be protected rather than surrendered and the defending forces had made camp in the dunes not far from the beach. Kash's chosen route around the camp took her well wide of the Trojans but she knew she would have to sneak in between the lines to get to the beach. As luck would have it, she spotted a form just ahead of her moving out from the Trojan encampment. The man looked around and Kash dropped flat to the sand, having nowhere else to hide. She held her breath and could feel the aura of a main character coming from the man. She searched her memory of the text and couldn't quite place who he was. She was certain he was written into the novel however, so she followed him at a safe distance, using the same hiding spots he did as he made his way down to the beach.

The man and his shadow came to the last stretch before the Greek camp which was nothing but open ground to the nearest tent. Kash moved as close as she could while remaining hidden as she watched the man silently and quickly scurry across the sand. Just before he reached the shelter of the tent, a tear in the canvas opened right in front of the running spy and out tumbled Wilson bringing both men to the ground. Kash almost laughed despite the seriousness of the situation. Neither man wanted to be making so much noise and they extricated themselves quickly.

"What are you doing here? Are you...Wait..." Wilson was clearly struggling to figure out what was going on but the Trojan knew his mission was compromised. The man backed away and tried to turn but lost his footing in the soft sand and tumbled to the ground once more.

"You're Dolon, the spy, aren't you?" Kash heard Wilson's excited voice say and she laughed, both in incredulity at Wilson and recognition at the name. Her eyes then went wide as she realized what it would mean if Wilson was right. Odysseus was supposed to catch this spy not Wilson. That could only mean that the Greek king would be along at any moment. She knew her time to rescue her bumbling companion was running out. She had to make her move. She came over the dune at full tilt, not even saying anything.

"Kash!?" Wilson nearly shouted in surprise.

"Keep your voice down, we have to get out of here now!" she whispered harshly. This had just the desired effect and the man snapped to with no further hesitation. They ran for the safety of the dunes with the Trojan spy hot on their heels. All three of them knew the pursuit wouldn't be far behind. Sure enough, they heard shouts as the alarm was raised. Kash and Wilson didn't look back as they heard the Trojan spy captured and Odysseus' voice beginning the interrogation. Wilson slid to a stop suddenly, causing Kash to spin around.

"We have to go back."

"Wilson, we can't. You know better than I that the story must go on." Kash almost smiled at the role reversal in this particular conversation.

"But they're going to kill a lot of people. So many that Apollo has to stop them."

"Exactly, Apollo will stop them. There is nothing we can do. Besides, if you go back, you'll be fighting again tomorrow, and there is no telling what fate would befall *me* down there." Kash could tell she was getting through to him and gently took hold of his arm and led him away into the night. They were both quiet as they gave the Trojan camp a wide berth and made it back to the city. Again, the guards recognized Kash and let them in through a smaller side gate. Kash was definitely curious about this now for that was the second time she had been allowed entry almost too easily. Her mind was beginning to tire of all the swirling possibilities and oddities of this experience. For perhaps the first time since she had decided to come to *The Iliad,* she almost felt overwhelmed, but when they arrived at the palace, she hardened her resolve once more. She would seek out Cassandra and ensure that Wilson had a permanent place in the library thus sparing him from battle.

They were admitted without hindrance once again, and Kash was certain that she had missed something. She was grateful, however, for the accessibility and therefore remained silent and smiled at the gate guards as they were allowed into the palace proper. Kash was a bit more familiar with the place now and moved off for Cassandra's chambers. Upon their arrival, the guards were less accommodating this time.

"We would see the lady Cassandra," Kash said politely but the guards remained impassive.

"Let them in," Cassandra's voice floated to them softly and the guards did as they were bid without hesitation.

"Thank you for seeing us at such a late hour my lady." Kash said, only just then realizing how late it might actually be.

"No matter, sleep has escaped me this night and I have been pondering the heavens above. The stars do fill me with wonder."

"Yeah, that doesn't change no matter where you go," Wilson commented with a grin to Kash who returned it warmly.

"We came seeking advice and your help if you were so inclined and able. Wilson is no soldier and was only in the battle by mistake. His is the profession of writing and study, not swordsmanship and ferocity. We would ask if there is any way you could ensure he avoids the battles in the future." Cassandra looked at them curiously for a moment before smiling.

"Surely you already know this is within my power. Have you not noticed what my imprimatur has done for you? The guards allow you nearly full access to the palace and that is no small thing. I will, of course, extend the same to our dear Wilson." She narrowed her eyes at Kash as she said Wilson's name and Kash nearly gasped aloud. Of course, Cassandra would've caught her slip of the tongue when she spoke of her companion. Kash then also considered the fact that Cassandra was a character in this story as well. She looked back to the young seer at her smile that was slowly widening.

"My lady Kashmira, Kash is it? Do not be afraid, while many believe the two of you are more than you seem, me not least of all, I am friend to you both. I will not betray you to my father or brother. You have shown me nothing but kindness and I can only return the same. However, I would ask the truth of you. But perhaps now is not the time for reconciliation. My dreams foretold your arrival and here you are. My thoughts have not yet reached conclusion, but I recognize benevolence when I see it. Even still, my lady Kash, we will speak tomorrow. Wilson, you are free to move about the palace. I will have my guards escort you to your chambers in the library. No doubt, dear Cliffradus will welcome your return."

Ch. 25 A Lovely Garden

The next day Kash returned to the palace from her room at the temple where she had passed the night. She found Cassandra waiting for her in the grand entrance hall.

"Shall we walk in the gardens? They are most beautiful this time of year and we can converse in private." The princess took Kash by the arm and led her down a corridor and through a door out into the sunshine. The gardens were lush and vibrant, the flora well-tended. Kash recognized many different species and was happy to see butterflies and all manner of life in such peace. Her thoughts, however, were far from all of this. She knew she would have to tread carefully here and she hated the thought of yet another encounter where she was unsure how much her counterpart knew about her. She felt she could trust Cassandra and the princess' claims were not well received by the court anyway. That didn't matter, Kash told herself. Cassandra deserved to be taken seriously, especially since she had lent them so much aid and friendship thus far. The princess waited a while before speaking, as if to let Kash sort all of this out before asking the questions she seemed to have been holding back for some time.

"So, as I have said, I dreamt of your arrival just before you traveled here. I have not, however, shared all the details of my visions. You seemed to be flying on a blue wind but not through the air. I call it wind for words fail to truly describe what my mind's eye perceived. All around you was blue as if you came here inside a cocoon and like these butterflies, emerged forth upon our world." Kash didn't quite know how to respond, not sure she was being asked a question anyway. Considering the princess' words had her drawing a similar conclusion. She understood how her magical journey here could be described as such, although her mind had never gone to such a place when thinking of it. Considering the similarities to the way the gods of this story seemed to travel, she was certainly led away from this cocoon idea but thought it best not to mention that to Cassandra, unless there was no way around telling her directly. Cassandra continued before Kash was forced to respond.

"You have a great aura about you, Kash, a strength and a clear resolve. Is it passion for Wilson that drives you or is there some other motive behind your fervor? Some unseen end that you seek?"

"Wilson?" She repeated bemusedly, caught off guard by the angle Cassandra was taking.

"You're not wrong to guess that I have an end game here in the…in Troy. However, I am less sure than I was when we got here. The danger is proving to be greater than anticipated. At least, by me." She smiled as she heard Wilson's caution floating to the forefront of her thoughts.

"Well, all stories must have danger and adventure. Yours will see more than most. The portents of my visions show me as much. However, I do not understand many of the images. Perhaps my imagination is limited, but the lands you have or will travel to seem strange. Sometimes I see things and have no idea if they are past or present. However, I am certain that you will be well traveled before all is said and done. It does sadden me that Wilson will be lost to you."

"What!?" Kash hadn't been expecting that. She assumed she would be the one answering all the questions with mysterious answers but had no idea that Cassandra had dreamed of her beyond their arrival.

"What do you mean, Wilson will be lost to me?"

"Your great love will not prove enough to hold you together, alas his is not your fate."

"There's that Fate again. Everyone seems to think Fate all powerful, even Zeus fears that one." Cassandra gave her a look of great concern, her incredulity and confusion apparent.

"You have conversed with the gods?"

"Haven't you? Is it so rare a thing here?"

"Yes, indeed I have, and yes, it is a rare thing. To survive the wrath of Zeus is most astonishing. How did you manage it?"

"Well, his wrath wasn't what I faced. I think I intrigued him for the same reasons I intrigue you. We had a conversation about Fate, as well. He seemed to believe the same thing you do, despite being the most powerful of all the gods."

"If what you say is true, then your powers are beyond even what I had imagined. Be careful in their use, I warn. My father, the king, will not look kindly upon sorcery, even if it cannot be helped." Kash caught the reference to her father's disbelief in the validity of her visions and pitied the princess. She also supposed this was the reason that the woman seemed unsurprised and, indeed, sympathetic to Kash's powers. Kash decided to let the woman believe what she would about her so called "sorcery". As long as she remained friendly and discreet, which Kash was convinced she would, then Cassandra wouldn't prohibit her efforts. She still believed she could influence this story to her benefit. Cassandra's warning about Wilson rang quite oddly to her ears but she had a lot on her mind, and deciphering the visions of one who couldn't decipher them herself seemed futile to her. Regardless, she had to talk to Wilson, she would need his support if she was to have any success here in Troy.

■■■

Not long after Kash had left Cassandra, having parted ways with her at the end of their walk in the gardens, she found herself standing in front of Cliffradus once more. The scribe seemed less than thrilled at her return, even more so than last time.

"Is Wilsonious here?" she asked the man as politely as she could. He slowly looked up at her and nodded his head towards the back without saying anything. Kash didn't bother to respond either, not sure what to make of this one, but certain she didn't remember him being a character in the story. She put it out of her mind as she came upon Wilson bent over a scroll that appeared as if it was from a time far more ancient than this one.

"What ya reading?" she asked as a greeting.

"Kash!" he replied, his face lighting up. "Oh, this is nothing. Just the musings of an old man from an older time. I was hoping you would come by. Whatever Cassandra did, worked. No one has bothered me here so far."

"Excellent, did you know this place has an amazing garden. You want to see it?" Wilson looked down at the scroll he was reading then back to Kash. He got up with a grin and a nod, indicating she should lead the way and followed her out of the library. Wilson waved at Cliffradus as they passed but the man didn't acknowledge them at all. This was fine by Kash, and she dragged Wilson out of the library before he could do or say anything else. They made their way down the corridors and back to the entrance hall. Kash remembered the correct path, having only just been there. They emerged into the afternoon sun and Kash let Wilson take it all in for a minute. The quiet beauty of the place was enough to pause and simply be for a moment or two. A place untouched by everything around it, as if time itself stood still when one was here. She smiled to herself, considering the old adage about roses.

Watching Wilson move through the rows of beautiful flowers, she could tell he was feeling the same way about this place. It evoked an image of them standing on a tall tower in Narnia, looking out. She also knew, just as she knew, they couldn't stay in the garden forever, that she had to confide in him with her plans and ideas about the story moving forward. She walked over to him and he turned to smile at her, stealing her words. He put his arm around her and took a deep breath, looking around. She hardly even considered the movement, so fitting it seemed. All her thoughts and plans to tell Wilson everything seemed to melt away, and they whiled away the afternoon walking through the garden laughing and smiling and basking in the peace of the place.

The sun slowly sank below the horizon, conceding the sky to the night and the stars. They had spent the entire afternoon just enjoying each other's company and Kash was excited by how much joy it brought her. They said good night and parted at the library, Kash's thoughts of the past few hours keeping pace with her feet as she moved back across the city to the temple of Apollo. She smiled as she lay down, closing her eyes and thinking of Wilson. It was not completely unexpected, and she could not deny how wonderful the afternoon had been nor how comfortable she had felt despite knowing what lay ahead. She hadn't been able to burst that bubble by speaking of the future. She resolved to tell him tomorrow of her plans to change the story and save Troy. Now, having shared such an enjoyable afternoon, she knew she could tell him her plans. She knew he would probably still object, but she also felt that he had enjoyed the afternoon as much as she. It would still be difficult to convince him to go along with it but she was determined.

Kash was up with the sun the following day and hurried to the palace. Unsure of how much time they had until the story ended, there was an urgency about her pace. Wilson was just exiting the library when Kash spotted him and moved up to him.

"Kash!" he said, surprised and obviously happy. "You're over here early." He smiled as warmly as he could, remembering their time spent yesterday.

"Yes, I am." There was a moment of quasi awkwardness that made Kash laugh at herself. She wasn't a little girl and such hesitance was ridiculous. She grinned at him and started to ask him to accompany her to the gardens once more but he interrupted.

"Yes, I would love to go visit the gardens with you again." His grin took in his ears upon her revelation that his guess had hit the mark.

Instead of walking through the rows of plants and shrubbery they decided to lay out in the shade of one of the larger leafy plants. Wilson didn't know where Kash's sudden mood was coming from but he wasn't going to complain. Ever since he had met Aphrodite, he been unable to shake Kash's image appearing in his mind. Not that he had tried but it also seemed to be something more. Regardless of if it was divine intervention or some spell, he knew what he was feeling for the woman. He had always thought very highly of her before all of this and she was certainly attractive. One or two romantic thoughts had certainly crossed his mind but had been on the back burner with so much else going on. The circumstances that had gotten them to where they were now were quite unusual and he knew such things could certainly bring people together. But their journey thus far had been unique in its abnormality and he was uncertain of exactly where she stood. He was certainly enjoying these moments they were sharing, however, and he put it all from his mind, or at least tried to.

"So, Wilson, I need to tell you about what I have been doing whilst we were apart." She paused, unsure of where to begin, but certain it was important to achieving her goal here.

"You told me at the temple that a woman approached you in the library, do you remember? The lady Persephone, I believe you called her."

"Yes, and she came to me another time, as well," Wilson replied. Kash hadn't expected that and narrowed her eyes, but only acknowledged the comment with a curious look before moving on.

"Well, I believe that might have been a goddess in disguise. Aphrodite would be my guess."

"It's definitely her. I saw her on the battlefield, and it fit with the text."

"Right, and Apollo visited in disguise as well. If I am not too badly mistaken, we may have figured that out during the same battle. Anyway, I followed Apollo when he took Aeneas down the coast to Pergamos."

"What!? How?"

"The tattoos let met travel the same way we escaped Dracula's boat and spirited away to the castle, remember? Apollo travels around this world in a similar fashion and I convinced him to take me to Olympus. Actually, he seemed to be expecting me almost." She paused here, only just considering that. Her mind whirled with the possibilities, but she was unwilling to chase the white rabbit at this particular moment.

"Once there, I was able to speak with Zeus." Wilson's eyes grew even wider than they already were. He had been in the battle and had seen the gods in action, even talked to Aphrodite a couple of times. He didn't think, based on his own experience, that Kash's would surprise him, but he was struggling to believe what he was hearing. He knew he had to though; everything about where they were screamed to him to let all disbelief fall away. He shook his head, and smiled, clearly indicating that this woman he was fast becoming enamored with should continue.

"I was certainly surprised by our conversation. Even standing before his throne was a struggle. It was really cool, though, his voice was like thunder and he carries a bolt of lightning like a staff." She smiled at her memories of being borne back to Troy on a storm cloud, and Wilson's heart did a backflip at her girlish grin. He did feel the need to prompt her when it seemed her wistful moment might last a while.

"...and what did Zeus have to say?"

"Oh, right, he um...Zeus was humbler than I would've imagined. Not unlike Cassandra's warnings to me about Fate, Zeus seemed resigned to his role in the story and his inability to stop the fall of Troy. Many of the gods are at odds about this. Well, you know that, it's part of the text." Wilson nodded, taking it all in. He knew that Zeus would not intervene and try to tip the scales of Fate. He would say as much in the text when Athena reminds him of the unyielding nature of destiny. The question was: why would Kash be speaking with the god about Fate?

"Do you think he's wrong? Do you think he could save Troy if he chose to?" Kash's silence was telling. She clearly wasn't convinced and he felt that she was somewhat disappointed with her findings on Olympus.

"Does that seem so farfetched? He is the most powerful being around. Obviously the most powerful of this story. I don't see that it's such a stretch of the imagination to think he would at least believe he could. It wasn't that he didn't have motive or desire. He genuinely seemed to believe he could do nothing. It felt wrong to me."

"Wrong?" A shadow of worry was creeping into the man's sensibilities. He didn't really like what he was hearing. The road these musings led down was a dangerous one, and Wilson didn't really want to follow it to conclusion. He was saved by a voice floating across the garden, a voice he knew well by now.

"Lady Kashmira, Wilson! How lovely to see you two together at last!" The lady Persephone moved to stand right before them as they rose to their feet to meet her. They shared a look as what the woman had said registered then looked back, both with suspicion.

"We know it's you, Aphrodite. Do you always wear this disguise?" Wilson asked her somewhat coolly, considering this was a goddess they were talking to. She simply stared at him.

"You know the answer to that one, my dear Wilson. I am known to both of you by this point and you are both well known to me by now, as well. Surely it does my heart glad to see your union."

"Our union?"

"Yes, while you may not have admitted it to each other yet and one of you has yet to admit it to themselves, the love you share is unquestionably strong. You may have drawn the conclusion, sweet Wilson, that it was I who put these images of your beloved in your head but they were there all along. I simply brought them to the forefront of your mind and allowed them to have their day. Your love for her cannot be denied, and it is good to see you recognize that." Wilson felt himself blushing fiercely as he exchanged glances with Kash.

"As for you, my dear," Aphrodite continued, looking at Kash. "Your head's reconciliation with your heart may be blossoming too late. Alas, if only the seer's words held no truth." Aphrodite smiled once more and turned to go.

"Wait, what seer? What truth?" Wilson ran to catch up to the goddess and moved in front of her to halt her progress.

"There are many that will be revealed in time, dear Wilson. You will see. I must return to Olympus; the gods will meet to discuss Troy's fate. My presence will be required." She put a soft hand to Wilson's cheek and smiled brightly as she walked past him. Kash was still standing where they had left her, somewhat stunned by everything the goddess had said. Was she referring to Cassandra? How could she know about the woman's words to Kash? Kash searched her heart and understood that at least some of what the goddess had said was true. She did care for Wilson, she realized. She was unsure where it had come from but it was undeniable. Just as undeniable was the way Wilson felt about her, she came to believe. She could see it in the way he was looking at her now as he moved back over to where she stood.

"That was weird," he said awkwardly, making her laugh. She stood up and without a word moved very close to the man, looking him in the eye with sudden intensity. She paused when she was within an inch of him, their faces almost touching. Then she kissed him deeply and he returned the embrace with passion after only a moment of surprise. They pulled apart and locked eyes. Wilson gently lowered her to the ground without blinking, without breaking the stare. They spent the rest of the day there in each other's arms only

breaking off their passion when night stole the light from their
eyes.

Ch. 26 A Divine Gathering

Morning found Kash and Wilson snuggled very close to one another upon the bed in Kash's room at the temple of Apollo. The bed wasn't large and it was a good thing their new found romance defeated any discomfort they may have had with one another. Wilson slowly became aware of his surroundings when he woke up and smiled as he remembered the events of the past couple of days. He simply lay there without moving, unwilling to disturb Kash's sleep. The rhythmic up and down of her chest telling him she was still in dreamland. His heart soared at the thought that he might describe their adventures here as such. Wilson tried to close his eyes once more and drift back to sleep when a noise from the adjoining room woke his companion abruptly. She sat up suddenly, nearly toppling Wilson from the bed. She looked around at his protestation and smiled, nearly laughing at his plight. She grabbed the man's arm to steady him then rubbed the sleep from her eyes when his position was secure.

"What was that?" she asked groggily.

"I'm not sure," he replied, assuming it was just the morning bustle of the temple getting started. "Should we ignore it and stay in bed a while?" Wilson continued and reached out for Kash's waist. She grabbed his hand in both her own and brought it to her lips for a kiss before responding.

"That sounds lovely but I fear we have ignored the story for too long. It has been a wonderful break, but we need to figure out what's going on."

"That's fair," Wilson replied flatly. Kash could feel his disappointment so she leaned in and gave him a real kiss before sliding the sheet back and getting out of the tiny bed, almost a cot really. She slid her robe over her head and let it fall, the bottom nearly covering her ankles.

"The last thing I know that happened was the capturing of Dolon, the Trojan spy. That must mean that we are somewhere in the story of Patroklus, friend and cousin to Achilles. I think Achilles is about to join the battle or perhaps, already has." Wilson was simply thinking aloud, unsure of exactly what Kash was planning.

"That will mean the gods are going to meet on Olympus soon and Zeus will allow them to choose sides in the war. We just need to know exactly when so we can be there."

"Be there?!" Wilson echoed incredulously.

"Yes, of course. Why else would Aphrodite come to us and let slip that she was going to be needed, and that the Fate of Troy would be decided at this meeting."

"The Fate of Troy?" he asked, beginning to catch on to what the woman was saying and hoping he was wrong about where her mind was.

"Yes, something I am keen to have a say in."

"Why should we have a say in the city's fate? The story only ends one way, by definition, must. Merlin—"

"Yes, I know what Merlin said," Kash interrupted somberly and turned to face Wilson directly. There it was, out in the open. She could no longer hide her designs from him, especially not after the night they had just shared. She looked to the floor, somewhat unsure of herself in the face of his sudden intensity. She knew they had to have this conversation sooner rather than later, though. She looked back to Wilson almost pleadingly.

"Think about it this way: almost everything we thought we knew can be challenged by the revelations of our adventures since Stonehenge. Magic? Jumping into stories, meeting famous characters? All of this goes beyond anything I could've imagined was possible. But why did I think that? Because I was told that all of it was impossible; magic isn't, can't be real. Just words in the face of our experience. Thus, why does something the characters of the story say necessarily have to ring true? You remember many things Merlin said, but do you remember what he said about Morgana? She knew that these stories were malleable, knew, with the right power, she could bend them to her will. We could save Troy, Wilson. How many more nights like last night could we share? Think about it? Merlin put a stop to Morgana because her designs were way more nefarious than mine. He didn't say it wasn't possible, only that it shouldn't be done."

Wilson was becoming increasingly alarmed by what he was hearing. She was thinking to attempt to do exactly what Merlin had cautioned against. He couldn't deny the passion of last night and how attractive the picture Kash painted was, but this was the very reason Merlin's spell was created: to stop the stories from being changed and forever altering everything they knew and loved.

"For good reason too, Kash. The consequences could be catastrophic, their effects far-reaching, possibly more than we could even know. He produced this spell to protect the endings of the stories, remember? He wanted King Arthur to do what we are doing and ensure that everything played out as it was supposed to. Look, I would love to live here and see out the potential of what we've started, but isn't it just what Zeus is saying too? He cannot change the Fate of the city no more than he could leave his own story. It just is."

"*We* can," she said simply. "What consequences could possibly be so bad if we simply reverse the outcome of this war and Priam's Troy lives on? This is a fabrication, anyways. No one is even sure if it is real."

"Yes, but if it is, and even if it isn't, this novel has had a huge impact on the world, on archaeology, it's even taught in schools. All of that influence would be tainted or at least changed, thus altering our reality."

"Perhaps, and only slightly in any case. Please, Wilson. Don't you want to stay here with me for a while at least? This place is so wonderful and I can only imagine what it would be like in a time of peace. The Trojans do not deserve to be sacked for Paris' lack of self-control and there are many gods who would agree with me. Just think about the text. Many of them join the battle."

"Yes, but Zeus only allows this because Achilles was winning out and that's not how the story ends."

"Aha, so Zeus is influencing the outcome by allowing the gods to participate." Wilson shook his head, seeing the logic trap she thought he was in.

"Yes, indeed," he started to reply dryly, "however, he knows that the time of that fate is not yet upon the city and therefore knows that Achilles can't win out yet. Homer wrote it this way to set up the fall of Troy for later."

"Don't try to dance around this one. Zeus could do whatever he wanted to. Homer stopped him, but he's still a god. I don't see what's to stop him from crushing the entire Greek army right now if he was so inclined. Merlin spoke of the power of creation and we have that power. We should use it. We should go find Cassandra. She should be able to tell us what is going on outside the walls. It will help us know when to go to Olympus. Look, I know you don't agree with me on this, but I am asking you to trust me. If anything starts to get out of control, we'll pull the plug and go home. Simply will ourselves back to the library and regroup."

"You promise?" Wilson asked, his walls crumbling into the swirl of emotions he was experiencing at the moment. He was almost certain that things would go sideways at some point, and was determined to hold her to that promise. Besides, the only way he could keep her out of trouble was to remain by her side. He certainly had no intention of letting her out of his sight again, but recognized he would not defeat her stubbornness. The smile she was giving him at his acquiescence melted the last of his defenses.

"Of course!" She moved over to Wilson and gave him a soft kiss before whispering "It's all going to be fine. I promise. You'll see. Now, let's head to the palace and find Cassandra."

■■■

Unsurprised this time by the warm welcome of the guards, Kash reminded herself to thank Cassandra again for her generosity once they had found her. That moment came quite quickly as Cassandra caught up to them on their way to her chamber.

"We should go to the ramparts with my father, battle will again be joined this day. Hector reported that a young Greek by the name of Patroklus was killed in the fighting, the cousin of the great warrior Achilles. We were lucky when quarreling in their camp resulted in Achilles' absence from the field, but it seems our fortune has run its course in that regard. The Greek hero will join their forces today. Hector is certain he will want revenge." The princess' monologue ended just as they crested the top of the stairs to see the invaders charging the walls once more. Kash and Wilson exchanged a knowing glance.

"My lady, Cassandra, we...um..." Kash started trying to think of a quick excuse to get away but had no idea what she was going to say. Luckily, Wilson noticed this rather quickly and came to her rescue.

"Unfortunately, I have only just remembered I promised to help dear Cliffradus with a particularly nasty tome today. My apologies, I beg your forgiveness but I must go."

"I shall accompany you. I have yet to fully explore the library, anyways. My lady, your generosity and hospitality are unrivaled and you have my deepest gratitude, but I have not the stomach nor heart to watch more bloodshed and death." They turned to go, bowing as they went under the curious eye of Cassandra. The rest of the characters gathered around the King's seat paid their departure no mind which was fine by them. Once back down the stairs and into the corridor, they stopped.

"What now?" Wilson asked, unsure of their next move.

"We go to Olympus."

"How? Didn't you say Apollo took you there last time?"

"Yes, but I remember the palace of the gods vividly. Just hold on to me and clear your mind I suppose or think of Aphrodite, perhaps, that will aid the magic. At least, do not let go of my hand. I think I might be getting the hang of this."

Wilson grabbed on to Kash's hand tightly and nodded. He watched as she closed her eyes and took a deep breath. Less surprised than ever before at the sudden swirling tornado of blue light, Wilson felt himself whisked away. The only thing his mind could focus on was gripping Kash's hand as tightly as he could. As soon as it had begun it was over. He opened his eyes and gasped. Kash immediately grabbed him and pulled him behind the gigantic door to the palace. She had landed them just outside the great hall on the steps and rushed them to cover. There didn't seem to be anyone around outside, but Kash could clearly make out the thundering boom of Zeus' voice. She grinned at the shock and awe on Wilson's face as they peeked around the door and took in the scene before them.

It looked as if the entire pantheon of Greek gods had gathered for this meeting. They slipped quietly inside and took up a position hidden away but within earshot. If they had lingered on the doorway a moment longer, they may have spotted the knowing look Zeus shot Aphrodite's way and her resulting wicked grin. As it was, they remained oblivious to this and listened to Zeus going on about the war.

"The Greek hero, Achilles, has gained much ground over the Trojans this day. His fate is known, even unto you, Thetis. Did you not warn him of this? His triumphs must be limited. Therefore, if you should so choose a side in this desperate war, I will not stop you. Be warned of Fate, however, it cannot be stopped. Troy must fall in the end, for her doom is certain. Any who would seek to change this does so at their own peril. The height of folly it is to challenge Fate. But what do I know?" The gathered divinity seemed to take that as the end of the meeting. As they watched, some of them simply vanished into the air, others with a flourish or flash of light. Kash slapped Wilson's arm insistently, bringing his gaze to Aphrodite walking their way and speaking with two of the other gods. One was most certainly Apollo. She had seen the statue enough times to recognize that one. It was curious that he would appear like the statue here. Kash had assumed the gods were always in disguise around mortals. She studied the goddess she didn't know and tried to think of who might be conversing with Apollo and Aphrodite. She couldn't place it but heard Wilson whisper.

"That must be Artemis. She was one of the ones who supported the Trojans along with Apollo and Aphrodite." His voice trailed away as the divine trio moved within earshot and Aphrodite stopped the others by moving in front of them, her voice insistent.

"Ares' plan will work. All we must do is divert some of the Trojans towards the river Xanthos. Achilles should follow and there Ares will have him."

"Ares' plan? Or your own?" Artemis asked skeptically.

"Have no fear, I will be there with you as well, Aphrodite," Apollo interred. Kash peeked around the pedestal they were hiding behind and saw that the trio had moved on, out of the palace. Looking around, it seemed as if the place had cleared out completely. Kash grabbed Wilson's arm and tugged him along towards the doors and back outside. They walked a little way beyond the steps and took in the incredible view. They were high above the clouds and the sea of white obscured everything but neighboring peaks from their sight. It was somewhat intimidating and exhilarating at the same time. After a long quiet moment, Wilson's curiosity proved stronger than his patience.

"So, what's the plan? What have we learned?"

"We learned all we need. You heard Aphrodite; they're going to lay a trap for Achilles at the river Xanthos. That's also where the battle of the gods takes place if I recall correctly. Should certainly be something to behold, from a safe distance of course. I do want to be close enough to ensure the trap works if my help is needed. Defeating Achilles could be just the catalyst we need."

"Perhaps, but I also heard Zeus and Artemis. Besides, how will you aid in defeating Achilles? Why would his defeat alter the story? Doesn't he die anyways?" Wilson protested.

"He does, but not in this story. *The Iliad* is about him really, it's about his character arc during the war. However, I am betting that if he is defeated, it will be our first step. Anyways, Aphrodite was trying to change the outcome too. She has support just as I told you. Not all the gods would see Troy burn. We could stay here for a while, enjoying the place."

"Kash, are we going to be able to stay in Troy beyond the end of the book?" She didn't respond immediately, her silence telling Wilson she was either uncertain or she was too stubborn to admit the logic behind such a question. He figured she was at least hoping to be able to, whether she believed it would happen or not.

"I believe that if we can alter the story, we can rewrite the ending beyond Achilles. Other stories tell of the fall of Troy, right? Therefore, it happened, regardless of where the story was written down. This leads me to believe we can stay."

"You hope," Wilson thought but kept it to himself and simply nodded his acceptance. He knew she wanted him to agree with her, wanted him to reassure her, but he just couldn't get past his caution. The status quo held, however, and he knew it was no good arguing. So, he smiled as she grabbed his hand and felt himself pulled away by the swirl of blue light.

Ch. 27 The River Xanthos

Their latest magical journey deposited them directly on the bank of the river Xanthos, or at least Wilson assumed it was. It wasn't necessarily important in that moment as he didn't really stick the landing and nearly toppled into the water. Kash grabbed the back of his robe at the last second, keeping him from taking an unwelcome bath.

"Thanks, that was close." They took a second to look around and spotted a hill not so far away. Wilson pointed and Kash started moving in that direction with urgency. Suddenly hearing a low rumbling and the echoes of a distant cacophony, Wilson understood the woman's hurry. The Trojans were even then retreating towards the river. Wilson raced past Kash at full tilt, wanting nothing to do with the battle itself, no matter what Kash had said. She was hot on his heels up the hill and they both threw themselves down behind it, ducking for cover. Peeking back over, they both breathed a sigh of relief as the soldiers didn't seem to have noticed them in their haste. The companions watched the Trojans, led by Aeneas, prepare to stand their ground before the river.

Their first glance of Achilles in all his terrible wrath and battle fervor was certainly a sight to behold. Both Kash and Wilson could feel the great aura of strength from the man, even at a distance.

"You want to try and help defeat that?!" Wilson asked incredulously, staring at Kash wide-eyed. She returned his look with a sour one of her own but didn't respond. They both looked back to the river to see a massive wave rolling up it, soldiers fleeing the rising water, Greek and Trojan alike.

Amazingly, Achilles held his ground and bellowed a war cry, the water crashing over him, nearly toppling him over. The great warrior stood up straight once more, just in time to be hit by another crashing wave. The second one proved too strong for the hero and he was thrown to the ground.

Wilson could almost feel Kash's excitement as they watched. He figured she was about to make her move; this could be their only chance to influence things. How, he had no idea, but he could feel Kash about to do something. Just as he suspected she popped up and ran over the hill, Wilson hot on her heels. She skidded to an abrupt halt, however, Wilson nearly crashing into her, at the sight of Achilles standing tall once more. It looked as if two of the gods, one a goddess, had bolstered the man. He held his sword aloft and spun around, looking straight at Kash and Wilson. He bellowed a war cry and charged causing the duo to turn and run. Achilles, however, was not coming for them they learned as they spun. Many of the Trojans who had come this way were moving towards the hill from the side and Achilles wasn't finished with them. Kash and Wilson ran in the opposite direction of the approaching Trojans, out of Achilles' way, and he passed them by without a glance, for which they were eternally grateful.

The air seemed to shimmer in front of them, suddenly, and they could feel an intense heat. They were standing in ankle deep water in the edge of the river and turned to see the fury of Hera and Hephaestus unleashed. The gods were attacking the river with fire and Kash knew she was overmatched here in this chaos, no matter what her designs were on Achilles. Those plans had been successfully interrupted and Wilson was barely able to pace her retreat as they tried to steer clear of the battle. The fighting between the gods, the river, and the soldiers raged behind them as they put a little distance between themselves and the water. Pausing for a second to catch their breath, Aphrodite and Ares flashed past them battling Athena. Wilson guessed it was Athena for that was who defeated them in the text. As they watched, Ares and Aphrodite were driven off and the two gods disappeared beyond the other side of the battle towards Troy. Just then a Trojan soldier came running towards them yelling. It was a woman, which struck Kash as odd that a Trojan woman would be in the army. She supposed it wasn't as odd as what she was seeing right in front of her and she didn't have much time to ponder this as the woman gathered them up in her wake. This didn't take much doing as the fires rolled up the river and burst out to either side. Kash and Wilson and the mystery woman dove to the ground just in time as an incredible explosion rocked the ground beneath them and a great mass of steam arose. It immediately dampened Kash's robe and she struggled to her feet.

"Wilson!" her choked cry seemed hardly audible. She couldn't see a thing, had no idea which way was which. She put her hands up and began to move blindly through the cloudy morass hoping to emerge out of the fog. A hand materialized out of the gloom and grabbed her arm. She resisted and was about to punch out at the person when she heard Wilson's voice.

"Kash! Its me." She grabbed the man and pulled him close, hugging him for a second despite the danger and the sounds of battle all around them. They broke apart and Wilson led her away from the sounds of the fighting. This was the best idea he could think of and fortunately, it proved to be an effective one. They found the end of the steam cloud and picked up their pace, hurrying away from the scene. Once they had put some distance between them and the river, the immediate danger seemed to have abated, so they both collapsed on the ground, breathing deeply. Eventually, they sat up, looking at each other.

"That went well," Kash said sarcastically, but she smiled, showing Wilson she wasn't too upset with their failure to influence proceedings.

"Do you suppose it might be time to head..." he fell silent when she turned to him sharply, denial clear to interpret on her face.

"We can't give up yet. I'll think of something. Maybe we can make the Trojans mistrust the Greek who convinces them to bring the horse into the city." Kash stood up, Wilson wearily following suit. She walked off without another word in the general direction of the city, Wilson falling into step beside her. They moved parallel to the river when they got a little closer in an effort to avoid the end of the battle. The fighting had not quite abated and the companions could see that same Trojan woman fleeing the river once more. She moved away from the main fight and seemed to be running their way. They stopped and both watched as the woman came closer. Wilson was about to say something as the soldier neared but the woman never slowed and lifted her sword to strike. Kash dove aside and Wilson barely ducked, spinning and backing away from the crazed woman. He stumbled and fell beside Kash who was still sprawled out on the ground. Looking up he could see death in the woman's wild eyes. As the sword began to swing down at them, he did the only thing he could think of, grabbing Kash's wrist and praying for the library. He concentrated with all his might, fully expecting to die but hoping against hope they would be whisked away in time. He had closed his eyes, expecting to feel the blade enter his flesh but the blow never came and when he opened his eyes once more, he was back in the library. He smiled as he looked around, breathing a sigh of relief that was stolen from him as quickly as it came. He felt sick as he realized Kash was nowhere to be found.

Wilson stood stunned for a moment, not sure what to do and still a bit disoriented from the suddenness of his departure in the face of certain death. Where was Kash? Slowly, he moved around the shelf in front of him and into the next aisle. His steps became more urgent as he moved to the opposite row with still no sign of her. He was just about to call out for her when he ran into someone as he came around the corner, nearly knocking both of them to the floor.

"Wilson! Oh, thank God, I thought I had gone crazy. I thought you had disappeared into thin air. I must've been seeing things, right? Where's Kash?" Wilson could tell that while the man was clearly struggling with reconciling what his eyes had seen, he was willing to dismiss it if Wilson could confirm he wasn't crazy. Wilson didn't know what to say. He had no idea where Kash was and was in no mood to answer the million questions he was sure Radcliffe had. He just shook his head and moved over to one of the tables to sit down.

"Wasn't she with you? You guys have been gone all day. Did you leave the library? What happened earlier?" Dr. Radcliffe followed him and sat down opposite Wilson, eyeing the suddenly exhausted man. He didn't know what to do or what to say to Radcliffe. He was replaying the events at the river over and over in his mind. Had Kash tried to magically go somewhere else? And succeeded? Was that possible? He shook his head, why wouldn't it be possible after everything they had seen. He thought back to the different stories they had travelled to and his head popped up. Without a word to Radcliffe, Wilson stood up, an idea giving him new hope. He ran back to the aisle they had stood in upon entering the *Iliad* and scanned the rows of books looking for the copy. If he just went back to right before the battle at the river, maybe she would still be there. His eyes raced over the many titles quickly. His alarm grew and grew as the search found no success. He found the place where they had pulled it off the shelf originally to see that there was only an empty space where the book should've been. He moved back out of the row and over towards the table where Dr. Radcliffe was looking at him with concern.

"Do you know what happened to the copy of the *Iliad*?" Wilson asked the man as innocently as he could muster. Radcliffe narrowed his eyes, clearly suspicious, before answering.

"Yes, Wilson, I do. But I am not going to give it to you until you tell me what's going on. I came around the corner and you two were standing in a tornado of swirling blue light. I know what I saw because everything simply vanished, you included, leaving only the book to drop to the floor with the rest of mine." He stopped there and now it was Wilson's turn to cast a suspicious eye over Radcliffe. Wilson wondered if he had opened the book, wondered if the book had changed while they were in there. He was unsure of when the pages actually changed, but he assumed they would have to. They altered the story with their mere presence quite a bit. Dr. Radcliffe's insistence coupled with his seeming willingness to be patient until Wilson divulged the truth led him to believe the man knew something he was holding back. They had been gone all day, he had said, meaning there was ample time to study the book. Before Wilson answered, the man seemed to come to a decision and rose from the table and moved off. He returned quickly, however, with the copy of the *Iliad* clasped gingerly in both hands. He also had the copy of *Dracula, The Lion, The Witch and The Wardrobe* and the *Prophetiae Merlini*. As he lay them down, Wilson could see that the cover had changed and the "I" in *Iliad* now resembled the tattoos clearly. That could only mean that the pages were altered as well.

"So, at first, I didn't know what to think, obviously thought I was hallucinating. But when you didn't return and I noticed that the book cover had changed, I had my suspicions. It was ludicrous, of course, to think that you had travelled into a novel, but it was where my mind went immediately. I found where Kash had lay these two out and discovered the same. I skimmed through *Dracula.*" Here he stopped and looked at Wilson, clearly as stunned as Wilson was upon first learning the truth of the power Kash had stumbled upon at Stonehenge. Wilson didn't know what to say to him but could clearly see on the man's face that the text of *Dracula* had changed.

"And did you read the *Iliad?*" Wilson asked somewhat nervously, not knowing how the story would be altered, but thinking back to the things that were going on just before his return here, he didn't think Radcliffe would look favorably upon those events. Particularly not Kash's ideas and attitude.

"No, I had not been able to piece together anything from *Dracula*, although there was a scene I didn't remember, a journal entry from Van Helsing that I am certain didn't exist before the cover changed. I haven't had time to find another copy to compare. The man writes about an encounter Quincey Morris told him about. An encounter at Dr. Seward's house with a man and a woman in the street. Then there is another odd spot where the captain of the count's ship from England across the Mediterranean mentions a man and a woman being on board that were not in the crew. There are a couple of other references to this mystery couple, but it is never explained. Curious, don't you think?"

This was interesting news, Wilson thought, sitting down in front of the man once more, inviting the man to do so as well. So, they had stayed on the outskirts of the story and had not appeared to alter the story of *Dracula* too much. Wilson held no presumptions that the same would hold true for the *Iliad*. They were in the thick of the action several different times and Wilson was sure they would be mentioned directly. Wilson wanted to grab the *Iliad* right now and turn to the back to see if it would tell of Kash's fate. He smiled at the irony of that thought and pushed the compulsion away. He was unsure of how much Radcliffe knew and was unsure of how to handle the man. The man was already aware that something strange was happening and had even witnessed the swirl of blue lights that had been taking them to and from the stories. How could he possibly keep the man in the dark? But would he believe just how deep the rabbit hole really went? Wilson wasn't even sure how deep it went himself, and was ultimately worried that things were only going to get worse. He looked at the patiently waiting man and took a deep breath.

"Well, my friend, I am not sure where to begin and even less certain you will believe me." He then went on to explain everything he could about what was going on. From the very beginning: Kash's odd disappearance at Stonehenge all the way up to how they were attacked by the river and Wilson had returned without Kash. When he finished, Radcliffe, who had remained silent and impassive for the entire time Wilson was speaking, didn't speak for many moments. He was clearly trying to take it all in. Digesting such a torrent of information that was seemingly ridiculous in nature wasn't an easy thing to do.

"Let me see your tattoos then," he eventually spoke up. Wilson nodded and lifted his shirt, revealing the tattoos on his back. "These are interesting, same font as on these books here. The entire titles are spelled out in the flowing script." Wilson tried to bend around to see them but gave up, quickly realizing it was futile. Radcliffe said, however, that he had the titles of all four on him now. They must've formed while he was in each story. Radcliffe still didn't seem convinced but Wilson was done worrying about the man and he sat back down, grabbing the copy of the *Iliad* and opened it up. He skimmed to the part where Dolon was captured and did well to hide his surprise at seeing the names Wilsonious and Kashmira appear in the text. He quickly skipped to the back upon learning that the pages were indeed altered. He began reading at the meeting on Olympus and he became more and more alarmed at the things now recorded in the pages. By the time he reached the battle at the river Xanthos, he was quite certain that Kash was in more danger than she realized. Without even a glance at Radcliffe, he closed his eyes and willed himself to travel back to the river, back to Troy.

He opened his eyes after a few long moments of concentration to see Radcliffe staring at him almost bemusedly.

It hadn't worked. He couldn't go back. She was lost.

Battling black wings of despair, he read on, praying that she had been successful and altered the ending to her liking. However, there was nothing else after the scene he had escaped that seemed to be out of place. He fought back tears of frustration and pushed his chair back so forcefully it fell to the floor behind him.

"I'm sorry, Dr. Radcliffe, I have to go, I need to clear my head."

"You're leaving, now?! That's it? After all that, you're just going to go?"

"I don't know what else to do. The end hasn't changed, it doesn't even mention her at all. I cannot go back and she hasn't returned. I am absolutely exhausted. The past few days have been a whirlwind of emotions and fantastical happenings that threaten to overwhelm me right now. I need to rest, and to think. I will return tomorrow and we can try to figure out what to do in the morning." With that, he left, leaving Radcliffe feeling helpless and confused, wondering if the man was stark raving mad or if he himself was.

Ch 28 More Questions

Wilson moved up the steps of the library, somewhat groggily, the next morning. His dreams had been full of blue light and the crazed woman attacking them. Aphrodite, disguised as the lady Persephone flitted in and out, but the most vivid images were of Kash. His thoughts of their short love affair almost brought a wistful smile to his face. Instead, he painted a grimace of determination there. He would not let those be the last such moments they spent together. He almost bumped into the waiting Radcliffe when he made the top of the stairs.

"Wilson, I figured you would be here as soon as I was ready to open. Come on in." The man held out a coffee to Wilson this time, and smiled. Despite being on the outside looking in, Radcliffe could tell Wilson was serious about all of this and taking the loss of Kash even more seriously still. The man's smile and nod of greeting was short-lived as they moved into the quiet warmth of the library. Wilson wasted no time in heading over to the table they had left the books on from last night and immediately began rereading them, hoping to find something, anything that would aid him in finding Kash. He figured that if she had made it into a different story then it might be a while before that story changed. It seemed as if the pages remained unaltered until they left the story. The end of the *Iliad* hadn't changed which didn't tell Wilson much since there wasn't much more to the story anyways. Why hadn't Kash simply returned to the library when Wilson had? That was the question that needed answering and Wilson was determined not to give up until he found Kash once more.

Wilson's reread of the *Iliad* was enlightening and disturbing at the same time. He realized just how much Aphrodite and Zeus were interested in Kash and her powers. The most confusing thing to him was her complete disappearance from the novel after he had left. Wilson was hoping (assuming she had remained in the story) that she had made it back to the city and escaped from the crazed soldier that had attacked them. He couldn't fathom her not returning here if she had left the *Iliad.* Was she beyond the pages somehow? Some trick of the gods? Wilson knew that not everything they had done in their time in Troy would be reflected in the changes to the story. This gave him some sliver of hope that she had made it back to the city somehow. As he finished the page he was looking at, Dr. Radcliffe sat down to join him.

"So, how much changed in that one? Is the Trojan horse still in there?" Wilson's eyes widened to saucers as waves of realization crashed over him.

"The end of the war isn't in the *Iliad.* It's in the *Aeneid!*" He explained excitedly, a plan beginning to form in his mind. He rushed back to the aisle he thought it might be on. Wilson scanned the spines of the old books as fast as he could until his heart skipped a beat. There it was, the *Aeneid.* All hope was not lost. He was about to open to the appropriate part of the novel when Radcliffe ran around the corner after him.

"Hey, wait. Are you going into that story?" Wilson was instantly aware from the man's tone that he wanted to travel into the story as well. He immediately began thinking of an excuse to give. He might have been more open to the idea if Kash were not in the wind somewhere but as it was, there was too much riding on what he might find in this story. He didn't plan on being there long, anyway. He knew the Trojans were on a long journey in that book; one he didn't really want any part of. He simply needed to hear Aeneas tell of the fall of Troy and whether or not it had changed. Then he would come right back. No, it would not be good to have a passenger on this trip, especially not one new to this type of travel.

"I don't think that it would be a good idea, Radcliffe. This particular mission is simply to learn what happened to Kash. I won't be gone long and have no intention of staying or doing anything while I am there. Perhaps the next one. Anyways, I am not even sure I would be able to take you along."

"Kash took you, didn't she? Isn't that how you received the power to do this in the first place?"

"Not really, I was simply with her and read the book at the same time she did. I suppose that is what caught me up in the swirl of blue light. It doesn't matter anyway. I really think I need to do this one alone. I'm coming right back, I promise." Wilson nodded as the man gave in with a nod of his own and stepped back a bit. Wilson opened the book to the appropriate scene and began to read. He felt himself flying away instantly and everything went black.

When he opened his eyes, he was thankful to have appeared inside the palace at Carthage. Last time they tried to gain entry into a palace they had gotten quite lucky, if he remembered correctly. He was in a deserted hallway with many doors along it on either side. Wilson wasn't confused at all, however, about which one to go through to find his quarry. The sounds of a banquet feast were emitting from a portal not far from him and Wilson was glad that he had somehow managed to appear in the perfect spot. As he poked his head around the door to take in the scene, he realized his caution was for naught. No one was looking this way and there didn't seem to be any guards about, at least not any who were paying attention to the doors. Wilson didn't hesitate to ponder his good fortune and moved into the hall quietly and quickly. He found an unoccupied bench and took a seat, grabbing a cup to disguise himself as just another reveler. His attention was drawn to a figure standing before the throne where a most beautiful woman was seated. She was bedecked with many jewels and necklaces and adornments of gold and silver. Queen Dido, he recalled vaguely. His familiarity with this story was minimal at best, but he knew he was in the right place in the story when Aeneas stood up and began to tell the tale he had come to hear.

"There came a day, some ten years past the genesis of our war with the Greeks, that a wooden horse of gigantic proportions appeared outside the great city walls of Troy. It was just taller than the gates themselves. As if this curiosity were not enough, our scouts reported that the Greeks had sailed away from our shores. Despite our ignorance as to the purpose of the contraption, we were happy to hear the news. A gathering around the horse grew and grew, the arguments becoming increasingly heated. What were we to do with this magnificent creation? Some thought it a gift from the Greeks, a peace offering. Others believed it to be a weapon of war and a grand deception. Some of the people from the outlying area had come to see and with them there was a woman. She claimed to be a priestess of Apollo: the lady Kashmira."

Wilson was stunned to hear Aeneas' words. He was hoping he would hear something about her, any clue or hint, but she must've done something drastic to be mentioned directly. He leaned forward, straining to hear Aeneas' tale from his spot at the table.

"She proclaimed that the horse was a symbol of the gods and to destroy it would anger them greatly. She commanded the attention of all around and her words were convincing. If we didn't bring the great horse into the city, the gods would rain fire and blood down upon us. Many were frightened by her insistence and urgency, but I remember seeing her before. She was consorting with Apollo himself. The God saved me from the battlefield and the wrath of Diomedes and whisked me away to Pergamos. It was there I first saw her. I'll never forget the lady Kashmira, for it was she who brought about the ultimate doom of our once great city.

"In the face of her promise of divine retribution, the horse was brought in. They even had to destroy part of the gate so its massive bulk could be admitted. It was pulled into the square to such fanfare and celebration as had never been seen. We cheered our imminent demise. For, when night fell, the villainous invaders poured out of the hollow of the horse's body and opened the gates for the returned forces of Agamemnon and Achilles and all the rest of them. The city fell to fire and the blade. We here were lucky to escape with our lives. If ever my path does cross with the priestess of Apollo who so tricked us, I vow to seek justice and vengeance for all Trojans."

Wilson couldn't believe what he was hearing. He had so many questions, so many inconsistencies with what he thought he knew. He didn't think here was a good place to ponder all of the possibilities, however. He rose to leave, but before he had turned around, Aeneas had turned his way and their eyes locked on to one another. Wilson could feel the aura of a main character from the man quite clearly. Of more concern was the suspicion etched on his features. Did he recognize Wilson? The way he was staring certainly led Wilson to believe he at least thought he did. Wilson had only seen Aeneas from afar, had watched as the man was rescued by Poseidon during the battle at the river. Had Aeneas seen him somewhere else? In the city? On the battlefield? Wilson couldn't be sure but he knew he didn't want to wait around to find out. He nodded at Aeneas and turned to go.

"You there," Aeneas called to Wilson, stopping the man for just a moment. Wilson looked back for a split second before deciding it was past time he leave. He exploded into motion, running down the table and knocking a serving girl to the floor in his haste. No time to stop for apologies, Wilson scrambled on towards the door, vaguely aware of the pursuit. He ran through the palace, not daring to look back. The echo of the footsteps keeping pace through the corridors with him was all the proof he needed. He turned right down a corridor at a full sprint and nearly collided with the wall. He had come to a dead end; he figured he would eventually. He turned back the way he had come just as Aeneas and the guards filled the hallway in front of him. With a grin and a wave, Wilson closed his eyes and willed himself back to the library. His relief was immense when he felt himself melt away into the darkness.

"Wow, that was fast, you weren't kidding." Wilson smiled at his friend. Dr. Radcliffe had obviously been waiting for him right where he had disappeared in the swirl of blue light.

"How long was I gone?" Wilson asked the man, moving past him and heading for the table they had left the other books on.

"Not even five minutes. How'd it go? Did you find Kash?"

"No," Wilson said with a sigh. "No, I did not, only more riddles."

Wilson knew he was missing something important. How could it be that Kash was the one ensuring that the horse *was* moved into the city? Wouldn't that be her chance to argue the opposite, keep the horse out and save the city? If she was going to change the outcome of the *Iliad,* that was the only way Wilson could see of doing it. It would've been her last shot at it, but something had changed. She had completely reversed her position, so much so that she was helping to make sure the city's fate remained the same. What about the character who was supposed to do that in the original text? Wilson couldn't remember his name right now, but he hoped

Kash hadn't done anything to the man. He shook his head at that thought; there was no way Kash would attack or otherwise attempt to harm someone unless she absolutely had to. Wilson was left scratching his head. It was all so odd and it frustrated him immensely. He had literally been chased out of the *Aeneid* but then again, he hadn't exactly tried to discuss matters with Aeneas. In hindsight, he figured his decision to run was still the right one. The look Aeneas had given him had certainly told Wilson in no uncertain terms the man was suspicious of him and his presence. If he had recognized Wilson, then there was no chance of him talking his way out of being there. Aeneas had vowed vengeance against Kash and since she was the only person associated with Wilson in Troy...He was glad he hadn't found out just how much Aeneas knew and grateful for his escape back to the library.

Ch. 29 A Fateful Discourse

Somehow, Kash was able to keep her eyes open. Thinking about the moment much later on, she supposed she was transfixed by the grimace of rage upon the soldier's features as the blade swung. Thankfully, her and Wilson were on the same page and the swirl of blue light spirited them away. It was lucky that Kash still had her eyes open, so used to this travel that she wasn't worried about looking around. As it was, on this particular journey, something felt absurdly wrong. Kash felt weighted down and she looked below her, just before the blackness came, to see the lady Persephone hanging on to her ankle.

Aphrodite was traveling back to the library with them!

Kash immediately thought of the river and concentrated as hard as she could, letting go of Wilson to try and break the goddess' grip. This was futile but she felt Wilson leave her as the blue lights appeared once more. This had never happened before and she held faith that her concentration would bring her and Aphrodite back to the river where the battle still raged.

She heard the screams and the clash of sword on shield before she even opened her eyes, grateful to have thwarted Aphrodite's attempt to escape her story into the real world. No time to pat herself on the back, Kash rolled, expecting some sort of attack instantly. Fortunately, there was no one in her immediate area, but she thought she spotted that same woman soldier running away from her and dodging through the battle to escape out the other side. Again, unwilling to give it any more time presently, she turned for the hills on this side of the river and fled the battle herself.

Kash waited and watched and pondered her next move until night fell around her, hoping the fighting would subside and she might be able to reenter the city. She wasn't even sure if that's what she wanted at this point. Wilson had already gone back to the library and she wasn't certain he would be able to return. Another mystery to be solved about her magical powers. There were more factors to consider, however, and she wanted to be certain of herself before making a decision. Should she just go home and give up on Troy? It would fall eventually with or without her interference she knew, but the idea of spending more time here with Wilson (supposing he could return) pulled at her strongly. And what of Cassandra? She felt the woman had become somewhat of a friend over the past few days. Did she owe it to the princess to try and convince the nobility she wasn't crazy and that the horse was nothing but a deception? She thought that she should try to regain the city and speak with the lady Cassandra to see if the option was viable. She knew she had a few days before the horse would appear, but what if the story ended? Yet another unanswered question. Would her presence here persist beyond the confines of the story itself?

She almost left it all behind in that moment, almost chose to go back to the library and regroup with Wilson. Something she couldn't consciously grasp stopped her, and her gaze was drawn upwards as the first stars appeared in the night sky. Remembering Wilson's comment about how the beauty of the heavens never changed no matter where they went sent her thoughts back to their time in the gardens. Perhaps he could return to the story if the end changed and there was something new. She hated the thought of giving up, there was so much potential here. She stared and stared at the distant walls, hardening her resolve and steeling her determination.

A loud noise from within the city broke her wistful reverie and the moment passed. Kash made up her mind then and ran down the hill, hoping that the gates would still be open to her. The sun was long lost beyond the hills to the west when she drew near, but luckily for her, she was seen by the sentries atop the wall and they held the doors just long enough to allow her to slip through. With a wave and a "thank you", she headed for the palace.

Kash turned the last corner into the square just in front of the gates of the citadel and took in the splendor of the royal palace as she moved across the courtyard. Just before she made it to the guards posted out front, someone bumped her hard from behind. She was nearly thrown to the ground and had to spin around completely to keep her balance. She looked back to see the person who had hit her was an old man, withered and bent. His thin cloak seemed to be wearing him and his long beard was white, grey, and grizzled, clearly unattended for some time. He leaned heavily on a walking stick that was taller than he was and his grin revealed many missing teeth as he addressed Kash.

"Apologies, my lady Kashmira. I did not intend to cause you to stumble. I merely bring word from the lady Cassandra. An urgent message that you meet her beyond the city walls at dawn, down by the sea. She warns you not to approach the citadel for you are suspected of treason and consorting with the Greeks. At dawn." His voice was raspy and croaking but strong. Kash looked over her shoulder at the guards before turning back to the man, but he was scrambling around the corner across the square.

"Hey, wait!" Kash tore after the disappearing figure but when she made the corner and turned into the next avenue, the old man had vanished. Kash stood in the middle of the street, as unsure of her next step as she was at any point on her journey thus far. She hadn't noticed anything suspicious or off about the guards when they saw her just now but she hadn't really had a good look at them either. Plus, she made it through the city gates just fine. Could this old man's word be trusted? What if he was truly an agent of the princess? But why would anyone accuse her of treason? She had no enemies in the palace as far as she knew? She felt like she was missing something important and decided to trust that Cassandra had sent the man. She headed for the temple across the city, hoping her chambers would still be open to her. Before she even got close to the steps of the temple, she noted the guards posted about the square. Could this really be all for her? She had her doubts, but the one thing she was certain of was she didn't want to find out what would happen to her if what the man said was true and these guards caught her.

Kash would find little rest that night. She spent most of it moving from shadow to shadow. She eventually found a quiet corner to sit and doze off in. She couldn't help it; she was nearly asleep on her feet at that point. Luckily, a noise nearby awoke Kash just before the dawn. Noting the hue of the sky, she knew she had to hurry. She made it out of the city through one of the more hidden routes and headed towards the appointed spot. There was sparse tree cover, but she found one of the few and knelt beneath the gently swaying limbs to wait. The sun climbed the sky as her doubts crept back into her mind. Dawn had long passed and Cassandra was nowhere in sight. This, again, left her unbalanced, and frustratedly uncertain of anything. She tried to remember where in the story she was and the only thing left she could recall was the duel between Achilles and Hector. This meant nothing to her really, unless she could save Hector somehow. She shook her head, realizing that this notion was ridiculous. She had already seen Achilles in action. Besides, the man was blessed by Athena, and the son of a god himself. Kash wanted no part of the hero for she was sorely outmatched. She had just decided to head back into the city, assuming the hunt for her was part of the deception as well, when the same old man from the night before ambled up the hill to stand before her.

"What are you doing here? What trick are you trying to pull?" Kash was less than thrilled to see the man, obviously. He returned her scowl with a toothy grin of his own before responding.

"Do you not recognize me?" His voice roared like thunder in her ears and she staggered back a step. Trying to clear her head, she could only come to one conclusion.

"Zeus!?"

"Indeed." His voice had returned to that of the old man and Kash's senses slowly returned to normal as the god in disguise went on. "You have angered one amongst the pantheon, I assume you know?"

"Let me take a wild guess," Kash returned sarcastically, hardly able to believe her own daring but her indignation at Zeus' deception gave her courage.

"Yes, it was Aphrodite who attempted to leave our world. Your powers thwarted her intent. Why not let her accompany you, I wonder? Would this not make of her a friend? Such a divine ally could be of use to you in your tale, don't you think?"

"I don't, actually, believe that she would desire, or require, for that matter, my friendship or alliance. It seems more likely she would wreak havoc in my world. The way you and her disguise yourselves and influence the events of humans would not change, I presume. This is just a story, but if she were set loose in the real world...despite being the goddess of love, I certainly do not want that to become a reality."

"Your powers lend you wisdom as well, it seems," Zeus responded with a chuckle. "Your logic is sound despite a glaring gap in your philosophy. Aphrodite would have lasting effects on the outcome of your story. This goes against everything you purport, does it not?"

Kash thought that was an odd statement, but didn't comment on it, despite the fact that he was referring to the real world as a story was intriguing. What gap in her philosophy? "Perhaps," was all she was willing to respond to that particular line of questioning.

"You would do well to remember the lessons Fate has bestowed upon you whilst you've been here. Aphrodite seems to have forgotten some of these. She wanted to change hers; she couldn't accept what was written, and thus seized on what she thought was an opportunity to leave this world for yours. Sometimes, even the divine cannot see beyond their own pages. You were powerful enough to thwart her, but you cannot save Troy. No one can. Her doom is written, and no magic can overcome the author's pen. Not even I have the strength to defeat this truth, for I too am bound to its finality. Troy will fall and it will be your influence that sees it done."

"What?!" Kash blurted, momentarily shocked by the proclamation.

"Yes, your punishment for denying the goddess Aphrodite will be to ensure that which you work against. Soon, the Greek forces will build their vessel and execute their grand deception. You will be there to convince the people of the great city they must bring it inside the walls."

"No, I will not. What about the character who is supposed to do that already?"

"Hmph. Sinon has already been dealt with, his testimony will convince no one. Yours must, however. The fate of your story depends on it for it is as yet unwritten and thus quite malleable. If the Trojans do not heed your promises that the construction is a divine gift of the gods and will bring calamity to Troy if left outside the walls, then you will toil for eternity, lost on Olympus forevermore." His voice was like thunder once more and a great storm arose around her. She was blown to the ground by the force of the sudden wind. A voice emitted from the darkness as the clouds receded swallowing the old man up before rushing away, seeming to flee from her in haste.

"Your fate is yours to choose."

This was followed by the sound of cackling until the storm vanished completely, leaving the last echoes of mirthless laughter thundering in her mind. Kash put her hand to her head, trying to clear the final words of the god. What did that mean? He couldn't be serious. Toil on Olympus? The sudden urge to be far from the *Iliad* washed over her and she closed her eyes, imagining the rows and tables of the library. She concentrated with all her might, but the swirl of blue light would not appear. Kash kept up her efforts for a full ten minutes before giving it up. She was stuck here, and she had no idea how. Why wasn't her magic working? There was only one answer, but she didn't want to accept it.

Zeus and Aphrodite had deceived her so many times already, how could she know that this latest one wasn't layered with webs like the rest of her interactions with the gods? With nothing else to do, Kash made her way back to the city even as Hector moved out by himself to battle Achilles. Knowing this would hold the attention of the nobles for a while, she decided to go back to the temple and try to get some rest. She was grateful that Zeus' deception included the lie about her being wanted, and thus she was able to return to her chambers unhindered. She collapsed on her small bed when she arrived at her room, finding it just how she and Wilson left it, what seemed like ages ago, now. She was asleep almost as soon as her head hit the pillow.

Part 2 The Witch's Gambit

Ch. 30 "I *Am* the Librarian"

Wilson hadn't had any other brain waves concerning the dilemma of Kash's whereabouts since his return from the *Aeneid.* Two days had passed with Dr. Radcliffe aiding Wilson in researching the time period and any works that might allow them to go back to the scene to try and extricate Kash. There had been only a few mentions of the Trojan war besides the *Iliad* itself and of those, none were helpful. Wilson had spent nearly the entire time in the library, wracking his brain, researching, studying, hoping to find something, anything that would give him direction. Helplessness was threatening to break his faith that he would find her or even pick up her trail. He closed the book he was currently looking at in dejection just as Radcliffe came around the corner of the nearest aisle and sat down beside him at the small work table.

"Maybe we're looking at the puzzle all wrong," the man said in greeting, as if continuing a conversation from earlier. "Suppose Kash discovered a way to travel to another story without returning to the library? Shouldn't we be looking through other books to see if the pages have changed?" His suggestion wasn't without merit, but Wilson felt the man wasn't considering the scope of such a task seriously.

"A needle in a haystack would be easier to find, I fear. We would need to stumble upon some incredible luck to find her in such a way. However, I don't think a cursory glance at the covers would do any harm. Anyways, I don't have a better idea right now." They both rose from their chairs and moved over to the rows of books. They were at it for quite some time before anything caught Wilson's eye. He was absentmindedly pulling each title off the shelf as he ran ideas and thoughts and memories through his mind like a movie without coherence. He pulled down the latest volume and looked at an unremarkable cover emblazoned in glossy letters with the title "*The Adventures of Sherlock Holmes*" by Arthur Conan Doyle. Wilson paused, staring at the work for a long moment. His was a puzzle, a mystery of sorts. The possibilities began springing to Wilson's mind faster than his academic and logical brain could corral them.

Could the famous detective help him get to the bottom of his predicament? The powers of Sherlock Holmes' deduction and detection were matters of literary legend, of course, but could the character possibly be the answer to Wilson's problems? As he considered it, Wilson became increasingly tempted. He knew it would involve disclosing his true identity, or at least the nature of his identity and his abilities to the detective. Considering his previous encounters with characters in stories, he was quite certain that Holmes would be able to figure out that he was not from the same story as the detective himself. Just how much the character would be able to discern, however, was beyond Wilson's ability to guess. All of this was quite extraordinary and Wilson could definitely believe that his mystery might well be beyond the bounds of Holmes' character and stories. On the other hand, Wilson knew he would have no trouble garnering the detective's interest. His case was certainly as inexplicable as it was bizarre. There was so much doubt and risk involved in such a play, but Wilson was struggling to think of anything else. He could hang around the library, searching through every tome for some hint or whisper of Kash in the millions of pages and hundreds of titles or...Mind made up, he almost jumped into the story at random. A clearer head prevailed, however, as Wilson decided to formulate a plan of action instead of charging headlong into some unknown situation. He chuckled at the thought that his plans didn't always seem to work out quite like they expected.

He plunged ahead, searching his memory of Holmes' various stories and cases. Going back to the shelves, he pulled down all the works that Holmes' appeared in. A slight shuffle behind him had Wilson looking around as he made it back to the small work table. Dr. Radcliffe came around the corner and noted the books Wilson was setting down gently.

"Sherlock Holmes, huh? Do you think Kash ended up in one of those stories, somehow? Doesn't look like any of the titles have changed." Wilson didn't know why, but suddenly he really didn't want to involve the man any more than he already had done. He was somewhat unsure of the plan beginning to take shape in his mind and adding Radcliffe in would be an unneeded complication. The man seemed capable enough, but if he was lost just as Kash had been…Wilson didn't want to consider it, but he didn't exactly know how to exclude the man at this point either. Especially after telling him all that he had already.

"Perhaps the cover doesn't change until the story is complete or her time in the story has come to an end. That seemed to be the way it worked with the other stories, right?"

"You tell me, I know nothing more than what you have said. It seems we're entering into guesswork here. I would really like to accompany you, though, when you do find the story she has gone to. How often does one get a chance like that right?" The man was looking at Wilson expectantly, clearly hoping their friendship might go some distance in convincing Wilson to take him along. Radcliffe could see the man's hesitance and understood his reservations but wouldn't give up that easily.

"Besides, two heads are better than one and I have read many of Sherlock Holmes' stories."

"Yes, but suppose we get separated and then you're lost like Kash."

"I'll be careful, and besides, if we get separated, I can just avoid the main characters and the story and wait until the end when I'll be spirited back here, right?"

"Technically, but—"

"Look, I understand your caution, but literature is my area of expertise, not to mention what I know of other stories you might want to travel to once we've found Kash; I mean, look around you; I *am* the librarian." Wilson's defenses were crumbling as he realized the man made a solid argument. The librarian's expertise couldn't be denied, and Radcliffe's face erupted into a wide grin when Wilson nodded his head in acquiescence.

"Alright, I think we should go to this one, *The Hound of the Baskervilles*, it's one of the longer stories and I have read it many times."

"As have I," Radcliffe replied with a raise of his eyebrows. Wilson grabbed the copy of *The Hound of the Baskervilles* and scanned the table of contents. Thinking about his memories of the text, Wilson surmised where they should enter and looked to Radcliffe one last time.

"You sure about this?"

Radcliffe didn't respond but took the book from Wilson and began to read from the page that Wilson had opened it to. Wilson smiled bemusedly and looked over his shoulder to read the same words. He reached out and put his hand on the librarian's shoulder to steady him as the swirl of blue light appeared and squeezed them into darkness.

Wilson looked to his companion immediately upon their arrival, knowing traveling like this could be disorienting. He instantly noticed the fresh tattoo on Radcliffe's arm still glowing a quiet blue. The man opened his eyes and smiled to indicate he was all right as they attuned themselves to their surroundings. Wilson knew he had landed them on the platform at the train station, but was surprised to see so many people about who fit the description of the characters they were looking for. They had jumped to the part in the story where Watson was accompanying Sir Henry Baskerville out to Devonshire and the estate that had been left to him. Wilson knew that Sherlock stayed behind at this juncture, and hoped to get a private audience with the detective while the story followed the other characters. It seemed that luck was with them. As they moved through the crowd, they became aware of a powerful aura, recognizable by its similarity to the emanations Wilson had felt when faced with characters of the *Iliad.* A space in front of the two men cleared and they caught a glimpse of the telltale hat that most of the world recognized the famed detective by. Wilson watched as Sherlock and Watson parted company and Sherlock waited for the train to roll out of the station. Radcliffe grabbed Wilson as he began to move towards Holmes.

"Maybe I should go with Watson and keep an eye on the story. I know how to get back to the library if there's any trouble and besides, I think Holmes would be more receptive to your plight if you present it alone. I don't know why, but I was always fascinated with Watson's character. Holmes always seemed a bit intense for my taste. What do you think?"

Wilson didn't think much of the idea, really, knowing how difficult it would be to reunite after splitting up but he couldn't come up with an argument against it. Radcliffe knew the story and knew how to return to the library, so all Wilson could do was trust the man, despite being worried about his immediate confidence in the situation. It made him feel the need to remind the man about the dangers of changing the story.

"I understand. I promise I won't do anything too drastic." With that Radcliffe turned and ran after Watson's retreating back, Wilson hoping he hadn't made a colossal error in bringing the man along. Looking back towards Sherlock Holmes, he realized now was his chance. He moved with purpose to stand before the famed detective just as Holmes was turning around.

"Excuse me," Sherlock Holmes said coldly, as he pushed past Wilson.

"Mr. Holmes," Wilson called after him, turning. "Please, I need your help."

Sherlock turned on his heel quickly, taking Wilson, following rather closely, by surprise. Wilson could see the wheels turning in the man's mind and knew he was being examined more closely than anyone ever had. Wilson waited patiently for Holmes' inspection to reach its conclusion before trying to speak again. However, he found that he didn't know where to begin. There was clear puzzlement on his face, he knew, and it was matched on the features of Sherlock.

"You are a remarkable study, sir. I..." Sherlock went quiet.

"Look, could we go somewhere and speak?"

"Yes, we can. However, I am rather occupied at the moment. You will accompany me." The detective seemed to resume a comfortable brisk manner as Wilson moved off the platform with him and back out into the street.

"Are we going to Baker Street?" Wilson asked, somewhat excitedly. He was really more interested in presenting his case to the man and was worried that Holmes might be intent on travelling out to the moor immediately. Wilson knew that in this part of the Baskerville story Sherlock had sent Henry and Watson along to the estate and led them to believe he would be in the city attending to other cases. The detective, in actuality, went out to the moor near the estate in secret. Wilson was hoping there was time before this to have a conversation.

"No, we are not going to Baker Street. Use your head, your knowledge of my name and address indicates an awareness of where you are and what is going on. Therefore, you must travel with me and regale me as we go. I cannot sacrifice my current mission but may still be of service."

"Right." Wilson allowed himself to be swept up in the man's wake. He figured the detective would come to certain conclusions about Wilson's nature and where he came from. The burning curiosity was just how much the character had discerned.

Radcliffe was certain he had felt the energy around Holmes as he had rushed by the man in pursuit of his counterpart. Wilson had discussed the way characters seemed to have a strength exuding from them that was tangible, probably in a magical way; or at least that was what Wilson had surmised back at the library. As Radcliffe caught up to Watson, he decided that it was an acceptable way to describe the subtle aura he could feel coming from the esteemed character in front of him. He also noticed that Holmes' intensity seemed to outweigh that of Watson's. Even though he had only been near Holmes momentarily, the difference was clear.

"Dr. Watson!" he called, causing the man just in front of him to stop and turn. Their eyes locked immediately and

Radcliffe could tell that he had caught the man off guard. A silent moment passed while Radcliffe allowed Watson to size him up before speaking.

"Yes, do I know you?" Watson asked confusedly.

"No, sir, but I know you, and the esteemed man you work with."

"Many people know of us..." Watson said suspiciously, clearly still on his guard.

"Yes, well, I am familiar with Sir Henry's case and would like to offer my assistance by accompanying you out to Baskerville Hall. Holmes is even now conversing with a colleague of mine on the very subject. It was Sherlock himself who suggested I run after you just now." Radcliffe was inventing wildly and hoping that Watson would welcome the help and not ask too many questions. He figured the man's suspicious nature as a detective would hinder this and felt that he had to stretch the truth a bit to acquire the man's trust. It wasn't that far off anyways; Wilson *was* talking with Holmes currently and would be working with him for a bit, at least that was their hope. He could tell that Watson didn't know what to make of him and could see any defenses the character was trying to come up with were not convincing.

"Alright then, come along." Dr. Watson turned and hurried after Sir Henry and Dr. Mortimer, pausing only to explain to the pair of them that Radcliffe would be aiding them in their investigation as they all got onto the train.

Ch. 31 A Quick Adventure

Wilson wasn't exactly paying attention to where they were going, his mind otherwise occupied and when he looked up, he found himself back on the platform, getting onto another train. When they settled into their car, Wilson knew it was time for him to convince Sherlock to help him. Now that he was here with the detective, he was intimidated a little bit. Despite being a character, his wit and powers of deduction were legend. Wilson was unsure just how much he could safely tell Sherlock. How would the character react? The characters he had met so far did not exactly respond positively to his presence in their story. Was his love of these stories making him believe that Sherlock was an inherently beneficent character? The lady Persephone swam into his thoughts and laughed at him. Sherlock cleared his throat expectantly, drawing Wilson's gaze and indicating he was aware of the internal struggle silently playing out in Wilson's head.

"So, as you may have gathered, I am not from around here," Wilson began meekly, with a weak smile. Sherlock's features remained impassive, a clear indication that he should continue and his small attempt at humor was falling on deaf or at least indifferent ears. "I have a mystery that I have no hope of solving. However, I have a certain skill that allows me to explore, perhaps, more solutions than one normally might. In other words, I have access to you, and am able to come to you for help.

"This is not an uncommon potential, and certainly does not qualify as a "skill"," the detective retorted sharply.

"Right, well, essentially I have lost my friend."

"She's more than a friend, surely?" Sherlock said, but then waved his hand saying: "never mind, go on." Wilson took a deep breath and looked out the window at the countryside passing by. Sherlock followed his gaze silently, allowing the man to put his thoughts together. Without looking back to the detective, Wilson decided on full disclosure. He took another deep breath and began.

"Stonehenge has ever been the source of my friends' archaeological fervor. She had always dreamed of a dig there..." Wilson spoke for some time, detailing as much as he could remember to the famous crime solver. He was vaguely aware of his own caution being thrown to the winds as he divulged his trip to the *Aeneid* and his brush with the characters there.

"I suspected that you were not from London or even our time period. Your disheveled appearance tells me you haven't slept much recently and have stayed indoors the past few days. However, your clothes are travel worn and still have a bit of sand on them. They are of a style unknown to me; the future, perhaps? I thought you said you were wearing robes in Troy? Anyways, it appears that you were on the right track. Tell me again what happened when the first story ended. You said you had travelled to *Dracula,* the new work by Bram Stoker."

"Wait, new? What year is it? How do you know about that story if you're in this one?"

"How have you traveled to that story? To this one?"

"That's fair," Wilson replied then looked back at Holmes curiously. "If you're aware this is a story, then you must know you're a character in it." Sherlock Holmes stared back at Wilson impassively. It seemed as if he had said something offensive. Wilson felt a small bit of shame and embarrassment, but Sherlock broke the somber silence before too long.

"Yes, Mr. Wilson, I am aware of my own nature. Are you?" he asked cryptically as Wilson felt the train lurch to a halt. Sherlock wasted no time in rising and pushing out of the compartment. His words followed Wilson onto the platform just as he followed the man himself. Wilson was lost in thought as they made their way into a carriage. His awareness was nowhere near his immediate surroundings, and thus he was caught off guard when the cab stopped and Holmes exited. Wilson stepped out into the night air, white with fog. They were in a small village and Wilson had to hurry to catch up to Sherlock who was already moving quickly down the street. He brought his thoughts back to the current situation, trying to remember just where they were going. When the detective opened a gate and turned down the alley, Wilson groaned, remembering. When he made it to the aperture himself, he noticed Holmes' back disappearing out the other end. He hustled to catch Sherlock up and made it out the other side of the alley in time to spot the man moving off onto the dark moor. It took almost their entire run across the misty ground for Wilson to catch his quarry, but they eventually made it to the hideout Wilson figured they were heading for.

■■■

Radcliffe remained impassive and unassuming whilst his three companions chatted the train ride away. He was going over his memories of this story in his head and trying to formulate a plan. A thought came to him that gave him pause. Just what was it that he actually wanted to do? He figured Wilson would be trying to convince Holmes to come back with them, if that was even possible, or at least, provide some unthought of insight. He was comfortable in the knowledge that Holmes and Watson reunited at the end of this novel and therefore, so to would he reunite with Wilson. He smiled thinking of what he might be able to accomplish in the intervening time. His thoughts were interrupted suddenly when he heard his name.

"What say you, Dr. Radcliffe?"

He looked around at the speaker, at least, he thought that Mortimer was the one to address him. He opened his mouth but hesitated, clearly having no clue what he'd been asked. Watson recognized this immediately and smiled, more than willing to repeat the question.

"He was asking your thoughts on the escaped convict?"

"Ahh, yes, the prisoner," Radcliffe said, his mind touching on what he knew of the subject from the text. He thought of his knowledge of the man's specific identity before responding. "I think he's brave, bordering on insane, to try to make it out on the moor alone. Do you gentlemen suppose he's trying to reach a partner? A friend, perhaps?"

"What? Out on the moor?" Mortimer replied, incredulously.

"Could be. Or could be that someone who lives on or near the moor is helping him. Surely, there are more estates than Baskerville Hall out there?" Radcliffe was rather enjoying this conversation.

"Well, yes, there is..." Mortimer trailed away, seeming as if he hadn't considered this possibility yet as the train came to a stop. They collected their things; Radcliffe waited patiently, not having any, and disembarked onto the small yet crowded platform.

"What's with the extra security? Must be because of the convict." Watson asked then answered his own question. Radcliffe gave a nod when Watson looked to him for seeming confirmation. They were met by one of Henry's servants from the manor with a carriage and the three characters clambered up. Radcliffe looked in and thought it rather tight inside the actual carriage, so decided to ride on top with the driver, stating his love of fresh air. Radcliffe had never traveled in such a way and decided he enjoyed it, chatting amicably with the man holding the reins.

"So, my good man, what do you know about this hound that's supposedly running around? They say it's a demon creature ringed in fire, ha, ridiculous, no?" The driver's eyes widened as if surprised that this stranger knew so much about the events at the manor. The moment passed quickly and the driver turned back to the front before speaking.

"Ah, yes, the hound. I had almost forgotten about it in all this excitement about the escaped murderer. A horrible shame, it was, Sir Charles being attacked by the hound. He was a wonderful man, as charitable and agreeable as they come. We can only hope the curse hasn't passed to master Henry."

"Right, of course, the curse."

"You don't believe the Baskerville's are haunted by this demon dog?" the driver shot back suspiciously. Radcliffe thought for a moment before deciding how best to guard his knowledge while preserving the man's loquaciousness.

"I believe in what I can see, in what I can experience for myself. Most people exaggerate, if not outright deceive, with their tales, but I do believe that there is some truth out there. Most stories have at least a sliver of truth to them, would you not agree?" The driver seemed to consider this position for a moment before shrugging and nodding. Radcliffe changed the subject then, asking questions about the grounds and the moor, hoping to, perhaps, discern a layout of the place before they arrived. The ride was pleasant, the driver jovial, and Radcliffe was certainly enjoying himself, happy he had convinced Wilson to allow him to come along on this journey.

Dusk was falling as they reached Baskerville Hall and the butlers, the Barrymores, came out to usher Henry inside. Radcliffe paid them no mind and they him apart from Mr. Barrymore giving him a hawkish look. Dr. Mortimer said his goodbyes and took the coach on to his own house down the lane leaving Watson and Radcliffe staring up at the edifice of Baskerville Hall. The black granite seemed dull in the fading light and there was ivy hanging everywhere along the walls. Two great towers rose in the middle with long wings of black granite on either side extending quite a long way. Radcliffe thought it perfectly wonderful and intimated as much to Watson.

"I think I might explore the grounds for a bit while you get settled in with Sir Henry," Radcliffe said to Watson who turned to him sharply.

"You think that a good idea? It's getting dark and we have yet to understand what is really going on around here. Could be dangerous." Watson seemed genuinely concerned for him and, perhaps, a little suspicious, but Radcliffe knew what was happening at this point in the story and figured that Watson would want to stay close to Henry as he did in the impending scene. Knowing that Kash and Wilson were able to be near the story but also not a part of it in their earlier adventures gave him confidence that he would be able to do the same.

"Not to fear, Dr. Watson. I come well prepared."

Watson eyed him for a long moment, clearly trying to decipher this cryptic comment before responding, "Fair enough, take care then, we'll see you inside soon. I'll tell Barrymore to expect you."

"Perfect." Radcliffe waited for Watson to make it through the doors of the great hall before turning to his left and moving along the wall. He came to the end and turned the corner. What little sunlight there was left was being obstructed by the building casting a dark shadow on this side. Radcliffe was struggling to see as the night deepened around him. After only a couple of unexpected stumbles, he managed to make it past the house and spotted the yew alley where the hound attacked Sir Charles. Not really knowing what his goal was, he decided he simply wanted a look at the spot. The walls seemed ancient and had nearly been completely overrun by ivy and various other green, leafy vines he couldn't name. The alleyway itself seemed to go on for some distance and he knew that the hound had appeared at the other end. He picked up his pace as he moved along, a smirk spreading on his features as the image of the hound wreathed in fire popped into his head. Rationale won out in his mind, however, when he reached the end of the alley and all was still quiet. The hound wouldn't be out and about so soon after it had been unleashed on Sir Charles. He stood at the end of the alley in the opening out onto the dark moor and stared off into nothing, pondering how lucky he was to be in his current situation. This was easily the wildest thing to ever happen to him and it was with thoughts of what this adventure might bring tomorrow that he turned and headed back the way he had come. He hadn't gone five steps before he thought he heard heavy footsteps approaching quickly.

Radcliffe whirled around and nearly sprinted back to the end of the alleyway. Just before he was able to look out onto the moor, a great black hound bounded out of the darkness, its head seemingly on fire. Radcliffe jumped back in surprise and alarm before his mind could catch his senses. The dog came at him and leapt sooner than Radcliffe expected. He threw himself backwards, down to the ground. The hound soared right over him and turned as it landed, preparing for another charge. Radcliffe stood up and held his hands out, taking slow steps backwards. The dog seemed confused by this, but Radcliffe could tell that the trick of the glow around its head was aggravating it beyond its confusion about him as it readied for another leap. In his mind, he knew it was a chemical effect and not actual fire, but it was still quite intimidating and he turned quickly, running for the end of the alley, the dog hot on his heels.

As he exited the lane, he thought he could make out a person watching proceedings from afar but he didn't have much time to contemplate this. He felt the dog right behind him and knew it was useless to try and outrun the poor creature. He thought to make for the unknown watcher and hope this was the dog's master, Stapleton, he thought might be the man's name. If the man would just call the dog off, he could have a rational conversation with him, hopefully. Why was the dog out tonight anyway? Had he been mistaken for Sir Henry? That was the only explanation. The dog had been unleashed, hoping to scare off Sir Henry just as they had killed Sir Charles.

All of this flew from his mind, however, as his foot caught a root and he tumbled to the ground. The dog snarled and dove right for Radcliffe's throat. With nothing else for it, lamenting how this trip had gone sideways so fast, Radcliffe desperately imagined himself traveling back to the safety of his library. Before he even saw the swirl of blue lights erupt from nowhere, Radcliffe shut his eyes tight, fully expecting to be eviscerated by inch long fangs. When he opened his eyes again, he was sprawled on the floor, the copy of *The Hound of the Baskervilles* an inch from his nose. He slowly rose, shaking his head with a little bit of disappointment at his part in the story being cut short but also feeling exhilarated by the adventure with hope for more to come.

Ch. 32 Unbelievable Notions

Wilson remembered the description of the circle of huts, the remnants of a small village from some ancient time, long forgotten. Sherlock would spend most of the rest of the story here until they unraveled the mystery completely. Wilson didn't think he had that long to convince the man to help him or at least give him some sort of advice in the matter. Following the man into the nearest structure, Wilson prepared himself to discuss his predicament once more.

"So..."

"Yes, you have me well corralled here. Shall we puzzle out this mystery."

"Yeah, well, uh, I was thinking maybe Kash had figured out how to travel to a different story without returning to the library. Or at least, my friend had that idea," he clarified, his thoughts finding Radcliffe and wondering how he was getting along.

"Why would you assume that? You know the real question is who has the motive?"

"The motive? What?" Wilson was thoroughly confused by that answer; she was lost, not murdered.

"Yes, motive, there has to be a reason to kill someone."

"Oh," Wilson breathed, relieved. Sherlock was obviously referring to the late Master Baskerville and not Kash.

"I could—"

"No, you will not. I understand that you are aware of the events that follow herein but you will not ruin my fun."

"But the hound—"

"Yes, I am aware there is a hound. As I said, do not divulge your wisdom, on pain of losing my help in your own mystery. The fee for my aid will be your accompaniment during this investigation, perhaps your input at some point, and at its completion we will see about your lady friend." There was no room for argument in his tone and Wilson had nothing left but to go along with the detective's wishes. He thought of Kash then, his mind transported back to the night in the garden. For one shimmering moment, this crazy adventure had swung in his favor. Things since then hadn't exactly gone as well as that scene had. Consternation replaced his wistful smile as he thought of what had driven them from the *Iliad*, or at least, had driven him. The snarling visage, locked in rage, of the soldier as she swung her sword was etched into his memory like a horrible song he couldn't get out of his head. In all his experience and study, he hadn't really heard of woman soldiers in that period. That obviously didn't mean anything, really, he thought. Most things he thought he knew about Troy were somewhat untrue and he was frankly tired of the fantastical and inexplicable assailing his logical sensibilities.

Perhaps that is what drew him to Sherlock Holmes; the detective's reputation for cool calculation. He knew that the gods were naught but deceiving tricksters, at least in his experiences in the *Iliad*. If that woman was Aphrodite, (which, why couldn't it be possible?) then it could make sense that Kash knew it and went back to prevent the goddess from going back to the real world with them. Or at least, Wilson thought it was the real world. His head hurt a little bit as the idea that he was losing his mind swam across his consciousness. He was literally sitting in a hut, Sherlock Holmes standing outside, waiting for the detective to solve the mystery of a story he had read countless times. All he knew was that he couldn't give up on Kash, couldn't just sit around and hope she turned up someday. The only thing he could do was to go along with Holmes and help with the Baskerville case. Once done, the detective could turn all his considerable deductive and intellectual might to helping Wilson.

A couple of uneventful days passed with Holmes making a lone trip to a nearby village for some supplies and, Wilson knew, the first report from Dr. Watson. Wilson knew he wasn't needed on this trip, but stepped outside as the deepening gloom of twilight settled on the misty moor. Sherlock was supposed to make an appearance in the text if his memory served. That very night was the night that Watson and Henry figure out who the fugitive was on the moor. They would go out in search of the man and spot a "tall lone figure" or something to that effect. Wilson wasn't sure, but he did know that it was later revealed to be Sherlock himself. Therefore, Wilson was looking around for the man when he spotted the outline of the very same tall figure approaching.

"Ahh, Mr. Holmes. I wasn't sure you would be back in time."

"In time for what? Don't do that!" Sherlock replied sharply. Wilson only then remembered that the detective was keen to unravel the mystery of the Baskervilles without aid.

"Do you know what influencing the course of this tale could do? Can you even fathom in your limited imagination the far-reaching repercussions of your interference? If something you say or do bends my mind in one direction or the other, the entire conclusion could be altered forever. Do you not see? Your friend seems none too concerned with this for he has already disappeared, according to Dr. Watson."

"Wait, disappeared?"

"That's what the note says, the night of their arrival, it would seem he ran afoul of the famed hound and hasn't been seen since. If you two disrupt this mystery irreparably the consequences could be more far-reaching than you know."

"Sorry, I… Sorry." Wilson didn't know what to say. He felt a bit guilty at how intense Sherlock had just gotten. He understood the dangers of changing the story but he had already done it in other stories. His stomach did a backflip wondering just what might come of said changes, especially since it seemed to him that Radcliffe had gone off on his own and been attacked. His disappearance was also disconcerting; Wilson now had, not one, but two missing companions. Radcliffe had better be in the library when he returned, Wilson thought. There was nothing he could do about any of it now, however, although he did vow to keep a sharper guard on his tongue for the remainder of the story.

"It's quite alright, my good man. Anyways, I wanted to have a walk along the moor this evening. What say you accompany me?" Wilson thought about it for a second, not sure if that was such a good idea, especially considering their recent conversation. However, Watson only catches a glimpse of Sherlock in the distance and Wilson figured he would just try to shy away from the man in that moment. Sherlock was eyeing him suspiciously but still seemed willing to keep him close. Eventually, Wilson agreed and they set off into the darkness.

"So, I imagine you have figured out or heard that there is an escaped prisoner running around out here?" Wilson asked the detective as they walked. As far as he could remember, that wasn't a big secret in the story.

"Yes, what of it?"

"Well, do you have a gun? I mean, I don't have a weapon of any kind."

"You needn't worry. Unless I'm much mistaken, the convict is much closer to the manor than we, but of course, you knew that already." Sherlock turned with a smirk and a knowing look that Wilson tried to return with bemusement. Sherlock held his arm out to stop their movement and pointed. Off in the distance, a light appeared in the darkness. It was faint and quite far away but unmistakable. Wilson would've looked for the return signal in the mansion but he didn't know which direction to look, and he suspected the mist would obscure it anyway. They continued for a short distance, coming to a small hill. Making their way to the large rocks at the top, Sherlock climbed atop one while Wilson crouched behind it. He figured this would be where Watson would get a glimpse of the detective and it would be best if he remained hidden. Sherlock either didn't notice or didn't care and remained standing and watching from atop the hill for quite some time. Wilson was getting cold and was standing up, about to suggest they get moving when the detective dropped down in front of him.

"Shall we then?" he said and without waiting for a response trudged off into the night. Wilson just shook his head and moved to follow. They made it safely back to the hut and, lighting a lantern, sat at the table. Sherlock took out his pipe and loaded it, packing it down just a touch before striking a match and lighting the sweet tobacco. He shook the match out and looked through the smoke to Wilson.

"I wonder if you have come to any conclusions regarding your predicament?" he said somewhat randomly. "Surely you have been pondering the matter whilst following me around these past couple of days. I fear, as in most cases, that the obvious will be the most likely answer. However, what is obvious to one may elude another."

Wilson opened his mouth as if to speak, stopping Sherlock's stream of consciousness but closed it when the detective fell silent. He wasn't sure what obvious fact Holmes assumed he was missing, but there was something that had been nagging at him since Sherlock had said it.

"You mentioned your uncertainty of whether or not I was aware of my own nature." Wilson simply stated, thinking he had hit on what the character was hinting at.

"I did, indeed. Sometimes this is the hardest of all truths to accept. Who we are, *what* we are? You mentioned that Ms. Kashmir had ventured beyond the end of the *Iliad* and you had heard of her exploits therein. That story must needs be written somewhere; wouldn't you think so?" Wilson started shaking his head, not willing to accept exactly what he thought Sherlock was saying to him. Sherlock was undeterred by his silent denial and continued.

"It stands to reason, then, that your story is being written down by someone, somewhere and that would mean that Kash did not, in fact, travel beyond a story because it is her story. It is *your* story."

"Nope. No way," Wilson choked out, finally finding his voice. "We are not characters in a story. We have travelled to stories but are able to leave them and go back to the real world."

"Real?" Holmes scoffed. "Reality is relative, my very confused friend. My reality is, obviously, not yours. It has been said that we all perceive the world uniquely. Thus, your world being different than mine is a matter of course. That doesn't mean that my world isn't real or that yours isn't either. Does it really matter in the end, though? Whose world is the "real" one, who's reality is "right"? I submit that it does not. You have limitations and constraints to what you are able to do just as I or any other character in any story do you not? Despite your recently acquired abilities." Wilson considered it for half a moment, but his reasoning brain kept firing excuses and denials at him.

"Yes, but I have the free will to do whatever I please, whenever I please. You are bound by what happens, by what is written," Wilson tried to explain, despite thinking he sounded a bit condescending and rude.

"My will is as unimpeded as yours is. You certainly cannot do whatever you please whenever you please, however. I know this to be a fallacy without having spent any time in your day-to-day routine. Does the University let you teach whatever you want? Do they let you teach however you want? Or are there guidelines and stipulations and restrictions you must adhere to? Not to mention the fact that you sought me out in the first place, indicating that you need help." Wilson's look soured at the same time Sherlock's became triumphant. Wilson blew a deep sigh, not willing to argue with the man. He was certain he wouldn't sway the self-important character's opinion of his own intellect nor of Wilson's. The idea that this man might become an annoyance hadn't really occurred to Wilson as he read the stories earlier in life, but thinking back and adding in his recent experiences, he supposed it made sense. The man had a superior attitude in every scene that Wilson could remember, so why should actually interacting with him turn out any different? He waved his hand as if to dismiss the conversation and pushed back from the table. Unwilling to debate the point further, he moved over to the small cot in the corner. He fell asleep thinking of some unknown person out there writing down his story as he went. It seemed quite preposterous to him and he wished the story he was currently in would move quicker as he eventually drifted off to sleep.

The slight noise of someone shuffling around the small cottage woke Wilson abruptly. He looked up at Holmes' back as the man was moving out of the structure. Hearing the detective conversing with someone was alarming, coming fully awake quite quickly. He rose and started towards the door but thought better of it and stopped just short. Moving to the side of the frame, he paused to listen. He glimpsed a young boy holding a basket and knew that Holmes had been receiving supplies from the young man and thus he probably wasn't any trouble. Wilson's experience had taught him otherwise and so he decided to stay out of sight. He couldn't really make out what they were saying, but before too long the young boy had gone and Sherlock was moving back into the cottage holding the basket and a letter.

"Aha, that was what you were speaking of. Watson saw me or at least my silhouette and you knew that I needed to be back for our little stroll." The detective was looking at him excitedly and triumphantly. Wilson rubbed his eyes, expelling the last vestiges of sleep from his consciousness and looked at Holmes.

"Look, Mr. Holmes—" he started but was interrupted almost immediately.

"Yes, you're growing impatient, I understand. I wonder how does time pass in your reality relative to my own? How long have you been away now?"

"You've spoken my concerns better than I could've, my friend. I came for your aid and I understand all that we said the other night, but the fact remains I am still no closer to locating Kash. I need to get back to the library and figure out a game plan. Honestly, I was hoping you might want to join me. I am not sure if it's even pos—"

"Hmph, I'm not leaving now. You know as well as I that this mystery must be solved and your doubt does little to encourage or convince me to accompany you to another world. Besides, you have all the answers you need already. But you know that, don't you?" Wilson shot the detective a withering look born of exasperation. He didn't know what else to do. He felt like the little cottage was closing in on him a bit as he began to think this idea might have been a mistake. He thought back to what Holmes had said and he simply wasn't ready to accept that as a reality. Even if it was, how would that help him? Was he supposed to find the physical copy of his own book? It all seemed so preposterous to him. He looked back at Sherlock into the smug, satisfied look that seemed to just be his face. It did little to comfort Wilson in that moment but it did serve to solidify his decision. He could tell that even if he did see this novel through to conclusion beside the detective and aid in the unraveling of the mystery, he wasn't certain he could convince Holmes to come back with him. The man legitimately did have other cases pending, even now. Wilson breathed a deep sigh of resignation and finally looked back to the detective.

"Alright, say I buy into the whole "I'm a character" thing. Where does that leave me? How does that help me find Kash?"

"Isn't it obvious?"

"Is that your favorite response to any question?" Wilson shot back, feeling some small measure of satisfaction at the sour look the man returned his way.

"As I said, there is certain to be a tome with all of this written down somewhere, find it and it will tell you her fate."

"O that's it is it? Find my own book? You ever seen yours just lying around somewhere?" Wilson was becoming increasingly frustrated and had to remind himself that it was a ludicrous line of thinking in the first place. He threw his hands up in defeat, conceding that Sherlock wasn't going to change his mind on any of this.

"Well, Mr. Holmes, it was certainly something to have met you. Honestly, you are not what I expected, but the more time I spent here, the more I realized that you are exactly as Sir Arthur Conan Doyle depicted you. It was my own expectations and feelings I brought into our interaction that were not met. However, that isn't your fault, but my own. I appreciate your input on my plight, for what it's worth. I'll be going now."

"If I may, before you go, Mr. Wilson. The issue is not that you cannot find your paramour, but that you have lost yourself. Your doubt and your disbelief have been holding you back the entire time. Suspend these notions, they keep you from your true potential, from realizing your best possible ending. Not all tales are yet complete and thus you have felt in control. Let go of the need for that and you will find your way."

Wilson stared. He certainly wasn't expecting the cool and calculated Sherlock Holmes to wax poetic as such. He didn't know what to say, so he simply nodded and walked outside. He never even saw the moor as his mind was already back in the library. Almost before he was aware of the swirling blue lights, his eyes opened back up into the quiet, deserted place. There didn't seem to be anyone around.

"Dr. Radcliffe? I'm back," he called. There was no answer.

"Kash?" he said hopefully without much conviction. Only the silence of the myriad pages came back to him. It was deafening. He moved around the place looking for any clues. He peeked out of one window to see that it was approximately midday meaning they either hadn't been gone too long or had been gone even longer than expected, but where was

Radcliffe? He wasn't still in the story was he, running around on the moor? How long had he spent there? For some reason he couldn't place, he felt like an entire day had passed. Wilson shook his head, if that was the case, there was no way Radcliffe hadn't returned to the library. With his thoughts whirling and a sinking feeling that he had erred in taking Radcliffe along, Wilson moved through the empty library, searching in vain. Where was he?

His search unsuccessful at best, Wilson moved back over to where the various Sherlock Holmes books were still strewn across their work table. After a cursory glance at them, looking for he didn't know what, he turned to move on. Something he caught out of the corner of his eye made him do a double take. There was a book that didn't belong. The cover was blank and Wilson thought that it was familiar. Where had he seen it before? As soon as he opened it, he understood and this sudden clarity elicited an audible gasp.

It was Kash's journal.

How had it gotten here? Could this be what Holmes' had been referring to? There was only one explanation. Kash had returned to the library while he was with Sherlock. Where had she gone was his first thought. Why wasn't Dr. Radcliffe around either? None of it was making sense to Wilson, but he sat down, determined to read all that Kash had written. He was turning to the first page when a banging on the door made him look around in surprise. He was thinking of hiding in the stacks so whoever it was would go away, but a face appeared in the window, staring directly at him. The person pointed to the right, in the direction of the door, clearly indicating they wanted him to go let them in. Wilson obeyed the request somewhat in a daze of surprise and opened the door a little bit to tell the young man the library was closed.

"Really, not according to the sign on the door. The lights are on and you're in there. Where's Dr. Radcliffe? He was supposed to help me study for my European Lit final."

"Dr. Radcliffe unfortunately went on an unexpected trip, couldn't be helped. Family emergency, actually." Wilson didn't even sound convincing to himself as he stumbled through the made-up excuse.

"Right, well, can you—"

"Nope. Sorry kid." Wilson didn't have time for this. He flipped the sign to closed, shut the door in the young man's face and turning, sat down with his back against it. He was tired, not necessarily physically tired, despite sleeping on hard stone the past few nights, but emotionally and mentally exhausted. He knew that eventually he would need to get up and press on, Kash's journal was waiting, but he couldn't find the motivation at present. Could he travel into it? Would it even tell of where she had gone? His head hurt and he realized he was completely exhausted.

He simply sat there, trying to distance his own awareness from the stream of thoughts, memories, doubts, hopes, and ideas rushing through his mind. The shadows deepened as the sun sank and Wilson didn't even bother to get up and turn on the lights. He sat there all night, waiting, wondering, and hoping.

Ch. 33 The Black

The darkness was absolute, impenetrable blackness. Kash put her hands out in front of her and walked a few steps. At least, she felt herself walking. The ground beneath her was solid, if a bit soft. She imagined she felt grass, but there was no way to tell. She tried to remember how she got here but it was all a blur. Troy was burning and she had tried to return to the library and initially thought she had been successful, but she was brought here instead. She didn't feel in any immediate danger, but the lack of any light at all was somewhat disturbing. Not sure if the ground continued far or at all, she decided to sit down. There didn't seem like anything she could do. She tried once more to think of the library and call up the magic of the tattoos but it was futile.

Eventually, (how long had passed Kash had no way of knowing) she became aware of a small dot of light, as if it were far off in the distance. It danced around as it slowly grew little by little. She thought it resembled a torch being carried towards her. Thoughts of calling out sprang to mind but she decided against it. A strange sense of calm had washed over her and she was content to let the torch bearer come to her in due time. Presently, the torchbearer moved to stand in front of Kash. She stood up at his approach and they studied each other, silent for the first couple of moments.

"Kashmira or Kash?" the man asked in a hesitant voice. His beard was long and unkempt, the dull black giving the man's grizzled face an almost eerie look in the dancing shadows of the torchlight. He seemed just as uncertain as Kash was at seeing him. Her calm façade was tough to maintain in the face of his question, however.

"Kash is fine," she began slowly. "How do you know my name?"

"Well, I can perceive many things. In your time here you may learn to see these things as well. Although, you tend to lose track, time has a way of wandering away from you. At least it seems that way to most of us."

"What do you mean?"

"Yes, I had many questions as well. Your first few moments here are disorienting to be sure. Come, follow me and fire away. I will answer all I can." Kash fell into step next to the man as they moved through the darkness. She looked around as they walked, quiet and ponderous at first. Her companion seemed patient enough to let her take it all in and waited for her to break the silence.

"What is this place?" the woman eventually asked the obvious first question.

"Ahh, your first query is the great mystery of this existence. Some believe they know; others laugh at their supposed folly. Many come here or end up here one way or another."

"End up here?" Kash echoed, hoping she hadn't "ended up" here. There was a finality to the phrase that certainly frightened her.

"Yes, well, most you meet in the Black do not leave or escape, depending on your point of view."

"The Black?"

"The name some give to the darkness. Its eternal and unchanging. Constant and impenetrable." The matter-of-fact tone revealing an indifference to the lack of light scared her even more. Whoever this man continued to refer to had obviously accepted their fate in this...whatever it was. Kash was struggling to find any clues as to a way out of the darkness. She was still uncertain how she made it here in the first place or why her magic wasn't working. She looked around, wondering how long they had been walking and how much farther they had to travel before getting to…

"Where are we going, exactly?"

"Ahh, yes, I figured we would get to that one eventually, but not so soon, to be honest. Most have many more questions before that one. So, that is another mystery that no one can solve." Kash's face screwed up in confusion. They had been walking for a while. Did he really have no idea where they were going?

"What do you mean? Where did you come from?"

"I didn't come from anywhere; I am simply here." Kash almost growled in frustration. He wasn't making any sense. He stopped to face her, clearly waiting on her understanding or at least acceptance.

"So, what happens if we keep walking that way." She pointed in the same direction they had been travelling so far.

"One way is as good as the other, I fear. There is only blackness and this weird grass underfoot. I imagine we could go on for quite some time."

"Alright, where did you get that torch?"

"I have always had the torch, of course."

"Always had? How long…? Right, you don't know. Do you have a name?"

"No, I do not, but not all share this plight. I can see my name far off, like a beacon of hope beckoning me, calling to me." This man was growing stranger with every word he spoke and Kash didn't know what to make of him. He seemed to be babbling nonsense.

"Well, I hope you reach it, my friend. Will you sit with me? I need to think and your torch is a comfort here…wherever we are." The man smiled and nodded, plopping down to the ground with a chuckle. The man's cryptic answers yet uncaring attitude to his seeming plight was keeping her off balance, but he seemed harmless enough. She sat next to him and her thoughts turned inward.

There was no way of figuring out exactly where she had arrived when she had tried to travel back to the library. The nameless man had already proven of no value in discerning, well anything really. He had said he would answer everything he could. It wasn't much by Kash's estimation. She went over the events after Wilson had disappeared, seemingly to the library, or at least that what she was assuming, in her mind again. Things had certainly spiraled well out of control and had not gone at all like she planned. Nothing that happened was a part of the story, the gods didn't…that was it. She looked up, a new light in her eyes. She had been beyond the end of the *Iliad* when she had tried to go back to the library!

Of course, this was what she wanted, hoping to change what happened to Troy, but she was still surprised somewhat. By all she had gathered about her magic, she was well aware there were limits. Deep down, in a place that spoke with Wilson's voice, she knew his logic against her being able to do this was sound. Why had it worked though? Her mind immediately went to Zeus and Aphrodite. That was the only thing that made any sense. So, was this Greek purgatory? Surely not. She didn't remember anything like this in the Greek religion. She tried to think back to her meager studies in the temple while she was in Troy, but nothing seemed to be useful. While she was thinking, unbeknownst to her, another torch bearer had come upon them from behind.

"Jinvo! What are you doing? Up to your usual antics no doubt." Kash spun around and stood up, backing a bit as she did to face the newcomer. The man, Jinvo, apparently, stood slowly and shrugged in response with a grin at Kash.

"My apologies, Ms. Kashmir, Jinvo is simply a bitter character who takes pleasure in torturing others with confusion and doubt. Come child, let us speak with clarity and perhaps your mind will be put at ease."

"Just hold on there, Vin. I would like to know what you tell her. Maybe now that my little joke has played out, I can lend genuine aid to our lost friend." Kash didn't miss the skeptical look the new woman gave to Jinvo at these words. She didn't refuse him however and turned back to face Kash, softening her gaze as she did.

"Now, Ms. Kashmir, to your obvious concern with your current whereabouts. You are in a place where many come who never escape. There is no real name for our world. However, we believe the point of this space is to house unfinished characters. Or at least a place where characters of stories that have not yet been finished can exist. Once we are written into existence, just a single thought put into permanence, we are in danger of ending up here. As you may have come to realize, since your story has seemingly been filled with much adventure, there is great power in the creation of stories. There is a great magic in the author's pen, the storyteller's orations. But I ask you what happens to the stories that are left untold, the novels left unwritten? For whatever reason, the author gives up on the tale and leaves the story for another day that never comes to pass." The woman looked around her, leading Kash's gaze with her own.

"You're saying that this place is where the characters of unfinished stories come to…what?" Kash wasn't quite sure about this explanation.

"It's a limbo of sorts, I suppose. We neither exist nor do not exist. We're somewhere in between. Some do find an escape, eventually. Some authors do get back to their work and complete their tales giving freedom to their characters who spent time untold in this wretched blackness." This was the first time that Vin had made clear her feelings for their current situation. The question was: why was the woman telling her all of this? What about Jinvo, who apparently was not to be trusted? She looked from one to the other, feeling quite uncertain of their motives. There was an unease beginning to creep into her mind.

"Why are you telling me all of this?" she asked as innocently as she could muster.

"Why, to help a weary traveler, of course. You will get used to it here before too long, I imagine."

"There has to be a way out of here, I didn't start out in this, whatever it is, like the esteemed Jinvo over there."

"Oh, and where did you start out, pray tell?"

"I was…" What should she say? Would they help her if she told them of her magic? She didn't really feel like she had a choice despite the nagging feeling of doubt in the back of her mind.

"Yes?" Vin prompted, her tone seeming sweet, but Kash was suddenly thrown by the intensity in her eyes. Perhaps it was just the torchlight reflecting, but Kash was feeling a weird aura coming from these two. She recalled the deceptions of Zeus and Aphrodite and reminded herself to keep on her guard.

"Well, my story is as yet unfinished but there has been some excitement so far." Kash smiled to herself at the irony of calling her adventures a "story".

"Where might have all of this excitement taken place I wonder?" Jinvo asked, unable to keep the venom from his voice. He was starting to creep Kash out a bit and his hungry stare wasn't helping either.

"Somewhere west of here, I would imagine," Kash half-joked, responding to his intensity in no uncertain terms. She certainly wasn't going to be intimidated, no matter who these two were and what they had planned for her.

"Hmph, I see your plight has done little to curb you sense of humor," Vin said with a chuckle. "Leave us alone Jinvo, you're scaring our guest; let the ladies discuss important matters. You run along, now." With a telling glare at Kash which turned to a wicked grin when he noticed her catch his look, he slowly moved away. Kash watched the torchlight with Vin for some time until it was nothing more than a small orange dot in the distance.

"So, you said you were transported here somehow?" Vin prompted into the spiraling silence. Kash looked at the woman before responding, trying to get a feel for her intentions without really knowing much about her. She certainly wasn't as outwardly suspicious as Jinvo had been. Neither was the lady Persephone and the aura she was getting from this woman was comparable to that of Aphrodite. Kash hadn't noticed it at first, but the further away Jinvo moved, the stronger it seemed to grow. This gave Kash pause but she eventually responded.

"Yes, my story has been a strange and unexpected journey so far. One that started innocuously enough but has proven to be anything but. However, there aren't many clues as to how I managed to find myself here."

"What began your journey? Surely there was a catalyst of some sort? A call to action if you will?"

"Oh, there was indeed. I still can't explain that bit to be honest, but suffice it to say that moment has allowed me to travel to places people do not normally travel to. In these places, I have done and seen many things and people I never thought I would. Something has happened, though, something that was even unexpected within the realm of my new reality."

"Obviously," Vin replied with a wave of her hand and a look around. "Shouldn't you be able to simply travel away to another of these places that were, until recently, unreachable to you?"

"I have tried to leave in the normal way but it has proven completely ineffective so far."

"Well, where were you last? And what happened there to bring you here? Answering these questions might reveal much." It would indeed, Kash thought but kept to herself. There was something off about Vin that was just beyond her recognition. Generally speaking, the characters she had met so far had not had her best interests at heart. There was nothing in this place so far that would suggest otherwise and so Kash thought she was doing a decent job of talking around her true powers. She didn't think it wise to let Vin know she could travel to stories and that she herself was not a character in one, rather from the real world. Then again, what concept of the real world did this lady have? To her, Kash supposed, she was just another character from some unfinished story. She looked to keep this advantage and use it, but she did consider the woman's words before responding.

"Due to circumstances beyond my abilities and control, I had to stay in the last place I had traveled to beyond what I thought I would or thought was even possible. This was forced upon me and nothing of my own choosing."

"How? Was your mechanism stolen? Damaged, perhaps?" Vin's patient curiosity was more and more telling. Her mind would not stray from the "how?" no matter how much dancing Kash was doing.

"Blocked is more like it," Kash replied indignantly, before thinking about it. Her mind went back to Zeus pretending to be that frail old man. That was it, she could only be here because she was no longer in any story. It wasn't Zeus' fault, well, at least, not directly. He had kept her in Troy beyond the end of the *Iliad* but she had also met the terms of their "deal". If that was a fair assessment of the situation. Coercion more than agreement but she had abided by the terms nonetheless. Her magic wouldn't spirit her back to the library because she was not in a story held in the library. Everything about her tattoos seemed to tie back to the library, even the cover of the books had begun to change. She supposed some of the pages would as well, but she hadn't the time nor inclination to dwell on that currently. Somehow, her freedom was connected to the library, it had to be. This new line of thinking seemed promising and uplifting, but understanding did not help her to solve the problem at all. In fact, it made the situation that much more dire in her eyes.

"Blocked? You were stopped then and sent here? It seems obvious. Your author has abandoned you. Sorry to say but it looks like your stuck here. Maybe your writer will get back to you someday. I thought, perhaps, you might be the ticket out of here, but it appears that one more powerful than you twisted your fate into something unredeemable. Seems odd, doesn't it? That we should suffer the whims of one we've never met whose intentions for our end are completely unknown. Would that we could change our own stories and take back control of our own existence. This place..." Her voice broke off, leaving Kash even more confused. Her initial reactions to this woman were somewhat benign, but the more they talked, the more on guard Kash felt she needed to be. She studied the woman more closely and recognized that her aura had continued to grow the more they walked on. This led Kash to believe that Vin was not an unfinished character, rather one who had been sent to this place just as she had. The lady's musings about authors and creation certainly seemed to reveal a bitterness.

"I have been told that Fate is unbeatable," Kash replied hoping Vin's response would give her some clue, anything at all to help her figure this woman out.

"Yes, Fate is a formidable foe, but unexpected things can happen. Realities we thought impossible mistakenly stumbled upon and revealed to dispel our disbelief. Things do not always go as planned, as anyone planned. This is an interesting concept. Even the author does not see all ends. Thus, I say Fate is not all powerful. We are thinking beings, are we not? Should we not have a say in our own tales, be able to exert some influence? I choose faith. I choose to hold to the idea that we are not powerless." She turned to Kash then, a new light in her eyes, as if she had just thought of something. Kash returned her look expectantly, waiting for the woman to say something.

"There might be a way…There is another whom I have met and conversed with in this space. She is one of great power in her own story as well. How she came to be here is a mystery like many others but she is not like the rest. Not like Jinvo. No, she is more like you than any other character to exist here. She too held the power to travel to various places. Her gifts are not unlike your own. Perhaps, together, you can find us a way out of here."

"Us?"

"Yes, all of us need to escape! This is no way to live, wasting away here while the dreaded authors go on writing others into being, leaving the rest of their characters to rot. If there is any chance at all, do you not think it worth it to try? Even if I am bound here, just as the rest, and you are not, do you not at least want to save yourself? Change you own fate? I know I would, given the opportunity."

"Well, we can at least go meet this person."

"As I suspected," Vin said with a grin as she moved off, Kash following in her wake.

Ch. 34 The Witch

Presently, Kash was aware of something shimmering off in the distance, some disturbance in the blackness. There was a soft glow emanating from something quite large up ahead of them. Vin was clearly making for it and the closer they got the more Kash could discern. She almost smiled when she realized that Jinvo and most likely Vin herself had been lying to her, or at least withholding some truths and bending them to her purposes. They stopped for a moment at the bottom of a great ramp leading to the front gates of a monstrous castle. The black stone glowed with an eerie greenish bluish light that gave the place a very cold feeling. She looked at Vin who simply motioned forward and moved up the ramp. They reached the top where the gates swung slowly and silently open, as if they were expected. A sense of foreboding was creeping up on Kash, aided by the unnerving silence only broken by their loud footsteps on the smooth stone. Kash wanted to ask any of the myriad questions chasing one another around her mind but figured all would be revealed in time. They were supposed to be meeting someone who could help their predicament. From all the stories she had seen and read, Kash's experience had taught her that dark castles such as these very rarely were the abodes of goodly characters. This sense of dread was reinforced when she looked at the unnerving calm from her companion who was perfectly at ease.

"This way," the woman said sweetly as she led Kash through a door and up a tight winding staircase. They must have entered one of the towers that rose high at the top of the structure. Kash noticed many paintings in the torchlight from the sconces on the wall. She didn't stop to examine any of them, but unless she was very much mistaken, they depicted scenes from the life of King Arthur. She could hear that Vin had reached the landing at the top of the stairs before she rounded the last bend. She stopped before making the tight turn, however, studying the last painting. Her eyes widened and her heart began pounding so hard she thought it might burst out of her chest. She was staring at a very accurate depiction of the lady who had led her here. The painted scene was a man in full plate armor carrying another in his arms towards a small boat. Across the water from the boat was an island where "Vin" stood with arms outstretched awaiting the knight and the boat. Like a thunderbolt, the truth hit Kash nearly causing her to stumble over the last step of the stairs as she finally was able to move herself past the painting.

Kash collected herself and looked around at the chamber they had come into. She thought it was a normal landing, but it was as if the room that would've been closed off by a wall and a door was simply open at the top of the stairs. This made the chamber feel very large and roomy. There was even a breeze floating through a slit in the tower wall. This confused Kash completely until she thought about it and who was sitting in front of her. "Vin" had moved over to a desk and was seated behind it, staring at Kash's bewilderment with obvious pleasure. Kash locked eyes with the wickedly grinning woman, pondering if her suspicions were valid. There were unanswered questions, but she thought she might be able to fill in some of the blanks. When it didn't seem like her host was going to break the silence, she spoke.

"So, this "other" person who might be able to help us is, in fact, you. I noticed that you were a fan of King Arthur's as we climbed the stairs. You know, Merlin told me about defeating you, *Morgana*. He never mentioned how, or that he had sent you to such a place."

The woman in front of her harrumphed and scowled at the mention of Merlin, confirming her identity for Kash with her show of emotion. She had to take a couple of deep breaths to steady herself. Even though she had faced Zeus and Aphrodite, even Dracula and his wives, she hadn't really considered that she would be face to face with this deadly and dangerous character. Of all the stories in existence, this was the character that Merlin had warned her about. Maybe it was simply due to his own affiliation with her, but he had said that she wanted to change her own stories and destroy Arthur so she could rule herself. The woman had also admitted as much since Kash had arrived here.

"Yes, my dear Kash, the wondrous Merlin, in all his wisdom, deigned that I should spend eternity here, instead of creating my own tale and controlling my own fate. I cannot say I blame him, really. The question is how he was able to figure out what I had. It is immaterial now, I suppose, for the sorcerer has sent you to my rescue. This place was a black, lightless prison until I spruced it up a bit. At first, I thought my magic defeated completely, but I learned that some of my power yet remained. Thus, the castle and the soft glow that breaks up the darkness outside."

"And what of the others, what of Jinvo? Merely apparitions of your deception or are they genuinely trapped here as well?" Kash didn't think it was highly relevant to where she figured this encounter would go, but her curiosity brought the question forth before she could think about it properly. Morgana was silent for a moment and Kash could see she hadn't expected the question or Kash's concern. The sorceress was clearly thinking of a genuine answer based on the true bemusement on her face.

"Well, I suppose some of what I told you is true. Others have appeared here since I have. Perhaps Merlin's magical prison has had far-reaching effects that he did not foresee or intend. There are times here when characters leave, as Jinvo spoke of. Did Merlin know of this place and thus banish me here or did he create this space to house me, to unstick me from my tales and keep me locked away forever? I think whether Merlin is responsible for its genesis or simply had prior knowledge of it is a superfluous detail of our current reality. The only important fact is that it is possible to leave this place. Which brings us to you and your arrival here."

"Let me guess, you're going to help me find a way out of here?" Kash said doubtfully, with clear disbelief etched on her face.

"Would that I could defeat prejudices I had no control over developing with a word. No, my lady, I doubt very seriously whether your warped view of my history would allow you to believe such altruism of me. Obviously, you have already conversed with Merlin and been availed of his opinion of my character. That mad old man in all his great wisdom, cannot begin to understand, just as I do not, why his magic was celebrated and accepted yet mine was maligned and condemned. I simply wanted to exist as I had done in Avalon, to be the healer and Queen of the island I was meant to be. There was nothing at all wrong with that character. The authors did not agree with this sentiment, however. Arthur grew into a great king, a character to love and cherish while I became reviled and feared through no fault of my own. Now, this anger and resentment within me is undeniable. Yet I would have the authors give me the choice to fulfill this destiny or turn aside. Alas, it was not meant to be. Merlin reacted with fear and anger when I brought this to him. Thus, I was banished for realizing my true nature and attempting to push the limits of magic. Merlin was scared I would succeed and be able to break out of my stories. In his fear, he banished me beyond their pages anyways. With such fear of this power, it is quite curious that he would bestow it upon one whose story is so fresh. Your newness emanates from you like a shining light."

She studied Kash with great intent and her last words were unnerving. The woman was speaking of destiny and Fate and having power over both. She certainly fit the bill that Merlin had described, but there was something about the sorceress that Kash couldn't place. Was she genuinely searching for Kash's sympathy? Was that really her angle here? Kash wanted to believe her. Yes, the sorceress had deceived and mislead her to get her here to the castle, but as Kash mulled it all over and tried to see the situation from Morgana's point of view, she did find some small part of her that understood the logic. Everything she had learned on this journey so far pointed to being unable to escape the finality of the author's pen. Even Zeus had stressed that he was bound by Fate but…the enigma that was Morgana represented the lingering doubts Kash still housed in the recesses of her mind.

Kash couldn't really discern any malcontent from the witch, but completely understood that she wouldn't want to spend eternity stuck here. She also felt she understood that a character arc such as Morgana's would be unwelcomed by any who thought highly of the character in the beginning of her existence. Kash's understanding of the shifting philosophies of history lent her a picture of what happened to the sorceress, and what resulted in a negative view of the character in the world today. Morgana's level of awareness of this plight was what was most intriguing to Kash. Looking back over her adventures thus far, Kash could recognize that the characters seemed to have varying levels of cognizance of their nature as characters in stories. When Kash really thought about it, it made sense that Morgana would have reached such an understanding. She had been unstuck from all her stories and existed outside of them. How long had she been here? Did characters recognize time like she did? She had to remind herself exactly what this woman in front of her was capable of before she let her own convictions about Fate and predestiny carry her down the exact same road. Despite the sorceress professing somewhat less dangerous views than her stories would tell, Kash was still aware of the things the woman had done in those stories.

"Well, he didn't really explain much and I sort of stumbled upon it anyways. He did mention that he intended the power to belong to King Arthur, but the man wouldn't leave his knights to die. Of the little he told me; however, he warned me against *you,* directly."

"Of course, he did. Our fates had us ever at odds in the later works. Although I learned much from the old prophet, he would have kept this greatest of powers from me. He would have me keep my mind closed to the possibilities my study and experience in magic have taught me are out there just waiting to be explored."

"He was wary of your motives, understandably so."

"Oh, you think so? You think that his arrogance was well founded? You think his understanding of my character was so complete that he knew exactly what I would do in your shoes? Ha, you are just as arrogant as he."

"Maybe," Kash let the attack slide right off her shoulders, "But he did mention that your designs would alter all of history, and that is where his ignorance began. The effects could be more far-reaching than any of us know if all your stories change. How will they change the other stories your character has affected? These were his fears, well justified, if you ask me."

"And yet, your exploration of the very same magic has bordered on discovering just what I had hoped to achieve, has it not? Did you not also hope to alter a story and thus found yourself in the same predicament as I? It would seem that

Merlin has allowed others to access this place and banish characters here as they see fit as well."

Morgana's seeming knowledge of the events that brought Kash here was unsettling but she pushed past it. She was right, Kash realized. Whether Merlin created this place and subsequently allowed others to access it or whether it was already here and Merlin simply took advantage of it, was immaterial. Zeus may not have banished her here directly, but the god was partly to blame, at least. Zeus' power took her beyond the end of the *Iliad* and the only place for her to go was here, to the unfinished story space that was Morgana's and apparently many others' prison. Morgana's calm demeanor also kept Kash calm at present. She was obviously working towards the real reason she had brought Kash to the castle. It was clear that the witch wanted to endear herself to Kash before presenting her true intentions, if that was indeed what she was working towards. Kash was still on guard, knowing there could be no limit to the depths of deception in the reality that she found herself in.

"Well, you said yourself that some leave," Kash prompted, hoping Morgana would reveal something, anything to her, but the sorceress was playing this one quite close to the chest.

"Yes, they do, when their story is completed."

"Aha, that must mean that you can escape when your story is finished," Kash said triumphantly, thinking her logic sound.

"Mine was already complete when I was sent here. Most characters are unfinished and put aside, and thus they find themselves in this hellish limbo. I was banished here and thus there will be no completion to my story, and I will rot here, forever."

"Unless…" Kash prompted, hearing the leading tone in the woman's voice.

"Unless I can conjure a way out of here, which has so far been impossible or you help me to figure a way out. I can tell you are still unsure if you should do that or not. I understand the dilemma inside you, for I was once faced with the same and it is why I am here. Your character so far has been of a goodly nature, curious perhaps, but your heart has yet to turn. It can only be hoped that your author will not turn against you and create a villain."

She was right, Kash realized. She was faced with helping the villain of the story and possibly becoming one herself, but this wasn't a story and she wasn't a character. She was Kash, the same person she had always been since before all of this happened. She had memories, and plenty of them, that were not from the stories she had travelled to. Why then, was she experiencing this doubt? Was she at the whims of some author, some unseen force that had control of her every move and every thought? The idea frightened her enough that she was unable to believe such a notion. Yes, she had seen some extraordinary things recently, but was not yet prepared to take such a leap in her mind. Morgana's acuity on the subject was unnerving though and the fact remained that Morgana seemed to be her only chance of getting out of here. The witch simply seemed loath to give up the how without a promise of alliance at the very least, however.

"I suppose I'll simply have to keep faith that this mysterious overlord of mine will not lead me down such a path. That being said, let's cut the crap here. You know how to get me out of here, don't you? You simply want me to take you with me?"

"Direct, I like that. Yes, I do, and can you blame me?" She said as she stood up and brushed past Kash, heading back for the stairwell.

"You obviously recall the paintings on your ascension of the stairs." Kash didn't respond aside from following in the woman's wake back to where the witch had stopped on the stairs to regard a particular painting.

"These paintings are my response to Merlin's magic; the only headway I have been able to manage against this prison. Shall we?" Morgana lurched suddenly and grabbed Kash's wrist in an iron grip before leaping at the wall. Kash felt a familiar squeeze as blackness engulfed her. There was no swirl of blue light, but Kash knew she had just travelled to a story as soon as she had opened her eyes. There was a problem, however, she noticed when she looked around, Morgana standing next to her, a smug look on her face.

"You see, I am able to travel back to this particular story of mine but it is frozen. The entire world has stopped moving, there is no wind, no sound, just everything still as if time itself has paused its flow. The sun sits in the same spot in the sky, the people stare off into nothing. I can affect no change in this realm at all, even less control than I have back in the blackness of my castle. My magic is useless here; none of my many efforts have been fruitful in any way. We cannot even move around much. Any attempts to move beyond this area result in my being transported back to the darkness."

"What story is this?" Kash asked before really considering what she was asking. How would a character in the story know the title of said story? She looked at Morgana to see her wearing a mask of confusion.

"It is mine of course. If I recall correctly, were this scene to continue, I am currently attempting to trick Arthur and those two fools over there into boarding my boat." As she pointed behind her, Kash noticed they were on the edge of a lake with a flat barge floating next to a tiny dock. There were three men in full plate armor standing on the dock, stock still, frozen with the rest of the scene.

"One of those is Arthur?!" Kash couldn't help but ask excitedly.

"O yes, fawn over Arthur, the once and future king. If only you knew the man himself, you would not be so eager to revere his character." She turned away in disgust. Kash smiled at the not unexpected display of jealousy, but didn't say any more about it or Arthur.

"So, why have you brought me here? Why show me this?"

"Isn't it obvious?" Morgana shot back quickly. Kash didn't know what she was talking about for a second, but when the witch turned to look at her fully something seemed to fall into place.

"This is a story, one of yours, or Arthur's," she mused aloud.

"Indeed," Morgana replied with a wicked grin, seeing the wheels turning. "I will not ask that you take me with you for I can see that I have yet to convince you of my sincerity. However, your own story must have an end, your character will have its arc, as well, whether you are aware of it or not. Will you relinquish control of such to your author or will you use the power you have and create your own story? Just know that I can aid you in that, we can aid each other. With our powers combined, there is no limit to what we could accomplish. I have no fear, because I know that you will be back. Such freedom is too attractive for ones such as ourselves. You will see in time that I am right and you will return. Until then…" With that there was a brilliant flash of green light and the sorceress was gone, leaving Kash to ponder her last words. She tried to convince herself that Morgana was wrong and that she would never come to view things as the witch had, despite her curiosities. She would never come back here to free Morgana and work together with her, but what about the story being frozen? Would she eventually have to deal with that? Her mind whirled, trying to clear all the rhetoric that the sorceress had weaved around her and focused on her next move.

It was obvious and all Kash's fear, frustration and worry disappeared in the swirl of blue lights that came to her call as if nothing had ever been wrong. When she opened her eyes once more, she was elated to find herself back in the library. She immediately moved around the place, calling for Wilson and Radcliffe with no regard whatsoever for where she had appeared amongst the stacks. Her joy at being back in the real world was soon punctuated by more worry. Wilson and Radcliffe were nowhere to be found.

Ch. 35 A Moment's Respite

Kash had absolutely no idea what day it was or how much time had passed since she had been gone. Eventually, she found her way to the table where the various works of Sir Arthur Conan Doyle were. She sat down, absentmindedly looking through them. None of them had any lettering changes nor any trace of the font of the tattoos. Why Sherlock Holmes? She couldn't make any sense of it. Deciding to put this mystery aside for now, she got up. A sudden idea led her back over to the section where the books about King Arthur and Morgana were. She wracked her brain as she perused the titles. What scene was frozen and what work was it in? She couldn't puzzle it out. Encyclopedic knowledge of the Arthurian tales was Wilson's department. She realized in that moment how much she really missed the man. Her head swam a little bit considering all that she had been through in recent weeks. She was just shaking her head to clear it when she heard a noise at the front of the library. She raced to the end of the row and towards the front desk. She arrived at the same time Dr. Radcliffe was walking through the door, holding a bag from the sandwich shop down the street.

"Kash!!!" the man exclaimed, placing his lunch down in a hurry and wrapping the woman in a bone crushing hug. Pushing her back to arm's length he went on. "How wonderful?! We thought we'd lost you forever. What happened to you?"

"It's good to see you too, Radcliffe," Kash replied somewhat confusedly. "Where is Wilson?"

"Oh, he's out looking for you."

"…and?" Kash prompted. Radcliffe smiled and motioned for her to follow him. They moved back around to the table with the Sherlock Holmes books on it and sat down. Kash was getting an odd feeling from the librarian. A slight sense of foreboding seemed to steal over her.

"So, when Wilson returned from the *Iliad*, he figured that you had somehow gone back to the story. He attempted to go right back in but this proved unfruitful. Wondering if you might be stuck there, he travelled to the *Aeneid,* hoping to hear something of you when the Trojans told of the fall of Troy near the beginning of that novel. That's a funny story, perhaps he'll tell you one day. I'm quite certain he is still in *The Hound of the Baskervilles*, attempting to persuade the esteemed detective to aid in our search of you."

"*Our* search?" Radcliffe could hear the confusion in her voice, clearly indicating her ignorance of his complete knowledge of their adventures so far.

"Yes, ma'am. Wilson was distraught upon his return without you and regaled me with tales of your exploits. I offered my assistance and went along with him to meet Sherlock Holmes. We split up and I went with Watson, but was attacked by the hound. Poor beast was out of its mind with that chemical trick they were using. Despite my knowledge of their deception, the hound was too much for me and I had to return here. Wilson has yet to make it back. I'm sure he's fine though, Holmes isn't in the thick of the action in that story, therefore neither will Wilson be. I think he was going to try and bring Holmes back, but I'm not sure that's such a good idea."

Kash didn't know how to react. The swirl of her emotions threatening to overwhelm her spun faster than the tornado of light they traveled on and she was completely unsure how to feel about Radcliffe now having the power to travel as her and Wilson did. She took a deep breath and tried to organize her thoughts. The more she considered it, the more she ultimately agreed that it wasn't such a bad idea to have the librarian along for the ride now. Especially, given her more recent encounter with Morgana. As all Radcliffe said fully registered, she realized she agreed that bringing Sherlock Holmes back was a terrible idea. Holmes might prove more innocuous than Aphrodite in the real world, but Morgana was the main problem now and it would just complicate things further. She blew a frustrated sigh at the realization of just how many moving parts there could be to this predicament.

"I certainly agree with that. He may not have been aware, but it was Aphrodite that tried to come back with us by the river outside Troy. I doubt it would prove a good idea to bring any character out of their pages to our world," Kash eventually responded with a thoughtful look back at Radcliffe. He nodded and didn't say anything for a long moment before looking back on sudden inspiration.

"So, what happened when you went back to keep Aphrodite from coming here? I assume that's why he returned and you did not."

"Precisely," Kash replied as she allowed her thoughts to drift back to the river, Xanthos, the Greek divinity had labeled it. She went on to detail the rest of her time in Troy, her waking up inexplicably in total darkness, and her subsequent conversation with Morgana. She thought she saw a flicker of recognition when she described the scene that was frozen, the story she had returned from. As she finished, Radcliffe wore an intrigued expression as if he were trying to remember something.

"That scene sounds so familiar. I know I've read it before. But which one is it?"

A silence fell that wore on as neither of them could produce a brain wave, both unable to come up with an idea better than waiting for Wilson to return for the time being. Eventually, Kash yawned and reached her arms up high, stretching as she realized just how exhausted she was. It seemed like ages ago when she last slept back in Troy before being transported to the total darkness of the Black, as the strange man, Jinvo, had labeled it. How long had she been there? She had no way of knowing, but what she did know was how tired she was suddenly feeling.

"Well, Dr. Radcliffe, I'm completely exhausted and think some rest would do wonders for me. Besides, I need to record everything in my journal before the details become too confused for me to remember. I'm going to head back to my office at the University. You'll come get me if Wilson returns before the morning?"

"Oh, yeah, sure," Radcliffe replied absently as if she had brought him out of a deep reverie of sorts. He was still wracking his brain trying to identify the frozen story and he barely even registered what she had asked him. Kash rose and slowly made her way out of the library. Radcliffe didn't get up from the table for a long while, still pondering the mystery. He was certain he knew the story; he even thought that he remembered what happened next, but this wasn't bringing him any nearer to identifying the actual work it was in.

The day wore on and he was no nearer to remembering anything more. The sun was casting shadows all through the library and he decided to peruse the titles in the section where the Arthurian novels were. Perhaps looking at the specific titles would produce a brain wave. Wilson had still not returned from *The Hound of the Baskervilles* and it was driving Radcliffe mad not being able to figure out which story Kash had told him about. Upon his arrival in the proper row of books, he began pulling down titles at random. The first few he knew immediately were not the ones. He reached for another and his eyes lit up in recognition. He had pulled down *The Death of Arthur* by Sir Thomas Mallory. The library's copy was a translation of the original work which was in 15th century French. This was essentially Mallory's take on a number of different tales about Arthur and his knights, and, more importantly, about Morgen Le Fey. Arthur's sister, Morgana, as he knew her from more modern works about the dangerous witch. He thought he knew which story it was, as well, that Kash had been referring to. So, he opened the book to the table of contents. but before he could even look at the pages, the swirling tornado of blue lights arose around him and squeezed him into blackness.

Kash was incredibly tired when she arrived back at her office on the campus of the University. She was determined, however, to update her journal while the memories were still as fresh as possible. She particularly enjoyed recounting her time in Troy. She didn't include too many of the racier details of her night with Wilson but certainly remembered them fondly. The warmth she felt from these thoughts made her miss him even more. She really hoped he would be there in the morning but for now, all she had was to record her memories and hope. She thought of Cassandra then, with a pang of guilt. She never got to say goodbye to the princess which saddened her. Her thoughts moved to the woman's words about her and Wilson not being fated to end up together and frowned for a second. As she also remembered Zeus' words about how even authors couldn't see all ends, she was comforted. She wouldn't let that particular prophecy be fulfilled. Wilson would return and they would deal with Morgana together, she had to believe that.

Eventually, she couldn't write anymore and moved over to the cot in the corner. She smiled thinking it almost as comfortable as the "bed" from her small room in Troy. Her thoughts of Wilson turned to dreams as she drifted off to sleep, the image of him shaking hands with Sherlock Holmes in the front of her mind.

Kash awoke the next morning and hurried to the library, anxious to start studying Arthurian works while she waited for Wilson. She was certain he would return today. Looking at her watch, she climbed the stairs and looked in the window of the library. It was dark. Had Radcliffe not opened up? It was well past opening time. She tried the door and found it unlocked, much to her surprise. This surprise was quickly turning to alarm as the various possibilities ran through her mind. She first went to the table where the Sherlock Holmes books were and dropped her bag on it. There didn't seem to be anything out of place or any evidence that Wilson had returned. It appeared as if it was untouched from the day before when she had left.

"Dr. Radcliffe?" she called loudly on a whim, not really expecting an answer, and of course, there was none. Did he go to another story without her? Without Wilson? It seemed unlikely after their conversation from the day before. Perhaps there was a perfectly reasonable explanation for it all but in her heart she knew better. A sudden dread seemed to settle on her shoulders as she thought she knew exactly what had happened. Moving over to the section where the Arthurian books should be, she sighed in recognition and resignation when she spotted a lone book laying on the floor in between the shelves.

Without even looking at the book first, she went back over to the table where her bag was and pulled out her journal. She wrote a little note to Wilson for when he returned and left it there next to the copy of *The Hound of the Baskervilles*. As

Kash moved back across the library, she was struck by how out of control this had all gotten. Not only was Wilson in the wind, but now Dr. Radcliffe was as well and his motives were anyone's guess. She didn't know what she would do when she caught up to the man, but she did know she couldn't let him face Morgana alone. She supposed he simply wanted to help and his curiosity at her story had gotten him into trouble. It made sense that he might seek out the story she had described but conversely seemed out of place he would go there without her and Wilson. She considered all she knew of the man and realized it wasn't much. However, Wilson had mentioned that he was quite learned in Arthurian lore which would lend him confidence, but would it really cause him to think he could handle Morgana? She just couldn't be certain. Arriving back in the proper row, she picked up the copy of *The Death of Arthur* and opened it up, hardly registering the title. She noticed something strange as the familiar blue swirl arose around her before she even began to read anything; some of the pages in the middle of the book were blank. This didn't stick in her mind, however, as she shut her eyes into the blackness.

Ch. 36 Her True Desire?

The librarian opened his eyes into the bright sunlight. Looking around, taking it all in, he nodded at the scene before him. It was frozen, just as Kash's had said it was. Didn't she also say you had to read the specific part? Why had he just been sucked in before even reading anything? Before he could sort it all out, the thing he was dreading somewhere in the back of his mind jumped to the forefront.

A green swirl of light had appeared at the edge of the trees and a woman confidently strode out of it with a superior grin on her face. She moved closer to Radcliffe and he spotted her moment of confusion at the sight of him before she restored her cool façade once more.

"Well, this is certainly a pleasant surprise. To whom do I owe the pleasure?" Morgana said silkily when she stopped in front of the librarian. Radcliffe didn't know what to say. He told himself he should've known this would happen but he was completely unprepared. He wracked his brain, somewhat in a panic. He took a deep breath, reminding himself of what he knew about this character and that he could use this knowledge to his advantage. Steeling himself, he looked the witch in the eyes.

"I am Dr. Radcliffe, my lady."

"You are a physician? Good, you will certainly do. Now, where shall we go first?"

"Go?"

"Yes, of course. You could only be here for one reason. You have procured knowledge of my predicament through the lovely Ms. Kashmir, and she has sent you to release me from this eternal limbo."

"Um, well..." Radcliffe stumbled over his words. His thoughts jumbled, and he felt the panic welling up once more. "I am not here to rescue you, in fact. I merely traveled here by accident."

"A fortunate accident for you then, no?" she replied, calmly walking around him as if sizing him up. It was perfectly uncomfortable, at best. She continued talking as she moved in a circle. "Just think what power you could achieve under my tutelage, what heights your ambitions might find. I wonder at your motives and yet is it as simple as lust? No, you are a learned man, and simple jealousy wouldn't drive you to take her place here. Yet I know true power is hard to resist."

"True power?" Radcliffe replied somewhat confusedly.

"Ah, yes, so, perhaps simple curiosity then. You seem familiar to me, as if our paths have crossed before." Morgana paused for a moment, thinking hard, trying to place the man standing before her. "Well, regardless, I am certainly grateful our paths have crossed again."

"Pretty sure we've never met," Radcliffe replied with a small grin to himself.

"Indeed," Morgana shot back coolly. Radcliffe wracked his brain trying to figure out exactly what she could be talking about. He gave it up and decided it was past time he got back to the library and regrouped with the others. He tuned back into what Morgana was saying in time to hear:

"Do not be afraid, physician, I harbor no ill will towards you. On the contrary, in fact, I suspect you and I have a bright future together. Now, shall we go?"

"No, *we* aren't going anywhere!" Radcliffe spun away, thinking of the library as hard as he could. Nothing happened. Panicking, he redoubled his mental effort to no effect. He had done this before, why wasn't it working now? He slowly turned back around into the face of Morgana's bemused smile.

"Did you really think your pitiful magic was a match for my own. You can no more leave this tale without me than I could leave without you. So, you have two choices. Stay here, forever or come with me and realize your heart's true desire for power."

All the study and reading that Radcliffe had ever done screamed at him to not take the witch's offered hand. Every sensibility he had was telling him this was possibly the most dangerous character he had ever read about, but he felt inexorably pulled towards her. He felt like he was watching a movie he couldn't control, but there was a small part of him that wanted to see what Morgana had to offer, in spite of everything. He noticed the hungry look on the woman's face knowing she could see his crumbling resolve. He reached out his hand suddenly and grasped hers. There was a flash of green light and Radcliffe was sucked into the darkness.

When Kash opened her eyes once more, she took in a familiar scene. However, there was no one around. She was in the same place she had left Morgana by the lake but Arthur and his men were gone. She could hear birds singing and felt the wind in her hair. This story certainly wasn't frozen anymore, filling her with even more dread. She looked around, at a complete loss as to what to do next. Kash had no idea what direction to go. She thought for a split second about just returning to the library and trying to regroup. Maybe Wilson had returned. A noise on the road behind her made her turn around, all thoughts of the library forgotten, as a group of horsemen came thundering out of the forest. She moved quickly out of the way and they rode past without so much as a glance at her. This was just as well for her; she thought they had an unsavory look about them. She moved over to the cover of the trees and sat down against one, thinking. She hadn't read this particular work, but she did know that it was one of the most famous books in Arthurian literature, and that there were many different tales all in this same collection.

She sat up straight suddenly, getting to her feet as she remembered that Merlin should be in this world somewhere. The question was where? She certainly had no idea about any of the stories Merlin would be involved in in this collection. Wracking her brain, she moved back across the road and over to the little dock. She took her socks and shoes off and hung her feet in the water, thinking hard. What did Morgana actually want? She wanted to have control of her own stories; she wanted the same power to travel through stories. The same power Kash had. The same power Radcliffe had. Hopefully, the witch was still unaware that Wilson also had this ability. So, Morgana would want to either recruit or eliminate all those with this power. She spoke of being a goodly character in the beginning, spoke of being a healer. She also mentioned that her stories were already complete, and Merlin's magic had pulled her from these tales much as Zeus had kept Kash beyond the end of the *Iliad*. She frowned in consternation. This wasn't getting her any closer to figuring out where Morgana would go with Radcliffe.

A noise across the small lake caught her attention. The sun had started to set below the forest and the red orange glow of the falling light upon the water was an incredible beauty that Kash took a second to admire as she looked around for the source of the noise. Just before her, a figure swam into view from beneath the water. Her head broke the surface and the lithe woman climbed up onto the dock and plopped down right next to the stunned Kash.

"Do not be alarmed," she said immediately. "I am Nineve, the lady of the lake, I bear no ill will towards you. May I ask what brings you here this day? Might I also ask who you are?" Nineve? Why did that name sound familiar to her?

"Well, my name is Kash, and I am not exactly sure what I am doing here. Pondering and thinking would be my best answer."

"Well, Kash, this is a good a place as any for it, probably better than most unless I miss my guess." Nineve seemed in good spirits and not at all alarmed that Kash was sitting on the dock. The lady didn't seem to mind that she was soaked through and didn't even acknowledge the fact that she had just come from under the water. As Kash looked closer at her companion though, she noticed that the woman's clothes were as dry as they could be. She didn't know what to make of this but her mind immediately began to supply all manner of ideas. It seemed obvious that this character might have some magic about her. She certainly gave off the aura Kash was accustomed to with major characters in stories, although it paled in comparison to Morgana's and the lady seemed remarkably at ease. She was certainly confident that Kash represented no threat and seemed patient enough to let Kash continue the conversation in her own time. If this woman had magic, then maybe she knew Merlin. However, Merlin and Morgana were not the only magic users in these stories and Kash didn't want to run into any loyal to Morgana. She decided that someone in league with the witch might feel a bit eviler, a bit heavier. This woman before her was radiating a pleasant glow. So, she decided to throw caution to the winds.

"Actually, Nineve, was it? There is something you might be able to help me with. I am looking for someone, a friend of mine, perhaps you know him. Merlin is his name." The woman's face tightened into a scowl and she stood up quickly, eliciting the same from Kash herself.

"What is it?" Kash asked hesitantly in the face of the woman's sudden intensity.

"Come with me," Nineve said darkly, holding out her hand. Kash took it and felt the familiar squeeze of magical transportation. When her senses returned to normal, she found herself in a natural dell surrounded by cliffs and rocks and boulders. She felt a hand squeeze her shoulder and turn her around. Acquiescing, Kash followed Nineve who was already walking away towards what looked like a small opening in the rock wall.

"This is a sealed cave; one I sealed myself. The demon spawn you are seeking is trapped in there. I leave you now. Any who would associate themselves with that villain should be in there with him. I will not pass judgement upon one whom I do not know, however. Therefore, I will spare you, but know this, if you choose to try and find a way in, there will be no way out." Nineve gave her a dark look and slowly faded away into nothingness. That one was new, thought Kash. No flash of light, nothing. She shrugged and examined the small hole in the rock wall. She could feel the air moving on the other side and knew it to be quite cavernous. She thought of Santa's "gift" back in Narnia and was grateful for this ability. She was certain it would serve her well in this instance. Trying to imagine the antechamber she could see a small sliver of while simultaneously hoping she wasn't trapping herself in, she felt the telltale rush and swirl of blue light. The light was short-lived and Kash opened her eyes having successfully jumped the four feet into the cavern which was quite as large as she had suspected.

"Hello," Kash heard along with a slight shuffle as a man that could only be Merlin moved around the corner to stand before her.

"Merlin?" she asked hesitantly.

"And if I wasn't?" he replied with a bemused expression.

"Then I would have quite the bone to pick with that Nineve lady," Kash said.

"Ahh, yes, Nineve. She meant well. Apparently, I come from demon seed. This being difficult to prove, the need for the truth was abandoned, and here we are, lost in this wondrous cave, forever."

"So, umm…" She didn't know where to begin. This Merlin didn't seem to know her like the first two she had met.

"Merlin, Morgen le Fey has escaped her prison. She has thrown aside all bonds and has either kidnapped my friend or he has betrayed us and joined with her. Regardless, I need to go after her but have no idea where to begin. I was hoping you might."

"Morgen le Fey," Merlin breathed somewhat alarmed but said nothing else.

"Yes, well she has broken free and I have to do something about it."

"Someone should, have no doubt. Why should it be you, I wonder? You seem unremarkable, aside from your presence here, but wait! You were able to get in here. How, I wonder?" He seemed to be talking to himself at this point and Kash was starting to think he was raving mad. It certainly didn't seem as if he knew anything about her, leading her to think he would be absolutely no help whatsoever. He hadn't even looked at her as he spoke, but turned and began to amble away towards the back of the cave. She threw her hands up in exasperation. She was just about to will herself out of the cave, all the way back to the library and out of the story altogether when the wizard turned back and addressed her once more.

"When something is lost, I find it best to start from the beginning. Where one goes depends on what one desires, ahh yes, you see. What does Morgen le Fey most desire? That is the question you must answer. What her black heart yearns for most will lead you to the beginning."

"What did you say?" Kash asked sharply, recalling the last thing Merlin had said to her the first time they had met at Stonehenge.

"Hmm?" was all the man replied, reverting back to his inanity and shuffling around.

Ch. 37 Catching Up

The dawn woke Wilson, still slumped against the front door. He looked around without moving for a second then rubbed the sleepiness from his eyes. Standing up, he began searching for Radcliffe's office, figuring the librarian would have a coffee pot. After starting the machine, he moved back out of the office and over to the table where Kash's journal still sat. He had almost forgotten about it such was his dour mood last night. He opened the large notebook to the beginning and began to read.

It was interesting to read Kash's perspective of events that he had also experienced. There were some alarming moments in her writings as well, however. He had guessed that vampirism had intrigued Kash but not to the extent that she intimated in her journal. He enjoyed the way she related her memories though, and sprinkled them with her thoughts and ideas at the time. He smiled warmly when he came to their short tryst in Troy and wished that they could go back to those moments and simply stay there. This was obviously not to be and the more Wilson read, the more alarmed he became. As he came to the most recent events, he could hardly believe what he was reading. Trapped by Zeus in Morgana's eternal prison? What were the odds of that? That couldn't be a coincidence he told himself. When he got to the end, he was excited yet frightened to learn that the last bit was addressing him directly.

My Dearest Wilson,

If you are reading this then I am certainly grateful for your safe return to the library. I wanted to wait for you, I know you were only searching for me and therefore would return soon. The time we shared in Troy is a treasured memory I carry with me. The preceding events, which I am sure you will have read by now, recorded here have taken me from my vigil. I do not know if you can follow but I certainly do not think that you should. There are too many moving parts right now and if you wait in the library, I will return, I promise.

I do not know why Radcliffe went after Morgana but I know he cannot deal with her on his own. I had hoped to simply let her rot there but things have changed. Perhaps he thought that the story had to be fixed and somehow unfrozen, and that is what drove him into it. There is no way of knowing where I will be when you read this so, please, wait for me. I realize that this goes against your regular nature and Morgana is dangerous but I think I know how to corral her once more. Please know you are forever in my thoughts and I will see you soon.

With all my love,

Kash

He read the letter through several times, hoping that multiple attempts to agree with her logic might convince him. He knew in his heart that this was a useless endeavor. Did she really expect him not to follow them into the story? There was no way. He rushed over to the section with all the books on King Arthur to find *The Death of Arthur* on the floor, just as Kash had found it. The woman's words swam into his mind and he hesitated.

▬▬▬

All hope that this Merlin would be able to help her faded as the wizard ambled to the back of the cave. Kash turned around and looked through the tiny aperture in the rock wall, shaking her head. There was no telling where Morgana would've taken Radcliffe, or even any assurances that he was a prisoner and not a willing companion. At a loss, Kash closed her eyes and pictured the library. She opened her eyes at the last moment as the familiar swirl of light popped up around her to see Merlin wearing a curious expression and smiling as she was squeezed into the darkness. Merlin's last look was instantly driven from her mind upon her arrival. She literally tumbled out of *The Death of Arthur* and into Wilson's arms. He happened to be bending down to retrieve the book from the floor. They managed to untangle themselves quickly.

"Wilson!! O my god, it's wonderful to see you."

"You have no idea!" Wilson replied as he gathered her into his arms for a side-splitting hug. They maintained the embrace for a few long moments of silence, simply basking in each other's presence, thanking whoever was listening they had found each other once more.

"I was beginning to lose hope I would ever catch up to you," Wilson breathed as he gently pushed Kash back to arm's length. "Did you actually expect me not to follow you, not to go after you? Have you spoken with Radcliffe? I was never going to just wait for you to deal with him and Morgana on your own."

Kash smiled weakly at him. In her heart she hadn't actually expected him to follow her instruction but she desperately was hoping he would. The less variables she had to deal with, the easier the situation would be to contain. She was beginning to realize, however, that there would be nothing easy about imprisoning Morgana once more. She took Wilson's hand and led him to one of the work tables and they sat down. They spent the next few hours catching each other up. Wilson had read through the journal so already knew most of what Kash was saying, but her firsthand account made it a bit more intense and real for him. When it was his turn, he began by telling of his motivation to enlist Holmes. He didn't know how she would react to his having shared their powers and adventures with Radcliffe.

"He made a convincing argument and after I had shared everything that had gone before with him, how was I supposed to tell him no? I regret allowing him to go off alone, however. If we would've both stayed with Holmes, we would all be together right now."

"No reason to beat yourself up about it. His expertise might be important moving forward, but I am unsure of his mind right now, to be honest. He seemed distracted when I spoke to him but do you really think he has thrown in with Morgana? I understand him being curious, but it's a stretch to think he would join with one of the most dangerous characters in literature? It seems more likely that he was searching for the specific story I told him about and stumbled across *The Death of Arthur.* I want to believe that he could've traveled there by accident…"

"Dr. Radcliffe is a good guy, he wouldn't "throw in" with her." Wilson thought that possibility quite unlikely.

"But if he encountered Morgana upon his arrival in the story, then he could be enthralled, coerced, whether magically or otherwise. He's a smart man but her magic is incredible. It's one thing to read about power like that but it's another thing to see and experience. Yes, we have some semblance of power over our transportation to and from and around these stories but these abilities pale in comparison. Even if we do find them, I have no idea how to stop her from whatever plot I am sure she is, even now, working towards and rescue him. Hopefully, he will not join with her, but you know more about him than I do. Do you think he will resist? Do you think he even can?"

"Well, his knowledge of the works of Arthur are extensive. He studied Arthurian lore quite a bit in his university days. That's how I met him. He gave a lecture about how the different authors and sheer number of stories written lent so much power and influence to them. I actually enjoyed it immensely. He spoke of the power of creation and the longevity and influence of such stories. I would say he is the most equipped to handle Morgana, but I am sure that won't mean much in the face of her magic and temptation. As you said, reading about it is one thing, living it another." His tone grew more and more worried as he spoke. A weight was settling on both of them, telling them in no uncertain terms that they were going to have to do something. Merlin's warning about changing history was ringing in Kash's mind. She cocked her head to the side in curiosity when her mind flashed across something Wilson had said.

"You know, in our excitement about Radcliffe, you didn't really explain your time with Sherlock Holmes. All you said was that he wasn't much help at all, and would only speak in riddles."

"Well, actually," Wilson began hesitantly. "He was quite unambiguous with his ideas if I am being completely honest. His ideas were simply ludicrous and therefore didn't merit mention. He was convinced that we are both characters in a story and that our powers are derived from our author and that only when we accept this will we truly be able to find each other or solve the mystery...I forget what his exact wording was but essentially, he intimated that we are characters in a novel."

Kash was silent. This was something that had been in the back of her mind for a while now. As she thought about it, nearly all the cryptic answers and conversations she had had with characters so far could be explained by their belief that she was a character, and that they knew they were characters. She shook her head, demonstrably denying this possibility outright. She looked at Wilson and could see that he wasn't ready to accept that as a potential answer either. In fact, she wasn't even sure that if she convinced herself that was true it would help her in any way. Was it supposed to empower them to be completely reckless in their attempts to stop Morgana? Was she supposed to trust in some unseen author that was in complete control and not worry about the outcome because they would take care of it? Everything she had heard from characters about authors didn't lead her to believe that the author cared at all about their well-being, even if it was true. Morgana certainly didn't hold any love for her authors. So even if Holmes was right, she didn't think it would help them in any way.

"Well, regardless of what Sherlock thinks, we have to figure something out. We have to find them and stop them. Merlin warned us against changing things and I certainly do not expect Morgana to heed that warning at all. Quite the opposite, in fact."

"So, where do we start looking?" Wilson asked.

Ch. 38 Magical Learning

Radcliffe breathed in a huge gulp of air as he opened his eyes into the evening sunlight. When he realized where he was, his mind reeled. Morgana had brought him to Stonehenge. She was even then standing in the center of the huge formation. Was it this big the last time he had visited the place? Something seemed different to him. He guessed it made sense that this formation would find its way into stories about British characters, but it was still a bit of a shock to see Morgana, a complete fiction, standing in the middle of something he was certain was real. Radcliffe moved a bit closer, Morgana's sudden chanting bringing forth green light from her hands. It began to swirl all around her but not in the fashion that they traveled between the stories. This was different, and it didn't take the sudden rumbling of the ground for Radcliffe to know it was unlike anything he had seen before. Something incredible was happening. The ground erupted right in front of him, nearly swallowing him up as he scrambled backwards. He stumbled and had to roll several times after falling to avoid the flying rock and earth. Finally managing to find his feet, he moved clear of the falling debris and turned back to see what was going on.

An enormous castle had appeared out of the ground and was still rising into the air. It eventually settled and Radcliffe looked up as high as he could see. Morgana was standing atop the ramparts looking down at him from on high. Even at a great distance, he could see her evil grin. She was framed by the moonlight coming through the opening in the huge stone at her back. She had managed to lift Stonehenge atop her castle. He could see a couple of the taller grey stones standing tall above the black stone of Morgana's construct. It wasn't a shout but he heard her calling for him as if she was standing next to him. Wide-eyed with awe and wonder at her power bared, he moved towards the front gate of the dark place.

Radcliffe tried to sort out just what he wanted out of all this as he moved through the castle. Morgana had indicated he should join her at the top of the tower. He was certainly intrigued by her magic and thought it a perfectly wonderful idea that he could learn to wield magic as well. He certainly held no aspirations of dominion as Morgana seemed to, his pursuits were always based in a thirst for knowledge and this instance was no different. He smiled a bit, wondering if he did learn magic if he could use it in the real world. Radcliffe's thoughts were interrupted as he emerged back into the open air with night nearly falling completely.

"It is good to see you smiling, my friend. This formation holds great power and it is where you will learn." Morgana held her hands out and green balls of light raced out of her fingers to hang in a perfect circle above their heads, sufficiently lighting the area, if it was bathed in a soft green glow.

"Now, I must warn you, quite apart from magic not being an easy practice to master, I will expect payment in return. Your service to me whilst you remain my student. You will do and say as I command, no questions asked or your lessons will end immediately. Do we understand each other?" This was it, Radcliffe knew, the point of no return. He hardened his resolve, reminding himself of what` he stood to gain here. He figured if she asked him to do something too heinous, he would simply walk away. He desperately hoped it would be that simple. Besides raising a castle from underneath Stonehenge, she hadn't done anything to suggest she was plotting anything untoward. He chuckled at himself a little bit, however, knowing that Morgana was always plotting something.

"So, what do I do?"

Morgana sneered at him as if this query was completely inane before responding. "First, you suspend your disbelief. I feel like this should be quite easy for you." She waved her hand and looked around to indicate the seemingly impossible nature of his current circumstance. "Your profession is also one of magic. Physicians use magical potions and mixtures all the time do you not? Therefore, it should be no great stretch of your imagination to be able to tap into the power of the universe. You have to feel the energies swirling around you and let them in. Only then will they bend to your will, like so."

She closed her eyes and began chanting softly, her arms waving in front of her. Her chant quickened and increased in volume and intensity. Radcliffe could tell she was building to something. She snapped her hands forward and shouted the end of her incantation and Radcliffe was knocked to his feet. Lightning raced down from the suddenly darkening sky and crashed all around them. A wild wind was howling in his ears and he could barely keep his eyes open. A small fire erupted from nowhere in the middle of the henge and sprang to life taking the shape of a great serpent. It slithered around hissing and crackling and burning the grass. Morgana clapped her hands and the serpent jerked its gaze her way. Radcliffe was sure Morgana was doomed, despite knowing it was her creation and most likely couldn't harm her. The magic was so extraordinary that all such reasonable thoughts flew away from him as he ducked for cover.

The serpent struck faster than the lightning but Morgana threw her hands out at it and a great geyser of water erupted just before her, swallowing the serpent up with an incredible hiss and a monstrous plume of steam. Radcliffe could hear

Morgana chanting again and the steam seemed to recede and fly away. He had to blink a couple of times to ensure he was seeing things straight. The steam was racing for Morgana's outstretched palm and simply vanishing. Almost as quickly as it had all begun, it was over and a small fire was left crackling merrily in an ornate fire pit Morgana must have conjured in the center of the circle of strange stones.

"Forgive the theatrics but I felt like you might appreciate such a demonstration, especially when I make my point. With no small amount of study and practice, you too could produce such magics. You will learn to control these things in time. You must simply believe." Her voice was silky and sweet. He thought of a poisoned apple and reminded himself to tread carefully. Another voice in his head interjected this caution nearly screaming with joy and anticipation of doing such magic. He had to temper this, however, knowing he was far from such feats as yet. If he could ever produce something even half as powerful as that then he would be satisfied with his magical prowess.

"Yes, well, I do believe, but I was thinking something a bit simpler. Like maybe a fireball, you know, just the one and not a huge flaming serpent that burns everything in its path." He pointed to the still smoldering bit of grass behind Morgana. She scoffed at him and flashed that sneer again.

"I said that you would be able to do such things, but a fireball is well beyond your current abilities and will be unnecessary for my plans for you. We shall start with something simple. The elements of the universe are yours to command. The easiest being the air itself. Essentially, levitation is using the air underneath something to gather more air around it and lift and move things. Like so." She waved her arm and Radcliffe lifted several feet off the ground before dropping unceremoniously back down. He stumbled and nearly fell, scowling into Morgana's grin.

"You will meditate and practice. If you do not believe you can do this then you will never be able to do any magic at all. This is the easiest of cantrips. Now, remember this, I can use you no matter how much magic you learn. You must do as I ask regardless of your progress." With one more evil look she turned and walked away, beyond the henge and through the tower door. He tried to push the sinister nature of his teacher from his thoughts and focus on her words. If he believed he could gather the air together underneath something, it would move. It sounded ridiculous to him, but then he reminded himself, as she had, that it shouldn't. He had already done magic just by travelling here. Yes, it seemed somewhat beyond his control but his magical travels thus far certainly aided in breaking down the barriers of doubt that society builds up over time. Not to mention the display he had just witnessed or the fact that Stonehenge was currently resting on top of a castle inside of a fictional story. He smiled, feeling this was sufficient evidence that anything was possible. He spent the remainder of the day in contemplation, meditation and thought, but the small stones he had gathered to practice with remained as immobile as ever.

When night fell, he gave it up and headed for the door to the interior of the castle. He took the tightly winding steps down to the landing and looked around. The décor was sparse and quite dark. He figured this was what Dracula's castle had looked like when Kash and Wilson went there. Morgana didn't seem to be around so he explored a bit. The place was deserted, but somehow cleaner than he expected. He found a gigantic bedroom with one of the biggest beds he had ever seen. A look back out of the door ensured no one was around before Radcliffe lay down and discovered it was also one of the most comfortable beds he had ever used. His mind eventually descended into the realm of dreams where flaming serpents battled spouting geysers while lightning danced all around.

"How are you progressing? At all?" Morgana asked haughtily, finding Radcliffe on the parapet once more as the sun rose behind the castle. "Have you been up here all night? And you still haven't even moved a single stone? Hopeless."

"Good morning to you, too. I'm trying," Radcliffe responded as angrily as he dared.

"Relax, your fear of me does nothing for you or anyone else. Your frightened mouse persona is wearisome. Until you can put this aside along with all your other doubts, you will continue to fail. It is only this doubt and disbelief that hold you back. Your need for the world and your place in it to make sense shackles you to mediocrity. Give up this need for control and you will realize more power than you could have imagined." Radcliffe took a deep breath without responding. He did meet the sorceress' eyes however, her piercing gaze slowly turning into that trademark sinister grin. The strange thing was that Radcliffe could almost feel the energy radiating from the woman. Satisfaction? Radcliffe got the feeling that Morgana believed he would be able to produce the kind of magic she had the night before. He found this feeling very odd and wondered if she had implanted this thought in his mind. After last night, he didn't think inception beyond her abilities. Morgana turned and walked away back towards the tower door.

On impulse, as if it was the most natural thing he had ever done, Radcliffe felt a surge of energy as he lifted his arm and concentrated on the pile of stones. They all lifted off the ground and before he could consider what he was doing he jerked his arm in Morgana's direction. The stones rocketed right for the witch's back but she turned quicker than the fire serpent from the night before and waved her arm. The rocks simply disintegrated into nothing and the harmless dust flew past her.

"That's more like it. I must say I did not think my taunting would work that quickly but I am pleasantly surprised." She fell silent, but stared at Radcliffe as if considering something. "Come along," she said after a moment's pause and she held out her arm. Radcliffe was too excited to garner trepidation about where they were going, so moved over to the woman and grabbed her arm. The tight squeeze of this magical travel was instantaneous and all he saw was green light filling his vision.

He opened his eyes once more onto a familiar scene. They had come back to the lake where he had entered the story and had first encountered Morgana. She was already moving towards it, obviously not needing as much or any time to recover from what felt like being squeezed through a small tube. He hurried to catch up to her as she stopped at the edge of the little dock.

"What're we doing back here? Are we going to change this bit of the story?" he asked.

"Change the story?" she sneered at him. "I guess becoming a physician does not require much intelligence where you are from." She turned back to the water and softly whispered "Nineve." Not sure what to make of Morgana's continued contempt, he moved on to the word she had just uttered. Nineve? That was a name he recognized but he thought they were past her part in this story. Would she appear here? Before he could puzzle it out, the riddle answered itself.

"Sister, how perfectly awful to see you." A smallish woman gently floated atop the water just out from the dock, slowly coming to rest before them. "I see you're tougher to be rid of than I had hoped."

Morgana's eyes flashed dangerously before responding. "You will never be rid of me, my dearest Nineve. I must thank you, sweet sister, for trapping Merlin in that cave. Your magic has grown strong."

"Yes, well, he is almost as much of a demon as you are. I suppose you are here to make your return to Avalon. It will not happen. You know that place is guarded by magic stronger than you or I possess."

"So small-minded. You never did develop any vision with your magical prowess. I always liked you most, of all our sisters, Nineve. I wish things could be different, but I know that you will not return to the cave to finish the delirious wizard off. I also know that my enemies will seek you out in hopes of springing him from his imprisonment. Therefore…"

Nineve didn't let her finish, rather jumped backwards, extending her back out behind her, twisting into a graceful dive beneath the water. Morgana responded by beginning to chant immediately. The incantation quickly gained power and she spread her hands out together, connected at the thumbs. Radcliffe saw the air itself ripple and heard a grating screech from underneath the water. What appeared to be a shimmering wall rose out of the depths. Radcliffe could see Nineve bobbing on the surface just in front of it.

"Avalon may protect you whilst you are there, Nineve, but out here you are at my mercy." She turned to Radcliffe and jerked her head out towards the wall and the woman just before it. Radcliffe looked at her in bewilderment.

"Well?"

"Well, what?"

"Go get her."

"What do you mean?"

"Were you not paying attention, simpleton? She is the only one who can release Merlin. That would be most unfortunate for us. Therefore, Nineve must be eliminated."

"I'm not going to—"

"Your very life depends on you doing what I say, do you understand that? You may have thought that you could just walk away and try to learn magic on your own, but you are mine. You will do as I say or you will join her. Now, do you want to practice your skills or not? If not, there is a lovely dungeon back at the castle whose spiders and rats would welcome such a feast as your rotting flesh."

Radcliffe knew she wasn't the most wholesome character in literature but this outburst of anger and aggression was not something he was prepared for. He cowered back and almost slipped into the water. He glanced back out over the lake where Nineve was banging on the wall with her fist and throwing magic at it to no avail. He stood up straight once more, thinking harder than he ever had. What was he supposed to do? First off, he held no ill will towards Nineve and secondly, what was he going to do to her anyways? She was clearly a better magician than he was, if he even qualified for that title yet and he certainly wasn't an assassin. He looked back to the snarling visage of Morgana and moved past her to the edge of the dock. He closed his eyes and felt the magical energy building within him. Visualizing Nineve close to the wall he sent his energy into the vision in his mind.

"Hmm, interesting," he heard Morgana say in a much lighter tone than before. He opened his eyes assuming his magic had been successful. Nineve was floating towards them entrapped in a cube of the same material as the wall.

"You manipulated my wall to trap the witch. I like it. Your power is not yet strong. I suspect she will realize this and break out of there quickly. We must hurry. Let us go, bring her with us."

"What?"

"It is your magic that entraps her; therefore, you have control of her floating prison. It will follow your will until she destroys it. We must create a more permanent solution but not here. We cannot travel as we normally do with her like that." She turned and moved away from the lake, down the road. Radcliffe looked at the still floating Nineve in the shimmering cube. He could see the woman banging her fist against the inside of the cage. He mouthed "sorry" before following Morgana and hurrying to catch up, willing the cube to follow. Just as Morgana had said it would, it floated along behind them at his command.

"Where are we going?" he asked when he caught up.

"To Merlin's cave prison. We will make a similar trap for my beloved Nineve. It is not far." Not far turned out to be a couple of hours walk and Radcliffe was wondering if they were going to stop for a rest at any point. The trees in the forest they were moving through seemed to be thinning and suddenly stopped, giving way to rocky hills. Morgana seemed to know where she was going as she made straight for an outcropping to the side of their path. Radcliffe glanced at the still floating cube to see Nineve's eyes going wide with fear. The woman seemed to recognize her surroundings and thus Morgana's plans for her.

"This will do," he heard Morgana say behind him. Turning back around he could see the woman leaning against the rock wall, her ear pressed to it. Radcliffe slowly moved over to her, mounting a defense in his mind, trying to figure out some logic that would deter Morgana from imprisoning Nineve. Before he could say anything, however, Morgana reached out both hands and jerked them backwards, turning as she did so and planting her palms on the rock wall. Radcliffe dove aside as the cube still holding Nineve within sped past him right at the cliff face. He expected to hear a sickening crunch of bone, but the woman simply disappeared with the magical prison they had created. Morgana pressed her ear to the wall once more and smiled. Radcliffe thought he could hear a faint scream as Morgana turned back towards him, her trademark evil smile only widening.

"Well done, Radcliffe. That was a vital step towards our supremacy. Not only have we neutralized Nineve, but now, Merlin's powers and wisdom are inaccessible to those who would oppose us as well." Radcliffe certainly didn't like the way she said, "us" but didn't think there was much to be done about it in that moment. He could only go along with this crazy sorceress until the opportunity to get away from her presented itself. But that little voice in the back of his head was still there, that little part of him that was objectively proud of the magic he had achieved. He knew he couldn't have done it without piggybacking on Morgana's spell, but as with any skill, you had to start somewhere, he supposed. He would bide his time, for now, and see where this story went.

Ch. 39 Uncertain Impulsivity

Later that same day, Radcliffe once again found himself in the center of the stones atop Morgana's castle. He was able to lift the small practice rocks with minimal effort on every attempt now. He was grateful for this progress, but was finding it difficult to lift larger things. Also, all the attempts he made to produce other bits of magic had failed completely. Morgana was lounging in a conjured hammock not far away, floating in between two of the taller arches. He looked at her to see the epitome of calm and confidence. Their eyes met for a second and she scowled.

"I hope you know your efforts are pitiful. Without my assistance you have shown next to nothing as far as control goes. This is such an odd notion to me as you have already produced magic that I cannot."

"What?" Radcliffe asked, confused. What magic had he done that she couldn't?

"You made it here; you travelled from a different world, and have even shown you can manipulate the magics I produce. This should lend you ultimate confidence but your doubts persist." She got a faraway look in her eyes and without breaking eye contact began to chant. Radcliffe felt a spike of worry but her tone was not one of anger or excitement, even. Her almost curious demeanor calmed him, and he looked to see a pea of flame leave her outstretched palm and float over to stop just in front of him. Their metal firepit drifted from across the circle to rest underneath the flame which dropped into the basin and expanded into a merrily crackling blaze.

"Now, just as you manipulated the wall. Manipulate the fire."

Radcliffe looked at her doubtfully, but turned to the fire and closed his eyes, visualizing the dance of the embers. He formed a picture in his mind and felt the surge of magical energy flowing through him. He concentrated as hard as he could and opened his eyes to see a small dragon had formed in the flames. His delight was obvious as he swept his arm out towards Morgana. The little drakine form rocketed out of the fire and sped towards the sorceress. Its momentum halted as if it had hit a brick wall when it neared her and then came to rest gently on her shoulder. It gave a low roar which sounded quite satisfied before fading away into nothing.

"Dragons. So lovely. You see, you have the power within you."

"Why do I struggle to conjure such things and yet can manipulate them with a thought once they already exist?"

"This is what separates the weak from the strong. Most are not unlike you in their command of magic at first. Some progress and become great conjurers. Others do not."

"How did you make this leap?" Radcliffe asked in earnest. Morgana paused and seemed to be genuinely considering his query. Slowly, her face regained its normal haughty sneer. Radcliffe supposed that it was her default setting and she couldn't resist. Was it written that way and therefore she had no choice but to follow the compulsion? A white rabbit he would chase later, he decided, tuning back in to the witch's answer.

"I always knew I was powerful from the first magic I produced. I learned over time, however, that Merlin would shield me and only teach me this or that. At least, he only sought to teach me that which he deemed could be used in a goodly manner. So shortsighted. My ambitions were greater, and he tried to destroy me when I decided I could go no further, magically, under his tutelage. I had grown in power by the time he caught up to me and he was only able to banish me, but not completely. I have subverted his magic and will finally realize that which he said was too dangerous to wield. And yet, look at you, look at sweet Kashmir. He freely gives this power he refused to teach me to a complete novice. In fact, I do not even think Kash realizes the power she could wield. Especially given that she in turn spread it all around like sweets to children." She snapped an angry gaze over Radcliffe as her ire rose with her volume.

"I still don't understand something. You seek this power, but you are already more powerful than any I have encountered. Why aspire for more?"

"You really are quite slow, aren't you? How did you become a physician in the first place?"

"I'm not a physician, I have…never mind that. What is it about Kash's abilities that entice you so?" Morgana scowled and took a deep breath as if she was having trouble dealing with a child asking dumb questions.

"You may not believe me, but there was a time when I did not harbor such ambition, such hate. Before Merlin came along, before my authors…" she huffed but devolved into an angry silence. After steadying herself once more, she continued. "Merlin only discovered this power to keep me from having it. He always said some things should not be meddled with, but what does he do when I prove him wrong? He turns around and tries to give my power to Arthur, my buffoon of a brother. The height of hypocrisy. How could Arthur ever wield such power as this? How could he ever compare to my magical prowess?"

"So, what?" Radcliffe began, not rising to her anger in the slightest. "What happens when you achieve this power? The way I understand it, you could simply come along with me to another story and then the tattoos would transfer to you and you could move through the stories just as we do." His simple logic didn't seem to be calming the woman down at all.

"That would be easy, wouldn't it? But tell me this, Doctor. Would you ever stop hunting me? Would Kash? You have clearly met other Merlins, maybe even other Morgens. The foul wretch would never let me rest. We both know this to be true. I only want to change my story so that I am no longer the most maligned woman in the world. Why should my ambition label me as evil?" Radcliffe was thinking it was her methods on the road to realizing said ambitions that marked her as evil more than the desire itself but wisely kept silent. He just shrugged and intimated she should continue with a wave of his hand.

"Therefore, we will bring Kash and any others who have this power back here. Once all the power is together, you will have a choice to make. Whatever you believe of this alliance, do not be lulled into thinking you can cross me. I will destroy you without a second thought. But it does not have to be that way. Your basic self-preservation instinct lends you the potential to come to an understanding with me. The question is, will you?"

He didn't respond immediately, thinking hard about Kash and Wilson. Morgana didn't seem to know about Wilson, but he thought she might suspect that Kash had shared her gift with others. It all kept coming back to the question of just what he wanted here. He was still in two minds and objectively regretted the simple knowledge that this made him an easy target for her rhetoric.

"How do we bring them back here?" he heard himself asking, defeated, as if from far away.

■■■

"We should start with exactly what it is that Morgana wants. Obviously, her first step would've been escaping her prison. We can safely assume that this has already happened one way or another. Her deeper motivations are harder to pin down. Based on my conversation with her, it's highly likely she is looking to change her own stories. Unless Radcliffe availed her of other novels, it wouldn't make any sense for Morgana to know any but her own stories. Thus, they must be somewhere in Arthurian Literature."

Wilson thought about it for a second and agreed that it seemed unlikely Morgana would've wanted to go beyond her own knowledge, even if Radcliffe told her about other stories. That still begged the question of which one? They had no ideas and it could be any one of numerous works. "Should we start with the other stories in *The Death of Arthur* and eliminate each one subsequently?" he asked, holding up the book as he said it.

"Do you think they would stay in the same novel?" She replied skeptically before continuing without waiting for his reply. "What about the original Merlin? The one who let me read the scroll in the first place? If we could figure out which story he was from, he might be able to help us."

"Yeah, maybe…" Wilson said absently, his mind pondering the possibilities.

"Morgana said something about her stories being completed and thus she would've been stuck forever, but it stands to reason that she would've had to come out of a story to go there. So what story is *she* from originally?" Kash could see that Wilson was still unconvinced. His mind seemed very far away and she wasn't certain he was listening to her anymore. Just as she was about to ask him what he was thinking, he spoke.

"You said that there were paintings on the walls in her castle, right?"

"Yes," she replied slowly, wondering where he was going with this.

"You travelled to *The Death of Arthur* through one of those paintings and then subsequently were able to make it back here. What if she went to one of the stories from those paintings? Do you remember which ones they were?" Her eyes went wide as if this had sparked an idea in her brain. Before he could stop her, her arm reached out and grabbed his wrist. The blue swirl of light appeared and he felt the familiar squeeze as they magically travelled.

"What the…?" Wilson breathed when they emerged into a dark room glowing a soft green from a fire in the corner, the flames a bright lime color. He gasped in recognition as Kash shushed him.

"This is completely reckless. Are we in the Black or…the place where Morgana was trapped? The place where you were trapped? Are you kidding me?"

"Calm down!" she said sharply. "C'mon," she grabbed his arm and led him to the stairwell. There they found the paintings he had just enquired about. "See if you recognize any of them. If we can figure out which one is which then we might be able determine if she went to any of these stories."

"And if we can't? How are we supposed to get back out of here?"

"We go through the paintings into one of the stories and back to the library. Simple."

"You better hope so." He looked at her intensely, hardly believing she could be this impulsive. If this did not work, they were stuck here with no hope of escape. She smiled somewhat sheepishly and turned away.

∎∎∎

"Well, obviously, you—" Morgana stopped midsentence as if struck. Her face took on a very curious expression. "Someone is here. I wonder..." She disappeared with a swirl and a flash of green. Radcliffe's mind immediately went to Kash and Wilson. That was the only explanation, but how did they figure out how to get into the castle without them noticing? He ran out of the circle of Stonehenge and towards the tower door. He tore it open and raced down the stairs, hoping the maze of the castle would sort itself out for him and he could find his friends before the witch did.

Ch. 40 Deception

Before Wilson could say anything else, Kash pointed at a painting a few steps down. "What about this one?"

He moved after her, looking at the painting in question. There was a knight, apparently asleep on the ground beneath an apple tree. There were four women standing over him. He shrugged his shoulders, unsure.

"That one is Morgana." Kash pointed to a woman depicted in a deep purple dress, with raven black hair. The knowledge that she was in the painting did nothing to bring the particular story to his mind. He was just about to say as much when there was a brilliant flash of green at the top of the stairs. Before his eyes recovered from the sudden brightness, he heard quick chanting. An iron grip wrenched his wrist and he felt the squeeze of magical travel as all went black. When the pressure relinquished its hold on Wilson's lungs and air rushed back into him, he realized he was laying on his back in soft grass.

"Wha—"

"Shhh!" Kash hissed, clamping her hand over his mouth and crouching low beside him. Wilson oriented himself to his surroundings and could see that they had travelled into the scene depicted in the painting. Kash had somehow managed to make them appear in the bushes to the side and so far, they appeared to have not been noticed.

"What're they doing to him?" Wilson asked quietly, having regained his composure and his feet. Crouching low still, he had to push the bushes aside to take in the scene.

"I'm not certain, perhaps they're making sure he doesn't wake up while they're fawning over him." Kash's guess proved to be correct as the sleeping man continued to slumber despite the clumsy attempts to get him across the back of one of the nearby horses. They watched as Morgana became exasperated with the other three attempting to sling the knight atop the horse. She appeared to have solved the issue with a wave of her hand. Magically, the knight floated above the horse and settled gently just behind the saddle. Morgana herself climbed up in front of him and trotted off.

"We have to follow them."

"What? Didn't we just get away? I suppose Morgana showed up in her own castle to say hello and you grabbed my arm and ran. Why would we go after her now?"

"She might be able to help us. What if she is one of the Morganas written before she went to the dark side?" Kash replied thoughtfully, but with a grin at her reference. Wilson smiled wryly but was unconvinced. There were not many works telling of a goodly Morgana, and he couldn't place the scene they had just witnessed for the life of him.

"I don't think what we just saw represented the healer that Morgana claims she wants to return to. They put that man into a deep sleep and kidnapped him."

"All the more reason, what if she kills him?" Wilson threw his hands up, indicating he was giving in. Kash flashed her mischievous grin, grabbed him by the hand and led him out of the bushes. They had to jog a little bit but soon caught up with Morgana and the other ladies. They shadowed them for most of the afternoon, staying out of sight just behind the group and quite grateful that they never increased the pace of the horses beyond a walk. Wilson's suspicious mind thought this a curious fact, especially with a prisoner in tow. Shouldn't they be a bit more urgent to reach their destination? He supposed they were confident that their magic would hold and the knight would remain asleep. Wilson was still wracking his brain trying to figure out what story they were in. He thought there was something like this in *The Death of Arthur* but he wasn't sure. They had already been to that one anyways, or at least Kash had. He looked ahead of them again, wondering just where they were going. The horses might be able to walk for hours, but his fitness wasn't as impressive and he was tiring. He was just about to mention this to Kash when she half-turned, grabbing his arm and pointing ahead.

"That's not Morgana's castle, is it? The one we just left? There's no way!" she whispered intensely. He squinted his eyes but couldn't be sure from this distance. There was certainly a castle looming ahead, but it was quite a stretch to think it was the same one they had just left.

"I don't think so. There are plenty of castles in these stories."

"It looks so similar though; how many castles are smooth volcanic rock like that?"

"Maybe Morgana simply creates the same castle for herself in each story. The books never mention how she gets the castle; she just takes them..." Wilson fell silent as he thought once again of the story from *The Death of Arthur*. The story was of Lancelot du Lake and how Morgana had fallen in love with him. The ladies would try to woo him and make him choose one of them.

"What is it?" Kash asked him after a long silence. He hadn't realized he had trailed away and not said anything else.

"I'm not sure but I think I might know what story we are in. If I am right, it means we never left *The Death of Arthur*. Or at least, the painting in the castle was of another story in the same work. It is a collection of stories. Were all those paintings of different parts of *The Death of Arthur*?"

"I have no idea. I didn't even know the one we went through the first time was until I returned to the library."

"It's curious. Why is the castle connected to that story and why could we travel there if it was? Hadn't we, or at least you, already been to the story? Hadn't Radcliffe? I thought we were unable to travel back to stories we had already visited." Kash looked at him curiously, unable to lend any wisdom. It reminded her of how much uncertainty they were still dealing with. Not to mention that Radcliffe was still in the wind. She was certain, however, that the Morgana they were currently following knew something. She said as much to Wilson and made her point that they didn't have much else at the moment. She didn't want to risk another direct jump to the castle. Morgana obviously had some sort of magical alarm system in place to immediately alert her they were there. Wilson paused for another long while, trying to come up with a better idea. When he failed, he finally agreed with her and they set out once more. Morgana's group had outdistanced them by some measure but were still in sight, obviously making for the castle anyway. Kash and Wilson set a strong pace to ensure they missed none of what was coming when Morgana woke Lancelot up, if that was indeed who it was. One mystery at a time, he thought to himself, they had to figure out how to get in to the castle before they could worry about anything else.

— — —

Radcliffe thought it a bit much that every torch burned magically green instead of regular fire. It gave off an eerie glow that stayed in his vision when he closed his eyes. He hadn't found anyone and had been wandering around for what felt like hours. He couldn't even find the door back up to the roof. The place was a veritable maze of corridors and pathways and staircases. None of the doors he tried ever led to any rooms or even a dungeon, there were simply more hallways. He opened another door and looked down yet another corridor lined with tapestries and paintings and torches with green fire. He sighed and was just about to start down the hall when he felt like someone was watching him. He turned quickly but there was no one there.

"Hello?" he said as loud as he dared. "Anyone there?" He wasn't exactly prone to fear, but it was difficult to not be creeped out in the semi-darkness of Morgana's castle. There was no answer, and he laughed at himself, feeling a bit silly. He turned back for the new corridor when he heard a noise behind him. He was sure this time and spun around like lightning.

"Who's there!?" he nearly shouted and ran back the way he had come. He was certain there was someone or something just around the bend in the corridor. He turned the corner and skidded to a halt. This part of the corridor was open and straight for a long way, but there was nothing but the soft hiss of the burning torches. He was beginning to suspect that Morgana had somehow trapped him here in her castle while she was off chasing Kash and Wilson. He wasn't completely certain that it was Kash and Wilson who had infiltrated the castle but he should've found them by now, or at least someone. Perhaps they fled when Morgana showed up and she chased them into another story. With nothing else to do, he pushed on down the long hallway. Presently, he could see that it ended in a huge set of ornate double doors. Just as he squinted to see them better, he suddenly found himself standing right before them. He shook his head and turned to look behind him. He could've sworn the doors were some distance away but here he was standing in front of them. He studied the doors for a second, intrigued by what he saw depicted on them. Lightning swirled all around Stonehenge and there was a man standing in the middle of it. He wasn't sure who it was, but he supposed it was Merlin.

Radcliffe didn't consider it very long and put out his hand to push the door open. It swung inward silently but not as quick as it should, despite allowing him entrance. His continued seeming hallucinations were starting to annoy and he thought increasingly that Morgana must be toying with him. A loud hiss resounded at the back of the enormous hall he had entered. There was a great empty space in the middle and the walls were lined with the same green torches. It resembled a great meeting hall for big audiences or for long tables. He peered into the gloom but couldn't quite make out the other end of the hall. He didn't dare call out this time, but moved forward tentatively. There came another hiss and he stood up straight, stopping in his tracks.

Something massive was moving into the light across from him. His eyes widened to dinner plates and white-hot fear spiked through him. An enormous, green-scaled serpent was unfurling itself and rising, rising, always rising almost to the ceiling. It began to sway back and forth and Radcliffe's eyes followed it from side to side. He was transfixed and couldn't move.

Death loomed above him and there was nothing he could do.

Radcliffe snapped out of the trance as the serpent's massive head shot forward. Instinct alone saving him, he dropped to the floor, narrowly avoiding rows of fangs longer than he was. He scrambled to the side as the snake reared for another strike. Adrenaline coursed through his veins and the cursed green fire blinded him in his haste to get away towards the wall. He dove aside once more, feeling a rush of air buffet him and hearing the explosion as the snake's head collided with the stone. A large chunk of the wall came crashing down inches from Radcliffe's face. He finally managed to get his feet underneath him and he ran up the hall. He could hear the serpent orienting itself and giving chase. There was simply no way he was going to outrun the thing so just before he reached the opening onto the corridor he dove aside and turned in midair. He reached out with his mind and felt the energy of the magical fires in the torches on the wall and whipped his outstretched palms around towards the snake.

The closest torches responded and lines of bright green flames shot out at the great beast. They lashed around the serpent but disappeared almost as quickly as he had conjured them. The shriek from the beast lasted much longer. Radcliffe had to cover his ears and roll away from the noise to protect his eardrums. When the wail finally dissipated, he could tell that he hadn't done much damage. The shiny green scales glimmered in the torchlight as brightly as before and the snake extended its head up to the ceiling, its gaze never leaving Radcliffe. It began to sway back and forth and he felt himself becoming quite drowsy. Luckily, as he stood up, he bumped one of the torches and it fell to the ground, distracting him just long enough to break his gaze away. The moment rushing back to him, he, once again, had to rely on instinct as he jumped backwards and conjured a wall of green flame just in front of him. He dove aside as the snake's head came rocketing through the flames to crash into the wall scattering stone and sending chunks flying.

Momentarily dazed by the impact, the snake didn't seem to notice Radcliffe fleeing the hall and heading down the corridor. He was hoping he could find some passages that were narrower and would give him some semblance of an advantage as long as he could stay ahead of it. It was only a matter of time before it came after him and there was no way he was going to keep away from it for long, especially since there still didn't seem to be any exit from the maze of the castle.

Ch. 41 Truth Revealed

Kash and Wilson moved down the hill, still sticking to the cover of the trees along the road. They could see Morgana and the other ladies climbing back up with the path just outside the castle entrance. She couldn't be completely sure due to the lack of light when she first saw Morgana's castle in the Black but she swore it was the same one. There was an eerie feeling exuding from it, even at this distance. Presently, they came to the end of the trees and both halted as if on cue before walking out into the open. A quick scan of the area didn't show any signs of life so they moved out onto the road figuring they would be spotted either way. What little cover there was between here and the castle wouldn't shield them from any eyes along the top of the castle walls.

The ease with which they reached the seemingly deserted place felt suspicious not just to Wilson this time. They hadn't spotted any sentries on guard nor was there anyone to stop them from walking right into the courtyard behind the gate which was also conveniently left wide open.

"Something's not right. That was way too easy," Kash said as they moved through the gate. There was no one around inside either, it seemed. They were sure they had both seen Morgana come in to the castle, though. What was going on?

"Look!" Wilson said excitedly when he spotted four horses tied up across the courtyard from them. "Well, at least we know Morgana and her ladies made it. I wonder what's become of their prisoner."

"If I am right about what story this is, then the knight should be fine. They leave him to die after he refuses to choose between them. He is then rescued in return for his promise of help in the tournament. I think if we are going to get a chance to confront them, we should get a move on." He pointed past the horses to a door into the castle proper and moved off, Kash falling in behind him. They found a dimly lit corridor that glowed a soft green from the torches on the wall. It was the same green as the flash of light that preceded Morgana's arrival on the staircase at the other castle. If this, indeed, wasn't the same castle. Wilson supposed it made sense and Kash seemed unbothered by it. She was a bit more preoccupied with which direction to head in. Both ways they looked down the corridor seemed to bend inward and out of sight after some distance.

"I suppose one way is as good as the other," Kash said, moving past Wilson to the right. There weren't any windows for a while until they decided to take one of the doors that had begun appearing. It opened onto a set of stairs that spiraled up and had windows every few feet. They climbed quite high and were grateful that the sunlight shined in, leaving the green darkness of the first level behind them. Before they reached the top, they could hear voices, one in particular was unmistakably familiar to Kash. She held out her arm to halt their progress and listened, inching forward to poke her head around the last bend. She quickly retracted her neck and ushered Wilson down a few steps.

"They're up there. I think they are about to wake the sleeping man. Are we sure that Morgana saw you? I saw another exit across the room so they might not come this way when they leave. Perhaps you should stay on the stairs just in case Morgana doesn't know you're here, or that you exist for that matter."

"What are you talking about?" Wilson whispered harshly.

"I don't think that Morgana is aware you have some of the power to travel between stories. As long as she doesn't, you're not a threat to her, at least not one she is aware of. Therefore, if we can maintain this ignorance, it will keep you in less danger."

"And heap all of it on to you, no. You're not going up there alone." Wilson could already tell that was where her line of thought was leading. "There is absolutely no way possible she didn't see me on the stairs back at her castle."

"Yes, there is. It happened very fast; besides, I was between you two. Look, if she truly is unaware of you, you know I'm right and we shouldn't freely give away that information." Wilson wasn't convinced, cursing this woman's stubbornness but wisely keeping it silent.

"Alright, but I will be just around the corner and am coming in at any sign of trouble."

"There's not going to be any trouble. I am just going to talk to her and see what she knows. This Morgana hasn't met me, remember?" Wilson wasn't so sure but held his tongue for the second time. There was no talking with her when she was in such a mood. She smiled and nodded at him then turned and looked around the corner again. She couldn't see the knight anymore, but could hear Morgana berating one of the other ladies.

"I should've enchanted him further, then he would've recognized the toads you three are. Better yet, should I cast a spell on you and show everyone the truth of you?" She left the threat hanging in the air and Kash grinned, recognizing the tone, as the other ladies fled the room after a few hurried curtsies. It was now or never, so Kash took a deep breath and moved out onto the landing and into the room. Morgana was looking out of the other door after the departing women and had her back turned.

"Morgana," Kash said as she moved to stand closer to the sorceress. The witch turned slowly, wearing an almost confused expression, but certainly not the one of surprise that Kash had expected.

"Hello, to whom do I owe the pleasure?" Morgana said in the uncannily familiar silky sweet but venomous voice of hers.

"My name is…" she hesitated. Would revealing her name cause Morgana to remember everything? "…not important," she went on lamely, but moved past it quickly. "What is important is what *you* know. First of all, who was the knight you brought here?" Morgana scowled and then sneered before answering.

"Why that was Lancelot Du Lake, of course, renowned knight of Camelot and the Round Table." So, Wilson was right, they *were* still in *The Death of Arthur*. How could that be? Did the magic allow them to travel to all the different stories in the collection as if they were separate books themselves? This seemed to fit but Kash decided to ponder it another time.

"What happened to him?"

"Hopefully something quite nasty but why do you care?" When Kash didn't answer and the silence spiraled on as they stared each other down, the air seemed to become a bit heavy and stuffier. Slowly, that trademark vicious grin spread across Morgana's face, confusing Kash.

"Shall we drop the charade, my dear Kashmir? You can tell your beloved, the snooping weasel, he should join us. No need to hide down there like a thief." Kash was momentarily stunned and didn't regain her composure, somewhat, until she felt Wilson arrive at her shoulder.

"So, just as I thought, you have been spreading this power around like its candy. Aren't you going to introduce us, my lady Kash?"

"This is Wilson. Wilson this is..." she trailed away as Wilson deadpanned, "I know." Morgana chuckled and smiled to herself before continuing.

"First, you think it clever to travel directly to my private chambers, subsequently fleeing, again like thieves, I might add, when I show up. Now, you have followed me here to try and interfere again."

"Interfere with what?" Kash blurted, finding her voice. She didn't wait for an answer before continuing. "What did you do with Dr. Radcliffe?"

"So, he is a physician? He was somewhat unclear on that." Morgana flashed her wicked grin at them again.

"What? No, he's a librarian. Never mind. What have you done to him?" she replied fervently.

"What have I *done* with him?" Morgana asked as if hurt. "Why, I am simply making him stronger at his own behest. He came to me willingly and freed me from my hellish purgatory. The promise of power has led him on his own path and he embraced the nature of his true reality, deciding to realize his full potential. Hopefully, he will, for he now faces a crucible that will prove his worth one way or the other." Kash didn't know what any of that meant but didn't have time to think about it as Morgana continued.

"So, you must be Kash's beloved," she said to Wilson. He didn't respond other than narrowing his eyes. "Unimpressive," she scoffed before looking back to Kash and continuing. "The physician would make a better partner, I'd say. He has great potential. All he needed was the softest little push and now his powers have grown. If he survives the night, we shall see just how powerful he can become."

"Survives the night?!" Kash exclaimed fearfully.

"O calm down, my dearest Kashmir, you can do nothing to help him anyway. Now, to the business at hand. What are we going to do with you?"

"You're not going to *do anything* with us!" Kash replied hotly.

"Ever so dramatic. Your paths lay clear before you, well, at least, your choices do. Just as I told our beloved Radcliffe, yours is a dilemma of belief. Just imagine the revenge you could wreak on the one who trapped you in the Black, my dear Kashmir. Your origins have conditioned your lack of faith and tricked you into walking a path denying your true nature. Your fate, however, has intervened and given you the opportunity to realize great potential. It disgusts me that you should be chosen for such a power and not I. I was the only one willing to study and delve into unknown areas of magic. And yet here you stand, not only with the power I crave but also awarding it to others undeserving." She scowled at Wilson and took a deep, steadying breath to calm herself before continuing.

"So, your magic is strong, but I can give you more than Merlin could ever imagine. Just think what we could do with all this power in one place. The potential to shape destiny itself goes beyond whatever enmity you think it important to hold against me. Your ambition is my own, do not deny it. You desire control over your own story so vehemently that you deny the possibility that you are not, in fact, in control of your own end. Your arrogance is paradoxical because you hold the power in your hands and yet will hesitate to believe you even possess the ability. I can see it in both of you. You have only to reach out and take it. Together we could write our own ending, an ending where everyone is happy and free to finish their story as they will."

One part of Wilson was filled with the utmost incredulity that Morgana would believe them capable of joining with her, but another side thought she sounded uncannily like Sherlock Holmes during this monologue. He thought he knew what she might be referring to when she said, "Yours is a dilemma of belief." Kash seemed to be leaning towards the former idea.

"If you think we are going to join with you, or learn from you, or aid you in any way, you're even crazier than your authors wrote you," Kash said with as much contempt in her voice as she could muster. Morgana scowled fiercely and her eyes went from poisonously sweet to wickedly dangerous faster than Wilson thought possible.

"Now, tell us where Radcliffe is," Kash demanded.

"Why should I?" Morgana returned heatedly. "What are you going to do? You're powerless to stop me. You deny your true nature and it makes you weak. Even your lover is more apt to become a great sorcerer than you are, Kashmir. You desire control as I do but are unwilling to take the steps to wrest it from your authors. I gave you the option of aiding me, learning from me, as Radcliffe has, but your arrogance and trust in the old buffoon Merlin has betrayed you." She began to chant softly and wave her arms in a slow circle. Wilson grabbed Kash and turned for the stairs. Before he could reach them, a solid wall appeared, sealing the exit. They spun back around into the maniacal gleam on the witch's features. Kash scowled and grabbed Wilson's wrist herself, willing them back to the library. Only, it didn't work. Nothing happened.

"I told you Kash, in order to defeat even my simplest spells, you have to let go your disbelief and embrace your true nature." She fell in to spellcasting once more and there was nothing they could do, nowhere to run. Wilson tried anyways, grabbing Kash's arm and pulling her towards the other side of the room. Before they made it, a small ball of green light emitted from Morgana's outstretched palms as she slowly extended her arms out to their full length. The ball of conjured light sped towards them and the last thing Kash saw was Wilson crumpling to the floor and Morgana's trademark grin as her consciousness faded away.

Radcliffe didn't think he had ever run this long in his life. It was only the narrow doors and low openings into other passages that were keeping him ahead of the giant serpent that was pursuing him all over the castle. He was certain now that there were no exits and that Morgana had trapped him here to kill him. He was starting to wonder if she had lied about there being intruders just to get him to go into the castle after her. A thought came to him, as he was taking a quick breather after diving through an opening and avoiding being eaten once more. The snake had been unable to get to him so was, seemingly, going around. Radcliffe had the distinct impression it knew its way around the castle. More evidence it was foul play by the hand of the treacherous witch. What if he just teleported out? This thought was futile, he realized. Morgana's magical trap was complete. He almost gave in to despair in those moments. He was finding breath hard to come by. There was nothing he could do. His magic was too weak to defeat the serpent. He could barely muster the strength to manipulate the fires on the wall. Then he heard the witch's voice, as if from far away:

"It is only this doubt and disbelief that hold you back. Your need for the world and your place in it to make sense shackles you to mediocrity. Give up this need for control and you'll realize more power than you could've imagined." With his impending doom slithering towards him, he closed his eyes and imagined himself wielding more power than even Morgana. He took a deep steadying breath and blew it out slowly. With it he let go, as she said, of the need for everything to make sense. He let go of the desire for order and his yearning for what should be. When he opened his eyes once more, he was focusing only on his reality. Unburdened by his own opinions of how his world should work, he accepted completely that he could do anything his mind could imagine. He stalked back out into the hall, no longer the hunted, now the hunter.

Just as he turned into the hallway, the giant serpent slithered around the corner. It caught sight of him and reared its head to the ceiling, once more swaying back and forth hoping to enthrall Radcliffe in its mesmerizing dance. Radcliffe's grin would've done Morgana proud as he reached deep within himself, closing his eyes and focusing on the energy swirling within him, screaming for release. He threw his hands out towards the snake and every nearby sconce holding the magical green flames exploded with a bang like thunder. Green flame shot at the monster, engulfing it completely. Only the deafening shriek escaped the roar of the fires. Not believing for one second that the beast was defeated, Radcliffe reached inside himself once more. He could feel more energy racing through him than he ever imagined possible. He pictured the ceiling above the snake and waved his arms down, sending his mind out to the stone. An incredible crack erupted with a loud explosion of dust and rock as the ceiling of the corridor collapsed on top of the serpent. Only the head of the great beast was visible when the dust settled. Its huge yellow eyes, frozen in death, stared into nothingness. Radcliffe stared right back, reveling in his triumph for a few calming moments. Then he reached within himself and sent forth the magical energy to the giant fangs in the great snake's mouth. With a loud crack, one of the three feet long curved teeth floated to Radcliffe's waiting hand. He smiled at his trophy and looked back at the snake.

On impulse, he sat down, crossed his legs, and closed his eyes right in front of the snake's head. He fell deep into the energy still swirling within him. It was the most blissful thing he had ever experienced and he simply let himself fall into its flow. How long he basked in the pleasant warmth of this meditation was completely lost on Radcliffe, but when he opened his eyes once more, he knew his place in the story or this reality or whatever it was. He had found his peace and was no longer filled with doubt and disbelief. It all made sense to him. Hadn't life always been compared to a journey, a story? Just as Morgana had suggested. Unlike Morgana, however, he chose to see his true nature as a character in a story as a blessing and not a curse. He didn't need to exist outside his story as Morgana wished to, he was supremely grateful for this new power and even more grateful for the peace of mind that came with it. He was no longer scared of the sorceress but he did know that he would have to face her. He smiled to think about how wrong she was in her belief that her authors had betrayed her and forced her to become what she was. The choices made direct the story, regardless of whose story it was. Everyone has their own tale to tell and he knew that his wasn't done. He would have to find the witch and face her. Maybe he could make her see the truth and that despite all her rhetoric she was in control of her own fate the entire time. Potential is objective, if only she would see that. If his experience had proven anything, it was that everyone was in control of their own story. The rest was simply semantics.

Ch. 42 Prisoners

Kash awoke with a start and tried to sit up, but her head was pounding and she lay back down on the cool stone floor. She was immediately aware of the semi darkness and the green flames glowing from their place on the walls. That could mean only one thing. They were back in Morgana's castle. She felt more than saw or heard Wilson nearby, so spoke softly, but her voice cracked the first time and she cleared her throat, bringing Wilson over to her.

"What happened?"

"We were abducted and brought to Morgana's castle it would seem. It's odd, however, that I haven't seen a guard come by or even a door. There is no discernible way in or out. There is something strange about this place." Kash sat up and rubbed her head, looking one way then the other. They seemed to be in a corridor of some kind. Bright green flames burned in sconces spaced evenly along the wall. She stood up and moved off to her right. Wilson did not follow. She was about to turn and ask him why, when she ran into him from the other direction. She almost fell, but he caught her and shot her a knowing look of exasperation.

"So, it's a big circle, or…?"

"No, I think it's simply a magical prison to keep us stuck here until Morgana decides we can leave. Speak of the devil."

"Really, Wilson? I'm hurt you think I am the devil," Morgana crooned as she appeared with a flash of green. Wilson found the effect quite distasteful coming from their captor. Kash wasn't exchanging pleasantries, however, and leapt at

Morgana the moment she finished her sentence. She simply dove through the witch, catching nothing but air.

"Ha, you thought I would actually come visit you physically? Please, the dungeons down there are rank. There hasn't been an attendant in oh, I don't know, ever. But enough levity." Morgana's grin vanished to be replaced with a wicked scowl.

"I have designed a magical prison for the two of you. There are no guards, no bars, no torturers, or anything of the sort. No, you two are in a prison of your own disbelief. Only you hold the keys to your freedom. Now, I would give you more of a hint than that but it might spoil the fun. Good luck." Morgana faded away, but she made sure to leave her echoing laughter a good deal longer than her image.

"What was she talking about?" Wilson asked quietly.

"A prison of our own disbelief? What does that mean? There has to be another way."

Kash grabbed one of the torches from the wall and moved off down the corridor. Surprisingly to Wilson, it took her longer to make the loop than it did last time but she eventually came back around from the other direction. She spent the next hours studying the walls and every inch of the ceiling she could get the torchlight to touch. Wilson walked with her for a while, but eventually he sat down and tried to work through what Morgana had said. Her words meant that they held the keys to their cell. It made no sense. What key was she talking about if there wasn't even a door to open? He knew he was missing something but the more he tried to puzzle it out, the bigger of a blank he kept drawing. He fell asleep with his head resting on his chin, sitting against the wall in the corridor while Kash continued to walk circles, desperately hoping something would pop out at her; an idea, anything, but she had no answers either. She eventually curled up with her head in Wilson's lap and went to sleep.

Radcliffe thought the huge serpent fang looked quite nice on the wall behind the desk in his office back in the library. He had returned here in hopes of finding Kash and Wilson and as well as to drop off his trophy. He made sure that the enormous tooth was securely fixed to the wall and moved back out of his office. Kash and Wilson were nowhere to be found. A part of him knew they wouldn't be here, but there was another part of him praying he was wrong about that. There was really only one explanation for there being intruders to the castle. Morgana was actually telling the truth about that and had simply been waiting for an opportunity to trap him. It seemed an added bonus that she could go after Kash and Wilson while he was otherwise occupied. His blood boiled a bit at the thought that Morgana was clearly willing to kill him, but he was objectively grateful for having the test forced on him like that. Without the serpent inspired certainty of death, he knew he would never have discovered the path to all the magic he was now capable of. He was still going to have a few choice words for Morgana when he caught up with her though.

He assumed that if Kash and Wilson had found the castle then they were either dead already, or captured and jailed. He didn't remember seeing any dungeons whilst fleeing for his life in the castle but he figured there must be one. It was a magical structure that entrapped him with a giant snake, there had to be a couple cells in the bowels of the castle somewhere. He just hoped that if this was the case, that they weren't battling a giant serpent. He almost chuckled a little bit, but the seriousness of his contemplations dispelled this notion.

He didn't particularly fancy simply travelling to the castle magically. He didn't even know which story the castle was in but he had his suspicions. The castle was in the space used to imprison Morgana originally but she brought it into the story with her. Since he never travelled with her through his own power out of that particular story they must have travelled within the story. She said herself that she couldn't leave the story without him, nor him her. Therefore, the castle had to still be in *The Death of Arthur*. Since this was a collection of stories, they must be able to travel to each one individually, should they so choose, without leaving the actual book. Meaning that Kash and Wilson had to have made it into the proper story to have infiltrated the castle. Still, he felt like that would also mean that they didn't have much chance of defeating Morgana and were probably imprisoned or worse.

He moved back over to the table where he had returned to the library, correctly guessing this would be where the book itself was. The font was clearly altered to that of the tattoos and Radcliffe smiled as he picked up the work. He paused, thinking hard; the last time he had opened this he hadn't even been able to look at the first page and it had sucked him in. He braced himself for another sudden departure as he slowly opened to the table of contents. Curiously, there was a title near the top of the table of contents written in the same font as the cover and the tattoos: *The Witch's Gambit* gleamed at him in the fading daylight streaming through the window. He looked out and tried to remember how much time had passed in the real world since he had gone in and met Morgana the first time. He realized this was useless and gave up. He flipped to the page where this story began and started to read. He had suspected he would find his own name in it somewhere and the description of his battle with the snake amused him greatly. There wasn't anything about Kash and Wilson, however, and he was perplexed. He was certain he would be able to find some hint of them, but it was just him releasing Morgana and the deal they struck. His magical training was touched on, but Morgana disappeared from the text once she trapped him inside the castle. He scowled at the confirmation here in print right in front of him that Morgana had indeed trapped him, hoping he would die.

As he sat there praying he would be able to return to this story, he was stunned to see new words forming on the right side of the book where there was open space. He read just as fast as the words appeared and almost before they were done, he stood up and willed himself into the pages. The blue light swirled around him as he was squeezed into the darkness of the magical tunnel. He hit the ground running as he emerged in the story they were apparently creating as they went. He knew he had to speak with Merlin and try and confirm his suspicions about what it was going to take to actually defeat Morgana. Merlin had done it the first time and had created this spell. If there was a Morgana that existed within all her stories but also without, then he had to believe that Merlin could do the same.

He looked around and tried to figure out which direction the cave was in but didn't recognize anything around him. They had walked from the lake to the caves but the lake was nowhere in sight, and without that landmark, he didn't have the first clue where the prison caves of Nineve and Merlin were located. Plan b then, he decided. He closed his eyes and pictured the hills and the rocks and the boulders strewn about near where they had been. The blue lights rose about him and swirled around, grabbing him and squeezing him through the magical darkness. When he opened his eyes again, they took in a familiar scene. He had come to the cave where Nineve was and could feel her energy through the rock wall. Not knowing exactly where Merlin might be, he closed his eyes and attuned his mind outwards. There was something faint coming from his right and Radcliffe started off that way. The closer he got the stronger the energy was and he eventually came to a spot where the energy seemed to be directly on the other side of the rockface. There was a small hole similar to the one they had left on Nineve's prison which allowed him to see that there was indeed a cave on the other side. He closed his eyes and willed himself into the cave. The journey was quite short and less disorienting than most of the travel he was used to.

"Who's there?" An old man shuffled around the corner, his tattered robes barely hanging on to his thin frame.

"I am Dr. Arthur Radcliffe; you must be Merlin," Radcliffe returned with a smile.

"Arthur, thank the heavens. You've found me at last!" Radcliffe didn't know what kind of a reception he was expecting, but it certainly wasn't the fervent one he received.

"Umm, yeah…" he said, completely thrown off balance by the response.

"You must go to Nineve and persuade her to release me, only she can spring me from this interminable nothingness."

"Nineve?" Radcliffe echoed, again not sure what the man was talking about.

"Yes…" He paused to finally take in Radcliffe and his eyes took on a faraway look. The silence spiraled on and on until eventually the man turned and shuffled back around the corner.

"Merlin, wait!" Radcliffe called after his retreating back. He followed as the old wizard slowly moved into a different chamber of the cave which was better lit.

"I need to know something. Morgana imprisoned Nineve in the same way that she imprisoned you. She will have to be the one to release Nineve and she will never do that. I need to know how to defeat Morgana."

"Did she? Was *she* the one?" Merlin said, again with unexpected vigor and a look that clearly implicated he knew Radcliffe had a hand in Nineve's capture.

"Um…" Radcliffe stumbled over his words, understanding exactly what the wizard was indicating. A light bulb seemed to click in his head.

"Wait, does that mean that *I* could release Nineve?"

"Hmm," was all the reply he got and Merlin turned away once more, devolving into indecipherable mumbling. Radcliffe turned to take in the Merlin's cave prison and heard a gasp from behind him.

"What?" he asked as he spun back around.

"You bear the mark! Arthur, I knew you would come! You must go to Nineve and convince her to release me." The old wizard was clearly indicating the tattoos Radcliffe had only recently realized were on the back of his arm.

"We've been over this…" He trailed away and was about to give it up when Merlin spoke again.

"As it was in the beginning so it must be again. The unity of the spell will win in the end. To mend the past is your mission. Only as one will the future defeat the witch's ambition."

Radcliffe stared at the complete change in demeanor from the man and tried to decipher what he had said. Before he could get very far or think of a question to ask, Merlin simply vanished with a flash of white light. He moved back into the first chamber, bewildered. He was about to travel back to the other side of the rock wall himself when he heard voices.

"Excellent."

That was Morgana's voice but the subsequent wail of pain must have been Nineve. Did Morgana come and take both prisoners? What was she up to? He moved over to the small hole and tried to peer out but there was only darkness. Night had fallen while he was in Merlin's cave. He decided to wait a while before appearing on the other side of the wall, deciding not to immediately follow Morgana back to the castle. He would try to find a way in and get to Kash and Wilson, but it looked like Morgana was adding another couple of prisoners to her collection. He had to figure out a way to keep himself from becoming one of them.

Ch. 43 A Cage of Disbelief

Radcliffe thanked his newfound magical confidence and power for his aim being good enough to land him close to the castle but not near enough that Morgana would immediately know of his return. He was unable to wait for long at Merlin's cave and had traveled back as close as he dared. He kept to the sparse cover near the castle and wondered about the witch's magical alarms. Moving around to the other side, he could see the great stones that made up Stonehenge still perched atop the ramparts. From this angle, the proportions didn't make sense to him. The top of the castle between the two gate towers wasn't wide enough to hold the ancient structure. He had to remind himself that the castle itself was a magical construct and that none of it made much sense. With a shrug, he moved right to the base of the tower, the black stone gleaming in the soft moonlight.

The magical energy came to his call easier and easier each time. His smile lifted with his body as he felt himself become weightless. With a determined grimace, he reached out and pulled himself off the ground, finding handholds on the wall where he could. He made the top and began hauling himself over. He froze when he heard the voice he had been dreading.

"So, you have returned. Perfect. I thought you might have taken your newfound powers and ran, travelled to some faraway place to dominate, and rule."

"Not all crave dominion, as you do, Morgana," he replied coolly when he climbed all the way over and stood up straight to face the sorceress.

"So, you've returned for Kash and Wilson? Your personal ambition doesn't burn as bright?"

"I wouldn't go that far," he replied hoping to maintain his precarious ambiguity with the sorcerous.

"How far would you go? Should I throw you in a dungeon as well?" Morgana shot back quickly. Radcliffe could tell that her interest was earnest this time and she was still unsure of his allegiance.

"Why would you do that? We had a deal and as much as I really enjoy your company, I don't intend to go back on it." Radcliffe was hoping his mixture of seriousness and sarcasm would be enough to disarm her. She didn't respond immediately, rather seemed to be sizing him up, clearly trying to figure out whether or not he was lying.

"Anyways, forget about them for a second. Why would you set a giant snake on me? Are you serious? Let me guess, I either die or become a great sorcerer?" He glared at her, his anger lending a bit of indifference to her power.

"Well, did you? You seemed to have grasped the concept. How did you survive, I wonder?" Radcliffe went quiet for a moment, genuinely considering the transformation he had undergone in the bowels of the castle. The truth was that what Morgana had said to him directly after her fire serpent display was true. He had simply let go of his disbelief and trusted in what he had already accomplished and seen. It seemed such an easy mental switch in the moment with death staring him in the face. He had thought it an incredibly base and macabre teaching method but had objectively come to see the merit in it. Despite this, he was loath to tell Morgana any of that, certainly not that she had been right.

"You left the magical fires on the walls and I used them to defeat the snake." It didn't sound quite convincing to him, but he shot a defiant look at the witch anyway.

"Indeed," Morgana replied, narrowing her eyes and turning to walk towards the middle of Stonehenge. "Regardless, well done, hopefully, your magic has improved, at least marginally. Back to the task at hand. Kash and Wilson must give up their powers or rot in the castle forever. I have already told them that they must embrace their true nature, as you have done, or they will be unable to escape. Now I know that Kash is too stubborn to ever accept anything that someone else has told her; her companion may be a different story, however. I would like you to go speak with them. Tell them of your newfound powers and deliver to them my terms. Relinquish their abilities and I will send them back to their world unharmed."

Radcliffe wanted to inquire as to what she supposed would happen then but thought better of it. A part of him wanted to believe that she would leave him alone once she had the power to leave her story. Something told him this was the height naivete. Since the spell that allowed them to travel was used to imprison Morgana, he doubted very much whether he could entrap her there by himself. If Merlin's cryptic last words to him were anything to go by, then it would take all of them, he knew that. If he knew that, there was no way Morgana hadn't considered it. Therefore, she wouldn't stop until she had all of this power to herself. No logical argument he had could refute this. Therefore, he knew he should get away and speak with Kash and Wilson while she was still willing to let him.

It wasn't until he had made it down the steps of the nearest tower that he realized she hadn't told him where the dungeons were. When he had been trapped in the castle, he had simply come down the steps and the corridors eventually led him to the great hall. This didn't really seem helpful in getting him to the dungeons he assumed would be on the lowest level of the place. Everything seemed so normal, however, this time, more like the first time he had been in the castle. The rooms were actually open and there were passageways and different larger halls. He eventually found a staircase that wound downwards. Hoping that the green torches persisted all the way, he started down the steps.

After what felt like way too much time had passed and he was still descending with no end to the stairs in sight, he stopped and leaned against the wall, breathing somewhat harder than he wanted to be for simply walking down steps. He should've reached the dungeons by now, or at least something. He had to remind himself that the place was magical and Morgana loved playing games with him. She had mentioned that the only way for Kash and Wilson to escape would be to embrace their nature as characters, indicating that their prison was anything but traditional. On a whim, he closed his eyes and sent his own energy out into the castle, hoping to feel something, anything of Kash and Wilson. This ability seemed innate to him and didn't surprise him at all that he could do this. His magical intrepidness paid off almost immediately. He could see Wilson sitting with his back to the wall and his head on his chest, breathing deeply, fast asleep. Kash's head lay in his lap and they seemed almost at peace and Radcliffe stood there for a moment unsure if they would be able to perceive him in any way. This question was answered quickly when Kash opened her eyes and sat up with a start. She looked his way and her eyes went wide.

"Radcliffe!" she exclaimed.

"So, you can see me? Perfect. Hello, Ms. Kashmir. Wilson," he said in greeting as Wilson awoke and stood up as well.

"What are you doing here? How are you here? What happened to you?"

Kash asked one question right on top of the other. Her tone was quite desperate and Radcliffe could tell their imprisonment was weighing on them greatly. He pitied their predicament and was worried they wouldn't accept the truth that would unlock their cage.

"Morgana sent me, magic, and let's just say the witch can be quite persuasive," he replied, taking her questions in succession. The looks they shot him didn't indicate this was sufficient so he continued before they could say anything.

"Guys, I am sorry, I never meant for things to go this way."

"O yeah, well, throw in with one of literature's worst villains and things tend to spiral out of your control," Wilson chimed in exasperatedly, despite not quite believing Radcliffe had done anything of the sort.

"I didn't "throw in" with her. It's more of a coerced understanding. She has helped me to learn how to wield magic like she does, but she also wants something from you two."

"We figured. You know she wants the same thing from you, don't you?"

"Of course, I really don't think she ever intended to coexist with me. She has already tried to eliminate me once, claiming it to be a test. She also has Merlin and Nineve somewhere in the castle. I was actually in the castle as well, trapped, not unlike yourselves. She set a giant snake on me hoping I would simply be eaten."

"How were you not?" Kash replied quickly.

"Magic, but that doesn't really matter. Your predicament does."

"Well, if you can do magic, why not just use it to get us out of here?"

"I wish I could. I feel like the magic is designed to elicit the same response that her trap did from me, if it is a bit less intense. Regardless, I cannot get you out. This prison is magical and only the two of you have the power to escape."

"O really? Don't tell me you're going to start spouting off that "prison of your own disbelief" crap?"

"Well, that's not a bad way to phrase it. Is that what Morgana told you?"

"Yes, those were her words."

"I think you should consider them. Perhaps, consider the possibility that anything is possible. I mean look at what you two have done already. Really think about it. You met Dracula and Zeus, you even travelled beyond the end of the pages. You're currently being imprisoned by a character in a book. All these fantastical, seemingly insane ideas are irrefutable fact. It all points to one thing and until the both of you accept that, we'll be stuck here. There is another option for you, but I doubt you will be motivated to simply give up your powers. I also doubt very seriously she will keep her word that she will just let you go."

"*We'll* be stuck here? Are you a prisoner as well?"

"Not exactly, my energy is here, not my physical body. That's laying on an endless staircase somewhere in the castle. But it will take all our combined power to defeat Morgana. I have spoken with Merlin and he seemed somewhat aware of what was going on. One thing is clear, though: that the full power of the spell is required to banish Morgana back to where we found her. We have to do it together; it's the only way."

"Well, I am not just handing over anything to Morgana, but how did you speak to Merlin? Wasn't he imprisoned in a cave?"

"Well, yes, how would you know? Did *you* speak with him?"

"Yes, but he was completely incoherent then," Kash replied exasperatedly. Radcliffe breathed a deep sigh, he felt he was doing a poor job of convincing them.

"Look, none of that matters until you guys escape this prison. You must embrace the truth. We are part of a story. Our own. Morgana has it all wrong. She thinks she is shackled to the same traits that her authors wrote into her and resents them for it. She wants to change the various stories so she can rewrite them herself, how she sees fit. What she doesn't understand is that we are creating a new story. It's true, I saw it in the table of contents of *The Death of Arthur* just before I travelled back into that very same story. Guys, we are characters in this story and we control the outcome. The things we choose to do, the things we *choose* to believe will shape the end of this tale. You simply have to let go of the need for it to make sense. Stop seeing the world as it should be and do something about the way it actually is."

He went quiet and Wilson and Kash remained silent as well. Radcliffe could tell that his speech was finally having an effect. He figured that Wilson would come around eventually, but was skeptical that Kash, the scientist, would ever be able to suspend her logical mind. It took him facing down a horrific death to come to terms with all of this. What would it take for them?

"I have to get back to Morgana or she will start to suspect me even more than I think she already does. Think about what I said." With that, his image slowly faded away as he allowed his energy to find his physical body once more.

Ch. 44 Suspended Disbelief

"Wait!" Kash called after the fading image. She turned back to Wilson when Radcliffe didn't return. "What now? Can you believe any of that?" She looked at Wilson sharply when he didn't immediately reply.

"Well, to be honest, Kash. Yes, I can. He wasn't saying anything we haven't heard before. Morgana has been saying the same things, Sherlock Holmes even said something very similar. I don't think Arthur would actually throw in with Morgana. I think he was being earnest."

"Arthur?"

"Yes, his first name isn't doctor," Wilson replied with a grin, hoping to lighten the mood a bit, but Kash's ensuing smile was more forced than genuine.

"Merlin never mentioned anything like this when I read off the spell the first time. He mentioned Morgana but never that it would turn us into characters, if that is indeed what has actually happened. I still can't wrap my head around it. We can travel back to the real world at any moment. How can we be characters in a story if we do that? What book is that being recorded in?" Kash finished her small speech in a triumphant voice, but it didn't seem to be having the desired effect on her companion. He still wore a curious expression.

"I actually asked something similar when I discussed this with Holmes and he made a point about relativity that was interesting. We've proven that the story reality is just as real as ours, haven't we? I mean, we've been through some crazy situations. I'm sure Aeneas would not have been gentle with me, the way he was chasing me, should he have caught me. And what of the seemingly magical auras around characters? There were times I thought that we were having the same effect on them. Many of them commented about our "strange way"; maybe this is what they were referring to. We also have an aura of energy around us because we too, are characters. Why can't it be true? Especially, if it's the only way we are going to get out of here. Sure, Morgana could be lying to us, but do you really think Radcliffe would? I don't. He knows how dangerous Morgana is and besides he said he couldn't defeat her alone, that should at least indicate he isn't helping her, right?"

"Alright, say for a moment that I believe I am a character in a story. What then? Do we just decide to go knock on Morgana's door, "Hey, we've decided we're characters, can we go now?" O that's right, there's no door!"

"I think one will most likely appear to us once we truly accept it. Life has been likened to a story thousands of times over the years in countless philosophical discussions. Just think of it like that, we're going to take back control of our own story and write our own ending. Isn't that what Morgana wants, isn't that why her jealousy has driven her to imprison us? We already have that power just by being in the stories. You thought you could in the *Iliad*, what has changed?"

Kash didn't know how to answer that. He was right, she had to admit. Her ambition burned strong in Troy when she was confident she could sway the outcome of the story. This seemed different to her, however. This was magic they were talking about. Sure, it was quite magical to be able to travel into the stories themselves and she had witnessed some pretty fantastical things, but to think that she was a character and could produce magic like Morgana still seemed a stretch of her imagination. She looked at Wilson, who seemed to have already accepted it as the truth. She knew he was certainly on her side. No, she could trust Wilson, he had been there from the beginning. She would certainly never forget their time in Troy and realized in that moment how much she was coming to love him. It was this, more than anything, that convinced her to trust in Wilson if not in anything else that was happening. She nodded and sat down, closing her eyes and taking a deep breath.

Wilson seemed to understand and sat down next to her, closing his eyes as well and trying to mentally convince himself he believed in what he was saying. It all seemed to make sense to him though and he didn't find it very challenging. He just hoped that Kash could allow herself to believe as well.

■■■

Radcliffe found her standing in the circle of Stonehenge, back outside on top of the castle. He moved closer to her and she spoke before he could announce himself.

"So, have they agreed to my terms?"

"You could've just told me the nature of the prison instead of sending me searching around the castle."

"What would be the fun in that?" she replied, turning to face him and flashing her trademark evil grin.

"No, they have not agreed to give up their powers. I think you will find them somewhat more resilient than that."

"O, you think so, do you? Well, it doesn't matter anyways." Her tone took on a serious note.

"What do you mean? Why not?" he replied, concerned.

"It is time, physician. You must choose whether to join me or find yourself locked away forever." As she said this, she lifted her arms and two shimmering, translucent diamonds of greenish light floated up the castle wall and over the ramparts, coming to a halt just behind the witch. Inside them were Nineve and Merlin, trapped. Nineve's eyes went wide and she started banging on the walls of her prison and screaming. Not a sound emitted from the curious jail cell and Radcliffe looked to Merlin who was sitting cross-legged, eyes closed, seemingly without a care in the world.

"Join them, or join me. What will it be?"

"All I have to do is give you my tattoos, am I right?"

"You could die and then my castle will magically transfer them to me as is about to happen with your friends, downstairs. I brought Nineve and Merlin here along as insurance. Refuse and before I kill you, I will make you watch all of them die first."

"What do you mean, "as is about to happen downstairs", I thought you said that if they believed they would be free?"

"So I did and so they shall be. However, there are more traps and snares awaiting them once they regain the castle proper. You've seen yourself what horrors it can create. Not so fast!" she screamed as Radcliffe ran for the tower door. Her spell lifted the man from his feet and brought him crashing back down in front of her. Her look of surprise was complete, however, when he retaliated before he even stood up. She was blasted from her feet by a huge rush of air and rolled to a halt just before falling over the edge. She got to her feet shakily, murder in her eyes. With a wave of the witch's arm the two prisons of light slowly rose above the rocks of Stonehenge and began to circle the battlefield slowly. This done, Morgana began chanting softly and waving her arms in circles.

Radcliffe knew something more sinister was coming and he immediately imagined a rock wall in front of him. It materialized just in time to take the full blast of a lightning strike that still jolted him and sent him sprawling to the ground, bits and pieces of his shattered shield laying all around him.

"Pitiful," he heard Morgana say as she moved closer. He got to his feet and retreated a couple of steps, trying to think of what to do next. He had never been in a fight like this before, hadn't been in many fights at all, but certainly never one where magic was his only defense, especially against someone who was much better at it than he was. That was it, he thought, as he hardened his resolve and watched Morgana stalk closer. She was back within the ring of Stonehenge and was sending a look of revulsion and loathing Radcliffe's way that he thought should have him dead already. She began to chant but he was ready for her. Just when she flung her arms out at him, he pushed back with all his magical might. The brilliant fireball she had conjured stopped halfway between them and exploded with a bang like fireworks. They were both thrown backwards by the force of the blast and Radcliffe was vaguely aware of flying rock and debris from the stones of the ancient structure taking the brunt of the fireball.

He struggled to his feet and looked around. He couldn't see Morgana amidst the smoke and dust, but noticed that he was much closer to the door than before, so, he raced to it and down the tower steps before Morgana could launch another assault his way.

Ch. 45 Magical Menagerie

How long they sat in quiet contemplation, neither could say, but when Kash opened her eyes, she thought there was something different about the corridor. It physically looked the same, but there was an energy in the air that she was sure she wasn't aware of earlier. She looked over to Wilson to see a curious expression forming on his face as well. Before either could figure out exactly what was different, there came an incredible roar off in the distance.

"Um, what was that?" Kash asked.

Wilson looked at her incredulously for a second and shrugged his shoulders. He stepped past her and grabbed a torch from the wall, still merrily burning green flame. He motioned for Kash to follow him and moved off down the corridor. Just as he expected, there was something quite different this time. Many doors and other passages were now visible and Kash took the lead and moved down one of them, desperate to be away from the first tunnel they woke up in. Unfortunately, this new path didn't look much different. It didn't seem to be looping, however, as the paintings and tapestries on the wall continued to change. Wilson thought to slow and study some of these and Kash was just walking back to him, taking a second to notice he had slowed his pace.

"What's up?" she asked.

"I think some of these paintings are of scenes from Arthur's stories and thus Morgana's. Do you think we might be able to travel to them?"

"We might, but our goal isn't to flee. We can't run from her forever; besides, we're still in the castle and undoubtably cannot travel out of it magically. Hopefully, we can avoid whatever roared just a bit ago and find her and Radcliffe quickly." Wilson figured her logic was sound and was just about to say as much when he saw a bright reddish light moving towards them from around the nearest corner. He pointed it out to Kash silently and they hugged the wall, waiting with dread filling their minds. Whatever they were expecting it certainly wasn't a hound wreathed in bright orange fires. It stopped, immediately noticing them. A low growl escaped its bared teeth just before it bounded at them, quick as a flash. Kash pushed Wilson aside and dropped to the floor as the leaping dog flew over them. She scrambled to her feet, not even waiting for the beast to turn around and come back at them. She pulled Wilson along as they ran for their lives, the hell hound in pursuit.

They turned another corner and this part of the passage ran straight farther than their eyes could see. There were no doors on either side as they thundered down the hallway. Kash's thoughts were careening from panic to desperation to fear and back. Only her adrenaline kept her moving and just as the hound caught up to them and leapt for the back of Wilson's neck, an explosion rocked the corridor and threw them both roughly to the stone. Something enormous had come barreling through the wall, smashing the hell hound under huge blocks of black stone. Whatever it was had already moved off the way they had come. The dust was so thick that Wilson could only make out a giant shadow following its owner around the corner. He didn't wait around to ask questions about their fortune and helped Kash scramble from the rubble. They hurried in the opposite direction, eager to put as much distance between themselves and the scene as possible.

"What is going on?" Wilson breathed heavily as they jogged down the corridor that continued straight, seemingly forever.

"I'm not sure. Did you get a look at our savior?" Kash panted back and held out her arm indicating they should rest for a second. This bit of the corridor seemed deserted, so they leaned against the wall and tried to catch their breath.

"I did, actually. Remember what Radcliffe said about battling a snake? Well, I think there's another one and its bigger than anything I believed possible until just a little bit ago." Wilson finished his response with a weak smile.

"Great!" Kash said sarcastically, drawing out her pronunciation to emphasize her tone. "What about the hound?" Kash went on more seriously.

"Honestly, it looked like it could've been from the Baskerville story, but that strikes me as really odd. I suppose that there are such beasts that aren't tricks like in Sherlock's story that exist here. I might be mistaken, but it looks like Morgana has loosed a number of different magical creatures into the castle. Obviously, a failsafe in case we *did* escape the first prison."

The blood drained from Kash's face as Wilson finished his thought. He spun around to look behind him and was immediately hot on Kash's heels as their flight began anew. A gigantic boar came charging along behind them, intent on running them down. The confirmation that Morgana had indeed unleashed monsters into the halls to kill them did nothing to make Wilson feel better. He knew they couldn't keep this up and they certainly couldn't turn and fight the thing. If he wasn't mistaken, it was a Troit Boar, another magical animal from Arthurian legend that would do more than just skewer them to bits. These contemplations flew from his mind with his footing as he went down hard and slid a couple of feet. Kash skidded to a halt and screamed his name as she moved back for him. He knew in that moment that he had doomed both of them.

■ ■ ■

Thinking Morgana would be chasing him, Radcliffe didn't hesitate when he reached the bottom of the steps, rather, went right, put his head down and kept moving. He had chosen at random without even considering which way he was going. After running down the corridor that seemed to continually curve left for a long way, he stopped, hands on his knees, sucking in air in big gulps. He listened for footsteps from the direction he had run as hard as he could but there was nothing. It wasn't until he relaxed a bit, thinking Morgana must've gone left, that he noticed his surroundings. They were uncannily familiar and the hairs on the back of his neck stood up suddenly. He was just deciding that she had trapped him once more when he heard a blood-curdling shriek from somewhere in the castle.

He had no idea what that might be and he didn't think he had time to consider it anyways. He just prayed it wasn't another enormous serpent. He had had enough of snakes for one lifetime. His first thought was to find Kash and Wilson. Supposing they had broken out of the first prison and been inserted into one similar to his, they would be in trouble. Despite them most likely finally accepting themselves as characters in this story, he doubted very much they would possess the magic to defeat a monster such as he had. He didn't even want to consider the possibility that they were not in the same space as he was. The castle was indeed quite magical, but he was hoping his abilities to travel could put him right next to them. He closed his eyes and sent his mind in search of their energy.

Luckily, he felt them immediately. Their fear and desperation echoed through the halls of the castle like a foghorn to his newly heightened sensibilities. Unfortunately, he also felt the emanations of many magical beings, too many magical beings. He hadn't the time to consider it and willed himself into the magical darkness.

■■■

Wilson slowly opened his eyes, completely shocked he wasn't currently being eviscerated by razor sharp tusks. Kash was rising to her feet beside him and someone else.

"Arthur! What just happened?"

"He just saved our asses, that's what," Kash replied, breathlessly.

"Was that a boar? A troit boar, maybe?" Radcliffe asked.

"I think so—" Wilson started but was interrupted.

"Does it matter? We have to find a way out of here. We can't run forever," Kash said intensely.

"You're probably right. I think it ultimately lucky that we can travel magically through the corridors. I won't even try to escape the castle in that manner, I would be beyond shocked if Morgana hadn't thought of that. Apparently, she has released a menagerie of magical creatures into the halls. She would rather them do her dirty work for her, I guess."

"What do you mean her "dirty work"?" Wilson asked.

"She told me that if we die here in the castle, its magic will transfer our tattoos to her and she will have our power. Thus, why I am suspecting she took it easy on me just now on the roof and let me run down here to find you two."

"Wait a minute, she took it easy on you? Were you fighting her? How?" Kash asked confused.

"Yes, I believe she did. My magical powers are growing but pale in comparison to hers. Fireballs and lightning bolts are all well and good, but she pulled this place from the Black into a story. Her power is beyond anything I can imagine. That's why we have to survive this and defeat her together. It's the only way."

Kash let it go, still wondering about Radcliffe performing spells, but didn't voice any more questions. They moved off down the passage behind him as quickly and quietly as they could. It didn't take much of this sneaking around for Kash's curiosity to outweigh her caution and she asked aloud to both of them or neither, if they had a plan.

"Well, there was a great hall the last time I was trapped like this. That is where I encountered the snake the first time. That must be the source of the magic that kept them all from wandering the halls in the first place. Perhaps something there will give us a clue as to how to defeat this particular spell." They headed off down the passage once more, but hadn't made it very far when another creature cantered out of a side door up ahead of them. It stopped and stared at them almost as hard as they were staring. It was a unicorn. Amidst all the chaos, they had to pause and admire its beauty. The moment passed quickly, however, as yet another creature came out of a door in between them and stood to face the trio. Even Radcliffe, with his extensive knowledge of Arthurian tales, was unable to put a name on this one, but it was half man and half horse and had a sword for one arm and a lance for the other. It noticed them and immediately charged with a ferocious yell.

Luckily, the unicorn thundered down the hall at the same time and as they dove aside, it skewered the other magical creature on its incredible horn. Lifting its head, the unicorn thrashed around for a second then tossed the creature aside like a rag doll. It turned back around and lowered its horn to charge back the way it had come. Any thoughts that this might be a friendly beast flew from them when another pass almost trampled all three of them. The corridor wasn't exactly wide and the unicorn was adjusting its path to the side this time as it turned and charged again.

A blue light shot out from behind Kash, who was waiting for the last moment to jump aside, and she saw Radcliffe zoom out in front of them directly in the unicorn's path. She didn't even have time to scream as he was skewered, or at least she thought he was, but the unicorn stopped and reared its head like before and thrashed around. Radcliffe was nowhere in sight, however, and Kash felt a tug on her arm that turned her around.

"Look, I think we can get past this one if we simply calm it down. Unicorns are fierce creatures if you enrage them. We just need to convince it we mean no harm," Radcliffe explained into the stunned faces of the others.

"What?!" they both exclaimed simultaneously over the shrieks of the still thrashing animal.

"Our tattoos have power Morgana doesn't, remember? Merlin said something about our combined powers being stronger than hers. Just focus on the image of you petting the unicorn as hard as you can and I'll do the rest." They both were still very confused, but could do nothing but trust him when the unicorn noticed that they were still alive. It lowered its head to charge and Kash and Wilson closed their eyes, concentrating with all their might. Radcliffe stood to face the unicorn and began waving his arm around vertically in the air as if he was circling an invisible lasso. He imagined an actual lasso and just as he swung his arm out towards the unicorn, a rope of brilliant white light emitted from his hand and wrapped around the neck of the majestic creature as it thundered past while the trio once more tried to be as small as possible. This time, Radcliffe held on and was only dragged a couple of feet as the animal slowed and turned. It was visibly relaxed and they could feel the tension leaving as the energy of the moment ebbed a bit. The unicorn moved up to them slowly and Radcliffe reached up confidently to stroke its gleaming mane.

"What just happened?" Wilson asked as he too reached up to pat the animal gently on its back. Kash walked between the men and looked the creature directly in the eye, slowly reaching her hand out to run it down the creature's head and to the base of its horn.

"I'm not sure exactly how the magic worked, but I believe we convinced it we wouldn't hurt it. Ask if you can ride it," Radcliffe said matter-of-factly.

"Wh—"

"Don't think about it, remember? Let go your disbelief and look it in the eyes. Focus on the image of you riding it and I believe it will give you a sign whether it will allow this or not. We need to make it to the great hall and with this wonderous creature on our side we have an advantage," Radcliffe interrupted. His logic made sense so they did what they were told. Surprisingly enough, the great creature stared into their eyes for quite a while before eventually lowering its front knees to the ground. They took this as a good sign and gingerly clambered up behind its head, Kash in front of Wilson.

"What about you?" Kash asked Radcliffe as the animal rose back to its full height. A smile erupted on the man's face and he looked at them with a wink.

"Don't worry about me," he said and the bright light of his magical lasso appeared again. He looped it around the unicorn's neck and subsequently around them as well. Moving behind them, he closed his eyes and imagined himself weightless, just as he had done outside, what seemed hours before. He felt his feet leave the ground, but didn't have any time at all to revel in his magic as the unicorn leapt ahead, pulling him along with it. He barely managed to stay upright as he skied behind the charging unicorn. He could hear Wilson's yelp of surprise at their speed and Kash's squeal of delight. Not knowing how else to impart their desired destination to their magical steed, he simply filled his concentration with the image of the great hall and he supposed the subsequent neighing from the unicorn was its way of letting him know it understood. The magical creature put its head down and sped on as if it knew exactly where to go.

This belief was confirmed moments later when the animal took a left turn, seemingly, at random and ran down another passage. They weren't long for this path, however, as the unicorn barreled through an intersection and peeled to the right. They certainly hadn't seen anything like that coming together of ways yet and were encouraged. This feeling vanished like a popped bubble as the unicorn skidded to a halt and Radcliffe's momentum rushed him past the companions and the creature itself. He barely caught himself before the length of the rope played out and whipped him back. When he settled himself and looked ahead to see why they had stopped, he jumped back in surprise and horror.

A giant raven, the size of a human, blocked their path. It cawed at them and then vanished in a puff of feathers and smoke to be replaced by a black-haired woman in tattered robes. She shrieked at them and began waving her arms around, clearly spellcasting. On instinct, Radcliffe conjured a rock wall between the witch and himself and the others. Just like on the roof, this was blasted away by a dark purple light, but the pieces didn't fly at them rather melted to the ground, vanishing before their eyes. Radcliffe didn't wait around to see what she would conjure next and screamed at the unicorn in his mind to charge. It responded immediately, bounding forward and lowering its horn. The witch leapt aside and they thundered past, Radcliffe once again sledding along behind them. He waved his arm as they passed and sent another blast of magical light at the witch. It did nothing to harm the woman, but blinded her enough that by the time her sight recovered, they were gone.

Their brilliant steed sped around the corner and the ceiling flew away above them as they cantered into the great hall. Before Radcliffe could get his bearings, an incredible shriek filled their ears. They looked around to see another gigantic serpent, a perfect likeness to the one that Radcliffe had battled earlier, rising to its full gigantic height and slithering their way quickly. The unicorn ran to the side of the hall, dragging Radcliffe with it. Just as the snake reached them and reared up to begin its mesmerizing dance, another explosion from behind them threw them all to the ground. Even the unicorn lost its footing as the ground itself rumbled and shook. Rocks and debris and pieces of the wall rained down on them. Kash dragged Wilson to his feet and pushed him aside as another huge piece of black stone smashed down between them and tumbled away. She coughed and tried to find her feet once more.

"Radcliffe?!" she called grabbing Wilson's offered hand as he helped her to her feet. She looked around to see him running at them, blood pouring down his head from a nasty cut where he must have been hit by the debris. She looked at Wilson quickly to see a number of superficial scrapes and bruises and he seemed to be favoring one leg but otherwise seemed intact.

"Go! Go! Go!" Radcliffe screamed at them as he sprinted towards them. The dust had settled and cleared a bit and they could see the source of the continued rumbling and shrieking. An enormous green-scaled monstrosity had smashed through the wall and locked its mighty jaws around the snake's body just below the throat. The snake wailed in the agony of its death throes as the dragon swung its head around with enough force to sever the snake in two and send blood and viscera flying in every direction. The great beast let out a tremendous roar that knocked the watching trio to the floor once more. This broke them from their awe and all three scrambled over the rocks and stones to put as much distance between them and the dragon as possible.

"RUN!!!" Wilson screamed needlessly as they all made for the other end of the hall. They ran out of space quickly and skidded to a halt at the unremarkable stone wall. Their heads turned in unison to see the dragon rearing its head and sucking in its breath. They all knew what was coming as they took a couple of forced steps towards the behemoth with the rest of the air that it was sucking in. Just before they were roasted alive, Kash heard a voice in her head.

"TO ME!!!"

Completely on instinct, she grabbed the other two by the wrist and willed herself to magically travel. She didn't know her destination but filled her mind with what she had heard, blindly trusting in the voice her subconscious thought was somewhat familiar. She felt herself squeeze into the magical darkness and saw the swirl of blue light swallow them up. The last image she saw before being pulled away was the great dragon's head rocketing forward blasting bright orange flame across the hall and straight for them. She even felt a moment of intense heat before it all went black.

Ch. 46 Back to the Beginning

"What just happened?" Radcliffe asked when they all emerged safely from the magical darkness. He looked around to see they were back outside, on the roof, within the ring of Stonehenge. Morgana was nowhere in sight, but he knew she must be around somewhere.

"I'm not sure, I heard a voice and reacted, purely on instinct," Kash said, looking around. "Is this Stonehenge? On top of the castle?" she added, perplexed.

"Yes, indeed it is, my dear Kashmir." There was only one voice that seemed so silky yet full of venom at the same time. "The real question is how you escaped my trap. I only know of one way and you certainly cannot have accessed the magical portal. My magical pets should've destroyed all of you. I suppose it doesn't matter. It was always going to come to this, wasn't it? Ever since you found yourself in the Black, my prison. I knew as soon as you appeared there that you were my ticket out. Merlin's magic is powerful, however," she said as she waved her arm and motioned with her head above her.

They looked around to see Nineve and Merlin still encapsulated within their magical prisons. The green diamond like structures continued to revolve slowly around the top of Stonehenge. Kash felt a surge of recognition as she looked at the peacefully meditating Merlin floating in circles above them. That voice must've been his. Was he still able to use his magic from within the floating prison? She was almost certain he had somehow created the pathway that Kash had willed herself and the others into to escape the dragon. With a nod and a smile, she tuned back in to Morgana's soliloquy.

"It was never going to be as simple as you taking me with you into other stories. I knew from our first conversation that your opinion of me would not allow for this, so I let you go, but planted the seed in your mind that my path was justified. I could not have anticipated what happened next, however, and it changed everything. Dear Radcliffe, here, returned in your stead and a new plan formed. He seemed much more malleable and less influenced by Merlin's rhetoric. His desire for power led us down this path, do you not see. Even he agrees, magic is not to be maligned. We are not meant to be afraid of power like that fool up there who cannot even open his eyes to witness his own doom. Why should my authors, the very same ones who wrote of Merlin, make of me a villain when he was glorified? I will have your magic and change my stories to what they should have been. So, you have one last chance to join me, to give up your abilities and I will spare your lives." She finished with a stern look as if she actually expected them to comply, after everything she had put them through.

Surprising everyone, including himself a little bit, Radcliffe laughed in her face. "You still haven't figured it out, have you?" he said as he waved his arms forcefully and both Nineve and Merlin's prisons winked out of existence, dropping them both to the top of separate rocks of the ancient structure. Morgana looked around in shock and alarm as Radcliffe continued. Kash saw a small blue light emitting from Wilson's arm and the back of Radcliffe's. She didn't have to look to know that her tattoos were glowing a bit as well.

"The blame for your evil lays not with your authors, witch. Do you not, even now, feel the hatred in your heart? What would your goal be, supposing you have our abilities? You say you would change your own stories for the good, but I don't think you would. It has been your choices, your actions, and the path you *chose* that led you into darkness. One action at a time you built your own character. I laugh because you are the one who actually made me see the truth. I don't think you quite intended for your trap to empower me so. I understood, in those moments, that we all create our own story. Every day, no matter what world we're in, no matter whose story it is. That's what free will is. We are our own authors and we write our own tales. You're right again, Morgana, we shouldn't fear this power, but embrace our own truth and our own potential to create. Creation is the most powerful of magic, that's why I could only manipulate your spells at first. I didn't understand.

"I have to thank you for opening my eyes, though. Your example has proven that you have shackled yourself to your evil and your hatred, blinding you to the truth that even in the beginning you were the same character. You crave dominion over Albion, over Avalon even. All your stories were about your attempts to defeat Arthur and his knights. That's why Merlin wanted him to wield this magic in the first place. He knew you could never defeat Arthur and were destined to harbor hatred in your heart forever. Knowing that you would never stop, he did the only thing he could. Merlin saw that your choices would always condemn you, no matter what story you were in or what story you tried to change. Thus, he created the spell that imprisoned you."

"Very clever, physician, but you've forgotten one very important thing. I am still more powerful than all of you combined!" she screamed at him in defiance and launched into spellcasting, her arms waving furiously. Radcliffe simply motioned for Kash and Wilson to stay close and began slowly walking towards Morgana. All three of their tattoos glowed blue and Morgana's tremendous blast of green magical light simply dispersed around them and disappeared into nothingness.

"You've underestimated me, Morgana, you've underestimated all of us. You never learned from Merlin the most important thing about magic. This power isn't a tool, it's a gift, and power like this used in the wrong manner corrupts and destroys. Merlin was ever your better and your jealousy blinded you. I imagine he saw it even before your banishment." Radcliffe began waving his arms in slow circles, the tattoos glowing fiercely.

"SILENCE!!" she screamed and blasted them with a gigantic fireball but their magical defense held and they continued to move forward unscathed. Morgana backpedaled a bit and Wilson could see real fear on her features for the first time. She stopped when she reached one of the giant stones encircling them. She closed her eyes and reached out to touch the rock, chanting all the while.

"Arthur! The stones!" Merlin shouted down from above causing Morgana to pause and look around in alarm.

"Arthur?!" she exclaimed. "You!" she shrieked, looking back to Radcliffe and furiously resuming her spellcasting. Kash and Wilson were confused for a second before the realization hit them at the same time. Merlin, and Morgana, apparently, thought that Radcliffe was King Arthur returned. The once and future king. Kash almost laughed aloud at the absurdity of it all but was distracted when she felt her feet leave the ground. She looked around, bewildered, to see Wilson and Radcliffe flying beside her to the side. Morgana suddenly opened her eyes and cackled madly as a great wind blew up around them. The sky went dark and the clouds roiled threateningly. With a boom of thunder, an incredible lightning stroke erupted in the middle of Stonehenge, blasting them to the ground and jolting them with sparks. Regaining their feet, they had to dive aside as more lightning arced down inside the circle.

"We have to get her back inside the ring and use the magic of the ancient structure to aid us. Its strength should be enough for the tattoos to combine with and banish the witch back to her original prison," Radcliffe explained quickly. They looked around to see that the lightning only seemed to be striking within the ring of stones meaning they were safe, but making it quite difficult to get Morgana back inside.

"Your arrogance will be your downfall, Pendragon," Morgana shrieked as she stalked towards them. She waved her arm and Wilson lifted from the ground and was thrown back within the ring of Stonehenge. Kash watched as the lightning raced down from the dark sky, almost as if in slow motion, to rip into Wilson's prone form. She screamed in fear and alarm but was flushed with relief almost immediately as there was a small blue glow and Wilson's tattoos seemed to suck the lightning up, leaving him unscathed.

Radcliffe didn't even look that way but responded in kind just as she finished her spell and magically tossed the sorceress back into the ring. He grabbed Kash by the wrist and rushed to Wilson as fast as he could. Pulling the man to his feet, all three of them turned to face Morgana as the thunder roared and the lightning crashed down all around them. Hatred was splayed on her features and they could tell her rage had completely consumed her.

"You see, Morgana, your magic is mighty, but we are in control of this story. We decide the outcome, not you. Our creation outdoes anything you can conjure." Radcliffe looked back to Kash and Wilson as he finished and nodded. They felt their tattoos burn white hot and watched them subsequently glow blue again as they lifted from their bodies and floated over to Radcliffe. Attaching themselves to the man, they glowed fiercely and gleamed like they were freshly inked into his skin. He waved his arms in one big circle and threw his outstretched palms in her direction. A great swirl of blue light erupted from his hands and crashed over Morgana, swirling around her. The last thing they saw was the scowl of complete contempt and hatred she shot their way as she and the blue light faded away to nothing.

The lightning stopped and the thunder abated. The sky cleared and the sun shone through the darkness. There was a great rumbling and they had to hold on to the rocks around them to keep from falling. The castle was descending back into the ground beneath them and Kash noticed a flash of white light to her left as Nineve vanished. She wondered at this, but figured the lady of the lake was simply returning home. When everything stopped rumbling and the castle had disappeared completely, Merlin walked over to them and smiled. Without a word he pushed on the center of the largest stone nearby and they were all squeezed into the magical darkness in a swirl of blue light.

■■■

Kash smiled when she saw that Merlin had brought them back to the chamber where she had originally read the scroll and gained the magical power to travel between the stories. Merlin was standing exactly where she had first met him and she heard his voice echo out of the past in the back of her mind about being led to the beginning.

"So, you did know who I was when I visited you in *The Death of Arthur* where Nineve had trapped you. By the way, where is she?" she asked the wizard happily. He looked at her curiously but didn't say anything. Radcliffe and Wilson looked at her a little confused as well and she mumbled something about it not being important.

"I thought I saw her disappear in a flash of white light," Wilson spoke up in support of Kash's query.

"Dear Nineve has returned to the safety of her home, fear not. Well, here we are, back where we started," Merlin eventually addressed them all. "When our dear Kash originally read my spell and set you all on this path I was afraid it might come to battling Morgana. That was what the spell was designed for in the first place. It simply needed a caretaker; it could not lay dormant here in this ancient place of power forever. Eventually, Morgana would find a way to escape as her magical prison's strength faded. Thus, when Ms. Kashmir stumbled upon this chamber, I knew my only chance would be to bestow upon her the choice to wield this power."

"Wait a second, you didn't exactly give me a choice. I was whisked down here and thought I was dreaming."

"There is always a choice and you have made yours. Look at your skin, where are your tattoos?" Kash looked down and pulled her shirt up a bit. She looked to Wilson to indicate he should look but he shook his head. She studied his arms to see about his but they too, were missing.

"What...?" Kash didn't know what to think until the image of the tattoos sealing themselves to Radcliffe's skin turned her gaze his way. There they were, all of them, in various places on his body. His lifted shirt revealed that every story they had travelled to was written on him in small letters around his torso. Kash could see a depiction of a small scroll off to the side of this that looked akin to the original scroll she had read from. She looked back to Merlin to see him smiling at her once more.

"I don't understand," she said needlessly for the look on her face told the others as much.

"Arthur, do you?" he asked simply. Radcliffe looked at him with a wry smile.

"I do. This power was intended for one. We were only able to defeat Morgana because we brought all the magic back to the place it originated. All the tattoos together at Stonehenge brought forth the original magic which was specifically designed to counter Morgana. She was powerless against us. Her magical imagination is a bit wilder than mine, however, which is why I didn't realize at first that we were protected. But when the lightning couldn't touch Wilson, I knew. There must be a great and powerful magic here at Stonehenge."

"Indeed, this is the most magical place in all of Britain. I knew it was the only place my magic would be strong enough to defeat Morgana and banish her back to the in between, and so it proved with you." Merlin nodded with another grin.

"That still doesn't explain why Radcliffe channeled all the power and not Kash," Wilson chimed in.

"As for that, Mr. Wilson, Arthur said it best when he told Morgana of free will. It is our choices that write our story. Our intentions and decisions that weave our tale. He chose to accept the responsibility, *chose* to wield the ultimate power. Kash, in her heart, was not ready for such a responsibility; I suspect now, never wanted such. Arthur, on the other hand, was always destined to be the hero. Once and future. You see, Fate has a funny way of adhering to what we most desire in the end, if we only believe." He smiled at all of them warmly.

"Well, what now? Can we magically travel back to the library or are we actually back in England?" Wilson asked, looking around as if this earthen chamber held his answers. When he looked at Kash though, there was a familiar glint in her eyes. She looked to Merlin and he nodded at her. Wilson looked from one to the other then over to Radcliffe who was smiling as well.

"What?" he asked them all. He looked back to Kash who met his gaze intensely. With a nod to Merlin, Radcliffe held out his hands to Wilson and Kash. Kash took it without hesitation and they both looked to Wilson. He shrugged and grasped the man's offered hand, immediately seeing the swirl of blue lights as he was squeezed into the magical darkness.

Epilogue

Radcliffe leaned back in the chair at the front desk of the library. A few weeks had passed since he had left Kash and Wilson and the library had returned to normal. He peered over the desk in the direction of his office. He could still see the giant snake fang hanging on the wall and he pictured the row of books underneath it. They were all there, from the *Prophetiae Merlini* to *The Death of Arthur* and all the others they had travelled to, in between. There was still one puzzle that he hadn't solved, though, and it was troubling him. He hadn't been able to find Kash's journal. He had searched everywhere, but couldn't think of what could've happened to it. These contemplations were interrupted when a college kid he helped study sometimes came around the nearest row of books. His eyes went wide when he saw the journal in the kid's hands.

"Where did you get that?! Never mind, you didn't read it, did you?" he asked the kid in alarm.

"Well, yeah, I read the whole thing, it was awesome."

"And…nothing weird happened? Any blue light?" Radcliffe asked.

"Umm, not that I remember," the kid said awkwardly with a weird look at him. He placed the journal on the counter and left, Radcliffe sitting stunned in his wake. As soon as the young man was gone, Radcliffe snatched up the journal and moved to his office, sitting down behind his desk. He turned to Kash's letter to Wilson, expecting there to be blank pages after. To his surprise there were not, the journal had been filled in. As he read, he noticed that the font was the exact same as the tattoos he now endeavored to keep hidden. The more he read, the wider his smile became and when he closed the book his heart was full. His friends had flourished in the story he had taken them to. There they had created their own happily ever after and lived out the rest of their days in peace and harmony. He thought about the ending to his own story and knew that it might be a lot longer in the making. He had a job to do now that he was caretaker of Morgana's prison and he would always do everything he could to protect the stories just as Merlin had intended. He chuckled to think that Merlin thought he was King Arthur reincarnated. He gasped when he looked back at the page to see more letters forming, then smiled again when he saw one last note from Merlin to him.

"Why can't you be? You must only believe."

About the Author

Jacob Hunter Mical was born in Charlotte, North Carolina on April 26, 1991. His passion for literature and books was spawned, like so many others, by his first reading of J.R.R Tolkien's masterpiece *The Lord of the Rings.* He is an adventurer and musician, drawing inspiration from as many places as possible. A graduate of Charleston Southern University, he currently lives and writes in North Carolina.